THE DARK AT THE BOTTOM OF THE STAIRS

"Vanessa," I yelled irritably. No answer. I went to the top of the stairs and yelled again. There was no sound from the cellar. Great, she probably passed out down there. I started down the steps, the dank, damp basement smell reaching up to meet me.

Moonlight filtered through a grimy basement window, splitting Vanessa's face neatly in half. Tears streaming down her cheek, one eye white and panicked. She struggled to swallow, something in the way. Just before the beam from a flashlight blinded me, I realized that the shadow behind her had her by the throat.

"Vanessa . . . ?" My voice shook, barely more than a whisper. I held up my hand and peered through my fingers, eyes fighting to adjust. Her head inclined ever so slightly and the arm encircling her neck jerked up and back. She choked and froze. The cellar whispered all around us, rustling, dripping.

Something glinted on Vanessa's cheek. A flat, rectangular blade . . .

"The plot is complex and the outcome unexpected."
—*Midwest Book Review*

"An exciting and tightly organized novel, *Watching Vanessa* is . . . amazing."
—*Syracuse Sunday Herald*

"Patricia Tiffin moves full throttle . . . in her fast-moving thriller."
—*Syracuse New Times*

WATCHING VANESSA

PATRICIA M. TIFFIN

St. Martin's Paperbacks

Published by arrangement with Baskerville Publishers, Inc.

WATCHING VANESSA

Copyright © 1997 by Patricia M. Tiffin.

Cover photograph by Ed Holub.

Library of Congress Catalog Card Number: 97-3560

ISBN: 0-312-97415-9

Printed in the United States of America

St. Martin's Press hardcover edition published 1997
St. Martin's Paperbacks edition / June 2000

St. Martin's Paperbacks are published by St. Martin's Press, 175 Fifth Avenue, New York, NY 10010.

10   9   8   7   6   5   4   3   2   1

To Marti Mann

WATCHING
VANESSA

1

Once a month we have lunch, me, Vanessa, Oola and my best friend Annie. We get together in Manhattan, eat too much and dish the dirt. The four of us have been friends since college.

Annie and I actually grew up together in Riverside, in the North Bronx. We'd been having lunch together since we shared soup from a Flintstone thermos. We met the others freshman year at NYU. Oola was an easy find, a standout. While the rest of us lived on Ho-Ho's and mystery meat, she subsisted on yogurt and nibbled homemade granola. Vanessa, on the other hand, loved Cokes and smokes in the student union, cramming Hostess cupcakes and biology in a desperate quest for decent grades. Scary but true, Vanessa was now teaching at Columbia.

Twelve years after graduation these lunches were our way to stay in touch. We each took turns picking the restaurant. If it was food you'd never seen before from a place you'd never heard of, it was Vanessa's turn. She liked the fast track—a hip, slick New Yorker-in-the-know. Oola on the other hand didn't do red meat or alcohol, caffeine or refined sugar. Those of us with less healthy lifestyles didn't begrudge her a spiritual path, but without sugar? Could that be anything but hell?

After a second scotch, Vanessa had been known to snipe about women who were slaves to their bodies. Oola would point out that her body housed her spirit and how she treated it reflected her self-worth. This was particularly irritating since Vanessa and I frequently had hangovers and always ordered dessert.

Oola was on a journey back to the Goddess. Vanessa said it was because she hated men. Actually, she couldn't have hated men too much since she'd been married to the same one for almost ten years. Andrew (never Andy or Drew) was an international computer something or other, and to this day I've never liked him. Fortunately the feeling was mutual. In fact none of us were good enough for old Andrew, though he tolerated our presence at Oola's annual Fourth of July party. Evidently there were enough of the right kind of people around to keep him from having to notice us. Annie said I'm too hard on him, but she said that about everyone I didn't like.

Being nice to people was what Annie did best. Her looks helped—her smile was almost corny the way it lit up her face. Fine, wispy brown hair floated around her shoulders in gentle waves. Her eyes were soft blue, and she had a great nose. People whose noses aren't so great always notice ones like Annie's. It was perfect, straight, with a little upturn at the end and just the right amount of sun freckles on the bridge.

Oola not only had a great nose, she had a great everything. She was slim and blond—natural, no matter what Vanessa said—and beautiful. In college, she'd driven men crazy and us women too. It's easier to hate someone gorgeous if they're stupid or stuck up or slutty. Oola was none of those things and eventually we lesser mortals had had to learn to live with a goddess in our midst. She was the last woman in the world I'd have figured to marry a man with a pocket protector.

Compared to the other two, Annie and I were pretty drab. I think that's why we all worked so well together. Oola and Vanessa were so defined—flamboyant, intelligent, successful—and both just a little bit weird. Annie and I didn't have the guts to be weird, though I was borderline, usually without intending to be. Still, drab is a perfect backdrop, so as a group, we balanced nicely.

Lately, our lunches had become a bright spot on my social calendar. Actually the only spot on my social calendar. Over appetizers and wine, we would talk of Annie's children, our jobs, Oola's latest meditation group, sex. Or in my case, the lack of it. Vanessa was good for outrageous stories of some underground warehouse where people with safety pins in their nipples danced until dawn.

Until recently, my divorce had been a primary topic of interest. But the papers had been signed six months ago and Kathleen Meriden had quietly gone back to being Kate Greerson, my maiden name. Interesting term: maiden name. It always made me think of Chuckie Greenfeld, who copped my virginity the night of his senior prom.

Everybody except Annie thought I needed to start using my old name immediately. Oola said it would help with the grieving process, and Vanessa couldn't understand why women took men's names anyway. "Get a grip on your identity!" Some identity, a 35-year-old failure with no life, no lover and no future. Whoa, hold on, big fun ahead!

Annie was mostly quiet about the whole thing. She was the only other married one now. She and David had two girls. She let the others toss my life around, organizing and repairing and rewriting its script. While Vanessa dictated strategy for my financial future—or my ex-husband's financial destruction, depending on how you looked at it—and Oola talked about the Goddess within, Annie would wink at me and smile. Sometimes she'd reach over and give my hand a squeeze. She was always there for me, all I had to do was ask. But her compassion made my eyes fill up, and I was afraid if I started crying, I'd never stop. So being a self-sufficient woman of the nineties I hid behind brightly smeared smiles. I was fine. As in Fucked-up, Insecure, Neurotic and Emotional.

I was the only one of us who lived in the city any more. Annie and David had a house in White Plains and Oola lived in Connecticut. Vanessa still kept a studio apartment on the upper West Side, but her barn, as she called it, was out on the north shore of Long Island.

The house really had been converted from a barn. It retained the original, darkly scarred beams and one entire wall was fieldstone, with fireplaces upstairs and down. The second floor hung open over the living room, so you could look down on it from the upstairs landing. Vanessa had added a porch around three sides of the house and a skylight in the master bedroom. Tucked in the front corner of the house was her office, a very special place for her—a respite from her flash and trash lifestyle.

The barn was where Vanessa wrote. As if being a professor of literature weren't enough, she secretly authored gory horror novels that sold faster than the bodies could pile up. Financial security, she called them. Skeletons in the closet, I think, since few of her oh-so-academic cohorts had a clue about her work. Her first book, *Headstone*, was a runaway best seller—soon to be a "major motion picture," with Vanessa, a.k.a. Gordon Sims, doing the screenplay. She had built a stock portfolio on death and dismemberment.

I still lived on Walker Street in Tribeca, without a mutual fund in sight. When Steve and I first married, we bought an old warehouse down there. This was before living in a truck stop had become trendy. You too could pay top dollar to be awakened by revving engines, diesel fumes and bilingual obscenities. We had rented out the bottom two floors to a sculptor and a clothing designer, and kept the top floors for ourselves. Unlike Steve, the sculptor still lived there. The designer had been replaced by a Russian interpreter and her husband.

When we met, Steve and I had both been in the advertising business. He still was. During our engagement, we had left our respective jobs to open a small agency of our own. We had worked hard and played hard. Building the agency was something I had been good at.

As a result of the divorce, I now owned the building with the Chemical Bank. I was also an unemployed graphic artist and a fugitive from the IRS. The way it worked out, I got the loft, Steve got the business. Wouldn't Gloria Steinem like to chat about that one.

At the time, though, the building was there. It was real, and it was where I lived. It was hard enough to lose my husband and my job . . .

The agency had taken off since we separated. Steve, the shithead, was doing very well for himself. Because of your hard work, whispered a little voice in my head. I nursed my grudges and licked my wounds and fantasized about blowing up their new offices. The bitch of it was, I had done it to myself, against all legal advice. He had bought me out for a song, though it seemed like a symphony at the time. *Nobody screws me like I do.* Maybe I could write Country and Western for a living.

We had had lunch in midtown; Annie's pick, so it was tourist hell. The only restaurants Annie knew in the city were the ones that advertise in theater programs at Broadway matinees. Bad food, separate checks, and lots of gawkers hoping that somebody who was somebody would show up. They never did. Still watching all the people, excited and dressed up for their big afternoon in the Big Apple, annoyed the hell out of me. If I didn't have a life, I certainly didn't need to be confronted by a busload of blue-haired ladies from Smithtown who did.

I got off the subway on Canal Street. A major bout of self-pity was brewing and I needed to stock up on supplies. Chocolate macadamia nut cookies with nine billion grams of fat, barbecued spare ribs, hot and sour soup and a bottle of chardonnay. Maybe two bottles, and this time I had to remember to ask if they delivered. It seemed I couldn't be at the loft these days without something to help me forget that I was alone.

Funny, for a long time I never minded being alone. I always had my own space in the loft, off limits even to Steve. I liked snuggling down in the faded brown couch, to read or watch old Disney movies on video. I'd tangle myself in an ancient quilt and sip cognac late at night. I never, ever wore panty-hose there.

Now I had the whole loft to myself, except for the cats. I moved the brown couch out into the living room, but it wasn't the same. Even scarier, I wasn't the same. I was afraid. Not of the usual New York stuff—muggers, rapists—that stuff I could handle. This was worse. Even my quilt didn't help.

Deep inside me was a place where fear gathered and stuck to me like tar. Sometimes I felt it tugging at me, like a soul-mate in despair. I danced around its edges, terrified but tempted nonetheless. How easy just to sink into the darkness, let the inevitable blackness come. The only thing that seemed to pull me back from the edge was a few drinks, and even that wasn't working like it used to.

Lately the booze seemed to be going down quicker and having less effect. It was amazing how often I'd pick up my glass and find nothing but ice. But I could hold my liquor, no question of that. My pop would have been proud. Pop had liked his booze, and as a kid I spent many an afternoon pub-crawling with him, playing pinball, signing the pill pool and doing Elvis imitations on the tables for nickels. It was a culturally fulfilling childhood until Pop dropped dead one day on the floor of Nelson's saloon. Heart attack, they said, but his liver was the size of a basketball. He was 51.

2

October was Oola's pick, and we were doing Middle Eastern. We had been waiting for Vanessa now for over a half hour. Oola was patiently explaining the difference between hummus and bean dip to Annie, and I was pouring my second wine when she finally arrived. Or should I say entered. Vanessa was so striking she always made an entrance, even when she was on time. She was tall, almost six foot, with dark brown skin, well-defined cheekbones and an endless array of hair extensions. Today she wore waist-length braids and a glorious red cape with a turban to match over a purple suede dress. Vanessa believed in being noticed and was rarely disappointed.

"I am soooo sorry, my nails just wouldn't dry," she explained, peeling off a red kidskin glove. Probably because they were as long as Michael Jordan's inseam, I thought. Vanessa's hands were slender and elegant, and she loved fake fingernails. Today's selection was squared porcelain tips that hung an inch over her fingers and perfectly matched her cape. I lived for the day she'd get one stuck up her nostril. All of us have to pick our noses sooner or later.

"Where's the waiter? I really need a drink." Vanessa's head could spin faster than Linda Blair's when she was looking for cocktails. Oola might have been a tad gleeful explaining that the restaurant did not serve liquor. Fortunately, the large bottle of cheap Bordeaux in my purse had survived the subway. With a quick flick of the wrist, I untwisted the top and solemnly offered it for sniffing. Good humor was restored as I slopped wine into our tea cups. Vanessa's and mine—Annie was abstaining too.

"So, I explained to Carla that little boys do pee standing up and she was so upset. Not that she had a problem with how they pee, but she hates being wrong." Annie laughed and shook her head. "Lord, that child is just like her father. Sweet as pie one minute, mad as hell the next. And she's only five! Can you imagine her at fifteen?"

"I don't want to imagine it, thank you very much," I put in. "About the only thing Steve and I agreed on was no kids. Thank God we didn't blow that like we blew everything else." The last of it came out more bitterly than I intended. Lately, thinking about Steve was really pissing me off. Actually, a lot of stuff was pissing me off. Oola gave me one of her patented looks, straight to the soul. She and Andrew were trying to adopt, as she couldn't have children.

The atmosphere was still strained as we gave our order to the waiter, with none of our usual joking and commentary. When he left the table, silence descended and I looked pleadingly at Oola, who smiled pleasantly but didn't respond. Where was the common ground?

I was almost through with my chicken charwarma when Vanessa made her announcement. "Speaking of men . . ."

"Were we speaking of men?" I asked.

". . . I met one." She sat back, smugly enjoying our reactions.

Not that men and Vanessa were an unusual topic, but the men themselves were always so unusual. Never a stockbroker or insurance salesman, always a 23-year-old sculptor, or a zydeco bandleader or an Ethiopian importer. There was a hint of Harlequin Romance in all of Vanessa's relationships and we ate them up. At first she was saturated with bliss but soon grew bored, usually before we did. She extracted herself with finesse, retiring to the barn on the pretext of dismembering yet another group of unsuspecting teenage campers. From sanctified isolation she would bid her lovers goodbye; the Long Island Railroad was the scene of many a choreographed farewell. After a month or so of seclusion, she would return to the social whirl and capture yet another pigeon. For those of us who believed there was no unattached male in the tri-state area who wasn't gay or on parole, Vanessa was a hero.

"Okay, spill it, Vanessa!" I said. "Who is he, a sailor on a banana boat, a disenfranchised French count?"

Envy prompted the sarcasm, even I could figure that out. My idea of a date was a chilled bottle of Absolut, moo shu chicken and an Alfred Hitchcock video. I had two male cats—

Harley and Ozzie—both testosterone-free, who were always willing to hang out with me. Honestly, I liked them better than most people. If you could pop the top of a Little Friskies can, you were never in danger of being dumped, even if you hadn't washed your hair for three days.

"Tell us, Vanessa. Where did you meet him, what does he do, what does he look like?" Annie asked eagerly. She loved Vanessa's dalliances and with the faith of a true romantic, firmly believed each was The One. You read enough fairy tales, you start believing in happily ever after.

Oola smiled at Annie and turned to Vanessa. "Truly, Vanessa, you are amazing. What happened to the last one—Elliot, wasn't it?" Oola shook out her hair a little as Vanessa dismissively waved away Elliot.

"A passing whim for the unwashed! The latest—that is another story altogether." Vanessa lit another cigarette and gestured toward her cup. Obligingly, I poured and the saga began.

"Remember I've been doing a lecture series on the appeal of horror—Stoker, Poe, Shelley? My Literature in Films class sponsors it, but it's open to the rest of the campus. Well, here I am explaining literary butchery to some of the strangest people I've ever seen . . ."

"Nice way to talk about your fans. You do write the stuff, remember?" I interrupted a little drunkenly. Red wine goes right to my head. An impatient grimace from Annie reminded me.

"I may write it, but they're not supposed to know that. The Vampire myth is about as contemporary as I get. Strange how that one has survived so long." Vanessa picked up the dessert menu. "I want crème brulée. Why doesn't this place serve crème brulée? Oola, if you don't start picking places with decent desserts, not to mention a bar, you will forfeit your right to choose."

"Vanessa, if you can't get through one meal without alcohol, perhaps you should consider a little self-evaluation. And as for dessert, whether you appreciate abstinence or not, your thighs will thank me."

I didn't care about crème brulée, but I was a little annoyed by the booze comment. People who don't drink are always harping on people who do. There was nothing wrong with some wine at lunch. To prove my point, I reached for the Bordeàux and emptied the bottle into my cup.

"Please get back to the story," Annie interjected.

"Only for you, Annie." Then turning up her nose at Oola: "My thighs have never given *me* anything to worry about, though I must say I wonder at your interest."

Once when we were having a drink, Vanessa had informed me that Oola might be a lesbian. I'd have put more stock in it if she had anything to back it up other than three margaritas. The goddess thing is hard on Vanessa's Southern Baptist background and very suspicious for a psychotherapist, according to her. I wasn't sure what was suspicious about it, but I knew better than to argue with Vanessa when we were drinking tequila. Personally, I couldn't have cared less what floated Oola's boat, but I'd have given my eyeteeth to be standing in front of Andrew on the day she came out of the closet.

". . . Anyway, I was asking for comments about contemporary authors whose work translates easily into other media and this guy who's standing in the side aisle calls out, 'How about Gordon Sims?' 'Gordon Sims,' I say. 'To the best of my knowledge, none of Mr. Sims's work has ever been filmed.' Pretty cool, huh?

". . . Then he says that my books were literally written for film and goes on for about ten minutes on how he would direct *Headstone*. Fascinating! And the whole while he's talking it was as if he and I were alone in the room. Suddenly, time's up and he gets kind of sheepish, you know, for talking so much. I knew he'd come up afterwards, so I took my time getting my stuff together. Sure enough, here he comes." She paused for a smoke, until a pleading look from Annie made her start again.

"He knows I'm looking him over. Doesn't faze him." She grinned impishly. "I think he liked it. He smiles, shakes my hand and says, 'After taking over your lecture, the least I can do is buy you a cup of coffee. I'm Jake Romano.' He sounds a little bit Brooklyn, but in a British sort of way, husky without being rough." She paused for a minute, savoring the memory of Jake Romano. "I don't know how to describe him, but what a voice."

"Let's get to the good stuff! What's he like in the sack?"

"Kate, not everything is about sex!" This from Annie who

thought that nothing was about sex. "It sounds so romantic, Vanessa. What happened next?"

"Well, for Kate's benefit, we didn't have sex. You know, dear, you're the one who needs to get laid. You're far too tense lately." Vanessa smiled bitchily at me. "Anyway, we talked a little bit more. He's a film maker, documentaries so far. Works out of a studio in Queens, near where they used to shoot Cosby. I had another class so I couldn't go for coffee, but I did watch him leave." Remembering the view she shimmied her shoulders.

"So I go to class and kinda forget about it, but then when it's over and I'm heading out, who's standing at the door?"

Silence now was more than even Oola could stand. "Come on, Vanessa . . ."

"So, he invited me to lunch and I went. He grew up in Massachusetts, went to Boston College and lives in Brooklyn Heights." The waiter set the check down on the table and Annie picked it up. "He's thirty-seven, seems financially solvent—as in, he paid for lunch—and likes jazz. That's it, you got it all." The inevitable digging in purses began.

"Wow, Vanessa, he sounds wonderful. Documentary films! That must be so interesting. What are the films about?" Annie counted out a five and seven singles into the pile of money next to the check. "Is that enough, Kate?" One of Annie's greatest fears was undertipping. She'd have left fifty percent if we let her.

"More than enough. You don't want to push this guy into a higher tax bracket." I added my money to the heap, making change for a twenty. "What's the next move, Vanessa? Two ships passing or are you going to see him again? Where'd you eat by the way?"

"Tavern on the Green, very chi-chi. Yeah, we're going to MOMA Saturday afternoon and I'm lucky to be able to do it, my schedule for *Headstone* is a bitch! I've got to meet with the studio people, suck up to the appropriate movie types, finish this semester's course load and turn the book into a screenplay by spring. I'll barely have time to call the guy, much less screw him."

"Thanks for the late-breaking revelations," Oola said, gathering up her bag, "but I have to run. I'm giving a lecture this afternoon and I'm already pushing it. Who's turn is it to pick?"

We pushed away from the table and headed to the door.

"I think it's Kate's turn, isn't it, Kate?" Annie was struggling into her coat, nearly knocking a large silk floral arrangement off a table in the foyer.

"Yes it is, ladies! Put it in your book, third Tuesday of the month," I replied, rescuing the flowers and waving away the hovering manager as we headed out the door.

"Kate, call me and let me know where. Peace everyone," Oola waved goodbye as she deftly flagged a cab that was doing sixty up Third Avenue. The woman was astounding; cabdrivers rarely recognized my existence, and they never let me in the cab until they were sure I wasn't going to Queens.

"Well, thank God Kate is picking, at least I'll be able to get a drink. Ladies, it's been a pleasure, as always. Kate, leave the restaurant with my secretary at school. I'll be hard to reach. Bye Annie."

Vanessa headed off, leaving Annie and me standing on the sidewalk.

"Kate, are you okay? Can you get home all right or do you want me to get you a cab?" Her concern touched off another one of those devils inside me, and I shook her hand off my arm.

"Of course, I'm okay, what the hell is wrong with you people?" I snapped. "Christ, can't a person have a drink without everyone giving her a load of crap!" Annie's eyes widened and her face kind of shut down. My anger receded as fast as it flared. Being mean to Annie was like kicking a kitten.

"Annie, hey, wait." She had started down the street to the subway station and I caught up with her halfway down the block. "Annie, I'm sorry. I don't what's going on with me lately." Even the short jog had me unsteady; that damned red wine. Amazingly, my eyes filled up with tears and my voice caught in my throat. "Annie, please, I just don't seem to know anything anymore and it's making me crazy. Look at me, I'm a basket case, a poster child for PMS." My laugh came out half-funny, half-gulpy and next thing you know, I was sobbing in the street, snuffling in the shoulder of Annie's coat. As if I were Carla or Lindsay she held me and softly stroked my hair, murmuring mother-stuff until I self-consciously raised my head.

"Kate, why don't I call the sitter and ask her to pick up the girls. Then you and I can go someplace and talk," Annie coaxed gently.

Danger. I didn't want comfort, couldn't bear pity. I shook my head, tears too close for talking, and backed away. She watched me till I turned and headed downtown. I went directly to Petrillo's, my neighborhood bar. I did not pass go, didn't quite spend two hundred dollars, and didn't remember getting home. Blessed oblivion, cheap at twice the price.

3

It was the end of November, our lunch date a week late because of Thanksgiving. We were waiting for Annie at a long, dark restaurant in Little Italy. Steve and I had found it years ago. Family owned and staffed, the kitchen turned out heavenly concoctions from Northern Italy. A huge espresso machine hulked in the corner of the bar and the candle holders—empty bottles of the house chianti—were layered with years of wax. I was playing with ours, flicking off pieces with my fingernail, studiously avoiding the bottle of Anisette that also adorned each table.

After that crying escapade with Annie, I had decided to be more careful. Maybe I was hitting the sauce a little hard since the divorce. But I had taken control of the situation. For the last three weeks, I'd allowed myself two glasses of wine a day, anytime after five. Civilized drinking. Sometimes I even skipped a day. If I had a drinking problem, I'd have been adding a lemon twist to my Listerine or making Nyquil Manhattans.

Of course, I did make an exception on Saturdays and Sundays. I'm a big football fan, college especially. Every week I did a football parlay at Petrillo's. It was only a couple of bucks, and the bar threw a small party. They put out some wings and pizza at half-time; it was pretty harmless. Just to be sociable, I shared a few pitchers and knocked back a few shots with the rest of the regulars. Even though most of the guys were my pop's age, we had a good time. Of course, if you wanted to talk about drinking problems, the regulars at Petrillo's wrote the book.

Vanessa and I ordered some mussels marinara while we waited. Annie had left a message with Oola's secretary that she would be late. Oola was in her glory, skimming the menu and debating the merits of spinach ravioli with pignoli nuts versus greens and beans. Vanessa and I—carrion and proud of it—were greedily sucking little mussels from their shells and dipping our bread in the sauce. Annie's entrance put a stop to it all when she struggled out of her coat.

"My God, there's a cast on your arm!" This from Vanessa. I wiped mussel juice from my chin and shrieked, "Annie, you hurt yourself!" Like I believed that! He finally did it, the son of a bitch. Some innocent remark of Annie's, and David cracked her, probably with a tire iron. David had been going out with Annie since tenth grade and I had seen things change between them. Annie would never admit it, but he definitely bossed her around. He could be a real prick, always picking at her, putting her down. It was so bad, a couple of times Annie actually flared back. Gave it to him good. It didn't look like this was one of those times.

Oola, the only one with common sense, rose to free Annie from her scarf and left sleeve. Annie flopped into the booth, self-consciously begging for silence. We fussed a little longer, then finally shut up long enough to hear what happened.

"Oh thank goodness, I thought I would never get here," Annie sighed, settling against the high wooden back of the booth. She set her arm gingerly on the table, the cast pristine and obviously fresh. "Kate, will you order me a glass of wine? Red please. I'm chilled to the bone."

A glass of wine sounded good, just what I needed to settle my nerves. I waved to the waiter, pointed to our wine glasses and flapped my hand in a circle over our heads.

"Sorry I'm late," Annie added. "Thanks for waiting. I took a cab from the doctor's office on Sixty-third Street and we got stuck in traffic on Lex."

"Sixty-third Street? Why did you have to go to a doctor in the city?" Oola's question was solicitous, but with a tiny undercurrent. Watch out, Annie, I thought, Oola's on to you. "Did you have to go to a specialist for some reason?"

"I'm afraid there's nothing dramatic about this, guys." She winced in mid-shrug. "I was going down to do laundry and I fell. How could that happen to someone who's the picture of grace, right?" When she mocked herself with that small smile we all loved her. "I have a hairline fracture of the tibia, as in I broke my arm. It's still real sore. That's it, honest." Annie looked around the table and laughed so good-naturedly, I almost bought her story. The waiter arrived and she gratefully accepted her wine.

There was a lull in the action while we heard a recital of the specials and Vanessa asked for more bread. We ordered the antipasto to start—no anchovies!—and dishes of fettucini with pesto, spinach ravioli and veal piccata to share. Oola wasn't thrilled with the veal but refrained from the usual baby-cow stories because it was Annie's favorite. This was enough food to feed Rhode Island, which pleased me no end.

"Annie, we need more detail than that, give it up," Vanessa said, as she signaled the waiter for another round. I was going to say no, but I really didn't have time and didn't want to make a big deal out of a little glass of wine.

"There's no more to tell, Vanessa," Annie replied. "I was carrying a pile of dirty clothes down the basement steps. Lindsay had left one of her toys on the stairs, my foot hit it and the rest is history." She giggled a little. "Especially my arm! Six weeks before this cast comes off! David's going to be really angry."

"Angry? Annie, why would your husband be angry that you've been injured?" Oola was still awfully intent. I personally focused my attention on the antipasto, which the waiter had dropped off on his way to the bar.

"Oola, for God's sake, stop fussing," Annie's voice rose along with Vanessa's eyebrows. Annie never talked back to Oola. Ever. "Look," she continued more quietly, finally realizing that Oola would have to be dealt with if we were to have a normal lunch. "I don't mean angry, I mean annoyed. You know, inconvenienced." We all looked blank. Inconvenienced by the fact that his wife had broken her arm? Even I, fresh with festering, male-inflicted wounds of the heart, did not get it.

Annie continued weakly, "David is really into his routine. He likes everything to be just so and with my arm laid up there's going to be some upheaval. That's what I meant when I said he'd be annoyed." She gave a shrill, tinkly, un-Annie-like laugh. It was so fake it scratched my ears. "I'm sure he and the kids will do everything they can to help keep things running smoothly. He's concerned about me, Oola. He does love me."

I was scarfing as many artichoke hearts from the salad as possible. Vanessa was doing the same number on the roasted peppers.

"And the doctor in the city?" Oola prompted.

"God, Oola, give it a rest!" Vanessa interrupted. "What is the big deal? Eat something, will you, before Kate swipes all the good stuff!" I would have protested, but my mouth was full of prosciutto. It was merely circumstantial.

"Oola, once and for all, I went to a doctor in the city so I could make this lunch. Also, Dr. Bernard is on vacation, and I hate the guy she's got taking her calls while she's gone. Case closed, okay?" Annie tried to dish up some salad, gave up and let Vanessa help her. "So Vanessa, what's the latest on the current male?" Oola's expression remained thoughtful, but she surrendered to group conscience and dropped the interrogation.

"The current male is fine, and I do mean fine," Vanessa purred. She cut her eyes at me, smiling the way women do when they want you to know they're getting great sex. I rolled my eyes and stuck a finger down my throat. "You know, Kate, if you weren't such a bitch, you might have a date in this century," Vanessa observed.

Before I could defend myself, Annie interjected a request for more details. I think she was hoping to redirect Oola's attention. Vanessa was happy to comply, filling us in on their afternoon at the museum, a night out dancing, an intimate dinner for two. So what? The cats and I have dinner by candlelight all the time, a little white wine and tuna fish for three.

"I just wish we had more time together, but I've really had to settle down to work. I've got deadlines all over the place. Jake waiting in the wings is just another reason to get it done," Vanessa added.

"Ah, here it comes, the beginning of the end," I sniped. "I think I'll start a pool. Whadda ya say, Oola, put in a buck and pick a date for his demise." Vanessa nailed me with a stream of smoke.

"Oh Kate, some relationships work out," Annie said.

"And some just get worse because the partners refuse to look at their problems," Oola added. Annie sank back in the booth, plainly unhappy at Oola's renewed interest.

She was saved by lunch, served with many flourishes by

our proud waiter. I took the liberty of ordering another round, but Annie said no and Vanessa was still working on the last glass, so it was wine for one. Okay by me. We spent the next few minutes absorbing the marvelous odors, textures and tastes of the steaming plates set before us.

"So, Vanessa, this sounds like it could get serious," Annie ventured, a million blissful calories later. We were on our third basket of bread—a must to mop up garlicky sauces. Even Oola, using wheat bread of course, dabbed at the leftover pesto. When the waiter arrived to clear and wrap we ordered double espressos and Oola's decaf cappuccino, as well as Sambuca for Vanessa and me with three coffee beans for luck.

"You never know, Annie," Vanessa replied, unwilling to commit. "Right now, I've got other things to worry about."

"Ooooh, I am so full. What other things, Vanessa? Are you having problems with the script?" Oola leaned back against the high wall of the booth, hands soothing her stomach.

"No, it's okay, I just have to make time to do it. And I explained to Jake, so that's okay . . ."

"And did he take it well? Poor boy, how will he survive without the light of his life."

"Shut up, Kate."

"If the script's okay and Jake's okay, what's not?" Oola asked.

"Well, this might sound stupid, but . . . have you ever felt like you're being watched?" She looked around the table and then down into her Sambuca. "I feel almost embarrassed saying it. It's just a feeling, a creepy feeling, like there's someone watching me. You know how your stomach feels when something's not right?" Vanessa looked to us for affirmation. We nodded; there wasn't a woman alive who didn't know that stomach feeling, all queasy and knotted up.

"Has anything else happened, Vanessa? Is there a reason for your feeling?" Oola slid right into therapist mode. She had her doctorate in psychology, and ran her own practice in Manhattan. Oola worked primarily with women who had survived something—incest, rape, domestic violence. Between Annie's arm and Vanessa's paranoia, she could bill out this lunch. I was preparing a clever comment on empty couch syndrome when Vanessa said, "Maybe . . ."

I looked at her in surprise and took a gulp of Sambuca. It

went down the wrong way and I coughed, pinching my nostrils together to keep it from coming out my nose. Oola shook her head at me and Annie patted my hand.

"Maybe?"

Reluctantly, Vanessa continued. "I've been getting some weird phone calls . . . Don't even say it, Kate!" God, I didn't even have a chance to open my mouth! "Hang-up calls. A lot of them. Sometimes I can hear somebody on the line, you know. Breathing." She lit another cigarette off the candle and took a deep drag. "See, stupid. It's nothing, probably just some kids getting their jollies." She laughed. We didn't.

"Vanessa, this doesn't sound like nothing. Too many women end up beaten, raped or dead because they don't trust their own instincts." Oola brooked no argument. "Do you know how many of my clients have told me about that very same feeling? But they disregarded it. They didn't want to appear foolish, overreact, admit they were scared. Well, they didn't want to be attacked either, but that's what happened."

"It just makes me feel stupid. Like I'm a baby or something. It's not like anything's happened . . . except maybe the flower thing. But even that doesn't mean anything. It's not like I'm being threatened or somebody's trying to hurt me. It's just . . . there's someone watching me. I feel it, at class, sometimes in stores, especially at home. And there are never any calls on my machine. Only when I'm home. Calls at the apartment too, and I'm hardly ever there."

"Van, it's probably just somebody you dumped, you know, some guy who can't give it up. Of course that doesn't narrow the field much." I swirled my Sambuca while I talked. I loved places that serve it in big snifters. It seemed to me we were making way too big a deal out of this whole thing. The way Vanessa made the rounds, there were bound to be repercussions.

"That would be kind of romantic," Annie suggested. Oola just looked at her and she added quickly, "But I don't blame you for being scared, Vanessa. If he never talks to you, that might be because you'd recognize his voice."

"Maybe you're right. It could that guy from the embassy. He was really persistent."

"Vanessa, you said something about flowers. What flowers?"

Before she could answer, I said, "You know, Vanessa, maybe this is a sign. One too many male sacrifices," I nodded sagely with a little burp. "Of course," I said, turning my attention to Oola, "if God really is a woman, then why would She care." I raised my eyebrows and Oola took my snifter.

"I want to hear about the flowers, Vanessa. And quite frankly, whether this is someone you dated or not, there's nothing romantic about it. You have every right to stop seeing someone, and to have that choice respected," Oola said. Annie ducked her head with a guilty look. It would take more than Oola to make me feel guilty, but I did want my snifter back. "What happened with the flowers? Kate, enough. Stop it— ow!" Oola scolded me crossly, frowning on my comic attempts to regain custody of the Sambuca. Annie shook her head at me. So my button got caught in Oola's hair—have me flogged and get it over with!

The waiter returned and Vanessa forestalled the check by ordering another round of coffees. Oola nixed any more Sambuca with one hand over my snifter. She was really getting annoying. This whole lunch was getting annoying. I couldn't drink any more, Vanessa was monopolizing the conversation, and I had to go to the bathroom. Bad. "Oola, can you let me out? I have to pee, don't start till I get back."

I took the turn to the ladies room a little early and bumped my hip on the wall. I struggled out of my pants—stupid zipper always gets stuck—peed and went to the sink. Out of the corner of my eye I saw a red-eyed woman with smeared lipstick. I wasn't sure if it was me or not and didn't stick around long enough to find out. I threw a little cold water on my face and headed back to the table. Evidently in my absence the conversation had turned to Vanessa's books.

". . . to my agent and the publishing house."

"So what did they say?" Annie asked.

"About what?"

"Oola wondered if this could have anything to do with Vanessa's novels, Kate. You know, like a fan. Someone afraid to come right up and talk to her. We're just assuming it's a man, it could be a woman."

"If that's the case, they'd be watching Gordon, and he'd be hoping it was a man." Gordon Sims, we had long ago decided in a similar wine-soaked environment, was gay, a Felix Unger run amuck, a flamboyant screaming queen who delighted in "outing" heterosexual Republicans. Gordon's name had appeared on caustic and very funny letters-to-the-editor in major metropolitan newspapers around the country until a humorless phone call from the legal department at Vanessa's publishers put a stop to it. No one wanted to piss off the Republicans.

Through the years, Gordon had become an amusing companion, the perfect imaginary friend for adults. Whenever Vanessa struggled with writer's block or dangling participles, Gordon took the rap. He could get bitchy and was sometimes uncooperative, but overall I highly recommend pretend men.

"Actually," Vanessa replied, sitting up a little straighter, "that makes sense, especially about the flowers."

"Could we please hear about the flowers?" By now, Oola was getting testy. She heard herself and flushed. "It will help us to understand, Vanessa."

"Okay, here's the thing. You know I hardly ever stay in the apartment. If it wasn't rent controlled I probably wouldn't even hold on to it. I mostly only sleep there if I'm out late and have an early class or . . ."

"Or you don't want to take the latest victim to a bedroom out of town."

"I'm getting sick and tired of you talking like I'm some kind of slut, Kate."

"I had no idea you were so sensitive."

"I had no idea you were so jealous."

"Jealous?"

"Could you two stop, please? I'm still waiting to hear about the flowers." Oola tapped her nails against the table. I looked at Vanessa.

"The Goddess speaks."

"The other day, I was up at school and I stopped at the apartment on my way home. There's a note on the door from the super saying I got a package. I go down and it's a huge bouquet of white roses that are half dead, been there almost a week. There was no note, no nothing. Just a couple dozen dead roses and some red ribbon." She shuddered.

"Maybe Jake sent them," Annie suggested, persistent in her hope that Vanessa had found true love at last.

"I hadn't mentioned the apartment to him. It just never came up. He knows I live on the island."

"Vanessa, you must've said something in passing, without even thinking. C'mon, he probably said something about a shop, or a restaurant, and you said, oh that's right near my apartment," I suggested reasonably. Now could I have my snifter back?

"I did not say where the apartment was. I'd remember if I told him. I'm not an idiot," Vanessa snapped.

"Well, maybe he saw you going into the building and wanted to surprise you," Annie suggested. "He does sound like he really likes you and maybe he . . ."

"He didn't send them! I asked him. He didn't even know what I was talking about. But what Kate said before, that makes some sense because the apartment is listed in Gordon's name. You know, on the intercom."

The book-buying masses believed in the reality of Gordon Sims, thanks to the efforts of her publisher's PR department. Talk about sexism! Vanessa's publisher—a woman, mind you—felt the public would better embrace mass murder and mutilation if a man wrote about it. It was a marketing thing.

"Gordon's name?" Oola repeated.

"Yeah, when we were making Gordon up, we gave him the apartment as an address. We were all sitting around one night celebrating the first book. I think you and Steve were there, Kate. Anyway, we baptized Gordon with some Nouveau Beaujolais and put his name on the mailbox. It's been there ever since."

"So if this is someone crazy, a fan, it makes sense that the flowers would go there."

"Yeah, and maybe they saw me at the mailbox or something and started following me."

"Maybe they've discovered Gordon is a cross-dresser. Oh my god, the secret's out!" I put the back of my wrist to my forehead in feigned horror and Annie giggled.

"Funny. But you know, now that the books are successful, they're less concerned about keeping me a secret. We've even talked about doing an article, the women behind the pseudonym. It wouldn't be too hard to find out who I am." She took the last sip of her coffee, eyes dark and thoughtful.

"That's kind of scary. I mean, your fans have got to be psychotic just to read the stuff." Oola pursed her lips and I hurried to avoid interruption. "No, I'm serious now. Have you talked to Mindy?" Mindy was Vanessa's editor at the publishing house. A thin, nervous, perky woman who alternately acted as babysitter, cheerleader or warden when Vanessa was under deadline.

"Please, the woman calls every day, they're waiting for an outline on the new book," Vanessa moaned. "I asked her about Gordon, you know, if they've gotten any calls."

"Well, have they?"

"A few, but Mindy didn't think it was anything out of the ordinary. Shit, what time is it?" Vanessa never wore a watch, probably another reason she was usually late. When Oola told her the time, she flipped over the check and divided it by four. "Jake's picking me up in ten minutes."

"Jake! You mean he's coming here? We get to meet him?" Annie was delighted. This was her big chance to sneak a peek at Prince Charming, particularly since she wasn't invited to the ball. No pun intended, whispered that little voice in my head. I finally found my wallet in the bottom of my purse. "Damn, I don't have any cash. I'll have to put this on my card, you guys can pay me."

"I shouldn't be doing it, but I promised I'd go with him while he scouts some locations in Staten Island. I really should be working, but this is kind of a last hurrah. At least for a little while." Vanessa threw some money at me and started gathering up her belongings.

"Vanessa, do me a favor. If these calls don't stop, change your number, both of them. Unlisted, okay?" Oola was ever practical. "And if that feeling doesn't stop, I want to know."

Vanessa nodded and pulled on yellow fur-lined gloves. We rolled out of the restaurant, full of food and bread and wine. I lagged behind the others, waiting by the front window for my credit card. It looked like a beautiful day. I should do something. I could walk home, take my time, shop a little, hit some galleries in Soho. Or I could stop at Petrillo's and check the pill pool. They drew the number today and I could definitely use some extra cash. I didn't know where all my money was going.

A silver BMW was carelessly double-parked on the narrow street. A man leaned against it, a tall, dark-haired man with sunglasses pushed up on his head. He was wiping the end of a long black cylinder, then raised it to one eye and squinted through it. In the sun, against the sleek car, he looked more like a magazine ad than a person. As I signed my slip, Vanessa went to him and they embraced. She kept a hold of his hand and waved the others over. No doubt Annie was wetting her pants.

He was undeniably attractive, more than that, really. His dark hair was fashionably cut and hung slightly over one of his startling blue eyes. He had olive skin and a faint dusting of beard. His jawline was well defined and the small indentation in one cheek might have passed for a dimple.

Slowly I walked out into the sunlight, all of a sudden on edge. Something prickled along my spine and settled in my stomach. Jake threw his head back and laughed at a comment of Annie's. Sunlight flashed on perfect teeth. Annie blushed and simpered. I didn't like it. Jealous? taunted the little voice. No, I thought quickly. Jealous, it declared again, sure this time. I stood at the curb, a few steps back as Oola said goodbye.

"Vanessa, I have to get going. Jake, so nice to meet you. Oh, there you are, Kate. We're going."

"It really was nice," Annie chimed. "I have to go too, my train, but I hope I get to see you again."

"I'd like that a great deal," he replied.

"Maybe you two can come out for dinner some weekend," she said eagerly. "I make great chicken divan and . . ."

"Annie," Oola said, sparing Vanessa the effort. "Why don't we share a cab. You don't want to take the subway with your arm."

Annie was trapped. "All right. Bye," she said, her lack of enthusiasm apparent as she followed Oola up the block.

"And this is Kate," Vanessa said, turning towards me. He stepped forward, gorgeous face creased in a smile, and extended his hand.

"Vanessa talks about you all the time," he said. His leather glove clung to my fingers, even after the shaking stopped. "It's nice to finally have a face to fit the stories. And a pretty one at that," he added gallantly. Liar, hissed the voice. I gave the tiniest nod of acknowledgment, civil but not quite polite. "You know, if I were the jealous type, you'd be stiff competition," he continued, grinning now, sharing his little joke of feigned insecurity. As if a man like him could be threatened by the likes of me.

"Yeah, well, stiff is what will keep you ahead of the competition," I replied, pulling my hand from his. I fought the urge to wipe it on my coat.

"Kate!"

"Just kidding," I added hastily. I saw him glance at Vanessa then cut his eyes back to me. "I'm sure you have nothing to worry about."

"I know I don't," he answered, pulling Vanessa possessively into his side, eyes still hooked to mine. A beat of silence. "Do I, babe?"

A rhetorical question at best, but Vanessa lapped it up. She pretended to ponder her answer until Jake wrapped her in a bear hug and lifted her from her feet.

"No, put me down. You have nothing to worry about, nothing," she giggled and gasped, feet wiggling until a shoe dropped. "Jake, my shoe! Put me down, you're so crazy!"

· He set her carefully in her pump and kissed her nose, then her lips. I stood awkwardly to the side, uncomfortable and angry. Angry?

"I'm gonna shove off, Van."

"Okay. I'll talk to you."

"You're welcome to join us, Kate," Jake said.

"No thanks, three's a crowd and all that."

"That's ridiculous, we'd love to have you."

"No, but thanks."

"Come on, I insist."

"I said no!" I shrugged his hand from my arm. Vanessa gave me a cross look. "I've got things to do," I mumbled, backing away with a tight smile. "See ya." A short way down the block, I turned to look back. He held the door as Vanessa got into the BMW and grabbed the lens off the hood. As he came around to the driver's side, he saw me looking. He stopped for a second, hand on the door, then raised the lens in flat salute. Neither of us smiled. He slid the sunglasses down over his eyes and slipped into the car. Uncertain and unsettled, I watched them pull away, then walked to Petrillo's alone.

4

We skipped lunch in December. Nobody could get their schedules together for the same day. I hated the holidays. All that fake sentiment, good will toward man. Ho fucking ho, my first unmarried Christmas.

Being without a family during the holidays was cold, wherever you happened to be. Even people who were perfectly happy living alone the rest of the year started disappearing the week after Thanksgiving. Some crawled into cocoons of quilts and flannel pajamas, feigning illness and slathering themselves with Vicks VapoRub. Some became super-committed to work—busy, busy, busy! "This shipment has to get out even if I have to work straight through Christmas!" Others fell face first into depression, hiding behind cheery holiday messages on their answering machines, as if they were hustling-bustling, cookie-frosting, mistle-toeing, party-hopping fools, in reality sitting home with Courvoisier in their tea, eating Chunky Monkey with Oreos for spoons, looking for a plum pudding recipe that called for Percodan. Some brave ones would make it out by mid-January, only to be massacred by the Valentine's Day marketing machine. Had I been a Hallmark executive, I'd have been working on a holiday for single people. There was a market out there just dying to be recognized.

I personally was in for the long haul. Isolation was my motto. I loaded up on staples—chocolate, booze, caffeine and toilet paper. I made copies of all my take-out menus and piled them near each phone, categorized by speed of delivery and fat content. I toyed with smoking cigarettes and even picked up a pack of Newports, which was what Vanessa had smoked in college. She was far too chic for that now and smoked long black Russian jobbies that she bought at a tobacco store in midtown. I may have been queen of the unhealthy lifestyle but I couldn't get through a single Newport.

I did venture out periodically, mostly to do some shopping. My mom and sister lived in Syracuse and I sent them stuff from Bloomie's. What was it about Bloomingdale's that got people upstate all atwitter? An overpriced K-mart whose sales clerks were in serious need of attitude adjustment. For the privilege of a Bloomingdale's shopping bag, which I now had to pay extra for, I could buy a towel with a 700% markup and be treated like dirt while doing it. Thank you for shopping with us, you stupid schmuck. But, it was Christmas and it made my sister happy to show off her Bloomingdale's sheets. So I came, I shopped, I went crazy.

About a week before Christmas I met Vanessa for cocktails. She was always good for a laugh, except of course this Christmas when I desperately needed one. I wanted her to come to Petrillo's but she was uptown and had stuff to do, so I met her at the Oak Bar on the condition that she buy.

The Oak Bar was a New York classic and if you don't mind a twenty-two-dollar burger and a seven-dollar martini, it's a great place. The booze was cold and they had big olives. I loved big olives. I would drink more martinis if more places had big olives. The Oak Bar made one hell of a martini, so that's what we were drinking.

It took time to make a good martini and the Oak Bar was never rushed. First they filled a shaker with the beverage of choice, Absolut for me, Bombay for Vanessa. Then they buried the shaker in the ice bin. Next, they filled each glass with crushed ice and drizzled dry vermouth over it. Then you waited, because the secret to a great martini was temperature. See, most bars just slammed the booze into a shaker and, within seconds, strained it into a glass with a moldy olive. God forbid the glass just came from the dishwasher, because then you were drinking tepid gin and olive brine.

After an appropriate interval, just long enough for anticipation to build, the bartender dumped the vermouth-soaked ice from the glass, shaking out the excess liquid. Then he strained the oh-so-cold vodka, or gin if you preferred, into the frosted glass. The final touch was a skewer of huge green olives, plucked from their own little rock glass of dry vermouth. A work of art. We were on our second.

Something was wrong with Vanessa. It took me a while to notice. I hadn't talked to a real person in almost a week, so I was in my Chatty Kathy mode. Right in the middle of a Bloomingdale's saga, it came to me: her nails. Ever since college, when all she could afford was Lee Press-On and Krazy Glue, her fingernails had been her statement. Dramatic, sometimes gem-studded, but always long and always there. Today nothing but stubby little nubs with chewed cuticles and ragged edges. And there were other fashion-related signs. Vanessa was dressed conservatively, almost as if she wanted to blend in. This was serious.

"What's wrong, Vanessa?"

"Nothing." She took a sip of her martini and chewed her thumb, gazing into space. Nothing? With all the wisdom of two martinis, I thought not.

"Hello?" I stretched forth my hands in supplication. "Is anybody home? What is going on and what are you wearing? Is that beige? Do you realize somebody might mistake you for a bank teller, or worse yet, some kind of account executive? What are you doing in a goddamn beige suit, with no fingernails yet?" I shook my head in disgust. "Hey Eddie, start us two more."

When I got off my high horse and looked at Vanessa, she was crying. Holy shit. Vanessa did not weep. She might reduce others to tears, but I had never seen her cry.

"Van, honey, I'm sorry, what's wrong . . ." Vanessa wiped her cheeks and fumbled for a cigarette. Eddie appeared from nowhere and smoothly lit it for her. Without any acknowledgement of her tears, a pile of napkins moved within reach and a tall glass of ice water and some Goldfish mix appeared. They definitely understand the difference between pampering and prying at the Oak Bar. Eddie moved on to check the chill of our third martini while I waited Vanessa out. Finally, she gave a shaky laugh.

"I have not now, nor have I ever, owned anything beige. This is oyster," she said, indicating the jacket with dignity. She took a deep drag and I noticed her hand shaking. This was not the time to argue about nondescript colors.

"Is it your mom, Van?" Vanessa's mom was well into her sixties and lived outside of Atlanta. Virginia Mae was strong, eccentric, a lot like Vanessa, and would probably outlive us all.

"No, Mom's fine. I'm going down for Christmas to stay the week."

"Is it the new guy?" I knew his name but didn't say it.

"No, Jake's wonderful. He's a little upset that I won't be here for New Year's but he's been wonderful through all this."

"Through what? Are you going to tell me or should we play charades?"

"Whoever's watching me." Her voice caught on the words like pantyhose on a stubbly leg. I had to lean in to hear her. "I don't know what to do anymore." She dragged again, her free hand systematically shredding a cocktail napkin.

"The phone calls? They're still happening?"

"He won't leave me alone, Kate. I get calls all the time, breathing, listening, never talking. He calls me at home, at school, even pulled me out of a meeting with Mindy. It's getting so I'm afraid to answer the phone."

"Oola told you to change the number. You have to get an unlisted number."

"I did. He called in less than a day. And he's following me, I know it. I can feel him. Watching. Sometimes when I'm alone, I find myself whirling around, sure he's right behind me. But he's not. I never see him, I just know he's there . . . and I'm not crazy . . . because the car . . . but I . . ." The words came out in gushes, punctuated with little pain sounds.

She degenerated into those awful hiccuping sobs that made you feel like a little girl when you had them and wrenched your heart when you heard them. Elbows on the bas she dropped her head and shook silently. I waved Eddie away and rubbed her back helplessly, repeating the noises Annie made when I cried. Finally, Vanessa drew a deep breath.

"I'm sorry Kate. I can't believe I'm losing it like this." She ran her hands over her face and hair. "Shit, do I have raccoon eyes?" She took a bar nap and swiped under her lashes, checking for displaced mascara. Satisfied, she lit another cigarette and gave Eddie the okay signal. We waited until he placed the fresh drinks, rang up our tab and discreetly left us alone.

"Vanessa, I'm sorry. This is so awful. What about the car?"

"The car! Jake's car, too." I thought she was going off again, but she swallowed a couple of sobs and pulled on her cigarette. "That scared me so much. But at least I know this is real. I'm not making it up, Kate, I'm not," she implored. I patted her hand and she continued.

"Jake and I haven't had a lot of time together. I've just been swamped and now it's finals, and Christmas. Shit, I've hardly seen him. He's not too pleased about it either. So last week, I invited him out for the weekend. I mean, he knew I had to work during the day, but he was gonna go get a tree and we could decorate that night. Just the two of us, have a fire, dinner, the whole deal."

"So what happened?"

"We got up Sunday morning and decided to go out for breakfast before I went back to work. When we went outside, all our tires were flat. All of them. My car was worse, all kinds of stuff was ripped out, they had to tow it to the garage. We started Jake's car to make sure it was okay, and the tape player kicked on. Kate, it was the audio cassette of *Headstone*, right at the part where the woman goes up in the attic. You know." I couldn't remember the specifics, but women who went into attics in Vanessa's novels never came back in one piece.

"Oh my god, did you call the police?"

"What am I, fucking stupid?" Vanessa snapped, then sighed. "I'm sorry, Kate, I'm flat out crazy. Of course we called the police. Jake talked to them, I was so upset. He told them about the phone calls and how I felt like I was being watched."

"And what did they say?"

"They were nice, and a little more interested once Jake told them about Gordon and the books. But Kate, do you honestly think they have the time to give priority to a guy who makes hang-up calls? Here's the cop: 'Now, when he breaks in or sexually assaults you, then we can nail the SOB.' Notice the use of the word 'when' as opposed to 'if.' "

"What about what happened to the cars? That's nothing you dreamed up."

"Evidently there've been other things like this in the neighborhood. The cops seemed to think it was kids."

"Yeah, and one of those kids has been reading your books and wants to apply what he's learned." She shuddered and I decided to proceed with more tact. "Did you complain to the phone company? How the hell did he get the new number?"

"They seem to think I gave it to him. Or gave it to someone who gave it to him. Christ, Kate, I didn't even have time to give you the number, so how the hell did he get it? They're going to change it again, but I don't think it will help," She shook her head. "Jake says I should be very careful about handing it out."

"Jake?"

"He was with me when I changed it. He's stuck with me through this whole thing. Even when I was sure I was nuts, he stood up for me."

Dark thoughts rumbled in my head. The after-effects of martinis, or were they real? I hunched over my drink, staring into the olives that stared back with their red pimento eyes. You're jealous, hissed the little voice.

"Vanessa, what if the phone company is right and it is someone you know?" I leaned closer to her, almost shoulder to shoulder. She turned to look at me, puzzled, when two hands came around from behind her and covered her eyes.

"Guess who!"

We both jumped, she upward and forward with a short yelp. Her martini glass toppled on its stem, cracking its rim and splattering gin everywhere. Eddie hurried over, bar rag in hand.

"You scared me half to death!" She glared at Jake. "What are you doing here?"

"I'm sorry," he said miserably. "I wanted to surprise you."

"Not the smartest move, given the current situation," I snapped, heart pounding, martinis spinning the room. "Idiot!" I felt his eyes rest on me for a second.

"Hey, it's just gin," Vanessa said. "Once my heart slows down, I'll be fine. Thanks, Eddie." Eddie handed her a rag and she wiped at a blotch of gin puddled in her skirt. Jake stood awkwardly, until Vanessa turned to him with a smile. "You wanna start again? Honey, what are you doing here?" she asked in a saccharine-sweet voice.

"I wanted to surprise you," he repeated sheepishly, hastening to produce a delicate spray of freesia from an empty bar seat.

"How sweet," Vanessa exclaimed, giving him a hug. "I didn't expect to see you, I thought we were meeting at four."

"Yeah, what are you doing here?" It came out more like an accusation than a question. Eddie never batted an eye but moved down the bar with new purpose.

"Am I interrupting? I can go . . ."

"No, of course not. I was telling Kate about the cars and the calls, everything. Right, Kate?" He pulled up a chair on her other side and she swiveled between us like a spectator at a tennis match. "What are you doing here, babe?"

"I missed you. I knew you were meeting Kate, so I decided to pop in and join you. Didn't think you'd mind."

"Lucky us," I muttered, swirling the remains of my martini and swallowing it with a gulp. Vanessa gave me a look.

"We've had a few martinis," she explained. "Jake and I are going up to Mindy's office. Jake had this great idea that we should look through Gordon's fan mail to see if there's anything we could show to the police."

"Very original."

Vanessa grabbed her soggy blouse with two fingers and flapped it, then slid from her seat. "I have to clean up, then we can go, okay, honey?" He smiled and pulled her to him for a kiss before she left. She's going to the bathroom, not Antarctica, I thought. Vanessa scooped up her purse and left me alone with Jake Romano.

We didn't say anything. Just sat until Eddie came over and asked if he wanted a drink. He ordered a draft and another drink for me. Stubborn, I refused.

"Something for the other lady?" Eddie asked.

"If she wants something, I'll let you know," Jake snapped, voice cold and dismissive. Eddie lowered his eyes and stiffly turned away. I tried to catch his eye, but he didn't look at me.

"That was classy."

"Was I rude? I didn't mean to be," he replied with a rueful smile. "I guess this thing with Van has me on edge. I'm scared for her, Kate."

"Me too. I think she should get out of town for a while. She's on sabbatical next semester, she should go someplace, get away from this guy."

"Did you tell her that?"

"Not yet, but I will."

"It's not a good idea. I don't want you to say that."

"Excuse me?"

"I don't think she should be alone. I'll take care of Vanessa."

"Vanessa can take care of herself. She's been doing it for years."

"Well, that's changed now, hasn't it?"

"Has it?" I turned in my chair to face him.

"Yes, it has. Whether you like it or not, I'm taking care of Vanessa now."

"Listen," I replied, "I've known Vanessa for years. I've watched a parade of guys before you, and I'll watch them after you're gone. So spare yourself some heartache, pal."

"I'm not your pal. And things have changed. The parade is over, Katie." No one called me Katie but my pop.

"Don't call me that!"

"I'm ready," Vanessa said. Jake rose from the stool, face composed in a loving smile. I sulked over the dregs of my martini as they paid the check. Vanessa leaned over and touched her cheek to mine. Before I knew what he was intending, Jake followed suit, his lips brushing my cheek.

"Bye Kate," she said, walking toward the door.

"Katie," he added, tipping his head with mocking smile.

"Fuck you," I muttered and ordered another martini.

I spent Christmas Day at Annie and David's, at Annie's insistence. It made me crazy, being dragged into a family celebration as if I were some good-will project. If I didn't want to spend the holidays with my own family, why the hell would I want to spend it with Annie's?

I'd gone to the bar on Christmas Eve, and from what I remembered, had a pretty good time. The next morning I boarded an almost empty commuter train with a hell of a hangover, two bottles of champagne, a pint of vodka and one slightly smushed, storebought pie. Once the train was moving, I got some orange juice and added a slug of vodka, taking care not to spill. Normally I would never drink in the morning, but this was a holiday. Besides, if you had a hangover like mine and were facing an afternoon of multiple children and a mother-in-law, you'd drink too. I did feel better, in fact—full of holiday cheer by the time we pulled into White Plains.

The day went okay. David and I got along all right, at least until the champagne was gone. Then the laughs died out and

I fidgeted uncomfortably until he took me to the station.

I slept on the train ride home and was ready for a nightcap when we hit the city, but Petrillo's was closed. That just frosted me! I spend all year in that bar and the one night I needed a place to go, they were closed. What did they think people wanted to do on holidays? I headed home, planning what to say next time I saw Roger Petrillo.

The cats were glad to see me at least, and I opened up a can of tuna for them, in lieu of Little Friskies. Harley and Ozzie were appropriately appreciative, curving their bodies around my legs, rubbing heads and tails. I poured myself a white wine and watched them eat until I noticed the blinking light on my machine. I debated whether to listen. Lately I'd been wishing people would just stop calling me. But it was Christmas and it could be my mother, so I hit the button.

It took a second to register. I had gone in the bedroom to change, but curiosity pulled me back. The tape was rolling yet the room was silent. The loft was dark, panels of faded street-light fighting the grubby windows to fall across the floor. Silence. Then I heard it. Breathing. Soft. Mesmerizing. Breathing. Unconsciously my own matched it. In. Out. Breath for breath. Goosepimples were signalling frantically all up and down my arms. In. Out. Waiting in the dark for a voice that didn't come. just breathing, in, out, in . . . Abruptly it stopped and I gasped, as if my air had been cut off. The machine whirred to rewind, and I sank slowly on to the couch. It was him. I knew it was him. I sat in the dark with my wine and my cats and wondered how he knew where to call.

5

The first thing I did was turn off the phone, the machine too. For almost a week. There was no reason not to. My mother had sent a care package with Christmas cookies, Russell Stover candy and a bottle of champagne. I drank champagne and orange juice until the citric acid made me sick, then I pulled on a hat and dark glasses and ventured as far as the liquor store. I bought a bottle of Jack Daniels, a half-gallon of vodka and on impulse some Kahlua. I don't normally like mixed drinks—mixers didn't sit well with my stomach, the orange juice a case in point—but I thought I would make some White Russians. When I got home, I put on my ratty bathrobe, mixed the Kahlua and vodka with some milk and ice and settled on the couch in front of the TV, feeling unbelievably depressed.

By day three I had run out of milk, but found an old container of Cremora that worked. I just added a teaspoon or two to each drink. A little clumpy, but not bad. Every once in a while, I'd check the machine, even though I knew it was off. The call Christmas night replayed itself inside my head, bigger and darker each day and each drink. How did Vanessa stand it? And why had he suddenly called me?

It didn't make sense. A deranged fan would hardly bother and I didn't really know any of Vanessa's exes. Except for lunch, our worlds barely touched. You know one, suggested the voice. "He's not an ex," I told Ozzie, "he's just an ass-hole."

But once the seed was planted the thought took hold. I rolled Jake Romano around, considering. He did know me, so that part worked. And he doesn't like you, whispered the voice. No one likes you, sniped a second. I don't like him either, I defended, there's something wrong with him. Wrong with *him*, hooted the little voice. Ha, said the second. I brooded, knowing their opinion would be the consensus. I switched to JD, not bothering with ice, and thought some more, debating the voices that kept denying me answers.

The day before New Year's Eve, the Jack had run out and I was back to vodka. Just vodka, on the rocks. I knew I had to tell someone what I knew—by now it made perfect sense—and decided to call Oola. Still, I picked up the phone several times before I dialed. It rang and rang until Andrew finally answered, slightly out of breath.

I tried to make polite chitchat, peace on earth and all that crap. It didn't fly well and when Andrew called Oola to the phone, I heard him say something about drinking. I sat a little straighter and pushed a greasy strand of hair out of my eyes. When had I taken a shower?

"Kate, Happy New Year!"

"Same to you."

"What's going on?"

"Have you talked to Vanessa lately?"

"Yes. It's horrible, isn't it? There was over $500 in damage to her car."

"Yeah, it sucks, but Oola . . ."

"I couldn't believe it," she continued. "This is more than Vanessa having a feeling. She's being stalked, Kate. As if she were some Neanderthal's dinner.

"I know. I don't like what's happening to her. We had a drink before Christmas and you should have seen her. She had no fingernails, Oola!"

Oola knew Vanessa well enough to take this seriously. She rattled on for a while about crimes against women and society's apathy. I listened with the phone tucked under one ear and reached for the vodka to replenish my drink. I dropped the phone as I tipped the bottle and it clinked against the glass.

"Kate, are you there?"

"Yeah, yeah, I just dropped the phone."

"Kate . . ." I could hear her debating. "Are you drinking?"

"No." Silence.

"Have you been drinking?"

"I had a glass of wine earlier." Shit, what time was it?

"Why did you call, Kate?"

"I've been thinking about this thing with Vanessa. Oola, what do you know about stalkers?"

"I've been pulling together some research since Vanessa and I talked. It's scary the things I found and I just started. Do you know that in 1990, one third of all the women murdered in this country—one in three—were killed by ex-husbands or lovers? Now listen to this, ninety percent of them were stalked prior to their deaths."

Jake Romano scared me more than ever now. "Oola, doesn't that make you think that whoever's stalking Vanessa is someone she knows?"

"It's a strong probability, Kate. It could very well be someone she rejected in the past. But according to what I've found so far, celebrity stalking is also on the rise. You and I might not think of Vanessa as famous, but somebody else could. Someone who reads her books. Remember that Stephen King story, *Misery*?"

"Yeah," I said dubiously. This was getting off the path I wanted to follow. "But what if it was somebody who just thought he was being rejected? Somebody still in Vanessa's life, but who wanted to play a bigger role than he'd been given?" Oola was quiet. I took a slurp of my drink, and the sound was louder than I intended.

"What is it you're trying to say, Kate. Just tell me."

"It's that guy, that Jake guy," I blurted. "Don't you think it's a coincidence that all this stuff started happening when Vanessa started dating him?"

"Jake. Jake? Why on earth would you think it's Jake?"

The suspicions tumbled out of me, mixed up with time and emotion and booze. I kept jumping around and fumbling for words and finally sputtered to a halt. "I don't like him, Oola. In my gut, I know there's something wrong about him."

"Kate, I don't want to be cruel, but it sounds like there's more liquor in your gut than anything. You have absolutely no basis for this."

"What about the bar? What about the message on my machine?"

"You don't have any idea who left that message." If there was a message at all, I could hear her thinking. "And quite frankly, Kate, the fact that you dislike Jake doesn't carry much weight. When have you ever liked anyone that Vanessa dated? Or me either, for that matter. Look at how you feel about Andrew."

"This has nothing to do with that."

"I think it does. Look Kate, I want you to stop drinking and eat something. Get out of that apartment for a while. Take a walk, go shopping, do something. I think you've blown this whole idea way out of proportion."

"Fine," I retorted angrily. "Thanks for the support. Have a great goddamn New Year." I slammed the phone down and gulped down the rest of my drink. Jesus, she sounded just like Steve, telling me to stop making a big deal out of things and always bitching about me having a drink. Holier-than-thou princess, little Miss I-Don't-Drink, she and my goddamn ex-husband were a match made in heaven! As I poured more vodka into my glass, anxiety crowded the anger. Could she be right? Oola's always right, whispered the voice. I hugged my glass to me and rocked.

I woke up New Year's Eve around noon, my face creased by the texture of the couch. I took my first shower in nearly a week and left the bathrobe on the floor. The living room was a disaster. As I threw away the bottles I stepped in a pile of potato chips, so I swept them up along with the paper candy cups and moved some books to cover the rings on coffee table. Oola was right about one thing, I thought: get out of here.

I had breakfast in a diner near Canal Street. The menu shook in my hands but I forced myself to order. Once I started eating, I was ravenous and got a second bagel after I finished my eggs. It was a little after two-thirty when I finished. I walked around Soho for a while, watching everyone go somewhere. It's very important in New York to be going somewhere all the time. I had nowhere to go and wandered aimlessly. There was just enough snow to be sooty and left-over Christmas decorations looked tacky and forlorn. Tourists strolled on Broadway, ears straining for the lullaby. At three-thirty, I gave it up and headed to Petrillo's.

Mr. Moriarty waved to me from his table by the window. I waved back as I took my usual stool and ordered a Molson, no glass. Roger Petrillo thought drinking from the bottle was unladylike, so he always gave me a glass anyway. I pushed it out of my way and skimmed through a newspaper left on the bar.

Sometime around four, Chubb came in with a guy who

looked vaguely familiar. Chubb was a regular, though not always a welcome one. He only drank whiskey when his Social Security check came in and invariably developed an aversion to plate glass windows and men in uniform. That's how I knew the other guy! He was Chubb's nephew, a retired cop. Bobby was his name. It was Bobby who saved Chubb's butt every time the shit hit the fan, footing the bill for damages and smoothing things over with New York's finest. If I remembered right, he still worked somewhere, doing security. Chubb was always boasting that Bobby was some kind of bigwig in a firm uptown. Not that I paid much attention to Chubb, but if even a part of what be said was true, this was a golden opportunity.

I ordered myself another Molson and told Roger to get one for Chubb and his nephew. They wished me a Happy New Year and I slid off my stool into the one next to Bobby.

"Mind if I join you? Hey Chubb." The old man grunted and downed his shot. "Hi, it's Bobby, right? I'm Kate."

"Hi Kate. Thanks for the drink."

"No problem."

Chubb cursed loudly. He was glaring at the TV screen at the other end of the bar, rheumy eyes squinting. Evidently the game's quarterback didn't have "a fuckin' idea what do with a fuckin' football." Chubb gave him a few off-color suggestions before Bobby suggested he go over and watch the game. Chubb toddled off to a seat near the TV and we settled back with our beers.

"Bobby, you're a security guy, right?"

"You could call it that, Kate, though the company I work for does a lot of different things. Why?"

"I have a problem, actually a friend of mine does, and I'd like to tell you about it. See what you think."

"Tell away."

I told him about the calls, the cars, the message on my machine. I left out Jake Romano, Oola's reaction still fresh in my mind.

"How long since it started?"

"I think October, maybe late September."

"So not very long."

"Not very long!" I shrieked. "It's been over three months! Shit, you have to see her! Well, you don't know her, but if you knew her and you saw her, you wouldn't know her! She's a mess, Bobby, a hostage. If those people in Iran had only been held three and a half months, would you have said, 'So, not very long!' "

"Slow down Kate, I know your friend's in trouble," Bobby replied. "It's just when one of these guys is serious, it's for the long haul. It can go on for years."

"Years?"

"Yeah, years. There was a case in California where a stalker pursued a woman for over eight years and eventually tried to kidnap her at gunpoint. Her husband was a football player, with the Dolphins, I think."

"Eight years! Holy shit. A celebrity thing, right?"

"Not really; I mean, no. I don't even think that he was playing when the whole thing started. No. The stalker was a guy the victim had gone to high school with. He had a speech impediment that made his voice very peculiar, that's how she was able to identify him. She had barely known him and hadn't seen him in years."

"You mean he just appeared out of nowhere?"

"Strange as it sounds, yes. Who knows how long he'd been fixated on her. Stalkers are very methodical about their obsession. They're intent on having the victim, owning her, so to speak. Everything they do is totally justified in their own minds, even though everyone else knows it's crazy."

"But what if the stalker isn't crazy? What if he has a good job or is handsome and charming?"

"It's a misconception that all these guys are skevey. Remember that judge in Albany? He looked great on the outside, but underneath? Totally wacked! Victims do this to themselves all the time, take responsibility, try and figure out what they've done, as if it's their fault."

"Why would he suddenly call me," I asked, wondering if I could lead into Jake.

"Your friend's an author, right? If he can't get to her, or wants to feel closer to her, who better to contact? Or he could be threatened by your relationship with her. It's not unusual for stalkers to involve victims' families or friends. Do you remember that woman, an actress, Italian, I think, Teresa something? She was stalked by some nut and he called her family, her agent, her business manager, anyone he could think of. Wrote them letters, too. She was scared to death, almost literally. The guy finally attacked her with a knife right outside her house." Roger came by and Bobby ordered us another round. I sat there and thought about being attacked with a knife.

"I remember her. I've seen her on talk shows. She was trying to keep him from getting out of jail."

"Yeah, good luck. But I suppose, sick as it sounds, legally she was better off than most women. If a stalker doesn't do anything violent, the police are almost impotent."

"That's reassuring." I shivered just thinking about it, then realized that Bobby was still talking. "What? I'm sorry, I got lost there for a minute.

"You remember that kid, young girl, Rebecca Shaefer? She was on some television show. The detective who covered her case . . ." He was interrupted by a sudden crash of broken glass, followed by a spate of familiar curses. Chubb had thrown a beer at the TV screen. Fortunately, neither his arm nor his eyesight were on the money. Chubb was squawking angrily at Roger who was yelling back. Bobby sighed and went to intervene.

After a few minutes of chaos, Bobby had Chubb subdued and Roger pacified. He hustled Chubb toward the door and stopped by my stool to gather their coats.

"Gotta go, Kate. Give me a call." He threw a business card on the bar. "I got some stuff you might wanna look at."

"Great! Thanks a lot, Bobby. Happy New Year, Chubb." Chubb flipped me the finger as he stumbled out into the street. Bobby shrugged and followed him out the door.

It was almost five-thirty, so there didn't seem much point in going home. It was New Year's Eve after all. I grabbed a slice from Nunzio's next door and hung out at the bar. Roger Petrillo bought me a shot of peppermint schnapps, so I bought him one back. When the night bartender came on at seven, he came around the bar and sat down. Then we started drinking.

It was a pretty good party at Petrillo's. Nothing like the clubs uptown, but then again I wasn't paying a hundred bucks just to be there. We played the jukebox loud and around nine o'clock there was garlic pizza, a meat tray, potato salad and chicken wings. Roger cleared out some of the tables in the back and we danced. Being one of the few dateless women under sixty, I was a hot ticket. Everything from free-form to cha cha, I whirled from partner to partner, drink to drink.

We had the TV on, goofing on all the idiots who had made the trek to Times Square. At five minutes to midnight, Roger sent me to the bar for a bottle of Asti Spumante. Petrillo's was a small place, so I had to fight my way through the people. I hooted to get Danny's attention behind the tap and stood on the bar rail hoping to catch his eye. Someone prodded my shoulder. I ignored them. They nudged me again, harder this time.

"Hey, wait your fucking turn! I was here . . ."

He was hopelessly out of place. The stunning face stood out among the ancient cronies and creeps and drunks like a beacon in the night. His eyes were waiting for mine and when they met, a slow smile spread across his face.

"Happy New Year, Katie." He raised his drink.

"I told you not to call me that! Danny!"

"Need a drink?" So solicitous. The smarmy bastard.

"What are you doing here?"

"I saw you through the window. You seemed to be all alone. I thought you might like some company."

"I've got plenty of company. Plenty of friends." Damn that Danny!

He let his eyes run over the crowd before they swung back to me, disdain apparent. "So I see."

"At least I've got someplace to go. What's the matter, Vanessa have another date?"

"Vanessa is in Georgia, you know that." He took a swallow.

"Oh right, Georgia, I forgot. That's what she told you, right." The inflection was deliberate, the intent malicious. His face darkened and I faked an innocent smile. "Hey Danny, what's a person gotta do to get a drink in this place!"

"Have you heard from her?"

"No, why should I?"

"I just thought you might have." He paused, raised his drink to his lips and looked directly into my eyes. "No messages on your machine?"

There was something in how he said it. I faltered, the bar and the background fading away, just him and me and danger in the air. Danny slapped the bar behind me with a loud crack. I jumped, then tore my eyes away and mumbled over my shoulder about Roger's champagne. I turned back to Jake. He smiled.

The hair rose on the back of my neck. I didn't wait for Danny, didn't make any excuses, just ducked past Jake and pushed my way to the ladies room, down a hall off the side of the bar. I slammed the door and locked it, heart racing, head reeling. The beers, the shots, the champagne cocktails haunted me, specters of self-doubt. The sound of my breathing filled the tiny room, bringing back the message on my machine. All at once the spirits solidified and I was furious, sure, at Jake, but mostly at myself. What the hell was I doing hiding in the fucking bathroom?

I threw open the door and stormed up the narrow hallway, I could hear the crowd counting, "Ten . . . Nine . . . Eight . . ." Jake Romano suddenly filled the end of the corridor, blocking the light and the way. "Seven . . . Six . . ." I stopped short, suddenly claustrophobic, heart once again racing.

"Get out of my way." He didn't move. "Five . . . Four . . ." chanted the crowd. I pushed forward, elbow first as if to shove by. "Three . . ." He caught my arm just above the wrist and jerked me forward against his chest. "Two . . ." I could feel his heart beating. "One!"

Horns shrieked and people yelled. "Let me go," I cried soundlessly, lost in the noise of the new year. Jake Romano's fingers dug into my chin and forced it up. He bent his dark head, lips moist and full, slightly open, a tip of tongue against the teeth. Closer, through the noise and the smoke, strangers kissing strangers, closer. I shut my eyes.

"Don't get your hopes up, Katie," he hissed, lips brushing my ear. "You'll end up getting hurt." His teeth closed on my lobe and bit down. I jerked my head with a cry of surprise, tears stinging like my ear. Without another word, he turned away. I watched him work his way to the door, fending off balloons and streamers and plastic glasses of champagne. He didn't look back. I huddled where he left me, apart from the horns and hugs and frolic, the room and the crowd swaying to "Auld Lang Syne."

6

I had stayed at the bar until things got blurry and the sky got light. Eventually I was escorted out, after standing on a chair and declaring all men to be motherfuckers at the top of my lungs. Being the only woman left in the bar, I didn't rally much support. Roger Petrillo got me down and insisted on walking me home despite my kicks and curses.

New Year's Day I nursed my hangover and tried to sort things out. I was right, I knew it. And it didn't matter if Oola believed me or not. But Vanessa, that was another story. She was coming home tomorrow. I had to tell her. Chances were good she wasn't going to believe me either. I turned my phone back on and listened while Oola left messages and then Annie did because Oola told her to, I guess. I played kitty-in-the-bag with the cats and ate microwave pizza. It was all I could cope with, not to mention all I had.

The next morning I went to Food Emporium and stocked up, overtipping the delivery boy so I'd have a chance of getting my groceries before the burritos could defrost. When I got back home, there was another message on the machine. Jesus, Oola needs to get a life. I ignored it and flicked on the TV, but the flashing light nagged me. Might as well get it over with. The machine whirred and the sound of Vanessa's voice snapped my head around.

"Kate, are you there? If you're there, please pick up. I'm scared, Kate." I could hear her waiting. "God, you're really not home are you? Kate, I flew back today and when we got to the barn, there were flowers on the porch and . . ." I heard her draw a ragged breath, maybe on a cigarette, maybe not. "And when we went inside, there was a rose, Kate, one white rose lying on the mantle." Her' voice broke up into little gasps.

"He's been in my house. In my house. And he took the picture, my dad, it's the only one. Gone . . ."

She sobbed until the tape ran out. I played it twice, catching the reference to we and wondering if Jake was still with her. In her house. You don't know it's him, jeered the little voice. What did he really say, scoffed the second. He said enough, I answered. You were drunk, they murmured in unison. Fine, so I was buzzed, but I wasn't stupid. And anyway, if we were gonna believe the feeling in Vanessa's stomach, then I was damn well gonna believe the one in mine.

I didn't stop to think, just grabbed a cab to the train station. I owned a car, if you could call it that, but it was garaged over in the east twenties and I didn't want to waste any time. I called Vanessa after I got my ticket and told her I was coming. She sounded so small, like a little girl. I asked if she was alone and she said that Jake was with her. I told her to pick me up without him. She was silent for a second, then agreed. I was surprised it was so easy.

The train seemed to take forever. When I finally stood on the platform, I looked around for Vanessa, but didn't see her. I was heading for the pay phone when I heard the Volvo's horn. Filled with relief, I waved and ran down the steps to the lot.

"Are you okay? I was so worried." I hugged her hard across the seats. She pressed her cheek to mine, taking not giving. When she pulled away her eyes were brimming with tears and tiredness and the weight of just not knowing what to do.

"It's horrible, Kate. The idea of him being in my house, touching my things. It makes me sick."

"What did the police say?"

"We haven't called them yet."

"What? They'd have to take this seriously, Vanessa. They told you when the guy breaks in . . ."

"The rose inside was almost dead, it might have been there the whole time. Jake looked all over and couldn't find any signs of a break-in. He said . . . I'm tired of trying to make them take this seriously."

"You're tired, or was this Jake's idea?"

"Don't start, Kate!" She slammed the car into gear and pealed out of the parking lot.

"What? What did I do?"

"Don't think I don't know about you and Jake. How could you, Kate? I know you've been unhappy lately, but does that mean you need me to be unhappy too?" She careened around a corner, one hand working a cigarette free.

"Wait a minute, what are you talking about?" I took the pack and pulled out a cigarette. She grabbed it from my hand and punched in the car lighter.

"He told me, so can the innocent act. I know all about what happened at that stupid bar. And you talk about me being a slut. At least I can find my own men."

"What?" I roared again. "Is that what he told you? That I came on to him? And you believed it?" She didn't answer, just stared straight ahead, hands clenched on the wheel. "Well, fuck you. If that's what you think then take me back to the goddamn train.

"Fine," she snapped and cranked the wheel to the left. The Volvo squealed around the turn into a tree-lined side street. She drove about half a block and then swerved to a halt at the curb. Resting her head on hands on the steering wheel, she sighed. "I don't want to fight with you. I can't take it."

I fought back my anger and said softly, "Vanessa, I am your friend. I would never do that, what he said, and certainly not with him," I added with bitter emphasis. "Why would you believe something like that without even talking to me?"

"He told me how drunk you were. He even tried to make excuses for you."

"What did he say?"

"He said he was coming from a party and saw you in the window. You waved him in, insisted he have a drink. You were pretty smashed, he said, it was hard to understand you. Something about a parade through my bedroom . . ."

"That isn't what I said," I interrupted hotly.

"Then he said you started crawling on him, playing with his hair, nibbling on his ear."

"*His* ear!"

"And when you tried to kiss him, he had to put you off, then you got mad. Told him you'd fix things between us. So here we are, Kate. With you asking me to leave him home. Did you have something you wanted to say, something you didn't want him to hear?"

The son of a bitch. He had blindsided me and there was

nothing I could do. "Look, Van, I did see him New Year's Eve, but it didn't happen the way he said. It isn't true."

"I don't know what the hell is true anymore."

"Vanessa," I pleaded. She turned and looked at me. After a minute, her eyes dropped to her lap.

"Kate, I have never let anyone, any man, get close to me. Oh, I know, I'm love-'em-and-leave-'em Vanessa. Never found a man who measures up. Has it ever occurred to you I might be the one who can't measure up?" She finally lit her cigarette and took a deep drag. "I don't do relationships well, Kate. I'm great at short hits and one-month stands, but I'm scared shitless of the real thing." She lifted her head for a second, then dropped it again. "I don't wanna be alone anymore, Kate. I'm sorry you don't like him, but this time I have to try." Her eyes brimmed over and I was filled with an aching sadness. More than just the fingernails, walls were tumbling down. I reached out and patted her hand. She started the car and we drove to the barn in silence.

He was watching for us out the window. Just the sight of him enraged me, but for Vanessa's sake, I tried to settle down. He met her on the front porch steps and she clung to him. Jake held her so gently I almost believed I was wrong. I forced a smile and brushed past them into the barn. I took an armchair in front of the fire and they sat on the couch, the three of us looking anywhere but at each other. Vanessa offered me a drink, Jake got us some beers, obviously at home. He put the drink in front of me and settled on the couch, leaning forward, elbows on his knees.

"I think we should clear the air," he said. "Kate, look, you and I have gotten off to a bad start. I'm sorry if I've offended you in any way and I'd really like to try again." He picked up Vanessa's hand. "We both love Vanessa. And right now, she needs us. Do you think we can be friends, for her sake?" He was so earnest and sincere I wanted to slap him. Vanessa sandwiched their entwined fingers with her other hand and waited for my response.

"Sure. Yeah. Sorry," I said flatly, surprised I didn't choke. "So where are the roses," I asked, indicating the empty mantle.

"They're over . . . Where are they? Where did they go?" Vanessa's voice had an edge of panic. Nothing was safe in her house.

"Honey, don't get worked up," he soothed. "You were so upset, I didn't like seeing you that way, so I took care of it. It's bad enough this is happening, you don't need the damn flowers to remind you." Vanessa curled into his side and Jake nuzzled her hair.

"What did you do with them?" Enough with the warm fuzzies, answer the question.

"I burned them." He looked straight at me. Was that a smirk?

"You burned them!" It was a smirk. "You stupid . . ." Vanessa sat up and I swallowed hard. "How are we gonna explain to the police?"

"Jake, I know you wanted to protect me but . . ."

"Vanessa," he answered, ignoring me completely. "The last time we called the police, what happened? They laughed it off and you were a wreck. I'm the one who spent all day calming you down, remember? I didn't want to put you through that again, for nothing."

"That really isn't your decision." I wanted for Vanessa's confirmation but it didn't come. "Van, you have to call the police."

"Maybe Jake's right, Kate. They didn't believe me."

"We'll make them believe you!"

"You weren't even here, you don't understand," Jake replied. "There's nothing you can do."

"There's always something to do," I insisted, eyes blazing. Still Vanessa said nothing. I bit my lip. "Didn't you say he stole something, a picture?"

Tears slid down her cheeks and she brushed at them with a nail-less finger. She opened her mouth but her chest heaved and nothing came out. Jake glared at me and pulled her into his shoulder, hands roving her back. Vanessa's face turned away, I took the opportunity to glare back.

"Ouch! Honey, your ring!" Vanessa pulled away. His eyes broke from mine.

"I'm sorry, babe," he said. "It got turned." Jake reached around her and twisted the base of a large ring on his right hand. The setting was lumpy, almost thorny, a chunk of tiger's eye imprisoned in gold prongs.

"I don't want to upset you . . ." I began.

"Then don't," he interrupted coldly.

"But, Van, what picture?" I knew what Vanessa had told me, but knowledge was a funny game at this stage. What if Jake knew more about the picture than Vanessa had told him?

"Of her parents," he answered. Are you satisfied? his eyes asked.

"Of Virginia Mae? Which one, Vanessa," I said, emphasizing her name.

"The wedding picture, Kate. On the mantle. That's where he left the rose." Her voice quivered and Jake put a hand on her arm. "Can you get me a cigarette, please? You know the one, Kate. Remember the funny hairdos?" He handed her the lit cigarette. "Thanks. It was the only picture I had of my father. I can't believe it's gone." Another tear escaped. "I don't know how I'll tell my mother."

Vanessa's father had been a migrant farm worker. When she was six, he went up north to follow the picking season and never came back. They never found out what happened to him, but Virginia Mae always insisted that he loved them and never let Vanessa believe anything else.

"Oh Van. Oh no. We have to call the police! How will you ever get it back?"

Jake snorted, his voice dripping sarcasm. "Even if we did report it, what do you think her chances are?"

"Better than if we don't!" Both our voices rose. He wasn't budging and I had no intention of letting this slide. The two of us were mirror images, full of righteousness and fury.

"Please . . ." Vanessa whispered, shaming us into remembering her.

"Okay, okay, what's done is done," I said, reaching past Jake to touch her knee. We could talk about this later, when he wasn't around. I looked up at the mantle and mused, "I wonder why he took that picture."

"The guy is sick, Kate. He wanted a souvenir, a trophy."

"I know how sick he is. I understand why he took something but how could he know how important that particular picture was?" I waved my arm around the room. "There are a ton of pictures here, a lot of them of Vanessa. Why wouldn't he take one like that, Jake?" It was a challenge.

The phone rang. Vanessa jumped at the sound and huddled against his side. He wrapped his arms around her and I got up and answered the phone. Oola. There was no escaping her. I explained what I was doing there and what had happened. She was so shocked she never mentioned my previous call. Evidently she had been trying to fax the stalking stuff to Vanessa's computer, but either the modem wasn't on or something wasn't working.

I told Vanessa and she headed for the office, grateful, I think, for the break in our conversation. I trailed behind her, Jake still on the couch. The back of the computer faced the door and Vanessa checked the cables and connections before going around the desk to her chair. It was only a second before she gasped and propelled herself backward as if she'd been burned.

"The blood of the woman he loved rolled down his cheek like a tear," said the large type running across the screen. It was the first line of *Headstone,* when the crazy guy explains why he had to butcher his wife. I hit the enter button, the space bar. This was a screen saver, it should go away when the computer was in use. Nothing happened. The words ran over and over, blood red on black.

"Jake, Jake," Vanessa sobbed. He rushed in, looking from her to me to the screen.

"Get rid of it," he ordered.

"I can't!"

He pushed me aside and took the mouse. His elegant fingers moved expertly. When the computer didn't respond, he tried a number of keystroke combinations. Nothing. Still the bloody words. He snapped the switch on the hard drive and it droned off with a sigh.

"It's frozen up. Looks like a virus. We had one in the office just last week. Same thing happened."

"Except this one happened on purpose."

"You're right about that," he said. "Vanessa, I've had enough. I want you to get your things and come to my apartment. Now."

"I can't," she protested. "I've got too much work to do. And no, I can't do it at your house. It's too distracting. I need to be home, so if something strikes me and I wanna work, I can." They argued back and forth, his face flushed and dark. Concern for her safety or anger at being disobeyed?

"Hey, I have an idea," I said. "Why don't I come out here and stay for a little while?" She looked up hopefully; his expression was less clear. "Sure," I said. "I've got nothing going on. Let's run into the city and get my stuff. Oh, and the cats. I'd have to bring the cats, but other than that, no problem."

I brushed off Vanessa's thanks, but couldn't resist a triumphant glance at Jake. I had to go to the bathroom and when I came back downstairs I heard him talking heatedly, Vanessa patient but thankfully firm. The second they saw me, conversation ceased.

"Ready?" I asked.

They scurried around for a few minutes, getting organized. Jake wanted to drive us, but how would we get back? I asked innocently. Vanessa got the keys to the Volvo and called Oola to give her the fax number at her office up at school. We'd swing by and pick up her info. We went out to our cars and I settled into the passenger seat while Jake kissed her goodbye. She had just started the engine when he came to the window.

"I'm not happy about this, Vanessa. I think you're making a mistake."

"Jake, we've been over this. I won't be alone, I'll be with Kate."

"I want you with me," he insisted.

"It'll be okay, honey. Honest. I'll call you later. Love you."

He stepped back from the car and we pulled away. He stood in the driveway and watched us go.

7

"I'll be right back," she said when we pulled up in front of the school. "It'll take two seconds for me to grab the fax." She slammed the door and I fiddled with the radio, trying to find a decent station. Suddenly the door opened and I jumped. When Vanessa stuck her head in, I could have throttled her.

"Sorry I scared you. Kate, I just want you to know . . . just thanks. For coming out. Especially after . . . well, thanks."

She was gone before I could reply, so I waited in the car, grinning like an idiot. Friendship was the savior of the spirit, yet we women so regularly sacrificed it for men. I was glad that Vanessa had believed me, or at least had forgiven me for Jake's lie. He might be what I thought he was, but even if he wasn't, Vanessa would still be my friend and there was nothing he could do about it.

She had been gone close to fifteen minutes. I was starting to get antsy when she bounded down the steps clutching fax curls to her chest. "God, it's spooky in there." She handed me the papers and pulled two diskettes from her coat pocket. "Sorry I took so long. I knew we had some virus software somewhere but it took a while to find it. This should clean up the computer."

We hopped on the expressway and headed downtown, finding a parking spot relatively close to the loft. The condition of the apartment was less than ideal. The litter box smell hit us in the elevator and there was a note from Food Emporium tacked to the door. The place was a wreck, mounds of unopened mail, dirty sweats and scattered glasses, a half-eaten pizza. I tried to write it off to feline mischief, buying only a raised eyebrow from Vanessa and an injured look from the cats.

We tidied things up a bit and grabbed some clothes, cat

litter and the kitty carrier. Harley and Ozzie were not thrilled at the prospect of traveling, associating any and all car rides with a visit to the dreaded veterinarian. We trapped Ozzie behind the bookcase and coaxed Harley out from behind the refrigerator with a can of white albacore.

Given the stench of my apartment, I suggested we look over Oola's fax at Petrillo's. We walked the few blocks, carrying the cats, who howled miserably, pleading for strangers to intervene. I settled them on a back table in the bar, bribing them with beef jerky, but knowing there would be hell to pay. Cats were vindictive and patient beasts.

"Give us a couple of Molsons, Roger," I called. I scooped a handful of beer nuts off the bar. I nodded happily to some regulars in the corner and waved to Mr. Moriarty. Chubb was sucking on a draft and bitching loudly about the Knicks.

"Kate, I don't get it. What do you see in this place?" Vanessa whispered, after the beers came and Roger had headed back down the bar. "It's an old man's bar, for God sakes. Smells like the holding room in a men's prison." Vanessa looked around cautiously. I took a long drink from my beer bottle and laughed.

"They know me, Vanessa. I can come here and have a drink and not worry about being hit on or robbed or followed home. I don't know, we kind of take care of each other, like I used to with my pop." I didn't have to defend myself. I belonged here. "Let's see what Oola sent."

She spread the fax out on the bar, anchoring the curls with the beer nut bowl, Tabasco sauce and a salt shaker. I nailed the last corner down with the beer glass I never used that Roger brought me regardless.

Oola's fax, like Oola, was well put together and full of enlightening information. There was also her penchant for the obvious: The most common stalker is a guy who has been rejected by women.

"Wow, Kate, listen! 'In 1990, 30 percent of female homicides . . .' "

"Yeah, I know, she told me." Vanessa drained her glass and refilled it, her movements mechanical. Anything to create some sense of normalcy, while her mind processed the radical implications of Oola's research.

"I know it's scary, Vanessa, but those women were stalked

by someone they knew. If you think this is a stranger, you've got nothing to worry about, right?"

"Oh sure. Those guys were willing to kill a woman they supposedly loved, so my nutjob will hold off until he gets to know me better. I feel so much safer now!" She lit a cigarette with shaking hands.

"We don't even know if it's a stranger."

"I think the message on my computer makes it pretty clear."

"What if that's what he wants you to think?"

Roger interrupted to see if we wanted more beers. We did. Vanessa ordered a cognac too, better known as brandy here at Petrillo's. She was so absorbed in her own thoughts she didn't even comment when it was served in a shot glass.

Oola's fax was fascinating. It broke stalking behavior down into three categories: the jilted lover, the narcissist and the out-and-out crazy. The jilted lover was obvious, but full of scary statistics.

"Do you see this? It says that one in twenty women will be stalked in their lifetime. One in twenty! Damn, I hate that stuff. Do you remember when the FBI put out the one about a woman being raped every six seconds?" I asked.

"And you wonder why I don't wear a watch. How about this one." She read out loud: " 'The narcissist's ego is so fragile that any hint of rejection can result in rage. The rage fuels the hatred and the hatred fuels revenge. He's consumed by a justified prerogative to destroy the victim's life.' "

"That sounds right. Especially if it's somebody you know."

"It could work for a stranger too. What if this is somebody who wrote Gordon a letter and didn't get an answer?" she suggested stubbornly, more comfortable with the enemy unknown than familiar.

"I think the last one works better for that. See," I kept reading, unnerved by what I found. If what this said was true, maybe Jake was just a creep, not a villain. " 'This stalker is deeply disturbed; he believes his devotion to the victim is predestined—their love must not be denied.' And look, Vanessa," I added, pointing to the page. "It says people with certain mental illnesses can believe that stuff, even if there's been no relationship."

"That's it, Kate. That's got to be it!" I ordered us another couple of beers and Vanessa had another brandy.

"I don't know. There's no doubt this guy is a few ants short of a picnic, but this seems awfully well executed for someone who's supposed to be mentally ill." I could be stubborn too. I wasn't giving up on Jake, but I had to admit there were other possibilities. "What is this Oola's written, down here on the side."

"I don't know, I can't read it."

Vanessa picked up the fax and peered at Oola's handwriting, sipping her drink.

"She's got a note here, something about property, I think. What's this word?" Vanessa held the paper in front of me, pointing. I tilted my head, trying to read the smudged fax.

"For some reason, Oola's lousy penmanship gives me hope. Does it say owners or ownership?"

"Ownership! Yeah, here. 'If I can't have her, no one else will.' " She squinted at the page. "Prehysteria, no, prehistoric. 'Basic to prehistoric males, the taking of mates, the right to sexual ownership.' I think that's what it says." She handed me the paper, and I took up the deciphering.

" 'Some stalkers stalk for the pleasure of the act. Similar to the hunting of animals.' Animals? Yeah, animals. 'Isolate prey from the pack, build up fear and apprehension, chase until exhausted, make the kill.' Jesus, make the kill!" I shuddered, dropping the paper like a spent match.

"She's talking about sport. He views this as a sport." Vanessa slapped the bar. "I hate to say it, but that feels so right. No matter what his reasons are—he likes this. He likes doing it. I'm not a human being. I'm an animal, a female animal that he has the right to hunt and subdue. And if I get hurt during the chase, well, that's just my fault for resisting, isn't it?"

"The chase can be the problem. Bobby was telling me about a woman . . ."

"Who's Bobby?"

We sat there drinking as I explained. Slowly Vanessa began to get angry. I was glad to see it, it was better than the fear. We pounded back a few more beers, discussed the merits of castration and sang the chorus from "I Am Woman" until people screamed at us to stop. By the time we pulled ourselves off our stools, Vanessa was slightly smashed.

"You drive, Kate. I gotta pee and I wanna call Jake. He's probably worried." She wobbled for a second, then headed for

the phone. I had finished off our beers by the time she returned. "He's not home," she pouted.

We were halfway down the block when Roger caught up
with us to remind me of the cats. Vanessa followed him back
while I got the car. I gunned the engine, and moved the car
behind me back a few feet with my bumper. It wasn't nice to
crowd other people's parking spaces. I rolled down the window and headed for the bar, one eye closed for enhanced night
vision. I laughed off the little voice that murmured something
about drinking and driving. Some people drove better after a
few drinks.

I screeched to a halt in front of Vanessa and the cats. She
clambered in the car, felines yowling, and we headed back to
the Island. It seemed like one minute we were in Manhattan,
the next minute we were at the barn. I knew I took the expressway, but I couldn't remember being on the road. I roared
into the driveway, the two of us giggling and singing to the
radio. The cats were still howling indignantly and Vanessa had
scratches all over her hands.

"What I think, I think we should give the li'l fucker something to watch, that's what I think," Vanessa said, lifting the
cat carrier from the back seat and smacking it against the door.
She dropped it on the ground, cupped her hands and hollered,
"Hey, stalker! You, yeah, you! Watch this, big boy!" She bent
from the waist, flipped up her coat and dropped her pants and
drawers. As I came around the side of the car, she waved at
me from upside down between her legs. I cracked up, rolling
against the car in the dark driveway as Vanessa tumbled to
the frozen ground. None of the floodlights were on and shadows stretched across her as clouds blew by the moon.

"Shhhhh," Vanessa scolded loudly as she rezipped her
pants, "neighbors." She waved her hand at the silent houses
as she struggled to her feet. I picked up the cats and tiptoed
toward the back stairs. I stumbled up them in the dark and
unlocked the door, Vanessa totally hopeless and still given to
fits of irrational giggles. Inside, I sat the cats down and opened
the carrier. They fled into the dark house as Vanessa flicked
on the lights. Nothing happened. She flicked the switch again.

"Shit!"

"What's a matter, you need a bulb?"

"No, I need a goddamn flashlight, that's what I need." She

pulled the drawer almost out of its slot. "Fucking electricians . . . happens all the goddamn . . . Aha!" She held up the flashlight triumphantly, a circle of light on the ceiling. "I gotta fix the fuse." She headed toward the basement stairs.

"What about me, it's dark up here?"

She stopped by the cellar door and hit me in the eyes with a beam of light. I cringed. "Cut it out!" She flashed a huge, drunken smile and disappeared down the stairs, snorting and chuckling.

"I'm glad you think you're funny," I muttered.

I dug around and found a beat-up candle, but no matches. I pulled the drawer all the way out and dumped it on the counter, pawing through the contents. The woman smoked like a chimney, I thought, then remembered the stove. I got the wick lit, started for the living room and the flame promptly blew out. Shit. I flicked the wall switch. Darkness. What the hell was taking her so long.

"Vanessa," I yelled irritably. No answer. I went to the top of the stairs and yelled again. There was no sound from the cellar. Great, she probably passed out down there. I started down the steps, the dank, damp basement smell reaching up to meet me.

"Where the hell are you, Vanessa? I can't keep . . ."

The light came from below me, out of nowhere. It slapped against my eyes, forcing my head to the side, lids squinting shut. I put out my hand to block the light. "Goddamn it, that's not funny!" She didn't laugh.

Gingerly I moved a foot forward, feeling for the step. A small furry body shot out of the darkness and disappeared down the cellar stairs—Harley making a run for it. I tried to catch my balance and managed to grab the rail, but nevertheless sat down hard and bounced a few steps. "Ow, fuck!"

It took only seconds for the light to find my eyes again, but that was enough. Moonlight filtered through a grimy basement window, splitting Vanessa's face neatly in half. Tears streaming down her cheek, one eye white and panicked. She struggled to swallow, something in the way. Just before the beam blinded me, I realized the shadow behind her had her by the throat.

"Vanessa . . . ?" My voice shook, barely more than a whisper. I held up my hand and peered between my fingers, eyes fighting to adjust. Her head inclined ever so slightly and the arm encircling her neck jerked up and back. She choked and froze. The cellar whispered all around us, rustling, dripping.

"I don't know what you want," I heard myself say calmly, "but you can have it. Just don't hurt her, okay? You don't wanna hurt her." The flashlight shifted slightly. Still the face was hidden. Something glinted on Vanessa's cheek. The moonlight toyed with it, flashes of quicksilver teasing the cinder block walls.

A flat rectangular blade slanted to an angle at the top. Gleaming from a black leather fist. It traced a path from Vanessa's chin to base of her throat. The blade lingered there, caressing the hollow. She whimpered and it slid lower, tweaking the buttons on her blouse. They jumped free and rolled off along the floor, every little plink a sonic boom. The blouse gaped and Vanessa moaned. I jumped to my feet and started running toward the phone.

"Kate!" I barely recognized her voice. I made myself turn. Look. Her bright white bra was iridescent in the dark. She was on her knees, eyes closed, head pulled back by the hair. "Please," she pleaded. I took another step. Moonlight shimmied on her throat and she cried out. I sat down, mind racing, heart pounding out of my chest.

"Look, you can't stay here forever. I'm putting my head down, closing my eyes. You should go now," I said, as if a cab were waiting. "Go. Please."

Cellar sounds, settling, shifting, blood pounding through the ears. Hoping, fearing, ready, not. Shhhhh. Faintly, footsteps. Leather soles lifting, landing. Crunching dirt. Every nerve shooting sparks. Closer. Hairs standing up on end. Passed. Quiet, far too quiet. Eyes closed to hide the dark. Footsteps fading, going? Stopped.

The screech was inhuman, shrill, metallic. It shot me to my feet, half running, head spinning, not knowing what or where. The storm door gaped open, rust-wrapped hinges still whining in protest. Vanessa lay in a pool of light, crumpled on the floor. He was gone.

I nearly fell down the steps, legs made of Jello, and gathered her up in my arms. She started to sob as I touched her. The relief was stronger than whiskey. Her neck was unmarked, not even a nick. I rocked her back and forth, crooning on the filthy cellar floor.

"He's gone, you're okay, he's gone, it's over."

"It'll never be over . . ." she mumbled, sobs choking her words.

"Who was it, Van? Did you see him?" I shook her, harder than I intended. She cried out.

"No! He was tall, very strong, and I smelled leather . . . That's all."

Drinking could do that. Jake was tall and strong, but if it hadn't been for all the alcohol in her I felt sure Vanessa would have smelled his cologne. Smelled *him*. Still, a knife like that. Was Jake that dangerous?

8

I was waiting for Oola and Annie at Grand Central. Somehow I'd gotten her out of the cellar last night, Vanessa flipping from hysterical to catatonic. I had tripped the circuit breaker but she was no safer in the light. When I'd gone upstairs to grab her some clothes, she followed me, clinging to the coat I had never taken off. We left the cats behind and ran, me driving lost in the night, every set of headlights on every deserted road a potential flashlight in the dark. Quite by accident, I had found the police station, but Vanessa went crazy when I pulled in, sobbing and screaming and pounding the dashboard and the door. When she started hitting her head against the window, I'd pulled out in a panic and headed for the city, not knowing where else to go.

I guess I had intended to go to the loft, but then remembered the message on my machine. We'd be all alone there. I'd settled instead on a somewhat seedy, tour-bus type hotel in midtown, with chain bolts on the doors and a security guard in the lobby. While Vanessa struggled in her sleep, I'd sat up most of the night, replaying the scene in the cellar a thousand different ways, thinking of all the things I could have done. You did nothing, sneered the little voice.

I fidgeted at the coffee counter at the Zabar's. A little before noon. I had another half an hour to wait. Plenty of time for a drink, suggested the little voice. Yes, I screamed inside. I gave up my stool and my coffee and headed into the lobby, climbing the stairs to the bar.

"Kate! Kate!" I heard Oola calling my name. She caught up with me on the steps. "Thank goodness I caught you. Where are you going?"

I looked longingly at the top of the stairs, then back down at Oola. I had to have a drink. I couldn't deal with this. "I was too antsy to sit. I thought I'd walk around."

"Oh Kate, this is so awful. Are you okay? Is Vanessa all right? What did the police say?"

"We didn't call them. Vanessa wouldn't let me." I took another step up. Oola followed.

"Wouldn't let you? Why? Oh Kate, you should have called them."

"I tried," I answered hotly. Your fault, sang the little voice, all your fault. "She was crazy, you just don't know. Every time I picked up the phone she started screaming, grabbing me, scratching at her face." Two more steps. "I had to get her out of there, she was crazy," I said again.

"Of course she was crazy, she was terrified. That's why we have to help her, have the courage for her."

We reached the landing with the bar. Oola continued up the steps, carrying on about what we should do. What you should have done, sniped the voice. You don't understand, I wanted to say. Courage wasn't something I had, I ordered it, bottled or canned, on the rocks or straight up. When she realized I'd stopped, she turned back in surprise. I lowered my head as I told her, embarrassed by the desperation in my voice.

"I have to have a drink, Oola."

"I'm sorry?"

"Before we go back to Vanessa, I need to have a drink." I waited humbly, eyes cast down. Her voice was sad, but kind.

"I know, Kate. I've known that for a long time."

We took a seat at the almost empty bar. Halfway through my Bloody Mary, the little voice was in full swing. You don't *need* to drink, it scoffed. Of course I didn't, I agreed. I'd always been melodramatic. My mother said so, my teachers said so, my husband said so, the list went on and on. I hated everyone on the list.

Oola wasn't saying anything. She hadn't touched her juice and appeared lost in thought. I knew she was thinking about me, thinking I *had* to drink. Like I was an alcoholic. A drunk, sneered the little voice. The idea rankled. Defiantly, I gulped my Bloody and raised my empty glass to catch the eye of the bartender, who nodded. I'd show her.

"Kate . . ."

"Listen Oola," I interrupted, the best defense being a good offense, "just because I want to have a drink to calm down doesn't mean I'm a drunk. And if you don't like it, well that's just tough, because I don't need your approval. So you can just . . ." I stopped to breathe, full of self-righteous anger, when her voice cut through my histrionics like a thunderclap.

"Kate, shut up!" Oola hissed, her eyes crackling blue like an ungrounded electrical charge. "For once in your life, let some light into that self-pitying, self-absorbed little world. This is not about you. If you want to drink yourself stupid, I'm sorry for you but that's your decision. Right now, I'm worried sick about Vanessa. She needs our help. But if you'd rather sit here and wallow in your own petty bullshit, then tell me so I can get the hell out of here."

It was like getting punched in the stomach by Santa Claus. I couldn't remember Oola ever losing her temper, except over some discriminatory injustice, and even then there was no cursing. I slumped back into my chair, righteousness deflating. The bartender reappeared, picking up my empty, setting out a fresh paper napkin and a new cocktail. Silently I handed over a crumpled five from my jacket pocket and waved him away. Oola was still waiting for my response.

"Jesus, Oola, I'm sorry. I know I sound like a selfish idiot. It's just last night . . . it scared me. I'm not thinking straight. I just thought a drink would settle me down." Tentatively, I reached over and touched her hand.

She gave my fingers a squeeze and sighed, looking at her watch. "C'mon, Kate, Annie will be here in a few minutes." She gathered up her purse and gloves.

I did the same, surreptitiously taking a final pull on my drink. Coming down the steps, we saw Annie in the crowd. She looked tired, weighed down by her cast and our news, frail but determined. No one would ever accuse her of being self-centered, I thought guiltily. Annie's voice interrupted my wallow.

"Kate, you're awfully quiet. This must have been horrible for you." Annie linked arms with me, patting my sleeve sympathetically. Guiltily I repeated my new mantra: this is not about me, this is not about me.

"This is not about me, Annie," I said.

I don't think they were really prepared for what they saw when I unlocked the room at the hotel. The carnage far exceeded expectations. The blinds were closed, the room dark and clouded with smoke. Vanessa clasped herself in an arm chair, cheeks puffy and tearstained, eyes dull and beaten.

Annie stepped forward with a tiny gasp. I closed the door and fastened the chain lock as they engulfed her. After several minutes of soothing, Oola bombarded her with questions and Vanessa straggled through the story.

"How did I ever think I was strong, huh? That I could take care of myself?" She shook her head in amazement. "I was so fucking stupid. All it took was someone watching me. Watching me! Every second of every fucking day! And here I am, crazy, hiding in this dump, afraid to answer the goddamn door." She slammed her fist on the chipped veneer of a bureau, once, twice, then repeatedly, tears streaming down her cheeks. Oola went to her and covered her hand, stopping the sound of flesh on wood. "I'm such a fucking idiot!"

"You are not an idiot." Oola took her shoulders and shook her gently. "You're being terrorized, Vanessa. No matter how strong a person is, terror takes its toll." A spasm shook Vanessa like a cold chill and she gulped back tears.

Annie stepped to their side and lay her hand on Vanessa's shoulder. "It's more than being watched, Vanessa. He tried to hurt you."

"And we're not going to let him do it again," Oola added.

"You don't get it, do you? We don't have a choice," she exploded. "He's relentless. He'll never stop until he wins and I don't even know how to give up!"

"Maybe giving up isn't the answer. Vanessa, why wouldn't you let Kate call the police?" Vanessa turned away from Oola. Oola looked at me.

"Do you wanna tell them, Van?" She didn't respond, just got up and walked to the window, toying with the blinds.

"We never saw his face. But he knew how to get in and how to fix the lights. He wanted to scare us."

"I still don't understand about the police," Annie said. "Why wouldn't you call them?" Vanessa kept her face turned.

"Vanessa was frightened, not just by what happened, but by who she thought it was." Everyone stared at me. I hoped that my fears about Jake had taken hold.

Vanessa snapped suddenly. "Just say it, Jesus Christ! It's a perfect example of how crazy I've gotten. Some guy's holding a knife to my throat and I'm wondering if it's my boyfriend."

She yanked the blind cord and they tipped crazily, light striping through the cracks. No one spoke. I glanced at Oola and she had the grace to look away.

I explained about the intruder's size and strength and threw in something on a hunch about sensing someone we know by the sound of their footsteps in the dark.

"Was there anything else that felt familiar?" Oola asked.

"Yes, but I couldn't put my finger on it. And I still can't!"

"But something made you think it might have been Jake!" I faced her down and she turned away. "Just because you can't figure it out yet doesn't mean it isn't true." I looked at the others. "Vanessa can pretend she's crazy, but I know she's not. And if she isn't, then maybe she was right, whether she wants to be or not."

No one had anything to say. After a minute of quiet, I laid out my theory, using information from Bobby and Oola's fax as support. I walked them through our conversation in the Oak Bar, the message on my machine, my version of New Year's Eve. "He burned the roses, even admitted he had access to a computer virus, said there had been one at work. So what was to stop him from copying it onto Vanessa's drive? And the picture, he knew what it meant to her. How could a stranger know that?"

Vanessa tried to interrupt, but I talked her down, speaking directly to Oola. If I had ever needed the Goddess, it was now. "Jake wants to own her, Oola, just like in your fax. He's trying to scare her into doing what he wants. He was furious that she wouldn't go with him and that I was coming to stay instead. Notice how Vanessa wasn't even scratched! Why would someone do that, huh? Go to all that trouble? He could have hurt her, even killed her, but he didn't want to! All he wanted was to drive her out of her house. And into his."

"I think we should let the police decide this. You have a point, Kate, but we don't know for sure."

"I'm not calling the police," Vanessa almost shrieked. "This man has stood by me through everything. I never knew what that felt like, to count on someone being there. And now you want me to throw it all away for a bunch of boozy, paranoid delusions that I can't even remember! Well I won't do it! I won't do it unless I know!"

Annie went to sit with her. She rubbed her back as Vanessa

cried and shot me dark looks. She hated me for what I was doing but I didn't care. He might have pulled everything else, but he wasn't getting away with this. I had been in that basement too.

"All right," said Oola. "Then we need a way to find out."

Despite protests from Vanessa, we kicked it around until we came up with a plan. If Jake was the one following her, we needed to set a trap without putting her in any more danger. Vanessa would tell him she was taking a trip. After what had happened, she needed to get away.

"He'll want to come with me."

"You can't tell him where you're going," I said. It was only pretend after all, we would never let Vanessa go someplace alone. "If he doesn't think you've left him in the dark, this isn't going to work."

"It isn't going to work anyway." We argued while Oola made a quick call to Andrew at work.

"It's all set," Oola said. "You can stay at InfoTech's corporate apartment. Andrew will take care of it," she said, writing down the address. While the stalker thought she was out of town, Vanessa would have a chance to rest and regroup.

"We'll have to book two flights, just in case. All you have to do, Vanessa, is call Jake and tell him you're already at the airport. You're leaving and you'll call him when you get back. Whatever you want to say. Meanwhile you put out the word at your publisher's and your school that you're leaving tomorrow by United for LA at such-and-such a time. Whoever the stalker is has been able to find out everything he wants to know about you from those sources . . . somehow. Tomorrow, you go home and pack and I'll drive you to the airport for the real flight. If Jake shows up, we know we have a problem."

"Don't we have another problem?" Annie asked. "Suppose he does show up and Vanessa's not on the plane? And what if it's not Jake, Vanessa's still being followed by someone. If she's going to be able to relax . . ."

"Good point, Annie," I said. "We need a live body in the seat. She wouldn't be in any danger, no matter who's following her even if he got himself booked onto the plane. Not when he found out he was following the wrong person. Who can we get, Vanessa?"

"How should I know?"

"Could you please make an effort?"

"I'm not going to trick the man I'm dating!"

"The man you're dating carries a cardboard cutter!"

"Vanessa," Annie interjected. "If we do this, there's just as good a chance it won't be Jake. Whoever it is seems to know every move you make, though, so showing up to keep tabs on you is a giveaway. If it's Jake, you'd know for sure it's been him all along, right? If it's not, your double might flush him out, whoever he is. You've got to find a double, though."

Vanessa thought for a minute then volunteered the name of a graduate student who worked in her office. Sandy would probably do it, without too many questions, and she was black too. They could make a switch in the rest room at the airport and Vanessa could hide out until I made sure no one was watching and then head back to InfoTech.

When the flights were booked, we ordered some food from the lunch counter in the lobby. Vanessa squared it with Sandy, who already knew a little about the phone calls and the cars. I forced Vanessa into calling Jake while we were still there. I wasn't sure she would lie to him alone. Fortunately his machine picked up and Vanessa left a halting message, probably all the more convincing as she stumbled for the words.

"He'll never forgive me for not trusting him."

"He won't find out," Annie soothed. Like hell he wouldn't! I had every faith that Jake would take the bait.

"One thing I am going to do is have an alarm put in. I can't be worrying all the time that he's gonna break in again. I don't want to be afraid in my home."

"That's a great idea," Annie approved.

"Don't give *anyone* the code," I added simultaneously.

"It's not going to be Jake, so you don't have to worry about it," Vanessa snapped, eyes flashing. My temper rose and I fought it down. This is not about me, this is not about me, this is not about me. A knock on the door scared her silent and Annie checked the peephole before opening it for our lunch. We chewed quietly until Oola spoke.

"No matter who it is, what's happening is horrible. Intellectually, I understand the motives, the behavior patterns, but it's totally different when you're actually dealing with it. It gives me some practical experience to relate with my patients."

"Glad to be of help," Vanessa muttered.

"You know what I mean."

"I've often wondered if people really understand the impact of their actions," Annie said pensively. "Like if they knew what it felt like to be screamed at all the time, maybe they'd stop." Oola and I exchanged glances while Annie nibbled thoughtfully on a wedge of club sandwich. The cast looked huge on her slender arm.

"It's my experience that people need consequences before they stop, Annie," Oola replied. "If they're protected by their victims, allowed to continue their abusive behavior, it only gets worse." Annie choked on a mouthful of sandwich and Vanessa slapped her on the back.

"I'd give him some consequences in a heartbeat! I wonder how he'd like being held in a basement. You gonna eat these?" I speared one of Annie's fries. "Yep, the Bible works for me, an eye for an eye and all that jazz," I added, mouth full of potato.

"That reminds me of a story I heard." Oola sat up straight and tossed her hair over her shoulder. "I can't remember for sure, but I think it was a true story, about some women in a little village in China. Let me think. Okay, in this village it was considered socially acceptable for men to beat their wives. Incidents of domestic violence were dreadfully high." She curled her legs underneath her and continued. "Finally, the women got fed up. They decided they didn't want to be beaten anymore, and they got together to find a solution."

"What did they do?" I interrupted. "Collect sperm samples, then kill the men in their sleep?"

"No, but they realized they could do together what could not be done alone. So all the wives went home to their husbands and told them they would no longer tolerate being beaten. The husbands laughed and the women waited. It wasn't long before one of them was beaten. She told the other wives and together all the women in the village went up the hill to see the first woman's husband. They explained to him that this was his last warning. The man was very amused, told the women to leave and the very next day, beat his wife over a pot of cold soup.

"The women gathered together and took up sticks and brooms and rocks and marched to the man's home. Though he tried to fight them off, there were too many. Some women were bruised and hurt, but that didn't stop them. They dragged him from his home and into the street for all to see, and they beat him. When it was done, they turned to the other men who had gathered and asserted again they wouldn't tolerate being hit anymore. This time, no one laughed. It took a few more beatings before the men realized they were to be taken seriously, but eventually domestic violence was virtually non-existent."

"What are you saying, Oola?"

"I'm saying that maybe we can do together what Vanessa can't do alone. Give him a taste of his own . . ."

"You mean stalk him! Stalk him back! Holy shit! What a great idea! Wouldn't that just blow Jake out of the water."

"It's not Jake!"

"That sounds too dangerous, Oola," Annie protested.

I butted in before Oola could reply. "Christ, Annie, of course it's dangerous. This is our chance to stand up, to fight back. We're mad as hell and we're not gonna take it anymore. You're always such a baby!"

As if I hadn't had enough surprises for one day, Annie jumped up before my words even had a chance to echo.

"How dare you call me a baby!" She pointed her finger at me accusingly. "You don't have children to worry about! You don't have to answer to a husband because you drove yours out of your life." She practically spit the words at me. I was shocked senseless, attacked by a kitten who knew right where to scratch. "Maybe if you weren't always shooting off your big mouth, you might have a family. You might have something to go home to besides those cats and a bottle of cheap wine!" We were both shaken by the time she finished, her skin ashen, mine bright red. It was over in less than thirty seconds and probably took as much out of her as it did out of me.

This was definitely not my day. First Oola, now Annie. What had happened to *this is not about me?* Resentment coursed through me, empowering and entitling. Screw them! I'm out of here, I thought, reaching behind me for my coat.

"Oh Kate . . . I'm sorry." Annie moved quickly to my chair. I turned my head and she squatted down in front of me, trying to look into my face. "I didn't mean it, Kate, I'm sorry. You're right. I am a baby and I hate it."

She clutched at my legs, ending any hope for a dignified

exit. I could feel her tears seeping through my pants. I should probably apologize or at least accept Annie's, but I didn't want to. Why should you, said the voice.

"Let me up, Annie."

"Please, Kate, I'm sorry."

"Fine, now let me up. I got hardly any sleep last night and I want to go home."

"I think we've all had enough for one day." Oola rose and stood between me and the door. "Annie, if I had Andrew send a laptop to your house, could you do some research for me? My schedule's pretty tight and we need to know more. Do you know how to use a computer?"

"I've been taking some classes at an adult learning center in Mamaroneck. I don't know, my teacher thinks I'm a quick study. Maybe in comparison to some of my classmates . . ."

"Why do you put yourself down all the time," Vanessa asked. "I'm a teacher, and I don't just say things. I try to motivate my students to reach their full potential."

"David thinks it's stupid for a housewife to have a computer."

"Christ, with the kids farmed out half the day, even June Cleaver would have time to learn Windows," I muttered, but she heard. They all heard. I inched toward the door, outwardly sullen, inwardly shamed. Why was I being mean to Annie? If she wasn't such a wimp you wouldn't have to be, defended the voice.

"Come on Annie, we can share a cab to the station. Kate, are you coming?" The last was a cool and token comment. Nobody could freeze you as politely as Oola.

"Please don't let me intrude. Vanessa, I'll pick you up here around ten-thirty, I have to get the car out of the garage. That should give us plenty of time to go to the barn and pack. Try and get some sleep, okay?"

I hugged her, ignoring my fellow stalkers, and headed out the door. Despite my best efforts, we got stuck riding down in the elevator together, Oola cool and silent, Annie trying to fix everything. I hated that. I much preferred people who pretended that nothing was happening when things like this were happening. Get it over with so you can go have a drink, whispered the little voice. For once, it was a welcome friend.

"Annie, I am not mad at you, okay?" I sighed as if I were

talking to a mental incompetent. She looked confused, but not Oola.

She took Annie's arm. "C'mon Annie, we'll miss our trains. Kate will be all right. She's just worried someone might grab her favorite barstool if she doesn't get downtown."

Well fine, if she wanted me to drink, I'd be happy to oblige. Rage pumped through my veins, and I started walking downtown, oblivious to the dangers of midtown Manhattan after dark. I stormed down Eighth Avenue, then cut over to Seventh, my mind racing faster than my feet. As I turned a corner, I careened into a man, nearly dropping my purse. "Watch where you're going, dickhead!" I snarled.

He glared back, hands on his hips. "You gotta a problem, lady? You're the one who oughta watch where she's going!"

I couldn't stop myself. It was like an out-of-body experience. As if one Kate was watching another Kate go wild. He had turned to continue on his way and I literally jumped in front of him, screaming, spittle flying all over his coat.

"Yeah, I gotta problem, asshole, and I'm looking at it. I oughta watch where I'm going? You oughta watch where you're going and stay the fuck out of my way!"

I was roaring near the end, up in his face, needing a reaction, craving a fight. Before I knew it, I pushed him. Hard. With both hands. Combined with the surprise, the shove knocked him off his feet and into a trash can at the side of a building. He sprawled there, shaking things out to determine the state of damage. The Kate that would never hurt another human being instinctively moved forward to help him up. He covered his face with his arms and kicked out at the Kate who had knocked him down. He caught me in the shin and both Kates hurt like hell. I jumped back and stood for a minute longer, frightened but fascinated by what I'd done. As he began to pull himself up, I turned and ran.

I ran and ran, from him, from myself, from the blackness and the pleasure. Maybe that scared me most of all. It had felt good to hit him. I had wanted to howl like a jackal over its prey. My whole body was humming with glory while my mind recoiled in shame. I couldn't wait for Petrillo's. I saw the familiar neon light of a Budweiser sign a block down and across the street. I ran there, leaning gratefully against the door for a second, breathing hard. I looked back, but there was no sign of him. I smoothed my hair, straightened my coat and opened the door, comforted by the smell of beer and laughter in the dark.

9

My head was screaming. I wasn't even awake and my head was being ripped off my neck. Instinctively I curled my legs up and squeezed my eyes shut. My body shook uncontrollably and I reached for my quilt to slow the shivering. I grabbed a blanket and froze, the unfamiliar roughness of wool forcing my eyes open. Where the hell was I?

It was dark, a small room with stiff drapes tightly pulled across two windows. They were rusty orange, ugly, but effective at keeping out the light. I was in a bed, on sheets that smelled of cigarette smoke and body odor. And sex, the undeniable odor of intercourse. Oh my God, what had happened to me! Panic and nausea rose together. I swallowed hard and whimpered involuntarily. He stirred in his sleep behind me. HE! Who was he? I couldn't remember who he was or how I had gotten here. If my head would just stop, maybe I could think. The pounding was relentless. The room started to swing lazily in front of me.

I jumped from the bed, and frantically looked around, finally locating a cracked toilet behind a partially open door. I managed to get there before I vomited, clinging to the rim. Sweat congealed on my face and I thought my head would explode. Each time the dizziness receded, I'd lift my head but my stomach still rebelled. I heaved again and again until nothing but yellow bile, thick and foul, dribbled from my mouth. What was happening to me! Please, somebody tell me! The blackness rose and the panic choked me, the smell of vomit filling my nose and throat. I sank to the floor and lay my face against the cool tile. The sobs were so deep within me they made no sound but my whole body was choking. Please God, let this be over. Let me die.

"Everything okay in there?" His voice made me jump. I

kicked the door shut and mumbled something in return. Don't come in, please don't come in. Who was this guy? I had to think. I remembered going into that place on Eighteenth St. Oh shit, my head would not stop pounding. I struggled to sit up, then used the dirty sink to pull myself off the floor. I made the mistake of looking in the mirror.

The woman I saw was nobody I had ever intended to be. Her eyes looked as if they were bleeding and the lines that etched her mouth and nose had been dug with a jackhammer. Her yellowish, blotchy skin was broken out, bloated bags emphasizing the dark circles under each eye. I watched her wipe sweat from her forehead and saw the specks of vomit on her hand. When had this happened! When had I become this woman? I wanted to scream. Somebody help me, I'm so tired and so scared.

I splashed cold water on my face, took some tissue and wiped the vomit from the toilet seat and lid. A wave of heat and dizziness pounded me and I leaned against the sink, supporting my weight on two wobbly arms. Suddenly, I flashed back to another bathroom, in another house at another time. I could see myself at the door, just a little girl, shy in her pajamas, watching her pop lean against the sink on two wobbly arms. She was very quiet, that little girl, 'cause she knew Daddy was sick again. And even though she had to go to the bathroom very badly, she never said a word. She tried to be very, very good when Daddy was sick. Even when the sounds from the bathroom had frightened her and the way his eyes looked and his hands shook had scared her she never said anything, and sometimes she waited till she peed her pants and her mother swatted her soundly. When I raised my eyes to the mirror again, I saw my father looking back. I gagged.

I heaved over the toilet once more, but there was nothing left. I returned to the sink, rinsed my mouth and opened the mirrored medicine cabinet looking for aspirin. I swallowed three Advil and prayed they'd stay put. I had to calm down and figure out where I was.

I vaguely remembered talking to the bartender at that place, some hole in the wall with an Irish name. McGavan's, McNally's, Mc-something. He knew one of the guys that used to tend bar at Petrillo's. Suddenly, it rushed back to me, bits and pieces, not necessarily in order. A guy had come in some-

time after midnight, a maintenance guy at some building in
midtown. A little coarse but nice enough. We all started playing liar's poker and I got mad at the guy who was winning.
The maintenance guy—Jesus Christ, what was his name—
came over to talk to me.

Mike, I realized suddenly, his name was Mike. I was filled
with relief, immediately replaced by shame. I had sat in that
bar, drunk as a skunk, sucking face with this complete
stranger. I could remember his whispered suggestions, my coy,
cockteasing responses. I felt his hand on my ass while we
danced to the jukebox, felt myself grinding against him, oh so
seductive and desirable as he bought me drinks and said what
I wanted to hear. The last clear thing I remembered was the
leers of our fellow patrons as we stumbled out the door. Mike
earned a smirking thumbs-up from the bartender, not because
I was any prize, but because they all knew an easy lay when
they saw one.

"Hey, you sure you're okay in there?" This time he
knocked on the door.

"Yeah, I'm fine, just feeling a little sick. Hungover, you
know." I put on a plaid flannel bathrobe that hung on the door.
Underneath I was naked. I smeared some toothpaste on my
finger and across my teeth. I had to get out of this rat-trap,
and I needed something to drink, something carbonated. "You
don't have a soda or something, do you? I feel pretty lousy."

"Sure," he said and I heard him walking away from the
door. I hurried out of the bathroom and found my clothes,
throwing on shirt and jeans, no time to waste looking for un-
derwear. I ran across my bra underneath a shoe and stuffed it
in my coat pocket. My panties could be in a cab for all I knew.
I heard him returning and jammed my arms in my coat. I
whirled around and saw the man from the bar standing in the
doorway, holding a Mountain Dew. He was wearing under-
pants with a rip in the elastic and looked as bad as I felt. What
would Vanessa say if she could see me now!

Holy shit, Vanessa! What time was it? Nausea rocked me
and I fought it back. What time was it!? I was frantic. My
watch and gold chain lay on a table next to the bed. I grabbed
them and headed for the door. I never once looked at him.

"Look, ummm, Mike, thanks a lot for everything, but I
gotta go." I edged past him in the doorway, desperate to es-

cape. "It was fun, I just gotta be someplace, you know, I got an appointment."

I kept talking even though he never tried to stop me, just handed me the soda as I went. I raced through a tiny littered living room that I'd have sworn I never saw before. I got out in the hall and ran down the stairs, overpowering protestations of stomach and head. It wasn't till I was outside in the cold bright air that I opened my trembling fist and checked the time. Fuck me, it was twenty after eleven.

I needed a phone. Wait, I needed to figure out where I was first. I hurried to the end of the street and looked at the sign. I was in Chelsea, right near the plant district. Thank goodness, the garage where I kept the car was over on East 24th St., just a short hop across town. I had leased the space when I was still working at the agency and kept the car there even after I quit. Once you'd found garage space in Manhattan you didn't give it up. I flagged a cab and hopped in, telling myself that New York cabbies had seen much worse in their back seats. He dropped me in record time and thankfully I had money to pay him. My head throbbed unmercifully, the soda and Advil were slam dancing in my gut. Don't let me puke on the garage guy, God, and I will never drink again.

Some pimply kid with a bizarre hair style went to find my car while I used the pay phone to call the hotel.

"Vanessa, hi, it's Kate," I said quickly. "I'm sorry, I know you must be wondering what happened to me, but I'm having trouble with the car," I chattered, making it up as I went along.

"Where have you been?" she interrupted, furious. "Do you know what time it is?"

"I'm at a gas station and the guy says it will be about half an hour. It's just a fuse or something, I'm not sure, but they're fixing it now." I took a breath. "I'm sorry, really. It's not my fault."

"God, Kate, why the hell didn't you call me! I've been worried sick. So has Oola."

"Oola! Why did you call Oola?"

"Well, Jesus, Kate! You left the hotel all pissed off. Then you blow me off this morning. I called and called and nobody answered. What was I supposed to think?" She exhaled loudly into the phone, pausing to light a cigarette. "Forgive me for worrying you were in a dumpster somewhere."

"All right, Vanessa, I'm sorry." I could see the front of my car coming down the ramp. It was an old Pontiac Phoenix with a few dents, some chipped paint and a sunroof. I hardly ever drove it, but I loved that sunroof. "Look, I just overslept. I was so tired last night I turned the phone off," I lied. "I'm sorry. Really. " She started to interrupt but I talked her down. "The guy's calling me about the car, Vanessa, I gotta go. What time's your flight?"

"Two forty-five out of Kennedy."

Relief coated me like cold sweat. It was only twenty of twelve. We could make it. We might be cutting it close, but we could make it. I could imagine Oola if I screwed this up.

"Oola's not coming or anything, is she? I mean, she doesn't need to."

"Well, I'll call her now and let her know you're among the living. She and Andrew are supposed to go to some party, but she said she'd come if you didn't show."

I felt a surge of resentment. Generous Oola, wonderful Oola, fucking reliable Oola. Always making me look bad. I heard the pimply guy tap the horn, none too gently.

"Vanessa, here's the car. I'm on my way."

I hung up before she could say anything else. I took the keys from the kid and threw him a five. It was all I had left. I'd have to stop and get some more cash. I pulled the car out to the street, waiting for traffic to break, when my mouth started to dry up. Suddenly my cheeks felt like I had blown up too many balloons. Shit, I was going to be sick again. I gagged a couple of times, trying to keep it down, but it was no go. I couldn't move, cars behind me, traffic ahead of me and I was going to toss lunch. If one could call warm green soda and ibuprofen lunch. So on top of everything else, I ended up barfing down the side of my car. Finally there was a lull in traffic and I made my escape, stuck with the taste in my mouth until the first red light, when I dug some gum from my purse. I wished I was dead.

Vanessa was pacing the lobby. When she saw the Phoenix, she practically flew out of the hotel, nervously glancing right, left, behind. Guilt surged upward like the vomit and I fought it down. A guy behind me slammed on his brakes, then his horn. I flipped him the finger. The stupid idiot. How hard was it to see that I was double-parked? Vanessa slid into the seat as he careened around me, the two of us tossing obscenities through panes of glass.

"Can we just go, please, without getting into a fist fight?"

"Good morning to you too," I muttered, moving the car into traffic. She didn't answer. *She knows where you've been,* sang the little voice.

I set my teeth and drove like an animal. Vanessa didn't speak, just grabbed the door handle periodically as I swerved from lane to lane. We needed gas so I stopped at a minimart and put twenty dollars of regular, some Breathsavers, a tiny container of Advil and a six-pack of Diet Pepsi on my Visa card. While Vanessa stayed slumped in her seat, I got the key for the rest room from an indifferent attendant and rinsed my mouth out with Pepsi, spitting into the already brown sink. I didn't look in the mirror.

Vanessa watched me walk back to the car, eyes narrowed thoughtfully. I tossed the six-pack across the seat and killed a Pepsi washing down a few Advil. As I pulled back on to the highway my body shuddered, the afterglow of last night's adventure.

"Where were you?" Flatly.

"I told you, the car wouldn't start and I . . ."

"Bullshit. Where were you?"

"I said I was sorry, let it go!" It came out a little angrier than I intended. I kept my eyes on the road as hers burned into my profile. She lit a cigarette and held her tongue. When we finally pulled into the barn it was a little after one.

"Let's get your stuff," I said, hopping out of the car. "We'll have to haul ass to make the flight." I was halfway up the driveway when I realized she wasn't with me. I turned back and she was still sitting in the car. "Vanessa, come on!"

Hands on hips, I tapped a foot impatiently. She didn't move. Finally I walked back to her door. She was facing straight ahead, eyes closed, lips thin, fingers snarled in her lap. I knocked on the window and she started like a deer in the darkness. As I reached for the door handle, she cowered back, head shaking no, tears tumbling. Her body twitched like mine, little shivers from muscles out of control. She was afraid to go in her own house. Compassion replaced irritation and gently, I opened the door.

"Come on, Van. It's okay." She shook her head. "Do you

want me to go in first?" She just stared, eyes wild. "Okay, I'll go in and check, make sure no one's there. You wait here, lock the doors. When I come back, if you still don't wanna go, I'll go up and get your stuff." Moving like an old lady, she reached in her pocket and gave me her keys. I closed the door and she locked it carefully.

The kitchen was silent. The contents of the drawer I'd dumped still lay on the counter, some of it on the floor. My heart sped up and I wasn't sure what prompted the film of sweat on my forehead. I could hear the soles of my sneakers lift from the floor. It was like being in a house where someone had died. I moved cautiously toward the living room and felt a stab of pain on top of my head.

"Ow!" I jumped up and back, flattening myself against the kitchen wall. Ozzie hissed at me from the top of the refrigerator, tail twitching wrathfully. The cats! I let my breath out in a whoosh. They hadn't eaten since we left the loft. Quickly, I pulled a box of food from the bag I'd brought from home and poured a bunch in a bowl. Harley appeared out of nowhere and they swarmed over the food, stopping only long enough to shoot me outraged glances. Is there anybody you haven't let down? asked the voice.

I went through the house, checking rooms and closets. The only time I paused was on the cellar steps. I forced myself down the stairs and checked the lock on the storm door, then I raced back to the kitchen and glanced at the clock. We had to get going.

Vanessa was still in the car, chewing her knuckles in between drags. I smiled as I approached, nodding, holding my hands up and out to let her know it was okay. She unlocked the door, but didn't open it.

"Everything's fine, Van. I checked everywhere." I pulled the door open. "Come on. We have to hurry or we'll miss the plane." I said it loudly, glancing nonchalantly toward the street, hoping for a glimpse of a sleek expensive car. She slid her legs to the ground, but stopped at getting out.

"I can't," she whispered.

"Sure you can. Think about it. What could be worse than letting me pick your clothes for the week?" Her lips pulled, not wanting to smile but not able to help it. Encouraged, I took her elbow and helped her from the car. At the back steps, she stopped again. I faced her. "Vanessa, this is your home. You worked hard to get it. Don't let him take it from you without a fight."

I walked her through the kitchen and up to her bedroom. When she started to pack, absorbed in her closet, I left her to it. I went back down to the kitchen and sucked up to the cats with a can of Salmon Surprise. I waited for Vanessa to finish, no longer distracted from my hangover. I still didn't remember how I got to Mike's apartment last night or what happened after I did. It was the only mercy shown to me so far today.

Vanessa finally came down the stairs but she turned into the living room. I heard muted voices and realized she was checking her machine. A lot of messages. I was waiting at the back door when she came into the kitchen. Her expression was strained, but she looked more normal than she had in a while. Though stubby, her nails were tawny pink and still smelled faintly of varnish. She wore a cowl-necked salmon sweater, short Zodiac boots, jeans and a long-billed cap that shaded her face. She carried a huge brown leather bag that concealed a duffel inside.

"You look great," I said as we headed down the back steps.

"I wish I could say the same about you. Kate, what is . . ." I scurried down the driveway before she could finish. I suddenly realized that I was still wearing yesterday's clothes, none the better for having spent the night on Mike's floor. The last thing I needed was an interrogation.

"You haven't been home, have you?" No escape. "Kate, what is going on with you?" The very question I'd been asking and still no answer in sight. So I didn't say anything, just started the car. She threw the bag in the back and slid into her seat. "I'm worried about you. Why won't you tell me what's wrong?"

Why wouldn't I? I had this need to keep everything secret, storing it up in that big black pit. She wouldn't understand. Nobody would. Even I didn't understand what was happening to me. I just couldn't seem to stop. Stop what? taunted the little voice. Things were getting scarier and scarier and the more scared I got, the more I had to drink and the more I drank, the more I did things that scared me. I was pathetic, anyone who knew the truth would see that. I put on my best fake smile.

"I stayed overnight at a friend's house, all right? Aren't you the one who's been telling me to get laid? Now back off and let's get going." I squealed the tires pulling out of the driveway and she gave me a look. Backing off was not Vanessa's strong suit. Before she could open her mouth, I asked if there had been any messages from Jake. Biting her lip, she nodded.

"He's really upset and wants me to call him as soon as I get my messages, wherever I am. He's so worried. I hate myself for doing this."

"This guy isn't any different from any other man you've been with. You never had any trouble skirting the truth when you wanted them gone."

"I don't want him gone. I thought you understood that." She played with the hem of her sweater. "I wish he was here, Kate. He makes me feel safe."

"You never needed a man to feel safe."

"Well, I've never been stalked before, have I?" She flared for a second, then sighed. "I had to fight with myself all morning not to call him."

"You didn't, did you?"

"No, Oola talked me out of it." She stopped for a cigarette. "Oola. Doesn't she just crack you up sometimes?"

"Oh yeah, she's a laugh a minute."

"I know she's really scared for me, but I can't shake the feeling that she's taking notes while we talk. As if this is some kind of psychological study and she's writing a thesis. AA— Assholes Anonymous! Then there's the advanced class, Absolute Assholes Anonymous, triple A!"

Though it was good to hear Vanessa joke, as far as I was concerned, AA was no laughing matter. I didn't really know what went on there, but I figured Alcoholics Anonymous was like a methadone clinic for drunks. The end of the line.

"Kate, don't tell me you're all right. You're shaking and you look like death."

"Thank you so much. Vanessa, I stayed out a little too late and had a little too much to drink, okay? Remind me to call you next time you have a hangover and give *you* a play-by-play." I laid on the horn for the benefit of the idiot in front of me who had just cut me off. He flipped me the finger and kept going. Shithead.

We drove in silence until Vanessa found a jazz station on the radio. In the close quarters of the car, I could smell myself, sour and used. I needed a shower more than a drink.

"Any sign of the BMW?" I asked, unnerved by the lack of conversation.

"No!" Triumphant.

"Any other calls?"

"No." More hesitant. "But I wasn't there. He never leaves calls on the machine."

"Just mine," I muttered. "What a coincidence. Jake thinks you're gone and all of a sudden the calls stop."

"*Jake's* calls didn't stop," she pointed out. "Even though he knew I wasn't there. Why won't you believe he cares about me?"

"Vanessa, it's hard to imagine a guy who wouldn't care about you. I'm not trying to hurt you. Look, if you can just do your part, for a little while longer, we'll know. And if I'm wrong, you can hate me as much as you want."

"I wish I never started this whole thing."

"Have you remembered anything?"

"No, and I don't want to. Just thinking about it scares me so much I start gagging and my stomach gets all funny, like I'm gonna puke."

I glanced at her, paranoid, and sniffed the air discreetly. I should have washed the car door while she was packing. All of a sudden, the Phoenix seemed to reek of vomit. How could she not know? Fears chased each other like squirrels in my head. When was she going to confront me, call me a slut and a drunk? When would my life be exposed so everyone could laugh or turn away in disgust?

I rolled down the window a little, despite the freezing temperatures, needing the air.

10

The drive to the airport took forever. When we finally pulled up we let a skycap take the bags. I left Vanessa off to get her boarding pass while I parked, promising to meet her at the gate. It felt so good to be alone I had trouble making myself leave the car. Life was so hard. I never meant for things like last night to happen. Why was I always getting in trouble when all I planned to do was have a couple of drinks? Your idea of a couple of drinks is a couple of cases, said the first little voice. You may be easy, sniped the second, but you sure ain't cheap.

"Get out of the car, Kate," said my own voice, the only one other people ever heard. I went to the terminal, reminding myself this was not about me and keeping a lookout for Jake Romano. Who was, after all, a much worse person than I was. Does he knock people down in the street? teased voice number one.

"Shut up!" I snapped crossly, drawing a nervous look from a woman who had no doubt just flown in from Idaho. When I stuck out my tongue and crossed my eyes she gave a little shriek and scuttled away. Tourists!

Vanessa was upstairs near the gate, wandering about, doing her part, leaving a trail. I joined her and we waited until the plane began to board. Casually, I mentioned the need for a bathroom, and started to hug her goodbye.

"I should go too," she said. "I hate peeing on the plane. It's so claustrophobic." She waved broadly to the flight attendant. "I have to run to the john, honey, hold the flight." The woman smiled blankly, as no doubt she was well paid to do.

We entered the bathroom where another woman waited by the sink. She was African-American, wearing jeans, short Zodiac boots and holding a large flat gym duffel. She and Vanessa hugged quickly. Vanessa introduced us—Kate, Sandy,

Sandy, Kate—while she stripped off her sweater and emptied her bag on the diaper-changing shelf. Sandy threw the sweater on over her Danskin and pulled the cowl up around her face. She took Vanessa's coat and cap and picked up the bag. Her nails were long and pink and press-on. She looked in the mirror and then at us. We nodded and I checked my watch. I hugged Vanessa. She would have to wait here in this bathroom for an hour before cabbing it to the InfoTech apartment.

"Let's go," I said.

Sandy and I walked quickly to the gate. I scolded her loudly about missing her flight. She kept her head down and her feet moving. I waved as she went down the ramp, careful not to show my relief as she disappeared into the plane. Alone at last.

I glanced around the terminal but didn't see any sign of Jake Romano. I didn't know if that was good or bad. I decided to hang out for a few minutes to see if he showed up. I felt like shit anyway and was sick of driving. My headache was better, but the dizziness and shakes were still going strong. I needed to try and get something in my stomach, so I headed to the nearest lounge.

The bar was crowded and just the thought of a beer made the room sway ominously, so I took a small, cramped table still littered with a previous lunch. After studying the menu I opted for a hot turkey sandwich with mashed potatoes—something filling to subdue my rowdy stomach. The waitress bustled over, swept the dirty dishes into a bus box and took my order.

"Something from the bar while you're waiting, ma'am?"

I ordered a large Diet Pepsi and sat alone with myself. I could see my reflection in the window, a lonely woman at an empty table. Other people laughed and joked at the bar, meeting family and friends, laughing with strangers over the common ground of a whiskey sour. No matter how hard I tried, I didn't fit in. I always felt alone. I ducked my head when the tears started and swallowed them down in a gulp.

"Kathleen? Kathleen is that you?"

I looked up, startled. The man speaking had been at my wedding. He was a business associate of Steve's, and of course I didn't have a clue what his name was. He was smiling, carrying a little overnight bag and looked genuinely pleased to see me. Obviously he didn't know a loser when he saw one. I forced a smile and extended my hand, conscious of my hung-over face and clothes.

"It's Jerry, Jerry Kintella. Great to see a familiar face in this crush, Kathleen. Mind if I join you?" He draped his coat over the other chair before I could think of an excuse. Great, a friend of Steve's, lucky me.

"Jerry, geez, it's been a long time." Small talk wasn't my long suit, even on a good day.

"Yeah, it has. Too long. Hey, where's Steve? Picking him up, or did you just send him off?" He looked around the room for my recently divorced, never-again-to-be-present husband. When his eyes came back to my face, he knew he'd hit a sore spot.

"Steve and I aren't together anymore," I mumbled. "We got divorced a few months ago." I'm sure he thought the tears in my eyes were his fault. I put up my hands to forestall his apology. "Hey, Jerry, it's okay. Shit happens, you know."

"Yeah, I do know, Kath. Suzanne and I got divorced three years ago. It's hard. I'm sorry."

He had nice eyes, kind of grayish and twinkly, and I think he really was sorry. The first nice, unmarried guy I'd met in months and I looked like I'd been hit by a train.

"Well, what can you do? We just couldn't beat the odds. I think working together makes it tougher. You know, every-thing was all jumbled together, the marriage, the partnership. Oh, I don't know. I've given up trying to figure it out." The waitress arrived with my sandwich. "Hey, let's have a drink for old times' sake. I'll have a Bloody Mary with lots of Worcestershire," I told her. "How 'bout you Jerry? It's on me."

"Thanks Kathy . . ."

"Kate," I interrupted, "it's Kate now."

"Kate," he said. Nice smile. "It suits you. I'll have a cheese-burger, medium, with sauteed onions and french fries." He handed the menu to the waitress.

"To drink, sir?" She waited, pen in hand.

I remembered now. A Jack Daniels man. When I was meet-ing Steve after work for a drink at a little joint on University Place where Jerry and some other guys partied. If I remembered correctly, he could pound 'em pretty good. Maybe this day was picking up after all.

"I'll have a club soda, thanks, with lemon if you've got it." The waitress hurried off.

"Too early?" I asked, a little defensively.

"Nah, it's never too early, but sometimes it's too late. I'm just not drinking today, Kate." He seemed awfully comfortable. It made me nervous.

"Why not?" I blurted, before I could stop myself. Then I slapped the side of my skull. Bad move. "How rude. I'm sorry, Jerry. If you don't want to drink, you don't have to drink. If I want to drink, I can have a drink, right? God knows I can handle it. I really can."

Apparently my stomach wasn't the only thing out of control. I sounded like an babbling idiot. Jerry was looking at me strangely, as if he suddenly recognized me. I wanted to crawl under the table but couldn't, so I shoveled a huge forkful of processed turkey breast and canned gravy into my mouth.

"You're absolutely right Kate. Folks who can handle a drink have every right to have one. Me, I'm one of the people who can't." I swallowed the gooey mess in my mouth with difficulty. What was he saying? "You don't have to look so worried, Kate, I'm not dying or anything. I'm an alcoholic. That was the main reason for my divorce. I finally joined the program and stopped drinking, but not soon enough for my marriage."

Shit, what had I gotten myself into? Of all the lousy people in this goddamn airport I had to end up with a holy roller. I heard Steve in my head, saying he was worried about me, that I was drinking too much, it was destroying our marriage. Heard me screaming that he was fucking crazy, to leave me alone, that his nagging was killing our marriage. My head spun. This day was too much. Time was getting all mixed up. I pushed my plate away and saw Jake Romano enter the bar. I choked.

"Kate, are you all right?" Jerry leaned across the table and nudged me on the shoulder. "What's the matter?" He swiveled around, trying to follow my line of vision. "You're white as a ghost."

No one could ever accuse me of being a boring lunch partner. Old Jerry would think twice before he joined another friend's ex-wife in an airport bar. Jake hadn't seen me yet. He had positioned himself by the door, leaning on one of those narrow shelves that pass for counters in places like this. I saw a couple of flight attendants at the bar give him the once-over, their approval apparent in the quick pats of hair and recrossing of legs.

"Kate, if you don't answer me . . ." Jerry threatened.

"Jerry," I hissed, "it's kind of involved. Look, there's someone here I don't want to see. I'll explain in a minute, just stop turning around, okay?" I slid down a little in my seat, trying to shield myself from Jake's view. When Jerry shifted again I told him, "Stop it, goddammit!"

The waitress arrived with his burger and my Bloody. I stirred it nervously and plucked the celery from the glass, biting down hard. Jerry sat still, watching me while he added ketchup to his burger.

"Kate, are you in trouble?"

"Kind of, but not really. You don't want to hear about this, Jerry. It's a long story and very complicated."

"I've got plenty of time, Kate." He was taking big bites, though.

"Okay, but you asked for it." I picked up my drink but the smell of the vodka rocked me. Don't let anyone ever tell you vodka has no smell—they're just the people who need to believe it. I set the glass down again and felt the sweat form under my arms. If I didn't get a shower . . .

"I have this friend, Vanessa, you might have met her at the wedding, tall, black, really striking?" He nodded. Men always remembered Vanessa. "Well, this guy's been following her, you know, stalking her, and we kind of set a trap for him. I brought her to the airport about an hour ago, and now he's just walked into the bar. Don't look!" I pinched his wrist, squeezing hard. His head stopped in mid-rotation.

"Ouch, Kate, cut it out."

"Well don't turn around then," I snapped, releasing my grip. "He hasn't seen me yet, and I don't want him to until I figure out what to do."

"But if she's already on the plane, what can he do?"

"She's not on the plane. Sandy's on the plane. She's in the bathroom," I whispered through clenched teeth, exasperated.

"In the bathroom? You brought her to the airport to hide in the bathroom?"

"Of course not! Jesus Christ, I told you you wouldn't understand."

He gave me a look to let me know whose fault that was. Men were so annoying.

"We want him to think that she went out of town for a week so we can get ready," I explained irritably, keeping an eye on Jake. "We put Sandy on the plane dressed like Vanessa and Vanessa is waiting until the coast is clear. Which it obviously isn't. Man, I gotta let her know." I looked at my watch. She'd been in there over fifty minutes. She could come out anytime now.

"So you can get ready for what? No offense, Kate, but this whole thing sounds crazy." Jerry had almost finished his burger and obviously still didn't get it. But he was here and I was going to need help.

"Jerry, look, I can't explain everything right now, but I need your help. Do you have to catch a plane?"

"No, I just got in from Atlanta. I was only going to grab something to eat before I caught a cab home."

"Great. Look, if you'll help me, I'll drive you home and explain everything. Please, Jerry, just help me. Please." I took his hand, this time gently. He let me hold it for a second, taking in my face and my generally pathetic condition. He'd have been heartless to refuse.

"All right, what do you want me to do?"

Quickly I outlined my plan. He agreed, more to humor me, I think, than anything else. I took a deep breath and got up from the table. I strolled around the back of the circular bar, carrying my Bloody Mary. I wanted to come up behind him. He was still looking out at the terminal, his eyes periodically sweeping past the bathroom where Vanessa waited.

I was less than two feet from him. Jerry waited at the table for his cue. He nodded at me and I nodded back. This was it.

"Well, if it isn't the lovely Jake Romano," I announced grandly, swinging my arms wide, drink sloshing about. He turned, and I was gratified by the quickly repressed flicker of surprise in those beautiful eyes. Get used to it, I thought, you ain't seen nothing yet. "Hey Jake, out here lookin' for hookers or you still having a problem gettin' it up?" My voice carried easily to the curious flight attendants. "What's a matter Jake, don't you remember me? It's Katie, from the basement. Katie!"

By now a number of people were watching, some under their lashes, some out-and-out staring. I was loud and apparently drunk.

He shrugged his coat back on his shoulders and smiled his model's smile. Nobody hit thirty-five with teeth that white.

"How could I forget you, the charming Katie? And what a stunning outfit." He looked me up and down, unruffled on the outside. We'd see what he was made of on the inside.

"Ya think so, Jake? Well thanks, cause it's one of Vanessa's. You remember Vanessa?" I slurred my words just a touch and posed awkwardly. I'd been around enough drunks in my day to imitate one. "I thought it was a real shame she dumped you when she found out about that incident with the little girl. I mean, once a guy has served his time, he shouldn't hafta keep paying for it. People don't understand, eleven-year-olds can be very sexually aggressive, right ole buddy?" Boy, the crowd was with me now. I was on a roll, loud and clear, and conversations throughout the lounge stumbled to halt. Jerry was moving toward us. I had to push harder. I was getting to him, I could feel it. I moved a little closer.

"Stuff like that must happen to you all the time, as good-lookin' as you are. What were you supposed to do when she forced herself into your car? So what if the kid tried to kill herself, you weren't her first blow job, no matter what the shrinks said." One of the flight attendants gasped. His jaw hardened and his face flushed.

"Don't fuck with me, Katie," he warned through gritted teeth.

I threw my hands up in mock innocence, the Bloody Mary swinging a little too close to his face. His response was a reflex. He couldn't help himself. He grabbed my wrist, the ring pinching my skin. I twisted myself in his grasp and threw the bright red Bloody Mary all over the front of my much maligned blouse. Some of it splashed on his coat and he dropped my arm like a hot pan. Too late, sucker.

"Hey," I practically shouted, "hey, let go of me! Look what you've done, you son of a bitch. Look at my shirt." Dramatically, I flung out my arms, palms upward—then stepped back, cowering, though he hadn't moved an inch. "Don't hit me, Jake, I'm on your side," I finished, aggrieved at his lack of trust. His eyes narrowed to slits. I might have been playacting, but he wasn't. If he could have killed me, he would have.

"What the hell are you doing, buddy? Are you okay, Kate?"

The cavalry had arrived in the form of Jerry. His intervention had mobilized the waitstaff and the bartender pushed a button on the phone, relaying a brief, terse message. We had to move. No way was I spending the day with airport security. I backed away from Jake, pushing Jerry with me.

"I think Katie's had too much to drink. I'm sorry about the mess. Send me a bill for the cleaning, or a new blouse." He smoothly extracted a business card from a small silver case in the pocket of his coat. Jerry took it without changing expression. Jake looked about and shrugged disparagingly at the crowd. "We just broke up a week ago, she's still a little upset." One smile from Adonis, one look at me and the fickle crowd was swayed. It didn't matter, he was leaving. '

"Kate and I have been in Atlanta for the last two weeks," Jerry declared, deceitfully sincere. "So maybe you oughta go look for whoever you broke up with and get the hell out of here." Nice improv, Jerry!

Jake wheeled and left the lounge without another word, joining the throng in the terminal. Five more minutes, Vanessa, I prayed, stay put five more minutes. Jerry was trying to sop my front with cocktail napkins offered by our solicitous waitress. Jake Romano had stopped at the water fountain in between the two bathrooms to sponge the tomato juice from his coat. Damn.

"Honey, I need to go to the ladies room and clean up. Take care of the check, will you?" I shoved the soggy napkins at him, and flew out of the bar. I was maybe twenty feet away from the bathroom door when I saw it start to open. No! I flew the last few yards and planted myself in front of it. Jake looked up coolly, tense and wary beneath the smooth veneer. He hadn't planned on me, that's for sure.

"You know, Jake Romano," I screeched, more for the benefit of those in the bathroom than those outside it, though it did catch the terminal's attention. "You'll pay for this and not just the blouse, you creep." The bathroom door eased shut. I added a few foul epithets for emphasis. Thank God I was beyond embarrassment. I'd have hated to know what people were thinking. "And if I were you, I'd stay the hell out of my way!" It was the perfect exit line, so I grandly slung my purse over one shoulder and turned to the bathroom.

His palm slammed into the door, stopping it cold.

"But you're not me, Katie."

"Hey," I said, yanking at the handle. His fingers curled around the edge of the door, the heavy gold ring standing up like a brass knuckle. He was so close behind me his overcoat brushed my legs, breath stirred my hair. A piece of Vanessa's face peered through the crack, then her eyes widened and she slithered out of view.

"Let go of the door." I yanked again but it didn't give.

"Don't make that mistake. Don't forget who I am."

I twisted over my shoulder, inches from his face.

"If you don't let go, I'm gonna scream my fucking head off!"

His jaw tightened, eyes glittering like blue marbles lit from behind. I opened my mouth wide, drawing the breath for a scream.

"You're stupid, Katie. You don't even know how much."

His hand dropped and he walked away, melting into the travelers roaming around the gates. I pulled the door harder than needed and gratefully slipped inside, shaking but triumphant. We'd flushed him out and now he had no place to hide.

Vanessa was sitting on the floor under the diaper-changing shelf. Her arms were wrapped around her knees and her eyes and nose ran. She looked dazed, hair every which way, mouth gaping like a goldfish. Mine was a victory she wouldn't share.

"Van, I know you didn't want it to be him, but we had to find out. He might have hurt you." She didn't answer. "I guess he did hurt you, didn't he. I'm sorry."

"You don't understand."

"I'm trying to." She shook her head no and buried her face in her knees. "Don't, Van; talk to me. Please."

When she raised her face, her eyes were lasers, bright with angry tears. "It's the ring. The fucking ring!"

"What?"

She untangled her long legs and paced the bathroom with a clenched fist. "Damn him! What I couldn't remember, it was the ring. That fucking ring. I can't tell you how many times he's stuck me with it or gotten it caught in my hair. That night, I felt it. Through the gloves. That's why I couldn't . . . when the knife . . . when he cut my buttons." She gagged for a second, fright fighting memory.

"You felt the ring? When he ran the blade down your chest?"

"Yes!" It escaped her in a whoosh. "The bastard, the fucking bastard! Comforting me, taking care of me! The son of a bitch!" Her voice rose in shock and disbelief.

"But now we've got him! Don't you *see*, Van, we've got him. He knows we know! It's like turning over a rock and watching the bugs scurry for cover. We've got him!"

"Oh no, Kate. He's got me. He's got me good." She bit her lip, remembering. "I was so busy, I barely had time to see him. Five, maybe six dates, you know. It wasn't till this starting happening . . . I started to need him. Rely on him. I never did that before . . . I couldn't, I . . . you know how I am." She turned away and forced a shaky laugh. "What a joke! I finally decide to have a relationship and the first man I pick is a fucking psycho!"

"Stop it, Vanessa. You didn't pick him—you might think you did—but trust me, he picked you."

The door opened with a whoosh and I turned to Vanessa as if to a stranger. "Honey, help me with this, will ya? Can you believe it, some idiot in the bar dumped a drink right down my blouse." For the first time, Vanessa registered the reddish stains on the front of my clothes. The woman went into the stall and she hissed, "Did he hurt you?"

"It's Bloody Mary! Can't you smell it?" Horseradish had taken over where hangover left off. All and all, I couldn't imagine smelling worse.

The toilet flushed, forestalling further thought. The woman avoided us and went about her business. Vanessa waited until she left before she lit a cigarette.

"It was like a bolt of lighting. I heard you yelling—Christ, Annie could have heard you yelling in White Plains—and then he grabbed the door. As soon as I saw the ring, I knew. It floored me. I felt stupid enough before, now I feel even dumber."

"Cut it out. You're the victim. All you did was believe someone who said he cared about you."

"Great. Says a lot about commitment in the nineties, doesn't it." She blew a stream of smoke. "Oh my God, what he said about you. I believed that too. Kate, I'm so sorry. I was such an ass."

"Look, Vanessa, ass you might be, but actually I was kind of flattered. It never occurred to me I could be competition. Hell, I should start practicing." I faced the mirror, pushed back a mat of hair and dropped my soggy blouse off one shoulder, rolling it seductively. "Say cowboy," I said in a throaty whisper, "wanna go to heaven for a buck?"

She smiled, but it wasn't the right time.

"All right, I'm gonna go, in case he's waiting," I said. "We don't wanna take any chances. I don't think he'll hang around, but stay until dark, okay?"

She nodded. "I've got a book and a couple of Snickers. I'll be fine." She tried to smile reassuringly, but failed. "This is real, isn't it, Kate? Even though we know who it is, that doesn't stop it. It's still happening to me, isn't it?"

Soggy shirt and all, I hugged her hard. "To us. It's happening to us, Van. And we're already winning." She nodded bravely and I hugged her again. She held on tight. "I gotta go," I said, disengaging her arms. "I love you, Vanessa."

"Love you, Kate."

Jerry was leaning against a pillar. I had forgotten all about him. He had both our coats and his carry-on. I took his arm, grateful that he'd waited and we headed out to the parking lot. For a woman with a hangover, I was having one hell of a day.

11

I could see Annie through the window of the diner. Her bright blue minivan was parked near the door, various Odies and Garfields stuck amid small raspberry hand prints.

She looked up as I came in and waved. It was funny to see her without her cast. A small laptop computer was open in front of her, along with a manila folder full of papers. Annie had been busy. It was just two days since the airport incident, three since our meeting in the midtown hotel.

"Kate, hi! How are you! How's everything out at the barn?"

I slid into the booth across from Annie. She looked very happy today, shining almost. I finally felt guilty about my computer crack at the hotel. Christ, how could I have begrudged Annie a little self-esteem? Some friend you are, said the voice.

". . . a modem and everything," Annie was saying. "I can't believe something this tiny can do so much. I've got lots of stuff already and I know I can get more. This is so exciting, Kate. I know it's, I mean, I know what's happening to Vanessa is awful and I hate it, but I can't help feeling good about what I'm doing. Do you think I'm terrible?"

"Of course I don't think you're terrible. You're a big help. When you have a talent it should feel good to use it." She nodded shyly. "Look, Annie, about how I acted at the hotel, I didn't mean to be such a bitch, I . . ."

"Kate, it's over. If you can't forget about that then I can't forget about the awful things I said to you."

The emotional rollercoaster I lived on crested a hill and took a sharp dive. I was always on the verge of tears lately—that, or I wanted to kill someone. A complex range of emotions, right on a par with a two-year-old's. I pulled my fingers from Annie's grasp and patted her hand briskly.

"Okay, moving on. Let's bring each other up to date. You wanna go first or me?"

"You, I'm dying to hear what happened in the airport. It really is him! I can't believe it. When I spoke to Vanessa yesterday, she said something about a ring?"

As Annie settled back for the story, our waitress arrived. She flipped my coffee cup and filled it without asking. Without ever addressing either of us, she mechanically recited the specials, then shifted her weight to one hip, waiting. Waitress, waiting—aha! she wanted us to order. It was hard to believe this woman could actually survive on tips. Obligingly, Annie scanned a menu that had more pages than some novels and ordered a hot turkey sandwich. I shuddered and ordered a tuna on pumpernickel, lettuce and tomato. The waitress pulled a pen from behind her ear—god knows what else was stuck up there—and scribbled on a pad. She ripped two pages from it, slapped them on the table and sauntered away without saying a word.

"Gee, I didn't know this was a four-star diner," I said, hoping she'd hear. "What were we talking about? Oh yeah, the airport." I laughed. "I was definitely a variable that Mr. Romano hadn't factored in."

I recounted the afternoon at the airport, encouraged by Annie's rapt attention and occasional gasps. Needless to say, I didn't feel it necessary to include my little rendezvous with Mike the maintenance man. There were some things you couldn't discuss in a brightly lit diner in Hempstead.

"I'm getting the alarm put in today. They're coming out at four."

"Kate, please be careful. I don't like you being there alone."

"I'll be okay. Has anybody heard from Sandy?"

"She called in. She's coming right back. But he's already called Mindy to find out where she'd gone. He said he knew she was leaving town but couldn't remember for where. If she was going to L.A. on the film, he wanted to alert his friends so they could be at her service. We figure he wants to get to Vanessa before you do so he'll have an explanation for being at the airport."

"How's Van doing?" We had agreed I shouldn't contact her, we didn't know if Jake was watching.

"Better. He hurt her so badly, Kate. But right now, she

seems more angry than anything else. Oola said it's pretty natural."

"Speaking of Oola, she wants us to meet up on Friday for lunch at the InfoTech place. I'm bringing Vanessa home, so we need to get our schedules organized. You know, for the stalking."

"I'm going to be limited to days when the girls are at school, but I might be able to free up a little time on the weekends. I just don't want David to find out."

"What do you mean 'find out'? Didn't you tell him? Annie, he's got to know!"

Our waitress returned, Miss Congeniality of 1964, two plates on her left arm, coffeepot in her right. She slid the plates across the table with practiced ease and refilled our cups. Before I could ask for a glass of water, she was gone, just a faint memory of large buttocks beneath a polyester skirt. I flagged down a busboy and requested water. He gave a shrug and struggled away with a busbox full of dirty plates.

"Annie, why didn't you tell David? He's your husband, for crissakes."

"Did you tell Steve everything, Kate? I did talk to him about it a little bit, right after lunch when Vanessa told us about the flowers. He thought we were all making a big deal out of nothing. I think it's hard for men to understand, you know? Women, we know, because we live with it." Annie swirled her fork in the instant mashed potatoes, watching the tracks fill with gravy.

"Something isn't right, Annie. Okay, so David thought we were overreacting, but after the break-in at the barn, he must have known this was serious."

"I didn't have a chance to tell him. He was pretty upset at how late I got home that night. He had to feed the kids and get them ready for bed. I tried to explain what happened, but he was too mad to listen. When David's mad, it's best if I keep quiet. Then maybe it will blow over without . . ." She stopped abruptly, stricken.

"Without what?" I spoke very calmly. My mind was racing. Was she finally going to tell me? What should I say if she did?

"Without what, Annie?" Try as I would, the urgency I felt carried into my voice.

"Nothing, Kate. I don't want to talk about it, okay?"

"No, it's not okay. Answer me, without what?"

"Without him . . . without him screaming at me and us getting into another fight. Look, Kate, I don't want to talk about David right now. Please, don't make me."

She couldn't even look up from her plate. I looked at that bent head and remembered a few secrets of my own. It wasn't fair to expect Annie to do what I couldn't do myself. I wanted to grab her and hold her and keep her safe, the way I used to on the playground when boys pulled her hair. But I couldn't even take care of myself.

Vanessa wasn't safe, Annie wasn't safe, I was a mess. So many delusions, so many myths had set us up to fail, so many expectations that would never be fulfilled. We women had become the caretakers of an ugly society, dooming ourselves by assuming responsibility for the actions of others.

"Annie." I pushed my half-eaten sandwich aside. "I can't believe that David, that he'd . . ." I didn't have the moral authority for this. "Promise me you'll talk to Oola."

"I promise to think about it, Kate. I'm not sure what to do yet. Our fights scare me and I worry about the girls. I don't know what's happening to us."

"Annie, do you think I drink too much?" It was out before I knew it was coming. My mouth dried up and my pulse quickened. She was surprised, but I knew with sinking certainty it was the question itself, not the content, that startled her.

"Yes."

That was all she said, just yes. We looked at each other, one damaged woman reflected in the eyes of another. Old teeter-totter partners and jungle gym explorers who had found life riskier than expected. I saw clearly she was as frightened for me as I for her.

"Okay, computer wizard, what have you learned?" She busied herself with the laptop, giving us time to get composed.

"When Vanessa and I talked, we decided we needed to know more about Jake. I chased down some stuff for Oola on the web and then Vanessa hooked me up with a professor friend of hers at Boston College. That's where Jake went to school. I used his access code and got into the school's mainframe." She turned the screen slightly to face me and brought a record up for view. Jacob Albert Romano had been born in

Springfield, Massachusetts on February 13, 1958. The day before Valentine's Day, how sweet. He had graduated from BC in 1980 with a 3.25 GPA. "There really wasn't a lot here. No clubs or fraternities, it looks like he was kind of a loner. Now here's the stuff on his family." Jake Romano had one older brother, James, Jr. who lived in Arizona. His parents, Margaret and James Romano, were both deceased by 1979.

"See how neat this is, Kate. Once I knew where he was born I tapped into the on-line services at the Springfield newspapers and got access to their archives. I did a search for Romano and hit the jackpot." She repeatedly stroked the enter key and page after page of news copy flipped across the small monitor.

"Here we go, this is the most recent stuff," she continued. "Jake's fourth documentary received some national recognition from an independent film-makers association. That was two years ago. The *Springfield Herald* wrote him up, kind of a local-boy-makes-good article. See his picture?" She pointed at the screen, thrilled by the technology. "He looks more like a movie star than a director. I just don't understand why someone who looks like that has to do something like this!"

"If it's one thing I'm learning, Annie, the outside means nothing. All it does is cover up what's inside, and sometimes what's inside has nothing to do with what we see." I grimaced self-consciously. "Look at me, I'm living proof." I paused. "You too, Annie."

She ignored that and pulled up yet another screen of data. "It says he did his graduate work at NYU. I haven't been able to access their computer yet, but I'm sure I can figure it out."

"God, Annie, you should become a detective or something."

"There's really not a lot to it, Kate. Everything's online these days, you just have to know where to look."

"Shit, Jacob Romano doesn't have a chance. Both his parents are dead?"

"Yeah, his dad had a heart attack not too long ago. But his mother, that was awful. She got hit by a drunk driver when he was twelve. The article said she was coming home from the supermarket. A guy named Harry McCarthy, driving on a suspended license, already had three DWIs. She died instantly. It's scary, Kate, that could have been me and the girls." Now it was my turn to ignore her. If Annie could have been Margaret Romano, I had been Harry McCarthy more times than I wanted to remember. The only difference was that I'd been lucky. I didn't feel lucky.

"So that's it for family, a brother in Arizona."

"Well, unless you count an ex-wife."

"Annie," I practically shrieked. "You bitch! A wife!" That floored me. I picked up my long-forgotten sandwich and chewed thoughtfully. What kind of woman would marry Jake Romano? Just about anyone who didn't know him, I realized. Annie was grinning a Cheshire Cat grin, very pleased with herself. "Okay, Annie, spill it. Tell me, not another minute!"

"Okay, I couldn't help myself, Kate." She typed in a file name and the screen changed. "It surprised me too. I guess his obsession with Vanessa blinded me to the possibility of other women in his life. When you think about it logically, a man who looks like him wouldn't lack for female companionship."

"Annie, tell me or I may have to kill you." The busboy reappeared, just when I was sure he'd moved back to Argentina, and set two glasses of water on the table. Annie smiled and said thank you as I impatiently waved him away. He flashed a gold tooth grin for Annie and murmured something uncomplimentary about my mother in Spanish.

"Hold on, Kate, I don't have a lot." She pulled a printout from the manila folder and handed it to me. I raced through it as she walked through the same information on screen. Jacob Romano had married Natalie Ellinwood in 1988. Natalie had been a theater major at NYU and at the time of her marriage had just landed the part of Cassie in the touring company of *A Chorus Line*.

"I didn't even know he was married until I read that article in the *Springfield Herald*. It mentions 'his 'brief, unfortunate marriage to actress Natalie Ellinwood,' so I did some looking around and finally talked to the people at Equity. She let her dues lapse in '90 and according to them, she never went on that tour."

"When did they get divorced?"

"I don't know. It didn't say."

"We have to find her, Annie. Do we know where she lives?"

"No. I wasn't sure how far I should go, you know. She has a right to her privacy, just like Vanessa."

Annie was so much nicer than I was. I didn't give a shit about Natalie Ellinwood Romano's privacy. I cared about stopping Jake Romano and the end would justify the means. This woman had been married to him. She had the inside track and I wanted to know everything, anything that would make him vulnerable.

"Annie, Vanessa's the reason we need to know," I said, back to telling half-truths.

"Kate, I don't feel comfortable. Judging from the article, they weren't married very long. He was quoted as saying that they were too young, their career goals took them in different directions. It sounded amicable, the split I mean." Annie finished her coffee and looked around for the waitress from hell. "I feel like dessert. You want some dessert? I saw a lemon meringue pie on the way in that looked fabulous."

"Sure, pie, fine."

Of course the split sounded amicable to Annie. It was Jake's version and she still hadn't grasped his propensity for lying. As an accomplished liar myself, I knew better.

"Annie, how about this? When Steve and I had the agency we used to hire actresses all the time. We worked with a couple of different agents, I was pretty friendly with one guy. Why don't I call him and just see if he knows who represents her. I could get a bio—public information that she makes available on request. I wouldn't be invading her privacy or anything. How's that sound?"

She was mulling it over when our waitress returned, obviously inconvenienced by our request for further service. She slopped coffee into our cups, sullenly added the pie to our checks and slammed them back down on the table. I was ready for her on the return trip and insisted that she remove our lunch plates after dropping the pies. Her expression reminded me of my cats, full of superior scorn for the petty needs of human beings. If she hadn't taken those plates, she'd have been wearing them.

"God, she's awful, isn't she." Annie shook her head. "But the pie is great. It must be hard to be a waitress, dealing with people all day, always on your feet."

"Annie, unless you are up for sainthood, I don't want to

hear another kind word about that woman. God, you are too much. So, what do you say? About Natalie, I mean."

"I guess it's okay to get her bio, but nothing else, Kate, until we all decide."

"That's fine, Annie. When are you going to talk to Vanessa again?"

"She's calling me this afternoon. We check in at four every day. I'll ask her then." Annie scraped the last bit of meringue from the plate and nodded. "She told me she feels more comfortable calling out than having to answer the phone. That must be terrible, being afraid to answer a phone. He's an awful man, Kate. I don't know if Vanessa will ever be the same."

"I know. I've always looked up to her so much. If this could happen to her, what chance do I have, you know?"

"We'll all be all right, Kate, I have to believe we'll be all right."

"Annie, I'm really frightened. I don't know if I can do this." I wasn't talking about Vanessa anymore.

"I know, Kate. I don't know if I can either." Neither was she.

We left the restaurant after arguing over the tip, but I let her slip an extra two bucks on the table. I really had to do something about money. I still hadn't collected the January rent. Like I had gotten December's. Crazy Carlos, my downstairs tenant and sometime sculptor, had been with me since Steve and if I totalled things up, probably owed me for at least a year. I didn't like totalling things up, and as a result hadn't looked a bank statement in almost two months. For some reason, I was afraid to open the mail. It was getting harder to even take it out of the box.

On the ride back to the barn, I thought about Annie. I thought about David, too. He'd always been a little macho and far too critical for my taste, but I have to admit I thought he was funny at times. I'd never hated him. Until now. He did pick on Annie a lot, but I was guilty of that too. We all joked about her simple ways, her optimistic outlook, her willingness to look for the good in everything. When had I started thinking those were laughable qualities?

I beat the alarm company by ten minutes. We toured the house with the alarm guy pointing out all the unlocked windows and the flimsy chain on the kitchen door. Not the biggest challenge for an adolescent burglar, much less someone like Jake Romano. We were proceeding to the basement to examine the wiring when the phone rang. I waved them to the stairs, reminding them of the storm door, and answered it.

"Hello Katie." His voice was sultry, almost sexy. My heart pounded and I knew I should hang up.

"What do you want?"

"I want to talk to you. I miss Vanessa so much that I thought talking to you would make me feel better."

"Well, I have better things to do now. And so does Vanessa."

"Ah yes, the alarm company," he replied, ignoring the reference to Van. "Such a waste of time and money."

"How do you know who's here?" I felt a little panic and it sharpened my reply.

He laughed softly. "Surely, you and I understand each other by now, Katie. Are you really surprised or just teasing me?"

"I wouldn't waste my time teasing a limp dick," I retorted. I had to be careful; I was getting angry. "Here's a news flash for you Jake. Vanessa knows. Get it, she knows! Take it from me, things aren't gonna be so easy anymore." I could hear him breathe into the phone.

"Is that supposed to scare me, Katie?"

"I don't need to scare you. Not everybody gets their rocks off playing with razors in the dark."

"You know even a sharp razor can slip . . ."

"Is that a threat, Jake? All it takes is one threat on tape and your little game is over."

"A threat? Shaving is a threat? Drinking already, are we Katie?"

I hated him passionately. "My drinking is none of your business."

"Well, you're right of course. I just worry about you."

"I bet."

"I enjoy our conversations, Katie. I'll be calling again soon. I hope you don't mind."

"I don't mind at all, Jake. You know, you told once me not to make a mistake and so I'm gonna do you the same favor. Don't ever think you scare me. That would be a mistake, a big fucking mistake." I slammed the phone down, shaking. Hardball, then, and this was just the beginning. I'd have to get in shape; this wasn't going to be easy.

I poured myself a glass of Chardonnay and sipped it while the electricians worked. They clumped up and downstairs, testing, drilling holes, mounting boxes and checking flashing lights. The wine was my first since the Mike incident and it didn't taste quite as good as I had hoped. Fortunately, with alcohol, the more you drink the better it gets. The second was smoother than the first, the fourth slid down my throat like liquid glass. I signed for the installation and watched them pull out of the driveway a little after seven. This would cost through the nose, a rush job complete with overtime. I sat in the dark, running my fingers over the curve of my wine glass. The little red light of the alarm was small comfort. I thought of my promise to Annie and poured another glass of wine.

There were messages on Vanessa's machine, its flashing light a twin to those mounted on the alarm by the door. The messages could wait until tomorrow. I didn't want to talk to anyone. My luck running true to form, the phone rang almost immediately. Screw it. The machine picked up and I heard Vanessa intoning instructions for after the beep. His voice was as clear as a bell. I froze in place, every fiber alert and listening.

"A mistake, Katie? Feel safe, do you, drinking alone in the dark?"

I didn't have time to move before the outside lights started coming on. First the ones in front of the garage, then the front and side porches, and on to the back. I whirled with them, following the path of light as it circled the house like a SWAT team. I couldn't see out the windows but I knew he must be out there. I felt dizzy and it was hard to breathe.

When the phone rang again I dropped my wine. It was so easy to plan on not being frightened, another thing to execute the plan. I thought I would hear his voice and steeled myself, but instead there were a series of beeps after Vanessa's greeting and the machine began to play back. It took a second before understanding dawned. The bastard had beeped her machine and was listening to the messages. I lunged at it, jabbing ineffectively at the buttons, until I finally ripped out the tape.

Instantly the lights began dousing themselves, reversing the order in which they were lit. I could barely swallow, choking, almost sobbing as darkness was restored one light at a time. I've got to get help, I thought, involuntarily running a hand through my hair as I reached for the phone. When it rang, it was so natural that I answer.

"Do you get it now, Katie? I don't care who knows, you stupid cunt. And don't fuck with me again!"

Even the dial tone he left behind was full of menace. I drew deep ragged breaths and tried to regain some calm. The alarm was on. If he tried to get in, the police would come. He just wants to scare you. I was talking myself down from my ledge. Turn on a light, that's a girl, turn it on. The lamp in the living room revealed a glistening pool of white wine and broken glass on the pale wood floor. Grateful for something, anything, mindless to do, I mopped it up with paper towels and replaced the glass.

He must have been outside, there were motion detectors on those lights. He must have been walking around the house, using a cellular phone. I didn't know how he turned them off, but it couldn't be too hard. There was probably some gadget for that; there were gadgets for just about everything. I wasn't thinking too clearly. I cursed the wine and the fear, not really sure which had muddled me more.

Out of the blue came the thought to call Jerry. He had helped me before, with no questions asked. Jerry was real and solid, the admitted alcoholic who didn't have to drink. I wasn't admitting anything, but I was pouring myself another glass of wine to help me straighten up. I dug through my purse and found his number, dialing quickly before I lost my nerve. He answered on the third ring.

"Jerry, it's Kate. You know, crazy Kate from the airport, Steve's ex-wife."

"I know who you are, Kate. What's up?"

"Are you busy? 'Cause if you're busy I can call someone else, it's just I don't want to be by myself and I keep drinking more wine . . . Oh it's so stupid, I'm sure you have other things to do, but I just thought . . . I just thought I'd call, but you're busy, so I'll talk to you later." The words poured out, tumbling on top of each other, punctuated by hiccups and snuffles. Once again I was an idiot. Every time I spoke to this man, I was an idiot.

"Kate, where are you? Have you eaten yet? Maybe we can

get something to eat. What do you think, honey?"

"Don't call me honey." I was crying in earnest now. "You don't know me. I'm not what you think. You don't know what I'm really like." Somewhere on my journey kindness had become the enemy.

"Okay, it's okay. Are you still out on the north shore, Kate?"

"Yes."

"I'm coming right now. I'm going to grab some Chinese food. You like Chinese food, don't you Kate?"

"Yes," I blubbered. "But you don't have to come all the way out here, Jerry."

"I wanna come, Kate. It's my responsibility. What's the address?"

Dutifully I recited the address of the barn. "You don't wanna be responsible for me, Jerry. Nobody wants to, not even me. I don't know what's happening to me. I just don't know." I trailed off, hitting an emotional plateau and resting in the void. My head hurt and I was suddenly exhausted.

"Kate, I know what's happening to you. Believe me, I know. I'll be there in a half hour." He hung up and I sat on the couch to wait, watching the steady red light of the alarm and sipping the Chardonnay.

He made it in less than thirty-five minutes, but that was long enough for me to feel mortified. I was determined to regain my poise, if not my dignity. Some secret, I was spilling my guts on a regular basis. I was in the kitchen when the doorbell rang. I punched the numbers into the alarm box and let him in.

I put out the Chinese on the coffee table in the living room while Jerry made a fire. It was the first one I'd had since I came. I went about the business of plates and napkins and tea without saying much. He ate and stoked the fire without a word about the broken answering machine or my state of hysteria.

I told him about Jake's latest escapade over General Tso's chicken. He listened carefully and went outside to check the lights. Every bulb in every floodlight appeared blown. Jerry thought it might be some kind of ultrasound device that popped the filaments. There was no doubt of deliberate intent and yet no proof of it. Classic Jake Romano. I felt better knowing Jake had made me so crazy, not the booze. I needed to settle my nerves, so I poured a snifter of Remy Martin while he was in the bathroom and waited in front of the fire. He came in and sat behind me on the couch.

"Kate, do you remember when we used to meet at Bruno's? You and me and the rest of the guys?"

"Sure, I remember."

"I felt so in tune with you, like we were kindred spirits."

"I remember the night you cornered me near the bathroom and told me we should run away together. God, I think you kissed me, too. Funny how things come back to you, Jerry. I forgot all about that."

"I'm sorry, Kate."

"Oh, there's nothing to be sorry about. It was a harmless little kiss and you were pretty sloshed." I twisted around to face him, the warmth of the brandy and fire kindling other flames. I leaned my breasts against his knees. "It wasn't such a bad kiss, was it?"

"I don't remember."

I understood now how mating dogs felt when people turned a hose on them. I jerked away from him, drawing my knees up to my chest.

"Hey, don't take that wrong. I'm the one who missed out." I was somewhat mollified, but not ready to give in. "Did that ever happen to you, Kate? Not being able to remember stuff when you drink?" I looked at him warily. This was dangerous territory. "It happened to me all the time. Sometimes just an hour or two, sometimes whole nights. It sucked. I hated waking up and not knowing where the car was, how I got home. Shit, sometimes I woke up places and didn't even know how I got there."

"I kinda had that happen to me. Not very often or anything, and nothing bad happened, but I couldn't remember everything." Cautious, I had to be very cautious.

"You're lucky. It happened to me a lot. And I couldn't be sure whether anything bad happened or not, so I always felt nervous and paranoid. It's hard to live that way. Pretty soon, I could turn on the flip of a coin, laughing one minute, enraged the next. Mood swings, I used to call them." He chuckled softly. "After a while, I didn't even have to be drunk for it to happen. I didn't know what was wrong with me, but I couldn't seem to stop."

I had turned to face him, involuntarily drawn by the story of my life. He told it all, the fights, the fear, the desperate need to make it all go away. He spoke of losing Suzanne, the endless cycle of bars and drinks and trying to belong, followed by unbearable depression, loneliness and despair. I cried as he talked. How could it be that this man I hadn't seen in years knew exactly how I lived.

Slowly, I started to tell him how it was for me. The rages, the voices in my head, the mystery bruises from forgotten falls. All the broken promises and exceptions to the rules. I told about Steve and about Mike and about the guys at Petrillo's. I told as much as I could, anxious to unburden myself. He listened, smoothed my hair and massaged my shoulders while I talked. Sometimes he threw in a story of his own and we laughed at the crazy things drunk people do. I never thought I'd tell most of this stuff, much less laugh at it. He pulled me up on the couch and I leaned comfortably into his side, safe at last. But not for long.

"So Kate, what will you do now?"

"Now? What do you mean?" I snuggled closer and he shifted his weight away from me. He reached under my chin and turned my face up.

"I mean now that you know you're not the only one who's done these things, what do you think you should do?"

"I don't know." The silence stretched. There was an obvious question to be asked. I thought about my promise to Annie and sighed. "What did you do?"

"When I finally couldn't take it anymore, I talked to a guy I knew. It was funny how it happened, I just bumped into him one day, the way it was with us. I hadn't seen him around much and he told me he was a recovering alcoholic. We talked for hours. He took me to my first AA meeting, Kate, and I've been going ever since. That was over four years ago and I haven't had a drink."

"You mean you go to those meetings? But Jerry, you were never a bum or anything."

He laughed. "Not a bum, Kate, just a drunk. Just somebody who couldn't stop drinking, no matter what it was doing to him and the people he loved. I always thought an alcoholic was somebody who slept on a park bench, drinking out of a brown paper bag. That kept me drunk a few extra years. And brought me closer to being there." He was pensive, saddened perhaps by the memory. Then he dropped the bombshell. "What about you Kate? Is it going to keep you drunk too?" For the first time, the cards were on the table. I could play the hand, bluff or fold.

"Are you saying I'm an alcoholic?" I sat straight up, defenses securely in place. Time for the finger-pointing, the lectures. I was used to that. I knew how to handle him. Defiantly, I picked up my snifter from the floor. He didn't appear offended, just lowered the glass to look in my face.

"I'm saying *I'm* an alcoholic. I'm sharing with you how I felt and what I did when I was drinking."

We stared at each other. It seemed like forever. I scratched my cheek and shook out my hair, but my face kept twisting up to fight the tears. I just wanted to feel the way I felt when we were talking about our lives. I set the snifter down.

"My pop was a drunk," I whispered haltingly. "I swore I'd never be like him. It killed him, you know." I tried for conversational tone, but my voice broke. "I'm so tired and so scared."

"Don't let it kill you, Kate." Then he was hugging me and while I drifted toward sleep he kept whispering about not doing it alone, that there were people who understood. Before I was gone I remember him promising that my life could get better beyond my wildest dreams.

12

I don't remember when Jerry left Tuesday night. I must have dropped like a log because all the dishes were washed and the Chinese containers thrown away. I woke up on the couch, neatly tucked under an afghan; even the alarm was reset. While I made coffee I thought about what had passed between us. I didn't like thinking about it. And I certainly didn't like thinking about doing anything about it. Vanessa's crystal snifter rested accusingly in the dish strainer.

All right, I wouldn't drink anymore, but I wasn't going to those meetings. I wasn't that bad. I just needed more self-discipline, no matter what Jerry thought. A life beyond my wildest dreams. Yeah, right. My wildest dreams involved being locked in a brewery with a man on parole.

Friday morning I busied myself with telephone calls. I went to the local coffee shop and monopolized the pay phone, afraid to use the one at the house. I talked to Charlie Harrington, my agent friend, about getting some info on Natalie Romano. We shot the breeze for a little while and he seemed glad to hear from me. I don't think he knew about me and Steve. I gave him the fax number at Oola's office and he promised to send over Natalie's bio as soon as he found it.

I had dug up Bobby's business card and called him at his office. The woman who answered the phone insisted he was busy, but I kept calling back until she put me through. I needed to see him, preferably today. I didn't give him time to argue, just went right into the cellar story. I had his full attention then and when I told him about the airport, he agreed to meet me for lunch, at Rockefeller Center. I called Oola's office, left a message that I'd be late for lunch and headed into the city.

I was feeling like dogmeat. My stomach cramped and gurgled and I hadn't slept for shit. Everything felt shaky and jangly, on edge. I blamed it on nerves and tried to ignore the idea that a quick screwdriver could fix everything. I hadn't had a drink in two days.

I figured Bobby would spring for lunch at the Rainbow Room, and toyed with the idea that a white wine spritzer wasn't really a drink. But when I got to the Plaza, I saw him standing at a vendor's cart, hotdogs in hand. I took the one he handed me and we walked to a nearby bench. Bobby was carrying an oversized briefcase.

"Geez, you'd think a Vice President would have an expense account," I said, wiping mustard from my sleeve.

"You'd think a Vice President would have paying customers."

I put my hands up in surrender and sauerkraut juice dribbled down my wrist over the mustard. My wardrobe was taking a beating these days. He pulled his case up on to his lap and I walked back to the cart for napkins and a couple of Pepsi's.

"So what ya got, Bobby?"

"First I want you to tell me everything. Right from the start, okay?" I walked him through it again, from the meeting in Vanessa's class to Jake at the airport and the lights at the barn. Bobby made notes in a little leather-bound book.

"There's a strong possibility that first meeting was no coincidence. You said he brought up a book she wrote under a pen name? I'd give you ten to one he knew exactly who wrote that book."

I was shaken. I thought about what Annie was doing, gathering information on Jake without his knowledge. When had this really started? I shivered just thinking about it.

"This is so bizarre. This doesn't happen, not to people I know."

It happened a lot more than people knew, Bobby said. The number of cases was growing, too, most of them single or divorced women, age 20 to 45. "Though male victims are probably underestimated because men are less liable to report it. That macho thing can work against us, you know."

"Please, there isn't a woman in the world who hasn't known that for years."

"Funny." He dug in his briefcase. "Here, remember I was

telling you about the Shaefer girl before? She did everything right, order of protection, bodyguard, the whole shebang, then one day she opened her front door and boom! The bastard blew her away."

"If this is supposed to be helping . . ."

The whole point was a survey the detective had done. Using 74 cases in Los Angeles as his baseline and despite it being Hollywood, less than a quarter of the victims were movie stars. The rest were normal people, most stalked by someone they knew. "So the fact that it's the boyfriend doesn't surprise me."

"What surprises me is that he picked Vanessa. She's a strong woman, Bobby. A success story, like something out of *Reader's Digest*. Poor rural background, scholarships through school, professor of literature, best-selling author, it's almost nauseating."

He nodded. "That fits. Attractive, intelligent women with some semblance of authority over themselves or others seem to draw these nuts like magnets."

"Or maybe they're just the ones who make people believe them. If a not-so-pretty woman is hounded, everyone assumes she's making it up. Guys think, 'You wish, Porky!' Men suck, Bobby."

"Hey, sexism isn't an all-male pastime, Kate. Believe it or not, most of us guys are just doing the best we can while the ground shifts under our feet. Not all of us are looking to screw everything that wiggles."

"Okay, okay. So what can we do? Anything?"

"Well the first thing is documentation. Get a tracer, like Caller ID, on the phone, all the phones. Log all the calls. I brought you a little recorder you can attach to the phone. Start taping immediately and save the answering machine tapes too.

"Okay, what else?"

"The cops, you have got to document stuff with the cops."

"The cops are assholes."

"Back off, Kate. I was a cop and it's not as easy as you think. The cops aren't the villains here, they can only enforce the law. What's the law?"

"What do you mean, what's the law?" I mimicked. Things were getting a little heated. I tried to slow down.

"I mean, do you have a clue what the law is before you go shooting off your mouth about what a shitty job the cops are doing? News flash, Kate! The law in New York State says a credible threat must be apparent for police intervention to occur. The guy got rid of the flowers, and the two of you chose not to report the break-in," he said. "So what are the cops supposed to have done, huh? The only two real crimes this guy committed you didn't even tell them about!"

"You're right. I'm sorry. Do you think I should report now? Is it too late?"

"You can try. You might at least be able to get it on record."

"What difference does it make if we can't prove it?"

"Credibility, Kate. You're in this for the long haul. Didn't you say this guy threatened you before he played his game with the lights?"

"Yeah, but I ripped the tape out trying to stop him from getting Vanessa's messages."

"Too bad. So you're starting from scratch. Anyway, you need to change your remote code right away. Save anything he sends you, notes, letters, gifts. Keep a master calendar where you enter any encounter, the number of phone calls, the time, everything. A calendar is considered a legal document in a court of law. That's what you're doing, Kate, building a court case."

"Okay, what else?"

"Do either of you have a gun?" he asked seriously. A gun! Jesus Christ, I didn't even like water pistols. "I didn't think so. It's probably just as well if you're not comfortable using it. Now look Kate, I brought you something, but I want you to be very careful how you use it because it's illegal." He looked around the busy plaza as he handed me a brown paper bag. I was hoping for some blow darts or at least some knock-out drops and was disappointed to find nothing but four tiny canisters.

"You brought me sample hair spray?"

"It's pepper spray, Kate. Kind of like Mace."

"Cool!" I looked at the cans with new interest. It struck me as ironic that this stuff was illegal, but I could trot to the nearest Wal-Mart for a hunting rifle and a case of ammo.

"Don't get any crazy ideas," he cautioned. "These are defensive weapons only." He checked his watch. "Look, I gotta go. Take the recorder and keep in touch. If this keeps going, and she can afford it, you need to bring in a professional. Don't get any crazy ideas about handling this, Kate, you're not qualified."

"I'll be a good girl, I promise," I lied. "Bye." He left me with the spray, the recorder and a rising temper. Not qualified? Bullshit. I was so tired of being perceived as helpless. Maybe that was the reason men thought they could get away with the things they did. It was time we started showing them exactly how capable we were.

Resolve in place, I pulled a ticket off the windshield and headed out for my Friday meeting with the other stalkers. It took forever to find a place to park, every hydrant I saw was already taken. I hated New York. What's the point of a city with everything if you can never get out of your car?

The building where InfoTech had its apartments was comfortingly nondescript. The doorman buzzed before he let me up. Oola opened the door and I could see the remains of their lunch on the kitchen table. Annie and Vanessa sat there, still sipping sodas, a cigarette burning in a saucer.

"Sorry I'm late." I went around the table saying hi. "I got some stuff from that guy Bobby. A recorder for the phone and some Mace." I handed Vanessa the bag and she pulled out one of the cans. Annie took the other, turning it over gingerly.

"This isn't Mace, it's pepper spray," Vanessa said.

"Same shit. What'd I miss?" I settled in the fourth chair. Vanessa got up and checked the fridge.

"You want something, Kate? I've got Diet Pepsi, a Snapple, raspberry ice tea I think, and some white wine." I could feel Annie's eyes on me.

"I'll have the ice tea, if no one else wants it."

Annie beamed. "I don't want it. No one wants it. You have it, Kate." The eagerness of her answer made me cringe. You're pathetic, whispered the little voice. Fuck you, I thought, I'm drinking Snapple. What more did people want.

Oola cleared her throat. "We need to set our schedules for next week, that is if we're all still in. This is a big commitment. Has everyone thought it through? Annie?"

"I can't honestly say I'm not frightened, but I have to do this. All my life, I just let things happen to me. I'm so tired of feeling helpless, not just about this, but about everything. Does that make sense?"

Annie had been thinking about her marriage. I wanted to tell her about Jerry and that I had decided not to drink anymore, but not in front of Oola.

."You know, Annie, I felt the same way when I talked to Bobby. He said that I wasn't qualified to handle this. I am so sick of men—no, not just men, people—deciding what I can and cannot handle. I am not helpless."

"Helpless is . what we've become, Kate," Oola replied. "Women as victims, dependents, women as trophies, tokens and weaklings. And what's even worse, we women encourage it." She sighed. "It's very trendy to blame men for what's happening, but doesn't that just perpetuate the problem? As if they're supposed to fix it! The quality of my life has to be my responsibility, no one else's. I dress for myself, I contribute my share, I own my choices and my feelings. Because of that, my life is enhanced by the presence of a partner, not fulfilled."

Annie was trembling. Sometimes I felt like Oola was from another planet. We had gone to the same college, shared so many common experiences, yet she had gleaned knowledge that I never knew was there. When I switched the subject back to stalking, I could feel Annie's relief.

"You know, I remember an article I read when I went upstate to visit my mom. It was about a girl who was being stalked, a waitress. For the longest time, she couldn't get anyone to believe her, not even her best friend. But the craziest part was what the guy said the last time she took him to court. The reporter asked him why he kept chasing this woman who so obviously wanted nothing to do with him and he said, 'If she didn't wanna see me, she wouldn't bring me here. I try to dress nice, she likes that.' Can you believe it! The guy thinks being on trial is a fucking date!"

"It's so frustrating! His crime is forcing her to see him against her will and then the law turns around and says he has the right to face his accuser!" The criminal justice system was one of Oola's favorite topics. I thought for sure the soapbox was coming out, but she held herself in check. "Stalkers have little or no fear of consequences, partially because they're ridiculously mild. But also because they perceive themselves above the law or so justified in what they're doing that they don't believe it's wrong."

"He knows it's wrong, Oola," Vanessa insisted.

"Stalking is about power, Vanessa, there are no rules. The way the uninformed think rape is about sex, stalking is seen as unrequited love run amuck. Uh-uh. It's about creating fear. Creating fear is like the way these men make love. The victim's fear is an aphrodisiac. And maybe a drug. An end in itself, since they're hooked on it."

"Then just like a drug, they need to up the dose," I put in.

"Right," said Oola. "Behavior like this gets serious quick. But because the stalker looks pathetic to most people, no one takes him seriously until it's too late. By the time the victim understands what's really happening, she's already playing catch-up. If she's had any interactions with the assailant, quite often she's blamed for the stalker's crime."

"I've thought that," Vanessa admitted. "When I read an article or saw a talk show, I'd think 'What a bimbo—playing games to keep some loser on the string.' " She paused, pain twisting her mouth. "I've always walked away. It was so easy. I never gave a thought to anyone's feelings."

There was an uneasy silence then.

"We have to remember this man is dangerous," Oola went on. "We don't know how he'll respond to our course of action. We need to think defensively and protect ourselves. I recommend that we never track him alone, always in pairs. Agreed?"

"Yes," we chorused.

"And one more thing. The drinking. Vanessa, I'm not saying the cellar would have turned out different, but I think we need to keep our minds clear at all times. No more nights out on the town, okay?" She looked from Vanessa to me.

Vanessa nodded. I didn't. Who the hell did Oola think she was, anyway? If I wanted to have a drink that was none of her business. I thought you quit drinking, prodded the voice. I did, but only if I said so.

"Okay, I have to get going. Kate, are you taking Vanessa home?"

"Yeah, but I thought we'd hit a couple of biker bars on the way."

"Oh, Kate," giggled Annie. They left together and Vanessa

and I picked up the kitchen until she settled down for a cigarette.

"It makes me so mad, Kate. The stuff Oola said. Especially the part about my fear being an aphrodisiac. I'm running around like a chicken with my head cut off and it's giving him a hard-on! Unbelievable!" She still avoided saying his name.

"Sometimes I can't believe any of it. No offense, Vanessa," I added, "but I thought stalkers were like the guy who went after John Lennon, or what's his name who went after Jodie Foster, via President Reagan."

"I think I can speak for Jodie when I say she wasn't interested." Vanessa took a drag and mused. "But you know, maybe part of it is the notion that women are on a perpetual manhunt. When we try and tell someone it's the other way around, they expect us to prove it."

"Yeah, what about David Letterman? He was stalked. I bet no one grilled him. 'So, Dave, tell us the truth.' " I stood, holding an imaginary microphone in front of an imaginary David Letterman. " 'How well do you know this woman? Are you sure you're not exaggerating this? C'mon Dave, did you lead her on, walking around the yard in those little blue Speedos?' " We laughed, but I felt sorry for David Letterman. He was still being hunted, and for all the manhood myths, he was just as incapable as Vanessa of stopping it.

"I thought about that when I watched his show last night. Of course I don't know what's going on now, but I kept thinking how normal he looked. Nothing's changed, he's just the same."

"You'll be the same again too."

"No. I don't think so." She got up and leaned against the counter, arms folded. "When someone is watching you, you can't help but watch yourself. Looking at everything, checking, judging the future, the past, every minute, every choice. Funny thing, Kate, I failed my review."

"Vanessa, stop beating yourself up. You're tired. God, if your life is lousy, then mine is screwed."

"I'm not beating myself up." She paced a little, then sat in the chair across from me. Her eyes burned with the same intensity as her words. "Here I am in this anonymous apartment, hiding from the world, nothing left but me. Don't you see?

Take away the outside and there's no reflection in the mirror. My life is a giant marketing plan that keeps me jumping through hoops."

"Van, you're a very successful woman. One man doesn't change that."

"Success is so relative, isn't it? I talked to Annie a lot this week, more than I ever have. I started thinking maybe she's the success."

"Annie is a mess!"

"But what if it's what she dreams of, not what she's got. Annie believes in things . . . Hope, that's what it is. Annie lives on hope. I live on bank statements and horror stories."

"Just because you're frightened now, it doesn't . . ."

"You think I was never frightened before, don't you?" She laughed and got up again. "I've been frightened all my life. Why do you think I built this Frankenstein? This woman made up of different pieces of other people, different colors, different accents . . . whatever it took I became it. To get somewhere, to be somebody." She picked up an empty soda can and twirled it on the counter. It spun gracefully for a second, then wobbled and fell, rolling to the edge of the sink. "Well, I'm somebody now, but I'm nobody I know. And no place I wanted to be."

I couldn't deny it. Stripped of fingernails, fashion and flair, she was a stranger. We had been friends for over a decade and I never even knew her. The thought of Vanessa being frightened scared me down deep inside where I wasn't willing to look.

"Let's go," I said. While she got her bag I washed the last two soda cans and left them by the sink. She waited at the door, face grim and tired and lined. I hesitated. "Are you sure you can do this, Van? It's not gonna stop. Probably get worse. Can you handle it?"

"I can handle this, Kate. It's the afterwards that scares the hell out of me." I picked up her bag and checked the hall before I let her walk out the door. I was a fragile shield at best, but better than none at all.

13

We did some shopping on the way home. Bought the ID box and a big calendar. Picked up a big pizza too. My idea. Vanessa had dutifully endured my self-important explanation of the barn's new security system. Fifteen seconds, Vanessa, you only have fifteen seconds to enter the code. I made her practice until she declared me a Nazi and flopped in front of the fire. We were lolling about on the living room floor, picking off the pepperoni and debating the definition of extra cheese, when the doorbell interrupted us.

Vanessa startled, then bit her lip.

"I'll get it," I said and peered out the window at the side of the door. A UPS truck was parked out side and a man waited on the porch, holding a package in his hand.

"Vanessa Clayton?" He asked, clipboard thrust forward.

"No."

"Sign here." I scratched my name on the paper and took the package. It was flat and square and felt familiar. I set it on the coffee table and we both looked at it, neither anxious to open it. The sender's name was smudged, but it looked like the last name was Smith. Not only was this guy an asshole, he had no imagination. I remembered what Bobby said about documentation and ripped the cellophane off the calendar.

"Get me a pen, Vanessa. We have to start writing things down." She got one from the office and I marked the date. The package was still unopened.

"I'll get the phone stuff hooked up," I suggested, "you can run the virus check on the computer. There's no hurry, Vanessa," I added with a glance at the package. She gave it one backward glance, and went into her office.

It took a while to figure out the wires, longer than it took to fix the computer. Vanessa went and got herself a Molson, sitting in the armchair, making suggestions until I threatened her life. She responded by pointing out a loose plug.

"Do you want to do this?" I demanded.

"I might have to."

I took a big gulp of diet Pepsi and watched Vanessa's throat move as she pulled on her Molson. I loved Molson and this one looked so good. Those little beads of moisture on the bottle, the icy bubbles, the crisp, almost bitter taste that left you wanting just another swallow. Maybe I should have a beer to see how it went, I thought. After all it had been almost a week. Wooo, a whole week, said the voice from hell.

"What, Kate? Jesus, you're looking at me like I'm Little Red Riding Hood and you're the Big Bad Wolf." Guiltily, I turned my gaze back to the wires.

"There! That should do it!" I sat down on the floor and grabbed another slice of pizza. All we needed was a phone call. Obligingly it rang. Oola of course. We talked for a second and then I hung up. Her number appeared on the machine and the tape had advanced an inch. Everything was working.

"Oola got the fax from Charlie on Jake's wife. She's still around the city, though Charlie said she hasn't worked in quite a while. She's supposed to be gorgeous—petite, with big green eyes."

Vanessa went quiet. I was in mid-bite when she asked softly, "Is she white?" I turned to look at her with strings of mozzarella on my chin.

"Is she what?" I said, wiping my face.

"You know, white. As in not black?"

"I guess white, she didn't say. What difference does that make?"

"I don't know. I can't figure out why he's doing this. I wondered if maybe it was a race thing."

"A race thing! Get real. This is about power, not civil rights."

"You're a jerk, Kate. 'I guess white, she didn't say'! Like white is the norm and if, God forbid, the woman is black, surely it would have been mentioned." Vanessa angrily lit a cigarette and threw the pack on the blanket. "Tell me you haven't thought it's strange that a gorgeous white man needs to chase around after a nigger!" The last was harsh—too harsh for Vanessa. Even a Vanessa pissed off at Jake or me.

She took a long swallow and killed her beer. Before I could think of an answer, she stormed into the kitchen and I heard the refrigerator door slam. A bottle hit the counter and a drawer closed loudly. I listened to the familiar pop of a bottle cap and thought longingly of the twelve-pack resting on the second shelf of the fridge. Vanessa's face was stony when she returned, cigarette dangling from the corner of her mouth.

"Vanessa, the word *nigger* is not in my reality," I began.

"Really! Where do you think the word came from? Some idiot white plantation owner who couldn't articulate the word Negro."

"Well, excuse me, I never owned a plantation! I don't even think of you as being black." As soon as the words were out of my mouth, I could have bitten off my tongue.

She paced the room and I shifted nervously when she stopped behind me. "You don't get to forget it as long as I can't." She turned her back on me.

"Vanessa, I'm sorry if I said something wrong. I've always wanted to be like you. You know I never thought I was better than you for any reason. Christ, if I'm an example of a superior life form, the world is in deep shit."

The phone rang and we both tensed. Vanessa and I turned toward the machine which picked up on the second ring. When we heard Annie's voice we released our held breath as one. Vanessa snatched the phone from its cradle and returned to the floor near the ashtray. I went to the kitchen, relieved at the break in our conversation.

I opened the refrigerator and stood, looking at the neat rows of Molsons, little soldiers standing at attention. I took one and smoothed the bottle lovingly. The glass was cold and hard in my hand. It fit perfectly and suddenly I knew it would be okay this time. It would be different now that I knew I might be an alcoholic. The key was moderate consumption. Everything in moderation, chirped the little voice. It seemed to take forever to open the bottle. My hand lifted to my mouth in slow motion and I felt like a woman on the verge of orgasm, just a little bit more, just a little higher, there! Oh God, it felt so good, that first deep swallow sliding down my throat. I was home.

Vanessa was still talking when I came back to the living room. She nodded acknowledgment of my return and I stretched out on the couch.

"Okay, Annie. No, he hasn't called yet. Yeah, I'm okay. Kate's here, we're just having a few beers and talking." I winced. Vanessa was such a blabbermouth. "Okay, well, we'll see you Tuesday, right? That's your day?" Vanessa paused, listening. "All right. Thanks. Love you." She hung up the phone. "Annie talked to Natalie Romano."

"She did! Great! What did she say? When are we meeting with her?"

"No dice, Kate. She doesn't want anything to do with this."

"Gimme the number. I'll call her. Mrs. Romano will talk to me, you can bet on it." I leaned across the coffee table for the phone, but Vanessa swiveled out of reach.

"Great, let's threaten the woman. That will really help." Vanessa rolled her eyes. "Look, Annie said she was petrified. Totally paranoid, kept asking how Annie got her number, did we know her address. She doesn't need you to beat her up, Kate."

I sulked over the dregs of my Molson. I was getting a little tired of being the group asshole. After all, wasn't I the one who'd figured this whole thing out? Came up with the whole idea? Poor Kate, crooned my secret self, no one ever gives you any credit. Okay, maybe it was Oola who told the Chinese story, but if I hadn't said the eye-for-an-eye thing, Vanessa would be living in Omaha under an assumed name. Screw it. I went for another beer.

"Get me one too, will you?"

I grabbed two beers and closed the refrigerator with what a deluded Los Angeles police officer would call necessary force. Suddenly I wanted to go home. I missed Petrillo's. And Vanessa was pissing me off. I kicked the pizza box out of my way as I handed her the beer.

"Getting your period?"

"No, us bigots can be bitchy any time of the month."

"If you're mad at me, just say so."

"Fine, I'm mad at you, okay? I'm really pissed. I've been a good friend to you and I think I've bent over backwards lately proving it. I don't know where you get off calling me prejudiced just because I'm white."

She started to respond in kind then bit back her reply. "Kate, I didn't mean to offend you. This thing with Jake, it's bringing up all kinds of feelings. I don't even know where they're coming from."

"Vanessa, I didn't mean it the way it came out. When I said I don't think of you as being black, I meant I don't think of you as downtrodden or beneath me."

"But Kate, that's the point. Why do you associate those things with being black?"

Even in college, I had thought white people who weren't prejudiced weren't supposed to notice if someone was black. I listened as she talked, squirming a little in my pale skin.

"Enough of this shit," she said, pulling me back to the present. She grinned. "I've been spending too much time with Oola. Get us a couple of more beers, Kate, and let's open this puppy. I'm ready now." When I came back, the paper was off, the package opened. She held a videotape up in one hand.

"How thoughtful, he sent us a movie."

"How much you wanna bet it's not *Thelma and Louise*?"

She popped the tape in the VCR and with false bravado, we settled back to watch. It was homemade, camcorder not professional, I could tell by the date in the corner. August 16th, 1:47 p.m. It was a street scene in Manhattan. The camera panned along storefronts, a vegetable stand, a cafe with tables outside. Suddenly it pulled up and zoomed in on the restaurant canopy. It looked vaguely familiar to me, but Vanessa jumped straight up in her seat.

"That's the São Paulo Pavilion! Oh my god!"

It was an Afro-Brazilian restaurant, one of Vanessa's picks. We had sat outside, drinking sugar cane rum and lime juice, during a break from the summer heat.

"There, see," she breathed. "Right behind the woman in the red dress, that's you, Kate." I stared in shock as the camera changed angles, coming around the other side. Vanessa blew smoke toward the back of Oola's blonde head and the waiter set food in front of Annie. The camera caught her nervous glance at the plate, before my arm cut across the view, drink sloshing in my hand.

"That was August," Vanessa whispered. She hadn't met Jake Romano for at least another month, maybe more.

"What's that?" The scene had changed again, so had the date. September 20, 3:13 p.m. Vanessa stood in front of her publisher's talking to Mindy. Vanessa kept shaking her head while Mindy chattered with a bright, insistent smile.

"She didn't like the outline I gave her. She was trying to get me to change the end." The scenes continued, Vanessa shopping, Vanessa getting into her car, Vanessa at the kitchen window washing dishes. The dates and times rolled with the tape. Then the screen darkened until it was hard to see. December 25th, 2:38 a.m.

A blob, somewhat darker than the background, roved around the screen, unrecognizable until it stepped in a pool of light. With morbid fascination, I watched myself bump into the streetlight. Rearing back my face expressed first surprise, then annoyance. Where the hell did that come from? I could see myself thinking. There was tinsel in my hair. As Vanessa and I stared, I pushed off the light, dropping my purse in the process, contents all over the sidewalk. I squatted down awkwardly and lost my balance, sprawling on the ground. Wiping drool with the back of my hand, I gathered the things within reach. I hauled myself up on my hands and knees, face toward the unseen camera. The skin hung loose, the muscles slack and sagging. I reached for a runaway lipstick and missed, my elbow hitting hard on the cement. Fuck, said the sloppy lips.

"Stop it! Just stop it!" I got up and walked away from the screen, from the woman on the tape. The beer was still in my hand and I automatically raised it to my mouth. I looked back where the other me was feeling her way along a brick wall. Vanessa hadn't said a word. I threw the beer at the fireplace and the bottle shattered.

"Oh my god," Vanessa gasped. I thought it was the beer until I turned back to the screen. December 28th, 4:05 a.m. A shade covered half the window, a flat plastic circle dangling from the string. Zoom past it to Vanessa sleeping in a strange room. The blankets were tangled and a brown arm snaked across the chenille spread. She tossed once, then again, a bare breast winked than vanished. The camera zoomed again, hoping for a second look.

I hit on the stop button so hard the VCR nearly slid off the TV My rage was overpowering. Vanessa sat, stunned. "That's my mother's house."

"Get your fucking coat," I ordered. She still didn't move. I went to the closet and pulled them out, tossing hers at her face. She caught it instinctively and looked over at me, eyes dark with pain. She started to speak. "Don't talk, I don't wanna talk anymore. Let's just go, right now, come on."

She followed me obediently, almost dazed. "Where are we going?" she whispered.

"We're gonna find the son of a bitch."

I went up the expressway ramp doing sixty and pushed the pedal to the floor. Signs and trees and homes flew by. Vanessa kept a death grip on her door handle as I weaved between the cars. I pounded the horn at a school bus hogging the middle lane and flipped off what appeared to be a CYO basketball team. I felt a little stupid giving the finger to a bunch of adolescent boys but knew they would understand.

"Kate, please slow down."

I ignored her. Everywhere I looked I saw that drunken face, turned up blindly in the light. I imagined him watching from the shadows, smile playing on his lips. If I had seen him right that second, I would have run him down.

"Kate, slow down!" I dodged around a pickup truck and almost hit a Camaro flying up the left-hand lane. The guy slammed on his horn and gave me the finger as he blew by. I jammed the gas pedal, chasing his bumper, looking for the fight. He easily left me behind.

"Where does he live, Vanessa?" No answer. "Tell me!" She did. I roared through Brooklyn until I came to the tree-lined streets in the Heights. I slammed to a stop in front of a pay phone. "Call him," I ordered.

"Stop yelling at me," she flared. I shut my mouth. She leaned her head against the dash. "He knows where my mother lives. Oh my god! My mother! My fault," she mumbled. "I didn't wanna believe you, all because I didn't want to believe."

"All because of him! Not us, not me or you, him!" I wanted to slap her, to make her mad, to inflame the dead eyes. "Are you just gonna sit here and let him get away with it?"

"No." But she did. I glared at her impatiently. "No, I'll call."

She got out of the car and went to the pay phone. I gripped the wheel and fought the voices in my head. She hung up twice and came back to the car. "There's no answer at home and his secretary said he was out of the office. Doesn't expect him for the rest of the day. I don't have the number of his cell phone with me."

We sat in the car, Vanessa smoking in silence, then I pounded the wheel in frustration. She jumped, eyes like deer. "Why aren't you angry?" I demanded. "Think of what he's done—what he's capable of doing. Dammit, Vanessa, feel something!"

"I can't. Let's go, Kate. We won't find him."

The hell we won't. "I'm not going home." She didn't bother to argue, just spoke in the same dull monotone.

"Fine. Let's go into the city. I have to get a publicity schedule from Mindy and we might as well do it now."

I barrelled over the bridge and ran us up to midtown, keeping up with the cabbies. I had great potential to be a cabbie. I parked on the edge of the corner, almost out in the intersection, across the street from the building. Vanessa pulled herself from the seat and disappeared into the lobby. I was waiting, drumming my fingers, kicking the floor, scanning the entrance. At first I thought I was hallucinating when Jake Romano approached the revolving door.

He moved with ease, turning into Vanessa's publisher's building as if he went there every day. Maybe he did. The prick, I should have realized he'd be looking for Vanessa while we were looking for him. I didn't know what to do. I wanted to warn her but if I found him first I was afraid of what I might do.

The minutes ticked by. My gaze flicked from the doorway to the little clock on the dash. Ten minutes. A half hour. No sign of Jake or Vanessa. I wriggled in my seat, battling a purely psychological urge to pee. Well, I wasn't losing my chance. I'd wet my pants before I'd leave this car. It was four-twenty.

Jake Romano walked out on the street, speaking to someone over his shoulder. I waited for Vanessa, but three women followed, one of them tucking a hand possessively through his arm. Jake was the center of attention, captivating this female audience with nothing more devious than charm. I recognized the woman with him. She had been at a book party Vanessa threw at the barn—somebody's assistant. I couldn't remember her name now, if I ever even knew it. But I knew her face and it was totally enthralled with Jake Romano.

They started up the street and I crawled behind them in the car. Two blocks up they turned into a trendy restaurant. I watched them thread their way through the crowd to find a space at the bar. I lost them when they moved to the back, vision obscured by a huge asparagus fern in the window. I double-parked the Phoenix where I stopped and followed them through the door.

I shimmied to the bar between two guys whose mothers must have dressed them and ordered a double vodka on the rocks. To hell with Oola, it was important to blend in. Looking around at the sleek, high-tech surroundings, full of high-powered people with even sleeker hairdos, I missed Petrillo's. I belonged there. Here I felt as obsolete as a forty-five record.

I craned my neck, trying to spot Jake in the crowd. Bingo! There he was, with his back to me, right behind a huge pea green vase holding a bizarre assortment of weeds and sticks. I worked my way closer and wedged myself in behind the vase. Jake was holding forth on the film business and the ladies were all ears.

A woman reeking of Joy stuck her elbow in my face waving her gold card at the bartender. I battled for position and never saw the sleazy little guy to her right. Out of nowhere, he ducked into an impossibly small opening in the crowd and pushed through. Me and my vodka tipped forward and rattled the sticks in the vase. I grabbed it with my free hand and found myself looking into the eyes of Jake Romano.

He never missed a beat in his conversation, but shifted position so he could see me. Rage rolled off him in waves and the hair stood up on my arms. I stared right back, hoping to raise a little hair of my own.

I set down my drink and deliberately brought my fist to my chin, cranking an imaginary movie camera with my other hand. He flushed angrily, and his companion looked my way, obviously wondering what the hell was so interesting. I let the film roll for a second longer, then carefully mouthed, "I'm watching you."

He slammed his drink down, so I lifted mine and tipped it toward him with false cheer. I tilted it up and let the vodka sear down my throat, draining the glass. His eyes burned into my back all the way out the door.

14

I stopped at a phone and called Mindy's office. Vanessa wasn't there. I prowled the streets for a while and then decided to head to the barn, figuring she'd go there. There was no one home. I swept the broken glass from the fireplace and poured myself a Remy. The longer I waited for Vanessa the more nervous I became.

She finally pulled up in cab and I met her on the porch. "Where were you? What happened! I was worried sick!" After I told her about Jake, she hugged me, then shook me, then hugged me again. I don't know which was worse. I hated huggers, always grabbing people without their permission. Still, I stayed put until she dropped her arms and we went into the house.

She went directly to the phone to call her mother. I didn't listen, it wasn't my place. I refilled my cognac, fed the cats and built a fire. She talked for nearly an hour.

"I love my mom," she said, coming up behind me.

"Everything okay?"

"Not really, but do you think I can talk any sense into that woman? I wanted to send her somewhere and she's going on about a church class she's teaching. So who gives a shit?"

"Evidently your mother. What happened? You wanna drink?" I gestured toward the Remy on the coffee table.

"Sure, if you promise not to tell Oola." I poured her a healthy dollop and added a topper to my own. "She's been getting flowers, Kate. The whole time I've been gone."

"White roses?" She nodded. We didn't talk. Just drank. "What are you gonna do?"

The phone rang and I answered.

"You left before I could buy you a drink."

"Believe it or not, I'm pretty choosy who I drink with."

"That's not what I hear, Katie."

"Well you hear wrong, Jakie."

I slammed down the phone and looked over at Vanessa. The fire tossed light and shadow around the room like autumn leaves in a storm. Her face was glowing, red embers lit her eyes. "If he goes near my mother again, I'm going to kill him." She was nodding her head with calm conviction. I raised my glass and she touched it with her own.

It started again the next morning. I let the machine pick up the first call while Vanessa took a shower. I'd polished off the cognac last night before passing . . . falling asleep on the couch. I was feeling none too perky this morning. I didn't understand why every time I had something important to do I seemed to have a hangover. It happened all the time. Oola warned you, reminded the voice.

While I poured myself some coffee, I checked the number on the ID box. It was Jake, all right, but he hadn't left a message. I was standing in front of the refrigerator scribbling the call on the calendar when the phone rang again. I rolled my eyes. I hadn't even had my coffee. On top of the refrigerator sat a big green whistle on a braided rope. It was Oola's idea. I picked up the phone.

"Could you hold on a minute please," I said, not giving him a chance to speak. I checked the box and made sure it was him. I held the phone six inches from my mouth, stuck the whistle between my lips and blew as hard as I could. It was incredibly loud. "Bye-bye," I said, hanging up the phone.

"What the hell was that," Vanessa growled from the doorway. She looked like shit too. "Listen, Kate, one of your goddamn cats peed on the fireplace rug!" She pointed an accusing finger at Ozzie, who stared back insolently. Harley lifted his leg and licked. We'd never know which one, cats don't rat each other out.

Neither Vanessa nor I could cope with cleaning it, so we doused the stain with spot remover and covered it with paper towels. Even that triggered my gag reflex and I was grateful to plant my shaky self back at the kitchen table. Coffee was my friend.

Oola called early and I waved away the phone when Vanessa tried to hand it off. She scowled at me, told her about.

the video tape and got stuck listening to Oola's analysis. She gestured irritably for a cigarette, then got pissed off that it wasn't lit. "Do you want me to smoke it for you too?" I said. Evidently not, since she flipped me the finger and took a deep drag, phone tucked under one ear. To make up, I poured her a cup of coffee and set it near her hand. She immediately bumped it with her elbow and slopped it on her arm.

"Ow! I gotta get off the phone, Oola. Kate just dumped hot coffee all over me."

"What a liar! Why don't you just tell her you're hung over."

"Thanks, Kate, you're a pal," she said, hanging up. "First your goddamned cats pee all over the place, then you narc me out."

"Make that hungover and cranky," I replied unfazed, carefully sipping from my mug. "I'm gonna take a shower. He's already called twice, so why don't you figure out today's strategy." I stood up and raised my fist in mock salute. "Let the stalking begin!"

"You are truly sick."

I stayed in the shower for a long time, scrubbing myself with Vanessa's loofah and trying all her hair junk. I used few cosmetics and never wore perfume, but I loved playing with other people's stuff. There was apricot scrub and avocado mask, a regular fruit salad. If it wasn't for the Remy wafting from my pores, I'd have felt like a real person.

I threw on a sweater and some jeans, but could only find one of my boots. Harley was curled up in the back of the closet, tail switching as my search disturbed his sleep. "Look, I'm sorry," I said, "but I need my other shoe." The heel of my boot stuck out from under his butt and I reached in bravely. Harley just watched, eyes narrowed, no response as I pulled it out from under him. When I tried to tie it up, the lace snapped in my hands, tiny teeth marks up and down the line.

"Damn! Vanessa," I yelled, hopping down the stairs, one boot off and one boot on. "Do you have any shoe laces? Holy shit!"

She turned from the mirror in a black silk double-breasted suit, cuffed pants, sleek lapels, no shirt. The fingernails were red, oh-baby oh-baby red, and matched her lipstick, her heels and the underside of a wide-brimmed, huge black hat.

"Did I miss something?"

"You wanted strategy, I got some. We're gonna pay Jake a little visit."

The phone rang. I picked it up. "Hello?" Nothing. "Hello," I said again. I could hear him breathing. "Don't make me get the whistle," I warned, hanging up the phone. Vanessa stood at the tracer.

"He's at work," she said, writing down the call. "Let's go."

I tried to get Vanessa to tell me the plan, but she was still paying me back for the cat pee. I grabbed a lace out of my Reeboks. If sitting next to an ad for Women's Wear Daily isn't bad enough for you, try it with one glow-in-the-dark green shoelace. The Volvo tore up the highway, Vanessa's red gloves steady on the wheel.

We pulled up in front of a low, painted brick building in Astoria. The guard at the gate of the parking lot smiled and waved Vanessa through. There were a few perks to being a stalker's significant other.

"What are we doing here, Van? You planning to sit here and wait until he comes out?"

"We're not waiting." She slammed the door and I followed her up the shoveled path to a tiny foyer. We climbed to the second floor of the building, Vanessa leading the way through a maze of halls. She finally slowed, then stopped, a few feet from an office door.

"Is that . . . ?" I whispered. She squared her shoulders in response and sailed through the door. I had no choice but to follow.

"Claire," she said warmly. "How are you? Is he in?" She barely broke stride, heading toward a closed door to the right of the woman's desk.

"Ms. Clayton! Hello. Yes, but he's with someone," she fluttered her hands. "Was he expecting?"

"No, definitely not. But he won't mind, Claire. Jake just loves to see me." She threw open his office door as I trailed in her wake, Claire in line behind me.

"Darling," exclaimed Vanessa, pulling off her gloves.

"What the . . ." Jake was rising from his chair.

"She told me it was all right, Mr. Romano," stammered Claire.

"Hi," I said to the three men around the table, just for something to say. Everybody waited.

"It's all right, Claire," Jake said, dismissing her and recovering nicely. "Well, sweetheart, this is a surprise." She turned her face up for his kiss, letting his lips skim her cheek. I plopped myself on the edge of his desk, swinging my feet. He took a step toward me, then rearranged his face.

"Gentlemen, I'd like you to meet a very special woman." He gave Vanessa a warm smile. She arched a brow and matched it. "A prof at Columbia and best-selling novelist. Jack, Ben, Harry, this is Vanessa Clayton." They stood politely, and Vanessa shook hands graciously. I coughed a couple of times but no one introduced me. Fine. So I'm a stepchild.

"If you can give me another, oh say, twenty minutes," Jake said checking his watch when the introductions were done, "I'll take you to lunch." He had returned to the conference table, assuming her compliance and took a seat at its head. The others, too, had sat.

"No," she answered, pretending to consider. "I don't think I want any lunch. Do we, Kate?" His eyes narrowed, reminding me of Harley. I tucked my one green-laced boot behind the other and mumbled a reply.

Vanessa breezed across the office and sat on the table next to his chair.

"I'm not going to bother you for long, Jake. I just have to tell you something. The boys don't mind, do you, gentlemen?" Vanessa's voice was eerily right for a Southern Belle and the men melted like butter in the Georgia sun. "Thank you."

"What is it that couldn't wait, Vanessa," Jake asked, an edge in his voice, eyes wary.

"Actually, this is a business trip. I guess what you talk about here is film, right? Documentaries?" Vanessa had stood and was addressing the whole table as if she were about to pitch them a hot idea. "Well, I got your latest effort, Jake, the one you've been compiling about me and my friends for months now . . ."

"I don't know what you're talking . . ."

"Oh yes, you do. You went all the way to Georgia to shoot pictures of me naked through the window of my mother's house. Tossing in my sleep, that is."

Jake leapt to his feet and went for the phone. "You'll have

to leave. I'll call security. There may be some problems with our relationship, but this is a hell of a way to retaliate . . ."

The other men had stood when Jake did with a sort of instinctive solidarity, but they were thinking about what they'd just heard. I got the impression they weren't his good friends.

"Only a dedicated artist could wait in the night outside an old lady's home as long as it would take for his subject to roll over in her sleep and give him a quick peep at her breast."

Jake was livid, but his voice was calm on the phone. "We have a situation here . . ." I noticed that he hadn't hit the intercom to ask Claire's help.

"As for the calls . . ." Vanessa dismissed his telephone with a sweeping gesture. "Why don't you stop the threats and go back to the heavy breathing. Oh, yes. And stop sending my mother flowers every day and breaking into people's houses when they aren't at home, taking out their light bulbs, letting the air out of their tires."

Jake was moving toward her now, flicking the backs of his hands toward the door.

"All right, that's enough for now. I'll leave. But Jake, just think, if you stop all this sick stuff, stop playing spy all over the place and scaring old ladies, think how much more time you'd have to devote to the films you're supposed to be making. Best of all, you won't have to worry that one of your victims will find a way to kill you."

She saluted his three guests, who were ashen, though their eyes were active, and stormed out the door with me right behind. Her exit would have been perfect except for catching one of her heels on his rug, so that she had to lurch through the outer office.

"Are you all right, Miss Clayton?" Claire looked up nervously.

"I'm gonna be, Claire," she answered, shrugging off my arm.

But she wasn't yet. She muttered to herself the whole way home, at first furious, then slowly not. I didn't say much; when I did she didn't answer, just chewed her lip and her cigarette, sinking deeper in her mind. The depression was in full flower by the time we made it home. She sank into a chair, ripped the hat from her head and sent it skidding across the kitchen floor. I went into the living room and poured a hefty dollop

of Irish whiskey into a snifter. I looked around sneakily before
I took a quick gulp, refilled the glass and capped the bottle.

"Vanessa, drink this," I said on my return, wrapping her
clammy fingers around the glass. "Take a sip, not a lot, just a
sip." Vanessa drank and some color came back to her cheeks.
There were three hangup calls on the machine, the numbers
all the same. I wrote them on the calendar and checked for
mail while Vanessa went and changed.

"Kate." I looked up. Harley slept blissfully on an end table
and Ozzie waged a life-and-death battle with a strip of cellophane from a cigarette pack. Vanessa leaned in the doorway,
wrapped in faded sweatshirt and baggy knit pants. I knew I
wasn't going to like what was coming, so I made an attempt
at heading it off.

"There was no mail again today. Can you believe it, not
even a Victoria's Secret catalogue."

"I'm done, Kate."

"I don't think we've gotten any mail at all, not since I've
been here . . ." I chattered.

"You heard me, Kate. I can't do this."

"What do you mean! After that performance? It was a mas-
terpiece! The man was friggin' blown away. You were so
powerful . . ."

"Powerful, that's a joke. All I did was play a scene, like
this is a movie script or TV show."

"It was way too good for TV, Vanessa."

"This isn't funny! Don't you get it! He does something, we
do something, he does something worse, so we do something
worse. Oola said we'd stop him, all we're doing is playing his
game! I can't do it, I know I said I could, but I can't." She
stamped her foot, voice rising. Mine followed suit.

"Yes you can. You don't have any choice! Are you going
to run now, is that it? Do you think that will stop him? Do
you think if you disappear he won't come looking for you!
Watch your mother, maybe hurt her just to flush you out?" I
was suddenly so angry I was shouting. "He started this and
I'm gonna finish it, whether you're with me or not!"

"This is not about you!"

"The hell it isn't!" We were face-to-face, each of us
breathing hard. I don't know who broke away first, but the
fight was out of us both. We had stirred up the cats, though.

Harley purred and Ozzie faked left, then·right, then pounced.
I wasn't sure at what.

The first delivery came at three. I did the sign-here thing and
took the package into the house. Vanessa turned away. I ripped
away the plain brown paper and lifted the lid from the box.

It was long and fat and black, almost menacing, with spikes
thrusting out of the top. Batteries included. Gingerly, I touched
the knubby plastic that was supposed to feel like skin. There
was a place in the Village that sold stuff like this. I'd been
there for bachelorette parties and showers, giggling like a teenager, embarrassed by my options and the variety of vibrators.
This one came with its own instructional video. Under different circumstances, we would have laughed.· Under these, we
didn't. Vanessa glared at me with stormy eyes, as if this
proved her point. We refused the other packages.

Mindy called and Vanessa talked in the kitchen. "Kate, did
you say something about the mail," she yelled. I had taken the
calendar off the fridge and was logging the latest device. I
tossed it into a box with the others.

"Yeah, there wasn't any."

"Mindy said she sent me some notes from our last story
meeting. I should have had them by now." Vanessa was off
the phone, standing in the· doorway.

"Christmas slows everything down. It takes the post office
till March to recover."

"What am I gonna do, Kate?" There was no more anger.

"Just what we've been doing, Vanessa. You have to give
it time. We're going to win, I know it."

"And that's the difference, isn't it? I don't wanna win. I
just wanna be safe." She turned away from me and went into
her office and softly shut the door. The defeat she left behind
was tangible.

I felt uncomfortable, tried and judged. There was nothing
wrong with winning. That was how she'd feel· safe, after all.
I paced the room and nearly tripped over the stupid box. I
kicked it, knocking it into the coffee table. The phone rang.

"Put her on," he said, without any preliminaries.

"Who?"

"Just get her on the fucking phone, Katie."

"Blow me."

"I said put her on the phone. Now, you stupid cow!" His tone was so careless. Something snapped.

"Don't you dare speak to me that way, you pathetic asshole!"

"Get her on the fucking phone!"

"What's the matter, Jake? Can't handle women if they don't run and hide? You're a regular ball-less wonder, aren't ya? Talk to me, Jake, I'm right here! I'm not going anywhere, so come on." There was too much saliva in my mouth. I swallowed hard.

"Oh I'm coming, Katie, you can count on that," he growled.

"From what I hear you can't even get it up. At least so somebody would notice. All these toys you sent, part of your own personal collect . . ." The dial tone cut off my question. I held the phone away from my ear, then back, completely surprised. I started laughing and turned to hang up the phone and saw Vanessa standing in the doorway.

"He hung up on me!" I laughed again. She smiled a little but didn't join in. "Come on, Van, this has got to make you feel better! We are definitely winning when the stalker hangs up on the stalkee!"

I opened the refrigerator and reached for a beer. The phone rang. I turned, still fresh from the win and ready for another fight.

"Please," Vanessa said, her hand covering mine on the phone. I let the machine pick up.

We listened to the greeting, bracing for his voice. I was so sure it was him it took a second to register that it wasn't. It sounded like Annie. I could hear the girls crying. Something about having to cancel tomorrow. Suddenly, I heard her say loudly, "Leave me alone! Stop it!" I grabbed the phone.

"Annie!" I said. "Annie, I'm here!"

"Kate, I . . ." David roared in the background, telling her to get off the phone or he'd rip it from the wall.

"Kate, I can't . . . David, I'm on the phone . . . tomorrow Kate, I . . . Stop it!" Then she was screaming with her hand over the receiver. He was screaming back, no muffler for the sound. I shouted her name.

For the second time, the only answer was a dial tone. I leaned against the wall, trembling. Vanessa took the phone from me and hung it on the wall. Our eyes locked. The secret was out. She dialed information and got the number for the White Plains police. I made the call and gave my name.

15

Annie didn't call the barn that night or the next day. No one was answering the phone at her house and we got nowhere talking to the cops. Finally Oola called with news.

"Well, I guess you're right. Kate and I could go out there, you know." Vanessa had taken the call. She listened for another minute. "I didn't think about that. Yeah. Will you call us if you hear from her again? Okay, I gotta go. Kate's going to chew my leg off if I don't tell her what's going on." She paused to look at me. "Oola says hi."

I just nodded.

"Kate says hi back. I'll talk to you later. Bye."

"What happened?"

"Annie called. I guess she's okay."

"What do you mean you guess? What did she say?"

Vanessa leaned against the counter, arms folded, face troubled. "She said she wants us to leave her alone."

"Leave her alone?" I freaked. "Is she nuts? Christ, he could have a gun to her head for all we know. We're going up there, right now!" I stood and grabbed my purse, fumbling for my car keys. What was wrong with everybody? Leave her alone? "Get your stuff, come on!"

"There goes Kate, off like a prom dress." Vanessa drawled.

"Excuse me if I don't stand idly by while Annie is beaten to death. What's the matter, Vanessa, has the spotlight shifted?" I snarled.

"Fuck you, Kate. That is really cold."

She wheeled and walked out of the kitchen, leaving me standing, arms flapping and lips moving. My coat was half on, sliding down my shoulders and my purse trailed on the floor. Okay, maybe that last remark was a little harsh, but Vanessa and Oola were taking this whole thing way too calmly. I was tired of being the responsible one—I had enough trouble managing my own life. With Vanessa, it was all for one and one for all, but when it was Annie, all of a sudden we were respecting her space. I didn't get it and I didn't like it.

Hearing Vanessa yell at one of the cats fueled the flame. I was going to Annie's and nobody was going to stop me. The phone rang and I pounced on it, sure it was Annie begging me to rescue her, telling me I was her only friend.

"Hello, Katie," he said, his voice calm and rich. As if yesterday never happened.

"Oh it's you," I said, annoyed. "What do you want?"

"Expecting someone else? I'm so sorry."

"Please, your picture is in the dictionary under sorry, as in sorry excuse for a man." I was in the perfect mood for this. Jake Romano, come on down.

"Where's Vanessa?"

"Out."

"I want to speak with her."

"Out." I said again. "Out, out, out. So I guess you can't talk to her today, too bad, so sad," I sang.

"Katie, my patience is wearing thin."

"Aaah, and patience is a virtue too. Gotta go." I hung up jauntily.

The phone rang again almost immediately. I picked it up and said, "Fuck off!" then hung up on him. I could do this all day. Call again, I thought, go ahead, I dare you.

"Was that him?" Vanessa's voice was strained. She had returned to the kitchen doorway.

"Did I hear something? Is there a chill in the room?" I gave an exaggerated shiver. When I looked at her, I was ashamed.

Her head was bowed and she was hugging herself. One of the cats was weaving in and out of her legs unnoticed. In the afternoon sunshine I saw tiny creases perpendicular to her taut upper lip, where lipstick cakes on little old ladies. They were new to Vanessa's face, adding to the stash of dark circles and harsh lines given to her by Jake Romano. The phone rang again and she quivered in response.

"What?" I answered.

"I know she's there, put her on the phone."

"She's not available, what part of that don't you understand?"

"I know where she is, Katie, and I want to speak to her."

"How do you know where she is? Are you telling me that you're following her? Speak clearly for the microphone, Jake," I added.

"Katie, you are becoming a problem. I don't like problems. They get fixed." He was under control, voice like silk.

"Too bad your old man didn't get fixed! Control the over-population of Romanos, neuter an idiot." Vanessa couldn't help but laugh.

"You give Vanessa a message for me, Katie. Tell her I love her, I'll love her forever and nothing she does can change that." Before I could think of a reply, he was gone. Vanessa was watching me.

Loved her. It suddenly made me think of Steve screaming, hurt and frustration in every word—I'm tired of hearing you tell me you love me, Kathleen, when the hell are you gonna show me! The darkness rose and I pushed it down.

I turned to Vanessa, but she walked away. I wrote the calls on the Jake calendar before I followed her. She wasn't in the living room, so I wandered into her office and found her standing in front of her desk, fingers trailing the top of her computer monitor. I hung by the doorway and cleared my throat a few times. Vanessa did, after all, deserve the opportunity to apologize and thank me.

"Kate, leave me alone. I don't want to talk to you." She never even turned around, just kept staring out the window.

"What?" I said, startled.

"You heard me. Please leave." She spoke in the same dull tone, lifeless and definite. Miserably I crept back to the living room and sank into a chair.

What had I done? I replayed our previous conversation and debated. I was never sure if the things I did were unreasonable or not. How did other people know? I was either a doormat or a Sherman tank, usually bombarding when I should lie back and vice versa. There had to be a middle ground but I was damned if I knew what it was. It seemed I was always saying and doing the wrong things, even when I was trying to do the right things. I pulled my knees up and rocked in the big chair, leaning my head into the plush cushions. What was wrong with me? Other than everything? sniped the nasty voice inside.

It drove me to my feet and I prowled restlessly, unable to sit still with only myself for company.

I wandered into the kitchen trailed by cats and went through the Little Friskies ritual. At least somebody likes me, I thought, as the cats purred their gratitude. I picked up the phone and dialed Annie's house, unsure what I would say if she answered. I needn't have worried, the machine picked up and I hung up without leaving a message. I flipped through a magazine on the kitchen table, feeling like a bored child with nothing to do. It's your fault no one likes you, said the first little voice. Who could? agreed the second.

"Nobody," I answered miserably. A tear or two slid down my cheek and I wiped them away with my fingers. I needed a drink. I started for the liquor cabinet when the phone rang. I wasn't in the mood anymore.

"Stop calling here, you jerk," I bellowed.

There was a brief silence. "Kate, it's Jerry. Are you okay?"

"Oh. Jerry, I'm sorry." Again, I was apologizing to this man. "I thought you were Jake. He's been playing phone games."

"Kate, have you talked to the police again? This guy is definitely out of line."

"Tell us about it!" I replied wearily. "So what's up, Jer?"

"I was just calling to see how you're doing."

"Oh, I'm doing, that's about it. Right now, I'm busy being the worst person on the planet, if you can believe Vanessa."

"What happened?" he asked sympathetically. It was all I needed and I unloaded my tale of woe, highlighting my noble motives and the tragedy of being misunderstood. Jerry would understand, I knew it.

"Kate, I think I understand," he started as I concluded my saga.

"I knew you would," I interrupted.

"I think I understand why Vanessa is upset," he continued firmly. Another one who's against me, I thought. Yeah, agreed the little voice, everyone in the world is an asshole except you. "Kate, did you find out why Oola didn't think you should go to Annie's?"

"No," I muttered.

"From what you've told me, Oola is an expert in these situations. She wouldn't just randomly decide to do something that would place Annie in jeopardy, would she?"

"No," I said again, "but Vanessa said . . ."

"Vanessa said what she said in response to what you said, Kate. Didn't she?" He prodded.

"Yes." I replied grudgingly. I had to make a comeback from monosyllabic responses. "But what about . . ." I trailed off, not sure what about what.

"Could Oola have a reason to recommend you stay away from Annie's, Kate? When I was drinking, people tried to steer me clear of emotionally charged situations. They had enough to worry about without me going off or getting crazy." That stung, like iodine on a scraped knee.

"I haven't been acting bad, Jerry. As a matter of fact, I haven't been drinking at all," I lied. "I stopped right after we talked. And without those stupid meetings either," I added defensively, sure he would ask. I fished around for a diversion and then a light came on. "But maybe it has something to do with Jake." I pondered this for minute and had to admit it made sense.

"Jake's still following Vanessa . . ."

"And if we went up to White Plains, he'd know where Annie lives! Shit, why didn't I think of that." I slapped my forehead with my palm.

"It's a little easier to understand why Vanessa was hurt," he finished gently.

It was so clear now. Poor Vanessa. What a shitty thing for me to say.

"Don't worry about it, Kate. Apologize and let it go. Vanessa knows you're under pressure, I'm sure she'll understand."

"Where did you get so smart, Jerry?"

"Well, my natural tendency is to pole vault over ant shit but AA helps me a lot with that." He laughed. "Sometimes the way I think is crazy." He went off on a drinking story about delusions of conspiracy between one of his customers and a cocktail waitress. "You should have seen me, Kate. Screaming, pointing my finger, demanding this poor waitress admit she was screwing this customer to get my job. It was nuts." He chuckled, but I didn't.

I knew what he was up to, the sneaky little drunk. Always talking about himself, never mentioning me or my drinking, he thought he was so smart. Like I wasn't supposed to draw parallels to my own drinking experiences from these little sagas. A regular 80 proof Aesop. Well, I wasn't going to bite.

"Fine, Jerry, AA is the answer to world peace and I'm delighted for you, but it's not for me. No more stories, okay?" Nobody was pushing me into some support group for winos.

"I'm sorry, Kate. I just thought it was funny. I didn't realize it would upset you."

"It doesn't upset me, I'm just sick of talking about it!" My voice was louder than I intended. I cleared my throat and continued. "Jerry, I appreciate your interest, I do. I just get the feeling you think I should be an alcoholic and I'm not, I'm really not."

"Hey, Kate, if that's the way I came off, I'm sorry. That's one thing you have to decide for yourself."

"I have," I replied firmly. "And I'm not."

"Okay, enough said. Why don't you give me a call next week. Maybe we can get together for dinner. I'd really like to see you again, Kate."

He seemed sincere, but I smelled a recovering rat. I put him off with a vague promise of checking my schedule and hung up. Dinner my ass, he wanted to give me another wildest dreams reality check. No way.

I went to the liquor cabinet and pulled out a bottle of Absolut, filling a glass half full. I wandered back to the kitchen, plunked a couple of ice cubes in the vodka and topped the remaining inch and a half with orange juice. A screwdriver was made right when you could read a newspaper through it. I set the glass on the kitchen table and contemplated it. Talking to Jerry had somehow taken the edge off my enthusiasm.

I probably shouldn't have a drink now, I thought. I have a lot going on. There's Annie, and I still have to make up with Vanessa. I looked at the kitchen clock. It was twenty after two. I wished it was later. Drinking after five was much more socially acceptable than drinking after two. Of course, drinking after two was much more socially acceptable than drinking before noon. I wavered, almost convinced. No, that was crazy, I could wait. I would wait.

Resolutely, I pushed away from the table to find Vanessa. I needed to apologize and hear what Oola had said. Annie certainly didn't need Jake camped on her doorstep. I entered the living room, with every intention of going to the office, when my feet slowed. What if Vanessa didn't understand. What if she was really mad and had already called Oola and the two of them wanted me to leave? I could feel the shame curdling in my stomach.

With no conscious thought I found myself back in the kitchen, staring into that perfect drink. If that's what they thought, I needed to fortify myself. I picked up the glass, fighting a losing battle of broken promises. I didn't care. If I was going to be thrown out, I deserved a drink. I touched it to my lips, suspended, its scent wafting and curling and calling my name. I finished it in two swallows. I felt better and worse.

As I walked to the office, I heard the postman on the stoop. I punched in the alarm code and caught him as he was leaving. He'd dropped a value pack coupon book, a newsletter from a devoted politician and two grocery circulars. Everything occupant, no real mail at all. When asked, he indifferently told me he delivered all the mail he had, but if there was a problem to call the post office. Gee thanks, my tax dollars at work.

Vanessa was sitting at her computer, pretending to work, gazing into the screen saver playing across her monitor. I knocked humbly and she started, then sagged.

"Kate, I can't take anymore right now, okay? Please leave me alone." She sounded so tired.

"Van, I just want to say I'm sorry. It was a shitty thing to say. The pressure's getting to me, you know?"

"Yeah, I know. It's okay, Kate, we're all strung pretty tight." Vanessa turned around and gave me a grimace that was her best effort at a smile. She heaved a deep sigh and rested her elbow on the chair arm and her chin in her hand. "I don't know how much longer I can take this. Whenever I think of the women who endure this for years, I go crazy inside."

"But we're getting to him, Vanessa." I sat in the chair next to her desk. "He hung up on me! He was so frustrated that he hung up. I beat him, Van." I reached over and grasped her wrist, needing to touch her. She shifted away and shook her head ruefully.

"Sometimes I don't know who's enjoying this more, you or Jake. Kate, this isn't a contest." She lit a cigarette with trembling hands. "You think you beat him. All that happens is he picks up the pace. He's going to have to try harder, do more."

Her words had hit their mark. This had become as personal for me as it was for him. Jake Romano had become a symbol for all that was wrong in my world and I relished each battle. I had forgotten there was a price for my pleasure and Vanessa was paying it.

"Look, Van, if I'm making you crazy, I'll stop." I wondered if I could. "I'll just hang up when he calls."

She shrugged. "Who knows what will work, maybe this is speeding up the process. I just wish I had a day, one day, where things were normal."

I didn't know what to say. There was no pat answer for what she needed and I didn't have a clue what normal meant. Then it came to me. When the going gets tough, the tough go shopping. Vanessa had a black belt in shopping and thanks to the wonder of modern technology, all we needed was a TV, cable and a touchtone phone.

"Vanessa, let's go shopping," I said, jumping up.

"I'm not going out," she replied listlessly.

"Not out shopping," I answered. "Armchair shopping!"

I forced an obnoxious level of enthusiasm that caught Vanessa's attention. She grinned tentatively and her eyes showed a little spark. I went around behind her and pushed her out of the room, chair and all.

"Ladies and gentlemen," I rumbled, "start your credit cards."

I had forgotten about the mildly pee-pungent fireplace rug. It grabbed the chair castors like quick-drying cement and sent first Vanessa, the chair and finally me tumbling head over heels. I fell to coughing while Vanessa alternately giggled and scolded. At least it felt like old times. I turned on the TV and found the home shopping channel.

Within minutes we were distracted by such shopping opportunities as porcelain clown cookie jars and polyester pants suits in a rainbow of unnatural hues. We watched in disbelief as our shopping guide warned of the near sold-out status of a rhinestone-encrusted lavender lampshade. Yours for the bargain price of only $28.95, she confided. Don't wait—get it while you can. Though we practiced restraint, the rest of

America eagerly jumped on the bandwagon, closing the item out with 47 seconds to spare. Don't tell me something isn't wrong with this country.

I went to the kitchen for microwave popcorn, returning with a huge bowl, two beers and a salt shaker. I could live without the butter, but try and take my salt away and you could lose an arm. I settled back on the couch next to Vanessa, placing the popcorn between us. The phone rang. We looked at it and each other.

"Fuck it," I said, crossing my legs and hunkering over the popcorn. "What did I miss?"

The machine picked up, the recorder whirred on and we listened. His voice was light and carefree, previous strife forgotten. He told Vanessa he loved her and missed her. He was going to a doctor this afternoon, but not to worry, he was fine. Bye for now. Vanessa flipped her machine the finger and I pushed the volume button on the remote. If we couldn't shut him up, we could certainly drown him out.

"Jewelry's coming up. I love buying jewelry," Vanessa said happily, munching on a handful of popcorn. We let the first few items pass by, with token comments on tackiness or poor taste. Then a pair of huge silver and ebony earrings were displayed on a red velvet backdrop. The announcer gave appropriate oohs and aahs and welcomed anyone who could blow $42.50 to call in. She talked at length of delicate artistry, quality metals and hypoallergenic posts. They weren't bad, I thought.

I turned to reach for the phone just as Vanessa did. We both hesitated and then she jumped. A split second ahead of me, she snatched up the receiver and held it out of reach.

"I saw them first, Kate."

"You did not!"

"I did too. You were looking out the window, I saw you." She held me off with her right hand, clumsily trying to dial with her left. "Shit, what's that number?"

"Like I'm going to tell you," I answered, taking another swipe at the phone. She replaced her right hand with her left foot, squarely planted in my sternum. Dialing hand now free, she triumphantly punched in the number and within seconds reached an operator who was standing by just to receive her call.

She went through a new-customer procedure and was assigned a home shopping ID number that entitled her to nothing more than the ease of spending money over the phone. She dug her wallet out of her purse while placing her order and, when asked, rattled off the number of her VISA. She went on hold while they processed her card.

"Kate, aren't they gorgeous?" she asked, pointing to the TV screen.

"Stunning, though I think they would look much better on me than on you. Your neck is too short." It was worth a shot.

"It is not." She threw her head back, stroking her long and elegant throat. "You're just mad I beat you to them," she said. "If you suck up a little, I might let you borrow them sometime." I opened my mouth to share my innermost feelings about her generosity when the operator came back on the line.

"What?" Vanessa said, looking puzzled. She held up a hand to silence me. "I don't understand." The operator must have responded. Vanessa listened and agreed. "Okay, let me give you another card." She went to the wallet again, leaving it open on the couch. I started getting a funny feeling in my stomach.

Vanessa carefully read the number off a gold card from her swath of plastic and waited. Eventually, her mouth twisted and she read another, then another. Her eyes blazed as she spit the numbers and expiration dates into the mouthpiece. Each was somehow unacceptable. I don't know how he did it, but I smelled the fine hand of Jake Romano. The operator finally begged off, leaving Vanessa hanging on to the phone, dazed.

"What happened?" I asked quietly.

"My cards are no good."

"All of them?" Vanessa liked to shop, but this was bizarre. "How could you be maxed out on all of them?"

"I'm not," she replied grimly. She dug through the small pile on the cushions and held up a platinum American Express. "There's no limit on this card. I just got it right before Christmas. I probably haven't used it twice. It's no good."

"Did she say why?"

"No," Vanessa answered angrily. "How could she? She's just a stupid phone operator who's never frigging met Jake Romano." Vanessa kicked her purse and gave the useless pile of plastic an angry backhand. The cards flew into the air, lit-

tering the rug, the coffee table and the popcorn. I fished a
MasterCard from the salty bowl and set it on the arm of the
couch.

"Calm down, this might not have anything to do with Jake,"
I ventured weakly. I had trouble believing myself. Vanessa
had no trouble. She snorted.

"Cut it out, Kate. We both know this is no coincidence."

"All right. We figure he did it, the question is how?" I
rolled ideas around in my head, waiting for illumination.
"When you were gone over Christmas, did you have your
purse with you?" She gave me a look. How stupid was I?

"I did not go away for week without my wallet. Plus if he's
had my card numbers since Christmas, why wait till now to
use them?"

"We don't know that he did," I reminded her gently. I had
visions of Jake Romano on an illicit Eddie Bauer binge.
"When was the last time you used one?"

"At that bar you go to, what's it called, Pumpkins?"

"Petrillo's," I said.

"Right. The night he . . . we ran out of money. The bartender even beefed up the check so we could have some traveling cash."

"Oh right, I remember." I didn't remember at all. Other
than the cellar, that night was kind of blurry. There was a
whole section of the Long Island Expressway that had been
lost in the void. "So it was good then," I mused. "But how do
we know he hasn't been using them for a while and they just
maxed out."

"I can get my bills. I'll be right back." She headed into the
office again and I heard files opening and slamming shut. She
was back before I had time to get another beer. "This bill is
from December. I should have had another statement by now."
She wore a pair of half glasses that settled comfortably on her
nose. "Did the mail come yet?"

"Yeah, but there wasn't any real mail, just junk." I pointed
to the pile on the pedestal table by the door. She got up and
perused it, then walked deliberately to the phone. Using one
of the old statements, she dialed customer service. She asked
for billing and waited on hold for at least three minutes. Credit
card companies could learn a lot from the home shopping
channel.

"I haven't received my statement this month and would like to find out if it was sent. If so, I need a duplicate." She gave her name, account number and other pertinent data. She waited, doodling on the bill while the woman did her search.

"It was sent? Well, I haven't received it. There might be some trouble with the mail delivery at this location, so may I have you send it to my work address? That would be great." She rattled off her office address at school and then the operator asked a question.

"Why did I close my account? Oh, too many cards. I shut this one down on Friday, right?" she asked casually. "Oh yeah, Tuesday. It was my American Express on Friday, if that's any consolation." She laughed pleasantly, sloughed off a sales pitch and hung up the phone. "Okay, he did it Tuesday. The account wasn't maxed, it was terminated by the cardholder, supposedly me. You gotta know the account number, card number, all kinds of stuff! How the hell did he do it?"

The phone rang. We both jumped, intimidated by the potential power of Jake Romano. What was he planning now? What schemes were already in play, unbeknownst to us? Just when I thought I was winning, the ground rolled under my feet and he landed on top. I grabbed the phone.

"Yes," I said bravely.

"Kate, it's Oola," she said. I could tell by her voice something was wrong. "I've got a problem. Jake's been here."

"Jake's been there? He just called us about an hour ago." Vanessa looked up warily. "Wait a minute, where's there?"

"At my office, Kate."

"Your office! What was he doing there?" Better yet, how did he know where there was?

"He must have checked me out, Kate. That video, he knew who I was, what I do. I can't believe this. I don't know what to do. My clients have to have a safe place." She sounded ready to cry, which is to say she didn't sound like Oola at all.

"What does this have to do with your clients, Oola? Calm down, just tell me what happened." Talk about role reversal! This might have been the first time in our friendship that I'd told Oola to calm down. Vanessa was sitting ramrod straight, credit cards forgotten, puffing furiously on a cigarette.

"Hold on, Oola," I said, turning the phone into my shoulder. "Jake showed up at Oola's office," I sidelined. Vanessa closed her eyes and I turned back to the phone. "What happened, Oola?"

The story was no more frightening than any other, but we were war-weary by now. She was having a session with one of her regular clients, she began in a halting voice. It was a given that Oola's patients had all physically survived something unthinkable. They came to her for emotional survival, to make the stumbling, painful journey back from existence to life.

When the session concluded, Oola walked the woman toward a door that opened into a public hallway. This second exit allowed those coming as well as going the privilege of anonymity. It was normal office procedure. Surprisingly, the woman turned and told Oola someone was waiting for her. Blushing like a teenager, she admitted it was a man. Genuinely pleased for her patient, Oola asked how they met.

"He picked her up in the hallway outside my office, Kate. He had asked for directions and then started a conversation. He's so sick, he must know how fragile these women are. It's Candyland for someone like him."

"Jesus, Oola, what happened?"

"It never dawned on me, Kate. She was so happy. She had met a guy and for the first time, she wasn't afraid. He was so nice, she said, he complimented her suit and hair. And so good-looking. I didn't pick up on it at first," she said bitterly. "When I asked his name, she said he wanted to surprise me, told her not to tell. I started to get a funny feeling, like the room got cold all of a sudden. She just kept talking, all happy and excited, delighted by the coincidence of him looking for me when that was where she was going. He told her he'd wait till after her session, say hi to me and then they could go for a drink."

Oola had opened the door with dread, wanting this man to be anyone but who he had to be. When they entered the waiting room, Jake Romano rose to his feet, smiling, his stunning blue eyes triumphantly meeting Oola's own. It was a perverse tableau, the client eagerly chatting, oblivious to the tension; Jake warmly stepping forward to take Oola's hand.

"I wanted to hit him, Kate, smash his stupid face. I can't believe the reaction it provoked in me. It took everything I had to suggest he come into my office for a second."

"You asked him into the office! Oola, you have to be careful."

Vanessa and I had gone to the kitchen, our Jake Romano conference center. Vanessa smoked and I drank beer, both of us mechanically replacing our drug of choice as soon as it was depleted. Periodically, I interrupted Oola's story to update Vanessa, both of us awed by Jake's ingenuity.

"This man is so evil. He didn't deny anything, He absolutely crowed, he was so pleased with himself." Her voice shuddered and I twitched in response, grateful for the quick release of a cold Heineken.

"What did you do?"

"I told him in no uncertain terms that I was documenting his behavior and had every intention of telling my patient who he was. He just laughed. He was so sure of himself. He said," she gulped, clearly having difficulty repeating his words, " 'Do you really think she'll believe you?' He said he could wrap the dumb bitch around his little finger. She was just another greedy cunt who'd do anything he told her to." Oola had to stop for a second. When she continued, her voice was falsetto, twisted with tears and outrage. "Did I wanna bet she'd suck him off in the cab, or should he call me later while he was fucking her up the ass?" Her voice broke completely. "He was toying with me, Kate. Teasing. He asked me if I wanted to watch, should he take some pictures. It was so ugly. And I was paralyzed, listening to him go on and on."

"How awful." I was nauseated, the beer and popcorn rolling in my stomach. I pushed my hair back from my forehead and waved away a cloud of Vanessa's smoke. She just kept puffing, spewing fumes like a belching furnace, eyes straight ahead.

"Finally, I came to my senses and told him to get out. I was practically screaming. I told him if anything happened to my patient, I'd hold him legally responsible. He just smiled and said it was Vanessa's fault. Vanessa could stop this anytime she wanted." Oola's voice cracked and she fought to finish. "Just before he closed the door, he told me to make sure to tell her. It would be a shame if someone got hurt."

Vanessa's gaze was on me now, waiting. I let my eyes slither away from hers and started fraying the label on my beer bottle. I couldn't repeat what Oola was saying. I knew Vanessa had a right to know, but I couldn't.

"What are you going to do," I asked helplessly, still avoiding Vanessa's persistent glare.

"I'm going to revise my calendar for the next two weeks. I can't take a chance with my clients' safety." She sighed heavily, burdened by this superficial solution. "I'm going to have my secretary call to say I have a family emergency. I hate to lie, but I don't want them to think I just abandoned them." Oola started to cry, an unfamiliar sound with no association in my mind.

"It will be okay, Oola. Don't cry," I murmured, conscious of Vanessa's reaction to my words. She had gone over to the Jake calendar, her back to me, her finger tracing the daily pattern of calls and encounters.

"I never even thought I might be putting them in jeopardy, Kate. I'm the one who spoke so blithely about everyone else's commitment. I never considered the ramifications of my own. These women need me and I put them at risk."

"No, dammit, he put them at risk!" I slammed my palm down on the table. Why was I the only one who could see this? "This is not about you or your patient or Vanessa, this is about Jake Romano! He's a sick son of a bitch and we're going to stop him, before he hurts Vanessa or anybody else. I'm tired of saying this—Jake is the problem! Not you, not me, not Vanessa—Jake!" I had stood by the time I finished, full of rage that had nowhere to go. There was one place.

"Oola, I have to go. I'll call you back or you call us, but I have to go right now."

She tried to hold me on the line, but I disconnected and started dialing the numbers I knew by heart. Vanessa had turned and watched me silently. There was no answer at his home and I punched in the car phone next. He answered cheerily, rock and roll blasting in the background.

I wasted no time on amenities. The rules had changed once again. My voice was hoarse with pent up emotion.

"All right you bastard, game's over. Vanessa can stop this anytime she wants, huh? Well, let me set you straight, you sick fuck, I'm stopping it right now! You stay away from us, you hear?" I barely knew what I was saying. The words flew from my gut, ripping clear of my throat. "If you bother any of us again, I'll find a way to kill you. Do you hear me, I will kill you! And I will gladly spend the rest of my life in jail if that's what it takes. Don't push me anymore, Jake, 'cause I'll hurt you, so help me God!"

I threw the phone as hard as I could, desperately needing physical release. It hit the wall next to the door, splintering its thin plastic cover and denting the sheetrock. My teeth and jaw were clamped shut and I swung my fist at the table, once, twice, three times. Vanessa bent and picked up the broken portable, checked for a dial tone and finding none, tossed it in the trash can. The thud of the phone in the can resounded in the kitchen, quiet now except for my ragged breathing. Vanessa sat calmly at the table, face expressionless, and motioned me to the other chair. I sat, an inmate facing execution. She signaled she was ready by raising her head slightly and I repeated what Oola had told me, flatly, bluntly, in its entirety. She listened without reaction, breathing slow. The blankness in her eyes mirrored the state of my soul.

She got up quietly when I finished and walked to the stationary phone hanging on the kitchen wall. Under a magnet on the refrigerator was a small scrap of paper with Natalie Romano's name. She dialed the number, listened for less than a minute. Then her face twisted up and she set the phone on the counter, leaning her face against the refrigerator, both hands buried in her hair. The recording continued like a ghost from the grave. Service at this number had been disconnected. No new number was given.

I rose from the table and gently put the phone back on the hook. Then I put my arms around her unyielding body until I felt it soften and lean into mine.

16

When I woke up the next day, it was raining. A gray, drizzly rain that could have no purpose but to depress mankind. I lay in bed, unwilling to get up. I swallowed the two Excedrin I'd left on the nightstand with a now stale glass of water. I chugged the water thirstily, my mouth drier than potting soil.

I had never understood how drinking could make you so dehydrated. There was a lot of water in beer! Magazines were always saying people needed to drink eight glasses of water a day. I had easily exceeded that quota last night, even got added nutrients from grains and hops. It didn't make sense that I felt like shit.

Last night had been awful. Vanessa had sunk into some personal abyss where I couldn't even find her, much less pull her out. Glassy-eyed, she had smoked cigarette after cigarette, sometimes letting them burn past the filter, then methodically lighting another. She hadn't been to her smoke shop in weeks. The elegant Russian gold tips had been replaced by stubby packs of Kools.

I'd called Annie again and left a message this time. I asked her to call us, told her we were worried. After a couple of hours with no response, I tried again. The machine had been turned off and the phone rang and rang. I sat in the kitchen, playing with the phone cord, watching Vanessa watching nothing, letting the phone ring endlessly. After thirty-some-odd rings, I hung up.

That was how the night played out, in silent despair. After curtly dispatching yet another seller of long distance services, I went through the barn, turning the ringers off on the phones and disconnecting the machine. With false cheer, I'd announced our safety from the outside world. Then I sat in the kitchen and drank the rest of the beer, closing the evening with a cognac or two after I'd killed the case. We were in bed by nine-thirty, each of us determined to sleep away our demons.

In the morning, waiting for the painkillers to kick in, I realized I needed a plan. We had to stop feeling like prisoners in this house and go do some normal things. We needed groceries and beer, Vanessa had to be running low on cigarettes. I got up carefully and headed for the shower. I'd get Vanessa up and dressed and we'd head into town.

She was already up when I got downstairs, sipping coffee, still noticeably subdued. I tried to sound cheerful.

"Vanessa, this isn't doing us any good. We can't just hide here, like ostriches. It's not like he doesn't know where we are." I poured myself a cup of coffee and sat down. I don't know how long she'd been up, but the ashtray was full of butts.

"Kate, I can't. I don't care what you think or say, I can't see him. And maybe this is working, he hasn't called," she finished hopefully, stubbing a butt and lighting another. She played with her Bic, turning it end over end, fingers in constant, nervous motion.

"Van, we turned the phones off, that's why he hasn't called. Come on, you've got to fight back."

"That's easy for you to say. 'Fight back, Vanessa,' " she repeated with a sneer. "There's nothing left, Kate. I don't have anything left to fight with. You may be getting your rocks off on this, but I'm not. I can't do it."

I let the comment slide. I couldn't afford to get pissed off right now. Though Vanessa might not believe it, I was running on fumes too. The man seemed all powerful. I still couldn't believe the business at Oola's office. Long before we ever knew Jake Romano, he had known us. It was an intimidating thought. How do you stay a step ahead of a man who had such a head start? But I was not giving up.

"Look, a moving target is harder to hit. Once we turn the phones back on, it's going to start again. If we get out of the house for a while, we can get some food and some fresh air. You need cigarettes, don't you?" I'd found the right button. The key to Vanessa's motivation was tar and nicotine. I could see her wavering.

"You go, Kate," she wheedled, looking for the easy way

out, to have her cigarettes and smoke them too.

"I'm not leaving you alone in this house. I promised Oola," I lied righteously to bolster my case. "If you won't go, then I suggest you slow down on the butts. They're going to have to last you a while."

I ignored the feral look she gave me, eyes narrowed, teeth slightly exposed. I poured more coffee and let her stew, checking the refrigerator and making a mental note to get tomato juice. A Bloody Mary would have hit the spot right now. I continued my inventory in the cupboards, humming tunelessly, filling time until she conceded.

"Oh all right," she said angrily. "This really sucks." She got up from the table and headed upstairs to dress, shouting back from the staircase, "Kate, stop the fucking humming before I scream!" Some people had no appreciation for music.

In the spirit of compromise, I stopped, skimming the morning paper for some contact with the outside world. Harley was asleep on top of the refrigerator, blissfully snoring. Ozzie sat at the kitchen door, meowing pitifully. The stupid cat spent his whole life in a New York City loft and in less than a week in the country was determined to get outside. "Ozzie," I threatened. He yowled again, louder this time, no doubt begging someone to call the animal welfare league. "Shut up!" I said, chasing him from the room.

When Vanessa returned, we sat and drank coffee and ate pieces of wheat toast with raspberry jam. I didn't say anything else, just waited until she was down to her last few cigarettes. Finally I stood, pulling my sheepskin jacket from a peg by the back door.

"Ready?"

"No," she grumbled, getting up and finding her purse. She reset the alarm and I reconnected the answering machine. We didn't want to worry Oola, or miss a call from Annie. Ozzie made a beeline for the door, but I blocked him with my foot.

"Let's take my car," I was saying as we went down the steps toward the garage. "It's less noticeable and . . ." I stopped in mid sentence, shocked.

The cars were parked in front of a dilapidated structure that served as a garage. It had probably been an outbuilding on the original farm, a chicken house or sheep shed. After she'd redone the barn itself, Vanessa's home improvement fervor had tapered off. There were occasional remarks about remodeling the garage, but it still remained in a state of disrepair. The roof leaked a little and it was crammed with so much junk there was barely room for Vanessa's Volvo. Most times, as now, the car was parked in back of the house, in front of the sagging garage door. Bold orange spray paint violated the weathered boards, letters so big they arched over the roofs of the cars. C-U-N-T.

We stared in disbelief. Slowly Vanessa walked to the door and ran her fingers down the wood, tracing the curve of the C.

"I guess I'll have to paint this now," she said, her whole body trembling though her voice was matter-of-fact. Tears behind the tone.

"We better check the cars," I said. We functioned in a state of siege. I circled both vehicles, looking for damage. Other than a delicate speckling of orange on the front bumper, the Volvo seemed okay. Nothing with the Phoenix either, until I walked to the driver's side. On the front seat lay an empty pint bottle in a brown paper bag. I knew I shouldn't touch it, but I couldn't help it. Wild Irish Rose, a buzz as cheap as it comes, ask any bum on the street.

Neither of us had a car alarm, me because an alarm would most likely cost more than my car, Vanessa because of their tackiness. Car alarms in most situations were a joke. I had never seen a single person respond to one by calling the police; mostly they just called the car and its owner foul names until the stupid thing stopped.

"He must have come after we went to bed," Vanessa continued, walking around the cars. "We'd have seen the motion lights otherwise." She could have been reciting a chocolate chip cookie recipe. "Gimme the keys, Kate, I'll see if it starts." She climbed behind the wheel of the Phoenix. I was still quiet, boxed in by the daring of our opponent. He had been outside the house last night, right below my bedroom window. I shivered. If you hadn't been passed out, suggested the little voice, you might have heard him. It would be over now if you hadn't been drunk, said the second.

"It's not my fault," I said, my voice lost in the roar of the Phoenix's engine. I stuck the bottle in my coat pocket. Vanessa turned the car off and checked the Volvo. I got out, walking to the Volvo. She turned the key with precision and it purred into compliance. She got out of the car and without thinking, we turned and stared at the letters on the door.

"I better call someone," she said finally. "I can't imagine what the neighbors think."

"Who cares about that! We're calling the police, that's who we're gonna call. I've had it with this shit."

We went inside and used the phone, making another pot of coffee while we waited. After the cops, I called Oola's office and left a message with her secretary. I tried Annie's again, still with no response. Vanessa thumbed through her phone book for the number of the contractor who'd done her renovations. She told about the garage and he promised to come today.

The police arrived about twenty minutes later. By then Vanessa was reduced to plucking butts from the ashtrays. It was for this reason they were first greeted by *her* butt sticking out the driver's door of my car as she foraged in the ashes. Somehow their presence stimulated a return of the Vanessa I had known for years. Undaunted by her position, she finished fishing a two-inch butt from the pile and regally asked for a light. One of the officers offered her a Marlboro and she went for it like a kid for a candy bar, lighting it as they walked to the garage. I trailed behind, once again the second banana I had always been in the long shadow of Vanessa.

"So that's it, Officer . . ." She waited.

"Clyde, Officer Clyde, and this is Officer Moroski," he said.

"Thank you so much for coming, Officers. Needless to say, this is very upsetting."

I was starting to get a little ticked off at Vanessa. This wasn't an art opening, for Christ sakes! So far, she hadn't said a word about Jake.

"We know who did it," I blurted from behind. They turned around in surprise, both officers resting their hands on the hips of their heavy leather belts. I smiled weakly.

"This is my friend, Kate Greerson," Vanessa said smoothly, still Queen of the May. "She's been staying with me." She dragged deeply on her second Marlboro, supplied by the obviously smitten Officer Clyde. Trust Vanessa to turn a crime into a dating opportunity.

"What do you mean, Ms. Greerson, that you know who did

it?" Officer Moroski asked benignly. There was something about cops that made me bristle. He sounded like he was talking to a kindergartner or a crazy person, ready to sweet talk me into a graham cracker or a straitjacket if I made any fast moves. My headache returned in a shooting pain behind my right eye. The resulting tic no doubt lent credence to my possible status as a nut job.

"There's a guy who's been stalking Vanessa, I mean Ms. Clayton, that's why I'm here and he calls her all the time and follows us and leaves roses in the house then scares Oola's patients and we have records on the calendar, I mean, I write it down every time and the videotape . . ."

Thank God I finally ran out of breath. I knew I wasn't making any sense. The bottle poked itself out of my pocket and almost fell. I caught it unconsciously, and saw them share a glance. They kept one eye on me, one eye on the pint, expressions stoic, but cynical. I had to slow down; they had to believe me. I remembered what Bobby said, that cops were good guys and we needed to document any illegal incident. I took a deep breath and tossed the bottle into the car. "Look, I know I'm talking too fast, it's 'cause I'm scared, but could you come inside and I can show you. Vanessa can help me explain," I said pointedly in her direction.

"Yes, please come in," she responded. "Kate's right, we have been having a problem. I just made fresh coffee," she added, opening the back door to the kitchen.

Everyone filed inside and stationed themselves around the kitchen table. I took the Jake calendar from the refrigerator and pulled the smaller daytimer from my purse. I started to explain when one of the officers broke in to ask about the video. Vanessa led the way to the living room, the tape was still in the machine. We rewound and watched in silence until the part about Christmas Eve. My face burned and Officer Moroski turned his head to stare at me.

"You get the idea," I said, pushing the stop button on the remote. Neither of them spoke, though a look passed between them. I went and got the stuff from the kitchen and slowly walked the officers through it, starting with Vanessa's first meeting. Occasionally they asked a question "Why didn't you report this, ma'am?" or Vanessa inserted a missing detail, "I didn't remember the ring till later," but basically it was me on center stage, chronicling our history with Jake Romano. I brought out the box with the vibrator and they looked from me to Vanessa, then Clyde made a note in his book. I could see the wheels turning, but didn't know in quite what direction. Hurriedly I concluded with his visit to Oola's office and my followup call to his car phone. I was just getting ready to tell about the tape recorder when one of them spoke.

"Ma'am," said Officer Moroski, "making threats against another person's life is a serious offense."

"You bet it is," I said, missing his point entirely. "I'm almost glad this happened, because at least now, you guys can arrest him."

"Ma'am, I'm referring to your phone call."

"What!" I shrieked, forgetting Bobby, forgetting good guys, documentation, and everything else. "Are you telling me that after everything I just showed you, your main concern is what I said to Jake on the phone?! What the fuck!"

I pushed my chair back from the table with a loud slap of my hands. Both cops responded instinctively, rising from their seats, hands sliding toward their belts. If this wasn't so pathetic it would be hysterical. Sarcastically, I threw my hands up in the air and cowered back.

"Don't shoot me, boys," I begged, "I'm unarmed." I dropped my hands in exasperation. "Jesus H. Christ!"

"Kate," Vanessa interjected, "please calm down. Officer, Kate was just defending us, me. This man is, I mean he followed me to Georgia. I was visiting my mother!"

"Ma'am," Officer Clyde said directly to Vanessa, "when people consume too much alcohol they get some pretty strange ideas. They can do things they wouldn't normally have done. And not even remember."

That's it! I'd had it. I spit the words at them. "So I'm delusional, is that it? A coupla beers and I start sending myself sex toys! Sure that works, that's easy." Vanessa made a move to quiet me, but there was no stopping now. "Hey," I said to Moroski, "could you call the precinct and get a coupla real cops out here? You two are a fucking joke!"

Moroski's face flushed dangerously. "Kate, stop," Vanessa ordered. "Officer, please excuse her, she's upset. Kate, go outside and calm down." I was still glaring at Moroski. "Kate!" I flounced from the kitchen, slamming the door hard.

I was hot! My head was pounding and I was so angry it was hard to swallow. At least the rain had stopped, but it figures we were out of beer. I was still shaking fifteen minutes later when I heard the back door open. I looked up at Officers Clyde and Moroski, followed closely by Vanessa. Everyone was stern and Vanessa's lips were pulled tight. No more smokes from Officer Clyde, it seemed. They halted in front of me. Here it comes, arrested for threatening Jake Romano—un-fucking-believable!

"Ms. Greerson, Ms. Clayton has explained the stress you've been under," said Officer Clyde.

"As long as Mr. Romano hasn't filed a complaint, we'll let this go with a warning," Officer Moroski finished. I made a rude noise, and shifted my weight to one hip with the classic defiance of a juvenile delinquent. "But, Ms. Greerson, this is not a joke. If there's another incident, we'll have to take action. Do you hear me?"

"Yes, I hear you. Now, I'd like to sign a statement or whatever it is I'm supposed to do so you can include what we told you in your report."

"We will file a report on the vandalism, ma'am. Unfortunately, these types of incidents are on the rise."

"Imagine, Kate, the mini-mart down the street gets graffitied on a regular basis," Vanessa mocked. Gone was the Queen of the May.

"I don't give a shit about the mini-mart." I put my hands on my hips and faced the men down. "And I'm not talking about graffiti. This a stalking, Officer," I continued through clenched teeth, "and it's my legal right to file a complaint. I have documentation of calls and encounters that have led up to this incident. Ms. Clayton, though you may be unaware, is a best-selling author. I'm sure her publishing company will be happy to alert the media about your lack of interest in her safety. Perhaps you'd prefer to wait until she's attacked before you take this seriously. Great career move, Moroski."

If my brain was half as big and half as fast as my mouth, I'd be a member of Mensa. I waited for the cuffs to hit my wrists, but the cops walked back to their car to use the radio. When they returned, Officer Moroski addressed Vanessa stolidly. He did not look at me at all.

"Ms. Clayton, I apologize if we seemed to make light of

your, uh, situation. My partner and I will file a report that includes all the information you and Ms. Greerson have provided. You can come to the station to make a formal statement if you so desire." He tipped his hat to her, scowled at me, and they started down the driveway.

"Hey, Officer Clyde," I called, never one to lose the last word, "how about another cigarette, for old times sake?" He stopped in his tracks, wheeled, then stiffly marched up the driveway and forked over a Marlboro. I was tempted to ask for a light, but even I wouldn't push my luck that far. Screw them, the report was on record. Jake Romano had a history now and that was the first step.

I handed Vanessa the cigarette and a smile spread across her face. She started laughing and I joined in. She pulled a lighter from her pants, lit her smoke, and blew ceremonious rings toward the sky.

"Kate, you are unbelievable. I thought I was going to have to raise bail! 'Great career move'! Jesus, you're nuts!"

Vanessa kept laughing and shaking her head at my audacity. It made me feel funny, like I had done something outrageous without realizing it. I didn't think my behavior was out of line. They were wrong. Just because they were cops didn't mean they deserved special treatment. Did it?

"Well, geez, Vanessa, what was I supposed to do? Sit there humbly while they protected the rights of the impeccable Jake Romano. I couldn't believe that!"

"Was the tape recorder hooked up then? When you called?"

"Yeah," I answered. "Good thing I forgot to pull it out or I'd be in custody right now. That's so fucking crazy!" I didn't like this. It had never dawned on me that if Jake was on tape so was I. You better watch yourself, said the little voice. They might find out, added the second, you're as bad as him. I wanted to deny it, but I knew. If it came down to playing nice on the phone with Jake or turning off the tape, there was no question what I would do. The bastard was not going to think I was scared.

"We might as well head to the market," I said, climbing behind the wheel of the Phoenix. "We'll stop at the police station on the way. Where is it?"

She gave me directions as I drove and I checked my mirrors regularly, watching for Jake's car. As I pulled into the police station, I thought I saw a BMW turn the corner, but it was heading the other way. The desk sergeant ushered us into a small windowless room with a table, four chairs and a crusty Mr. Coffee enshrined by stacks of styrofoam cups. We were interviewed by a lieutenant, Meese was his name.

He listened to our story, asked a number of questions and gently remonstrated with Vanessa for not reporting the break-ins. He left us for a minute and came back with a file on the earlier car incident and some new questions, obviously supplied by Officers Clyde and Moroski. I kept my mouth shut and let Vanessa do the talking. When she finished, he leaned back in his chair and looked at us.

"I think you should know, I've spoken with Mr. Romano," he said. Our jaws dropped. We'd only been here twenty minutes. Then he continued. "He stopped by here, just before you came." That had been his car! "Mr. Romano is concerned, Ms. Clayton. He said that he had recently terminated a relationship with you. That you had come to his office and threatened his life. In front of witnesses. Is that true?" He looked at her. She stared back, starting to rock, jaw clenched, lips folded. Slowly, she nodded, tears rolling down her cheeks.

"Wait a minute! She broke up with him!" I interjected angrily. Meese pulled a handkerchief from his pocket and handed it to Vanessa. "He's crazy, don't you understand! He's doing all these things and no one will help us. Why won't anyone believe us!" I understood now about the police. Jake had been right, there was nothing I could do.

The lieutenant didn't respond immediately, just kept watching Vanessa cry. "I didn't say I didn't believe you," he said. I stopped pacing, and Vanessa looked up. "His visit was too well timed. Almost like he knew you'd be here," he added thoughtfully. I was so relieved I could have kissed him. He gave us forms to fill out and promised to have a patrol car cruise the barn at regular intervals. We agreed to drop off the video and the other stuff. I didn't tell him about the tape. We signed our statements and he urged us to report any suspicious activity. I felt publicly served by the time we left. Somebody in authority had finally acknowledged the threat of Jake Romano.

I saw him when we turned into the parking lot at the supermarket. It gave me a jolt, but I really wasn't surprised.

"Lock the car," I said to Vanessa, "Jake's in the lot."

"Where?" She asked, her head swiveling

"Calm down, he's about three rows over, near the exit. He picked us up a few blocks ago." She sounded like a Lamaze graduate, alternately panting, puffing and whimpering. I felt my temper rising. Vanessa's martyrdom was getting old. "Vanessa, I don't want to seem unsympathetic, but get your shit together. I'm tired of you going off into hysterics every time you see him. It's only helping him, and I'm sick of it!"

I slammed the car door and locked stares with her over the roof. Her eyes flashed fire, but I didn't back down. She held it for a heartbeat longer, then slammed her door and stormed toward the market without another word. I followed her and Jake followed us, quite the caravan into the Grand Union.

She jerked a cart roughly from the line and sped up the produce aisle, barely missing an elderly woman feeling up the tomatoes. She threw random vegetables into the cart, bruising broccoli and string beans with equal vigor. I ignored her, gathering grapes and bananas without comment, carefully setting them in the childseat section of the cart. We moved on to baked goods at the same angry pace, when suddenly Vanessa stopped the cart. I tensed.

"Why am I fighting with you?" she asked. "You're right. I've been feeling real sorry for myself." She placed some onion rolls in the cart. "I'll try and do better, Kate. I promise."

We exchanged forgiving looks across the croissant selection and continued our shopping. We met up with him at the beer coolers where I struggled to remove a stubborn case of Coors. Normally I didn't drink Coors, but it was on sale and it was beer. Enough said.

"Can I help you?" he asked sweetly from behind me.

"No," I answered, checking Vanessa's reaction through the space between my armpit and ribcage. She was cool.

"Please step back," I said to him. He stepped closer.

The tomato lady tottered around the corner of the aisle, grayhaired husband now in tow. An audience, just what I needed.

"How dare you?" I shrieked, leaving the Coors hanging half out of the cooler. I crossed my arms across my chest, feigning virginal outrage. I cheated left toward Vanessa, making sure I was in clear view of the tomato couple. "He grabbed my, my," I stuttered for dramatic effect, "my breast!"

"No," exclaimed Vanessa, shocked to the very core. She lifted her purse menacingly. "You pig, you filthy pig," she screeched in her best imitation of a churchgoing matron. "Get the manager," she gestured to our goggle-eyed witnesses. "Hurry, please." The elderly woman scurried away and her husband hesitantly stepped forward, wanting to come to our defense but unsure what to do.

Jake stepped back quickly, flushed and angry. "I'm afraid they're teasing you," he reassured the older man. "It's a joke. I was helping her lift the case of beer. I'm her boyfriend." He gestured toward Vanessa, smugly. She rose to the occasion with style.

"My boyfriend?" she gasped. "I have never seen this man before in my life!" she informed our ancient protector. "Where's the manager, I want the manager!"

Jake moved quickly, brushing past me with a curt, under-his-breath, "Bitch!" I quivered and quailed and Vanessa draped her arm protectively around my shoulders. Jake pushed past the tomato woman and a young man with a clip-on tie and plastic name plate. The tomato lady fluttered her hands and pointed after him, but the young man didn't follow. Instead he approached us carefully and offered his apologies, unsure of store policy regarding breast-grabbing at the beer cooler. We thanked him and our elderly protectors, commiserating for a minute or two on life in America where women weren't safe at the supermarket.

17

We finished our shopping, struggling to keep straight faces, and could barely contain ourselves in the parking lot. We laughed in the car about my defiled bosom and debated the merits of a fake-fondling report to the sympathetic lieutenant. As appealing as it was at the moment, we reluctantly concluded that it wouldn't help much in the long run. We drove home cheerily, no sign of the BMW, but we didn't doubt he was around. We just didn't care.

The painters were there when we got home, putting on the second coat. The orange letters glowed eerily, like a hologram, still visible but only from certain angles. There were groceries to unload, so I started debagging while Vanessa checked her machine. Nothing from Jake or Annie, but there was a call from Oola and one from Mindy.

"I don't get it, Mindy's saying I missed a meeting yesterday. She's the one who faxed me the change in the schedule." Vanessa played the message again, frowning in concentration.

"Damn, Vanessa, there's something I forgot to tell you," I said, a can of peas in one hand, carton of Kools in the other. "When we got the video, I followed Jake, remember? I never told you what I found out." Quickly I explained about Jake's girlfriend from the publishing house. "He could have easily copped some letterhead from the kid's briefcase. I bet Mindy never sent that fax at all."

"Shit, I never even looked at the fax it was sent from."

"Why should you? You saw the letterhead, Mindy's initials. I should have told you."

"Well, it's no big deal, I can straighten it out. Describe the woman to me again, Kate. I think it's time I let Mindy in on what's going on."

I gave her as much information as I could and she went to

her office to call. I put away the rest of the groceries and made roast beef sandwiches on onion rolls with mustard and roasted peppers. I opened two beers and sat at the table, munching and swilling when she returned.

"Okay, that's set. There will be no more dates for Jake. Mindy thinks we should hire a bodyguard, the house will pick up the tab. I told her I'd think about it." She picked up her plate. "I've got to do some work, Kate. I'm way behind on the screenplay and for the first time in a while, I feel like working. Thanks for the boot in the butt, it really helped." She left the Coors on the table, grabbing a diet Pepsi and the second carton of Kools on her way to the office. I sat alone in the kitchen and finished my sandwich, my beer and her beer. Now what was I supposed to do? It was only one-thirty.

The afternoon yawned ahead of me. I did the dishes, played with the cats. I watched a soap opera, trying to remember who was boffing whom. I liked soaps, though I didn't watch on a daily basis unless I was in the throes of an agoraphobic depression. Then the glittering and glamorous tragedies of the ever well-dressed players sucked me in, and I could watch one after another, killing an entire day in Pine Valley and Lawnview. Today they just weren't cutting it.

I nursed my beer and tried to be interested in an eminent psychiatrist's psycho killer twin brother who had kidnaped a lovely blonde's illegitimate newborn. Somehow or other they had ended up in an abandoned amusement park with a mirrored funhouse conveniently open for a wild chase. Whoopee, I thought, as the evil twin captured two beautiful women, both perfectly dressed and coifed after running all over the place in heels. I flipped through the channels finding far too many talk shows and turned off the TV. I wandered into the kitchen for another beer and sat at the table.

I needed to get out for awhile. I'd been in this house too long. I walked to Vanessa's office door and heard the clicking of her keyboard. Nobody to play with there, I thought. You could go out for awhile, suggested the little voice. I could, I agreed, the idea taking hold. I brushed my teeth and finished my beer, rinsing the can and throwing it in the recycling bin. Quietly I crept around getting ready, changing my shirt, applying some blush. No need to bother Vanessa, I thought, scribbling her a note. It would only make her nervous to be in the house alone and I'd be back in an hour or so. She'd probably never even know I had left.

I pulled out of the driveway with a conscious sense of freedom, wild and impetuous. I cruised aimlessly for a few miles and then came across a small, neighborhood tavern promising Warm Beer, Bad Food and a pool table. Perfect! I took a fast, sharp right into the parking lot and checked my wallet. I had a little over twenty dollars, which was plenty for a couple of beers and a few games of pool.

I entered the dark bar eagerly, eyes adjusting quickly from the pale gray daylight. There was an old bowling machine like I hadn't seen since I used to go to bars with my pop. Two older men were hunched over a racing form at the end of the bar and a haggard middle-aged woman chewed a cigarette and nursed a draft by the window. Grimy Christmas tinsel still hung above the bottles and a dusty plastic mistletoe dangled over the entrance to the ladies room. A couple of guys with greasy hair shot pool in the back while two overweight women worked on a pitcher at a nearby table, one jiggling a baby in its stroller with her foot. I guess it was still too early for the after-work crowd.

I ordered a Molson Golden and strolled nonchalantly to the back, waiting until the shot was made before placing my quarter on the pool table. The two guys checked me out, the women too, and I wandered back to the bar to wait my turn.

I was a pretty good shot in pool. I had learned young and never quite lost my edge, no matter how long between games. I won the first game by luck, still warming up, and racked the balls for the second player. I got another beer, and we played for shots of peppermint schnapps. This time I won handily, earning the grudging respect and growing interest of my opponents. The games continued, this time for kamikazes, an appropriately named concoction of vodka, lime juice and triple sec served up in a bar shaker with a strainer for shots. We played several racks.

My buzz had kicked in by the time the bar started to fill up. The Happy Hour special was two-for-one Rolling Rocks and margaritas for a buck. I bought me and the boys a round of Rocks and threw in a margarita on the side for myself. I'd play this game and head home. Vanessa would probably be finishing up by now, I thought, with absolutely no idea of the time. I kept playing.

· Cash gone, I gave the bartender my VISA card to start a tab and was surprised to discover Happy Hour was over. I switched back to Molsons, skipping the margarita, and headed back to the table. Things were a little fuzzy, but I was okay. I'd lost the table a few games back, sinking the eight ball before its time. My quarter was up next. I'd play this game and go home.

The winning player shed his jacket and squatted down to rack the balls. I vaguely remembered him, my original opponents having long since left. I got up and evaluated cues, hefting each one and checking its tip.

"Hey, honey, this is my game," said a deep voice behind me. I turned to face a tall, big-bearded guy wearing a Cowboys sweatshirt. I hated the Cowboys.

"I don't think so, honey," I answered, dragging out the last word with a sneer.

"I put my quarter down when you were still playing the guy with the sweater," he persisted. "It's my game, honey, you're up next." He sauntered to the cue ball, stroking his cue behind it. I felt heat rising and followed, slapping my palm down on the felt between the cue ball and the rack.

"I'm not your honey, sport, and this ain't your game."

Things were about to get ugly. When the word *sport* came out of my mouth, it meant big trouble. The guy who won the table entered the fray, agreeing with the guy with the beard. Like I should be surprised men take each other's side against a woman. Things got louder and more heated with numerous onlookers choosing sides, decidedly in favor of the idiot with the beard who was trying to steal my game. The bartender finally came from behind the bar and after listening for about two seconds, settled it. The bearded guy would play, I would sit and sit quietly if I wanted to continue being served. Fuck you, I thought.

"Fine," I said, snatching a quarter from the line on the table. "Take the fucking game if it means that much to you. Creep!" I added under my breath, stalking away to a bar stool in the corner. I ordered a beer and a shot of tequila, Cuervo Gold. The bartender served it reluctantly, and I knew he was watching me. Well, let him, I thought. I had just about had it with men. Who the hell did they think they were! I snorted a couple of times and stared down two older ladies who were looking at me, shaking their heads. They turned away quickly, whispering. I hated these people. Did they have any idea what I was going through? No! They didn't know about Jake or Vanessa or Annie, but did they even ask?

"No," I said out loud to myself. I felt a tear slip down my cheek and wiped it quickly away. I looked around to see if anyone saw, but I couldn't tell. Christ, they'd probably think I was drunk, a maudlin baby crying in her beer. Showed what they knew, the small-town hicks. I popped the shot of tequila, sans salt and lemon, and enjoyed its harsh journey down my throat.

Annie, I thought suddenly. I wonder if Annie's okay. I pondered it for a while, hunched over my beer. Now there was a classic case of what men did to women. David was a bastard and a bully, a coward, afraid to pick on someone his own size. Let him go a few rounds with me and it would be a whole different ball game. You'd show him, said the little voice.

"You bet I would," I responded loudly, drawing strange looks from several patrons. A pack of giggling, man-hunting secretaries with big hair glanced at me, then deliberately moved their stools away like I was nuts or something. Absently I flipped them the finger, still thinking about Annie. I needed to get her out of there, that was very clear. Nobody else was willing to do anything, so it was up to me. Just like always, said voice number two.

Laboriously, I dug some change from my pocket and slid unsteadily from my stool. I held myself carefully upright and headed for the pay phone on the wall between the bathrooms, knowing the bartender was gauging my alcohol content step by step. Who cared! Once I called Annie and told her to get ready, I was blowing this puke joint anyway. I leaned against the wall and tried to remember the number. For some reason, I couldn't get the order right. A nasty woman hung up on me twice before I remembered to dial the area code. I was out of change so I charged the call to my phone card, slowly repeating Annie's number to a dense operator who seemed to have trouble understanding English. Finally she put the call through and the rings started.

"Hang on, Annie," I mumbled. "I'll be there as soon as I can."

"Hello," a man said sleepily. What time was it?

"Who is this?" I demanded.

"Who the hell is this?" he responded.

"This is Kate Greerson and I wanna speak to Annie."

"Kate, are you drunk?" David sounded disgusted. It suddenly clicked that I was actually speaking to him. David the wife beater, David who broke Annie's arm, David the man who had the gall to be disgusted by me.

"You lousy cocksucker!" I swore. "You son of a bitch, I should cut your balls off and shove them down your throat."

"Kate, sleep it off," he said angrily.

"Don't you dare hang up or I'll call the cops so fast your head will spin!" He must have thought me capable of anything because he stayed on the line. "How could you do this to Annie! You think we don't know what you are? Do you?" I raised my voice to be heard above the jukebox, forgetting David wasn't here in the bar. "Beating her up all the time! Breaking her arm! I'm going to make sure people know, your boss, your golf buddies, everybody you know, you prick. I'll take out a goddamned ad if I have to." There was so much blood rushing through my temples I felt dizzy. I leaned my forehead against the wall, and draped my arm over the phone. "Put Annie on, you fucker," I demanded to the dial tone. "Who cut me off?" I growled, peering suspiciously around the empty hallway.

I intended to dial the operator to demand an explanation when my stomach began to roll. I felt sweat gather in my armpits and swallowed hard, my mouth suddenly full of excess saliva. The phone seemed to tilt crazily and I stumbled. I staggered to the ladies room and fell against the door, balance all but lost as it swung open. I sunk to my knees gratefully and crawled to the nearest stall. A cigarette butt stuck on one palm and I scraped it off against the floor bolt of the john. I couldn't quite get the seat up before I heaved. Vomit splattered off the edge of the toilet, onto the floor, my face and hair. I hurled again and again, helplessly kneeling in the puke that missed its mark. I thought it would never stop. The vomit was tinged with blood.

I was lying there when she found me, one of the big-haired

girls. My face was in something wet, and I struggled to focus my eyes. She ran out and came back with someone else and they dragged me to my feet, faces twisted in distaste. What happened, I thought woozily, leaning on the sink. One of the women handed me a roll of toilet paper and told me to clean myself up. I looked in the mirror blearily, trying to wipe the mix of vomit and grit from my check. I started to cry, my rib cage playing like an accordion, snot cutting a path to my lip. I wanted to go home.

"I wanna go home," I sobbed. "Where are my keys?" I asked pitifully. "They're in my purse, I need my purse."

"You're in no shape to drive, honey," said one woman.

"I hafta go home. I want my keys," I whined again.

"I'll have the bartender call you a cab," she answered.

"NO! I want my keys!"

To make my point, in case they still didn't get it, I raised my fist and slammed it against my image in the mirror. We all jumped back, me as surprised as anyone, when the mirror shattered, huge cracks racing outward from my fist, tiny chunks of glass jumping free from the point of impact.

"I'm bleeding," I whimpered. "I cut myself." Now I began to cry in earnest, playing to a very unsympathetic crowd.

"Oh, great," bitched the woman with the toilet paper. "Get Joe," she ordered her friend. She wet a hunk of brown paper towel and applied it to the cut on the fatty side of my palm. It quickly turned a lovely shade of mauve.

"Vanessa, " I cried. "I want Vanessa."

Snuffling and sobbing, I repeated her number, over and over, long after the woman left for the phone. I held the soggy paper bandage in place and slid down the wall to the floor. The first woman returned with the bartender and the two of them carried me out of the ladies room, unceremoniously dumping me at table by the wall. I leaned my face against the sticky paneling and slept, minutes and years slipping by.

I heard Vanessa before I saw her.

"Where is she?"

I felt a hand under my chin and my face was turned. I had trouble seeing straight. There were three Vanessas, all overlapped, and I closed my eyes again in self-defense. The bloody paper towel had come unstuck and my hand oozed fresh, bright blood.

"Oh my lord, Kate. Are you all right?"

I wanted to answer but couldn't seem to make my mouth work. I tried to nod, but the motion was too much and I felt myself falling forward. She caught me with both hands and pushed me back against the wall. I heard her angrily grilling the bartender and forced my eyes open. There was a fuzzy crowd of people standing around me. They were too close, I couldn't focus. I looked past them, over the shoulder of the bearded guy, and saw him. What was he doing here?

I struggled upright and managed to get Vanessa's name past my lips. Someone pulled on her coat, interrupting her furious lecture of the bartender. She came to me immediately, my eyes more at speed with the blurry trail her movement left behind. Like the Road Runner at top speed, I thought drunkenly. Zoom.

"Hey Vanessa, you're the Road Runner," I giggled stupidly. "Meep, meep!" I called, slurring the sound. "Meep, meep, Jake, you can't catch us."

I grinned lopsidedly in his direction, my head lolling about on my neck. Vanessa wheeled about and stared at him. The bartender handed her my purse and she dug in it for the car keys. She signed my VISA bill, scribbled her phone number and slung my purse over her shoulder.

"C'mon, Kate, can you stand up?"

"Course," I answered, falling back against the wall.

"Need help, darling?" he offered sweetly. He had the best voice. He was a dickhead but he had the best voice.

"Ffffuck off," I sputtered loudly, spitting all over Vanessa's coat.

Without saying a word, she picked up a hi-ball glass one of the women had left behind and calmly threw its contents in his face. The crowd gasped, thrown by this new twist, and backed away from a drenched and enraged Jake Romano.

"Ha," I shrieked in delight, sucking the neck of my sweater into my mouth. "Ha, ha, ha!" Vanessa grabbed a hunk of my shoulder none too gently and jerked me to my feet. She ignored Jake completely and grasped me around the waist.

"Pinching me," I whined.

"Shut up," she hissed. "Get out of my way," she ordered flatly.

I started to cry again and she dragged me through the door.

The cold air hit me like a Mack truck and my stomach didn't like it.

"Sick," I mumbled, "sick."

Vanessa propped me against the hood of the car but I dropped to my-knees in the gravel. Doggy-fashion, I vomited again. Vanessa's cool hand found my forehead.

"Kate, Jesus, how much did you drink? Oh honey."

Why was everyone calling me honey?

"Cut it out," I said testily, wiping my mouth on my sleeve. I noticed that my hand was bleeding, but couldn't remember why. Someone pulled me up from under my armpits and poured me in the car. Vanessa started the engine and I flopped across the seat.

"Called Annie," I told her proudly. "Fucking Dave, fucking told him, all right."

My words trailed off and blackness seeped into the sides of my vision. I fought it, trying to remember something important. Jake was here? I wasn't sure but I had to warn Vanessa. Watch out, I thought, Jake's out there. I had to tell her. I passed out.

18

They were waiting for me downstairs. I could hear them. The clock said twelve-ten and it was only by the daylight streaming in the bedroom that I knew it was noon. I peeped cautiously through the back window, compensating for my lack of equilibrium by standing with one foot crossed behind the other, using my toes for balance. There was good news and bad news. The good news was that my car was in the driveway, so at least I had driven home last night. The bad news was that behind the Volvo sat a shiny, hunter green Blazer that could only have belonged to Oola.

I hoped I hadn't awakened Vanessa when I came in last night. I couldn't remember getting home or if I had talked to her when I did. She might well have been up. If I were to guesstimate my time of arrival, I'd have to put it at around nine. Of course I could be off by an hour or two either way, it was impossible to be sure. This had to be the worst part, not remembering. How could I prepare myself for the inevitable confrontation with Oola when I didn't have a clue what I'd done.

To be honest, there were a few clues, but I didn't like where they were leading. I woke up on top of the bedcovers, fully dressed with the exception of one shoe. The room reeked and it wasn't Vanessa's potpourri. There were stains on my sweater and my hair was matted. There was dried blood on one cuff and spots and smears dotted the thighs of my jeans. I located their source on my trembling right palm, a three-quarter-inch slice with bits of brown paper stuck to it. How the hell had I cut myself?

The bathroom seemed miles away. I resisted the temptation to crawl. Feeling my way across the room and into the hall, I collided with an antique Chinese cabinet that had no give whatsoever. I finally made it, then cringed against the door. Vanessa's bathroom had a huge double sink set in pale coral marble. Soft pink bulbs protruded from mirrored walls that extend from the sink cabinet around the corner to a jacuzzi tub and shower. There was no escape. Framed in pink dots, my reflection was duplicated over and over when once would have been more than enough.

My face was smudged with dirt and blood. There were nasty lumps clotting the hair that brushed my chin. Scarlet-webbed slits were barely distinguishable as eyes, and my clothes were a total loss. Their smell alone was putrid. The room suddenly began to shake and I spread my hands on each side of the door frame, cursing the Transit Authority. I braced my feet too, but my images still rattled and quivered. It slowly dawned on me there was no subway system on Long Island. The room wasn't shaking at all—I was, and I couldn't stop.

Stumbling to the sink, I shut my eyes and threw water on my face. Bending over, my brain clanked against my skull and shooting stars exploded behind my eyes, complementing the firestorm that engulfed my scalp and hair. The fuzz on my teeth was small potatoes compared to the pain. I felt fear and humiliation and guilt wash over me like the water, dripping and scalding, but never cleansing. I dropped to the fuzzy coral carpet wanting to die.

Not only did I not die, I continued to shake, so after a few minutes I hauled myself up. My stomach was signaling an emergency, but judging from the state of my clothes, there wasn't much left to purge. Finding no signs of sloppy regurgitation in the room, I was slightly heartened. Now if only Vanessa had been asleep when I came home, maybe I could pull this off. Hugging the thought to me like a blankie, I peeled off my clothing. Moving very slowly, each step carefully thought out, I got in the shower.

My back snuggled against the cold tile and the steaming water ran over me. Something washed onto my big toe and I yanked my foot away from the soggy cigarette butt as if it were acid. How did that get in my hair? I stood forever, the water pouring down, head throbbing, eyes aching. I was so tired.

I had to try and piece last night together somehow. Oola was downstairs. I needed to present a brave, if false front. I conjured up some jumbled images: a woman had her baby there. That was terrible, bringing your baby to a saloon. She needed to take a good long look at herself.

The pool table: I played pool. I did good, too, I remembered. There was some jerk, though. Something about a game, I couldn't recall the specifics. He was probably pissed 'cause I won. Men never liked women who beat them at their own games. I'd always been able to handle my liquor. Drink most men under the table and still pull off a perfect two-cushion bank on the eight ball. But there was something else, something about Annie. Damn, what the hell was it!

I tapped the tile for emphasis and left a bloody blemish on the wall. My hand hurt and I sucked the cut on my palm. The taste pulled up a tangled recollection of blood in a toilet. Just great! I must have gotten my period early on top of everything else. I'd worry about that later. I had decisions to make; like whether taking something for my head would put my stomach over the edge. Six of one, half a dozen of the other, I'd still feel like shit. Might as well give the aspirin a try.

I stepped out of the shower cautiously, toweling myself and doing the deodorant, toothpaste and mouthwash thing. The Listerine set off a familiar tingle that shivered down my spine. It was nearly 30% alcohol, almost the same as wine. That's what you need, said the little voice, in lieu of good morning. To settle your nerves, prompted the second . . . Oola's downstairs . . .

I looked nervously over each shoulder, making sure I was alone. The miniblinds on the shoulder-high window stood at half mast and I dropped them to their full length. They flapped noisily against the wall for a second, then quieted. I watched my reflected selves pick up the bottle of mouthwash and guiltily raise it to their lips. This is crazy, I thought. I won't be reduced to drinking mouthwash, that was truly pitiful.

The first swallow burned. My lips suckled the bottle neck greedily. I swallowed thankfully, feeling the release of body and mind, blood sugar rising and coursing through the tiny, broken, but barely visible capillaries in my face. I drank until I ran out of breath and set the bottle on the marble, wiping my mouth and avoiding the eyes in the mirror. Emergency situations called for emergency solutions, defended the first little voice. Anybody would have done what you did, facing what you have to face, said the next. Yes, I thought, willing myself to believe that other people turned to mouthwash in times of stress.

Fortified, I washed down three aspirin with some Mylanta and gathered my clothes, carrying them with me into the bedroom. Was I imagining it, or had my shaking slowed some? I crammed the clothes into the back of the closet and dressed, practicing opening lines for the critics awaiting my crucial first appearance. They knew I was out of bed. I'd have to go down soon, or they might come up here. I wasn't about to give up any control. Lights, camera, action, down the stairs I went.

"Hi!" I said breezily. "Oola, I didn't know you were coming. When did you get here?" They didn't say a word—not good. This was not good. Keep talking, Kate, just keep talking. "It's great to see you, has Vanessa filled you in?" I busied myself with the coffee pot, cursing my inability to control my movements. The pot bumped the burner, the cup, the counter; you name it, I hit it.

"I called her last night." Vanessa said flatly. Last night! This was definitely not good. Might be worse than not good.

"Oh really," I answered casually. "That's nice. I'm sorry I was gone so long. I stopped at the library and I . . ."

"Stop it, Kate! You are so full of shit!" Vanessa exploded.

"Lost track of time," I finished weakly. Yeah, worse than not good and probably worse than worse. At least I knew Vanessa had been up when I got home. That was a place I could backpedal from. Oola said nothing, watching the betrayal of my hands like a hawk. I spilled sugar into my cup and on the counter, nonchalantly brushing the residue into the sink. Oola stayed silent still, watching. Defiantly, I turned to face them.

"Okay, so I went out for a drink! What's the big deal?"

"What's the big deal? Do you have a clue what you put me through last night!" Vanessa screeched furiously. Oola touched her forearm across the table, ever the calming influence. "You don't, do you?"

This really sucked. She was right but there was no way in hell I could admit it. Something must have happened and frantically I cast around for some idea of what.

"Kate, do you remember anything that happened last night?" Oola at her best, direct, calm and ruthless.

"What do you mean?" I responded, still searching. "About what?"

"Jesus Christ!" Vanessa swore, getting up from the table and pacing the kitchen. I leaned uneasily against the counter, wanting to sip my coffee but afraid to pick it up. "You are pathetic! I didn't want to believe what Oola was saying, but she's right!"

I swiveled accusingly toward Oola. What had she said? I remembered the morning at the train station, the empty bar and the Bloody Mary. Anxiety flared, then anger. How dare she! That was in confidence, what I told her. And I was just exaggerating anyway! When was the last time I had a drink in the morning, I thought indignantly, Listerine forgotten.

"How could you!" I said to Oola at the same time Vanessa said to me, "You're a drunk, Kate, admit it!" Angry tears welled in my eyes and Vanessa shook her head in frustration.

"I think everybody needs to calm down. Vanessa, Kate, sit down," Oola said, indicating the kitchen chairs. "Please, we need to talk about this. Sit." Vanessa sat but I refused. Sit with these people, this traitor and her accomplice, accusing me of being a drunk and talking behind my back! I didn't need them, I didn't need anyone.

"Excuse me, Oola, but I'm not one of your stupid clients, so stop talking to me as if I were. As a matter of fact, I feel pretty sorry for your patients, since you're obviously incapable of keeping your big mouth shut when people tell you things in confidence. Thanks, Oola, thanks a lot," I jeered. "Yeah, I feel real comfortable letting you handle this. Go to hell!"

"That's it! I've had it!" Vanessa stood and grabbed me roughly by the arm. I had a quick and confusing flash of déjà vu, being yanked up from a chair. The coincidence ended a split second later as she shoved me down into one. "Now you are going to sit here and listen if I have to hold you down. Do you hear me, Kate?" she demanded as I struggled. "Hold you down!"

This was ridiculous. I would not sink to their level. I sat calmly in the chair until Vanessa dropped her hands from my shoulders. She remained behind me, ever watchful for an attempt at escape.

"I want my coffee." Oola looked at me and nodded at Vanessa, who slammed the mug in front of me, slopping coffee on the table. "Thank you so much," I said primly, anger boiling just below the surface. I fought back the trembling and brought the cup to my lips. What I wouldn't give for a nice slug of Tia Maria right now. I slurped some liquid from the brim, then pursed my lips. They wanted to talk, let them. I was not participating in their witch hunt.

"Kate, I can understand that you're upset. I'm sorry, but after Vanessa called and told me what happened, I felt it was in your best interest to share what I knew with her." Oola was such a good liar, so sweet and sincere. She made me sick. My look said as much and Oola sighed. "Kate, last night you got very, very drunk. Do you know that?"

I shut my eyes and hummed, ignoring her.

"Vanessa had to come get you, Kate." My eyes popped open in surprise. "You don't remember, do you? That's called a blackout, when you drink so much that though you continue to function, you can't remember it later."

I hummed louder now: Row, Row, Row Your Boat, the only tune I could manage. Nervously I drummed my fingers and jiggled my feet. If she would just shut up for a second, maybe I could figure this out. Shut up, please shut up, I thought.

"You got into an argument over a pool game, Kate. The bartender told Vanessa you'd been drinking pretty heavily, he wasn't planning on serving you any more. Evidently you used the pay phone because they found your phone card on top of it this morning. The owner told us when he called about the mirror." What mirror, I screamed in my head, humming louder and faster.

"Do you remember the mirror, Kate?" I couldn't stop my face from twisting. Why not just bring out the bamboo shoots and rubber hoses and get it over with? The acid in my stomach was lurching up into my mouth. Shut up, I yelled inside, the sound echoing in my hollowness.

"Some women found you lying on the bathroom floor, Kate, in a puddle of vomit." Oola was relentless. "You must have been sick, but you didn't make it to the toilet. They picked you up and tried to clean you off, but you got angry and punched the mirror. That's how you cut your hand."

I was shaking so badly I spilled my coffee without lifting the mug from the table. I had to block out the sound of her voice, the words of the story. I started to sing out loud, putting my hands over my ears. Bits and pieces of the night flashed in and out of my mind. I won't do this, I thought, you can't make me. Oola's lips kept moving and she leaned in toward me, face stern but compassionate.

"Row, row, row your boat," I sang.

Kate, her lips said.

"Gently down the stream."

Again, Kate.

"Merrily, merrily, merrily, merrily, life is but a . . ."

Bam! My head rocked forward. Vanessa's slap on the back of my skull wasn't intended to hurt, just to get my attention. It worked. Everything went blazing red. I was out of the chair and had her shirt bunched in my fists before Oola had time to react. I swung her around against the refrigerator and lifted her onto her toes.

"Don't you fucking hit me! Don't you ever fucking put your hands on me!"

I shook her, screaming through clenched, bared teeth. My ribs heaved and my heart blew shotgun blasts through my chest. I saw only red. Then Oola was peeling my fingers open, and I knew she had been calling my name long before I heard her. There was sweat on my forehead. My lip had cracked open, blood once again in my mouth. I remembered throwing up, there was blood. In the toilet. When was it? Time was all messed up in my head. Vanessa's face was in front of me—frightened now, frightened then, but for me, not of me. I started to cry, wilting and crumbling, allowing Oola to lead me to a chair.

"I'm sorry. I'm sorry. I can't remember," I sobbed. "I can't remember. I'm sorry." Oola touched the back of my hair and I shook my head. "No! No," I pleaded. "Leave me alone, please. Oh God, please. I'm sorry." My body was alive with pain, a crawling, living infestation. "Please," I begged, "please leave me alone."

No strength remaining, my communication dwindled to wracking, convulsing sobs. Oola and Vanessa silently left the room. Nothing more would be said right now. I couldn't have survived it, stabbed by remembered images and repeatedly thrust beyond my tolerance for pain.

I stayed at the table a long while, head down on the satiny

oak top. The phone rang twice and was answered in low, indistinct voices from the other room. Oola came into the kitchen, poured some juice and marked the calendar. I waited tensely for comment, but none came. She finished her business and left the room. The burden of their waiting sat heavy on my shoulders.

A CD carried weakly from the living room, an old Charlie Parker medley that Vanessa cherished. I got up for a soda, hungrily eying the beers on the bottom shelf. A diet Pepsi went down in three gulps. Opening another, I sat upright at the table. I would have to talk to them sooner or later. I got up and went to the living room, standing hesitantly in the doorway until Oola looked up. Vanessa ignored me.

"Feeling better?" I nodded mutely. Oola patted the couch next to her and I sat. "I'm glad. I hate to see you hurting like this." Oola put her arm around my shoulder and I leaned into her, gazing at Vanessa's turned back. I was so tired. My whole body ached, craving a beer. I couldn't get the thought out of my head. All I knew was if I could have a drink, everything would be better.

Oola starting telling me about their morning. Simple, soothing, as if her being here had nothing to do with me. She had driven in from Connecticut early, arriving around nine. Vanessa had reactivated three of her credit cards and they went out to buy a new portable phone and dropped the stuff for Lieutenant Meese. "The lieutenant, great," I replied weakly, feeling as if I was under water and wishing that I was. Vanessa didn't acknowledge me at all. "He was really great, Vanessa and I both thought so." Still nothing. "Let me know how much the phone was. I'm the one who broke it. I'll pay for it," I ventured, hoping this humble overture would break the silence.

"I'm sure the receipt's still in the bag," Oola replied.

"I'll pay for my own phone," Vanessa asserted venomously.

"We can work it out later," Oola murmured to me. "We don't have to worry about it right now." The phone rang. I was closest to it and my hand drifted to the receiver in slow motion.

"Hello," I said softly.

"Up and about, are we?" he asked cheerily. "The way you looked last night, Katie, I wasn't sure you'd make it."

"What do you mean," I whispered hoarsely. What did he mean?

"Of course, with all the puking you did, I guess you got most of it out of your system. Feeling shaky today though, I bet," he taunted.

Jake had been there. Suddenly I saw him standing at the bar, as if I was watching a big screen TV. Then he was closer; there was something dripping from his face. Was it raining? No, we were inside. I fought to remember. Abruptly, there it was: Vanessa pulling me, dead weight, Jake leaning in to help. The splash of a drink, his face contorted with anger, Vanessa dragging me away. I twitched convulsively.

"Get off the phone, Kate," Oola said, reaching for the receiver.

"There's nothing quite as vulgar as a drunken woman. You were a pitiful sight, Katie." Shellshocked, I was unable to muster a reply. What was there to say? Oola took the phone from my lifeless fingers and before she cut him off I heard him call, "Meep, meep."

"Kate," Oola said, "you don't have to deal with this right now." Vanessa snorted. I twitched again.

"I'm sorry, Vanessa," I pleaded.

"Sorry just doesn't cut it anymore, Kate." She got up and went into the kitchen. I picked up a throw pillow and buried my face. Oola soothed my hair.

"Alcoholism is a disease, Kate. A terminal illness. You need treatment."

"No!" I insisted stubbornly, pulling the pillow from my face and clasping it between tightly crossed arms. "I am not an alcoholic, I'm not!"

"Kate, I think you are, I really do. Part of the disease is denial. You want to believe you're not sick, but you have to face it. Whether you deny it or not, untreated it will just keep getting worse. Think of it as cancer, Kate. It will eat you alive if you let it."

"NO!" I twisted away from her. I wouldn't listen, I couldn't. Oola stopped talking. My mind raced frantically, thoughts rushing through at the speed of light, one after another until I thought I might be insane. Anything was better than not drinking when drinking was all I had.

She started speaking again. I shut her out until I realized

she was talking about Vanessa. My ears caught on the words "post office" and I turned my shoulder to listen.

"So it seems that someone, and of course we're assuming it was Jake, filed a change of address card for this address. Beginning December 30, mail was forwarded to a post office box in Manhattan." Simple, devious and effective. Jake had had access to Vanessa's mail for nearly two weeks.

"That explains the credit cards," I concluded wearily.

"That's what we figure. God, this man is so deviant. Who would think of doing something like that? I was flabbergasted. And it was so easy, too," Oola finished.

"Can't we prove he did it? That's mail fraud, isn't it?" You don't want to mess with the mail. The feds frown on it in a big way.

"You'd think so, wouldn't you," Oola said testily. "But no. Once the card is received, it's entered into a computer, then thrown away. Nice and neat. No records. Just a computer-generated label. "

"But what about the PO box? Somebody had to rent it."

"Somebody did, Kate." She surveyed my state of mind before adding, "It was rented by a Stephen Meriden. Paid cash, two months up front."

"Steve? My Steve?" Oola nodded in response. I sagged, air rushing out of me like a flyaway balloon. "You don't think Steve would have anything to do with this."

"Of course not. Jake just wanted to twist the knife."

I was too tired to summon any anger, depression was the way. It was hard even to speak. "Don't they ask for identification or anything?"

"Technically, they're supposed to, but does it really happen?" She tilted her head skeptically and took a sip of juice. "The woman on the phone swears that no one can get a box without ID, but I'm sure Jake didn't have much trouble."

"And now she needs to cover her ass."

"Hers or someone else's," Oola agreed. "It's a pretty big place. A lot of people work there, and nobody remembers renting that particular box."

"Did Vanessa tell the lieutenant? He said to report any suspicious activity."

"Yes," Oola said. "That's how we know about the box. No

one seems to have any time or interest, though. There's not a lot more he can do."

I could relate. There wasn't a lot more 1 could do. Vanessa stalked through the living room to the office and slammed the door. I jumped, the noise huge in my pounding head.

"She hates me."

"She doesn't hate you, she's angry and scared. It's frightening to watch what's happening to you, especially for people who care."

Leaving me to contemplate that, she disappeared into the kitchen. I heard her rattling around, the beep of the microwave, the close of a cupboard door. She came back carrying a tray with a can of Diet Pepsi, a steaming bowl of chicken noodle soup and a sleeve of saltines. She set it on the coffee table in front of the couch, handing me three vitamin capsules. Obediently I swallowed, listening halfheartedly as she endorsed the wonders of vitamin B.

"I'm going upstairs for a while, Kate. I thought I might take a bath. Will you be okay?" *Alone.* Why didn't she just say it? Will I be okay *alone?* Probably thought I would slit my wrists with a soup spoon.

"I'll be fine, Oola. I'm just going to eat my soup." I gestured toward the bowl. "Go ahead, I'm fine, really."

"I love you, Kate," she said, leaving the room. More guilt. Between Oola's understanding and Vanessa's closed door, I was consumed by it. A thought of Jerry danced through my mind, yet another burdock on my conscience. I felt exposed, tried and convicted by everything and everyone. Where was oblivion when I needed it?

I stayed on the couch, dawdling away the afternoon into dusk, locked in the misery of my own mind. I ate some soup, shuddering as the warm broth nestled into my belly, food an alien element. The crackers were easier. I finished half a sleeve, popping each salty wafer into my mouth whole, letting them dissolve on my tongue. In between, I scraped cracker crud from my teeth and felt sorry for myself, resolutely ignoring the liquor cabinet by the stereo.

No one understood. Drinking wasn't a disease, it was a cure-all. An escape hatch from life, complete with two doors. Granted one of them led straight to hell, but there was always the chance I'd pick the right one. I glanced at the clock; it was four-thirty.

I was still shaking, though not quite as bad, more tremors now than quakes. Oola remained upstairs and Vanessa's keyboard clacked furiously. The first tendril of desire crept in almost unnoticed, like a demonic vine. I found myself thinking of the cupboard above the refrigerator, a treasure trove of forbidden fruit. Dark sweet rum resided there, the finishing touch for Bananas Foster, one of Vanessa's favorite desserts. My can of Diet Pepsi sat lonely on the end table. It cried out for companionship and I who understood loneliness better than most knew what had to be done. I carried it to the kitchen and opened the cupboard doors, looking into the dark alcove. The yellow Myers label shone like a beacon. I reached for the bottle.

"What the hell do you think you're doing!"

I jumped straight up, bobbling the bottle and cracking my head on the corner of the cupboard door. Vanessa was inches behind me, hands on hips, expression outraged.

"Ow!" I whimpered, rubbing my head. "Jesus, you scared the hell out of me!"

"I'd like to do more than scare you! I can't believe you'd have the gall to try and sneak a drink! What is wrong with you?" she demanded loudly.

Defensive, I retorted just as angrily. "What's wrong with you? You're not exactly a teetotaler yourself, you know!"

"Me?!" She barked an angry laugh. "I'm not the one puking in a parking lot! How can you even think about drinking after what you did last night?" She jerked the bottle of rum from my hands and brandished it like a weapon. It danced provocatively in front of my eyes. "Is your mouth watering, Kate? You wanna drink it in the park!?" I turned my face away. Oola's footsteps pattered down the stairs.

"Shut the hell up! You drink, you should understand! You drink like a fish." I gestured wildly, grasping at any straw.

"You're the fish, Kate, and you're hooked. You're a goddamn junkie and it makes me sick."

"Go fuck yourself, or better yet, Jake Romano! If you weren't such a slut I wouldn't even be here!"

I stepped forward and so did she. Oola forced herself between us, in a space so tight that strands of her hair were sucked into my mouth.

"Stop it!" she ordered. "Just stop!"

Vanessa and I panted, securely joined by a current of rage and frustration. She broke off first, spinning away from Oola to stand by a kitchen chair. She pointed her finger at me and threatened, "And if you ever touch me again, so help me God, Kate, I'll beat the shit out of you, drunk or not!"

"Enough!" Oola pushed me back against the counter and silenced Vanessa with an upheld palm. I could barely breathe, dizzy and disoriented and overwhelmed with fear. I covered my face with my hands and the doorbell rang. All heads spun, the lilting ring a strident warning of an unexpected and perhaps unwelcome guest. It pealed again, then again, picking up speed until it was continuous, our visitor's finger surely stuck on the bell.

We moved forward as a group, Oola first, Vanessa next, me hanging slightly back. We advanced gingerly toward the front door, which seemed to grow bigger and more ominous with each step. I swallowed hard. Oola stopped a foot away and we piled up against her back, a humorless Three Stooges scenario. She reached out and pulled back the sheer cream curtain that dressed the window by the door. Leaning forward, Oola peered cautiously outside.

"Oh my God!" Frantically, she battled with the chain lock and the deadbolt, desperate to clear the entry. She finally worked them free, pushing us back as the door swung inward. I clapped a hand over my mouth, eyes wide with shock.

Annie stood on the doorstep, one entire side of her face purple, her eye swollen almost shut. Her lips gaped like a blistered radiator hose and a diagonal slice ripped across her chin, smeared with old brown blood. Carla and Lindsay huddled behind their mother, faces tear-stained and frightened. An angry red welt stood out on Lindsay's cheek. Annie fell forward into Oola's arms and Vanessa whirled accusingly toward me. I backed away.

"I knew it! You told me you called, that you told David off!" She advanced and I retreated. "This is your fault, Kate," she screamed at me as Oola soothed Annie. The children stood hesitantly in the doorway, adults oblivious, trapped in their grownup dramas. "Are you happy now! Do you want a fucking drink now, Kate!" My backside hit the rear of the couch and I could go no further. She came at me.

The alarm sounded with screaming clarity. We all jumped and Annie buried her head in Oola's shoulder, the children leaping forward to clutch at her legs. In her haste, Oola had forgotten to turn off the security system. Vanessa wrenched away from her quest for my blood and pounded the numbers into the box. The noise ceased instantly, the tension rose eternal. The phone rang next to my hand but I made no move to answer. Vanessa snatched it up and grimly repeated the code word to a solicitous alarm monitor. She slammed the phone down and turned to me again. Please, I begged silently, please don't.

"Look at her, Kate, look at her." Vanessa yanked my arm, forcing me around. "Tell me you don't have a problem! Look at her and tell me!" Fearfully I glanced at Annie, her broken face littered with threads of Oola's blonde hair. Her one good eye met mine and squeezed shut, tears glinting on the lashes.

"How could you, Kate," she whispered, then buried her face from view.

I started forward, but Vanessa stepped in the way. "Go have your goddamn drink," she snarled. "Do us all a favor and drink yourself to death." She wrapped her arms around Oola and Annie, shutting me out. I backed away, sickened by Annie's state, the children's faces, the memory of my call. But most of all, appalled by the knowledge that what I wanted more than anything else right now was a drink. Gagging, I ran from them and myself and vomited soup and saltines in the kitchen sink.

19

There wasn't much in my stomach. I let the water run and the evidence swirled down the drain with relative ease. Every place I looked I saw Annie's face. The grotesquely swollen eye, the raw sweep of scoured skin on her cheekbone, reminiscent of blush applied by Brooklyn girls with broad and garish strokes. I imagined David's fist on her face, knowing well the sound of flesh on flesh in anger. So help me God, I would never drink again.

I sat in the kitchen, exiled from the flurry of activity surrounding Annie and the girls. Any attempt to help would be misconstrued, I knew. The pain was searing and I sat in it, finally held accountable for my choices. There was no hope. I had destroyed everything important to me. Now I had to give up my only remaining source of consolation. I wondered how I would survive. *If* I could.

It seemed like hours, but the clock held fast to forty minutes. When Oola called me from the living room, I couldn't answer. She came to get me.

"Kate, please come in the living room. It's time to talk."

"No."

"Yes. It's not going to go away, Kate. Let's find a way to get through it."

"No."

"Yes." Stalemate.

"You saw her. You saw what I did to her," I mumbled. "Ask Vanessa, she knows."

"David did this to her, not you." Oola was firm. "You said it the other day, Kate, when I was so upset about Jake. This is not about you or me, it's about him. Why won't you believe that for yourself?"

"You weren't drunk, Oola. I was drunk out of my mind,

shooting off my big mouth, never a thought for the consequences," I spit out bitterly. "Probably 'cause I didn't have to pay them. I'm great at letting other people pick up my check, ask Annie."

"Stop feeling sorry for yourself, Kate. You have a problem with alcohol. If you stop drinking, you can be all that you're capable of being."

"We've seen what I'm capable of, so spare me the psychobabble. My best friends hate me and I don't blame them. I hate myself." There was not an ounce of emotion left in me. I was a blowup doll, a Kate held together by air pressure and plastic seams that buckled and strained at the joints.

"Annie wants you to come in, Kate," Oola said.

"Oola, let me speak to Kate alone please." When Vanessa had come in I don't know. She was just there, tall and righteous, the Clint Eastwood of my nightmares. "Oola, please. Kate and I need to talk." Oola nodded and abandoned me. I dropped my head and waited for her first strike.

"Oh, Kate, how did we get this way? We've always been so close, so much alike. Maybe that's why it's hard to get along sometimes." Surprised, my mind churned furiously, though I kept my face blank. This was not what I expected. Vanessa and I were nothing alike. She was good at everything and I was a loser. "I was really thankful when you came to stay with me, Kate. You're so strong. You made fun of Jake, turned my nightmare into something I could laugh at, sometimes. I felt so much safer with you here."

My throat tightened up and the tears started again. With all the crying I was doing I'm surprised my body hadn't shriveled like a grape.

"When I'm afraid, Kate, I get angry. Not the best coping mechanism, I know, but that's what I do. When I found you gone yesterday, I was frightened. I didn't know where you were and I was all alone. That made me angry. See, I wasn't thinking of you, Kate, I was thinking of myself. Later when the bar called, they said you were too drunk to drive home. I didn't want to leave your car, so I called a cab. I had a lot of trouble getting one, it was so late, you know." I didn't know. "That pissed me off too. How could you do this to me, just for a few laughs and a couple of beers." She smirked at her own words. "It wasn't until I saw you that I understood. I'm not trying to hurt you, Kate, but it was awful." I bowed my head further, guilt-ridden by a night I could barely remember. "I was losing you and it scared me." She sighed. "I've lost too many people, you know. I got mad. Mad because you were slipping away and I didn't know how to stop you. So I hurt you. I punished you for leaving me." My throat had closed now and air wheezed through my nostrils. Vanessa finished softly, "I'm sorry, Kate. I didn't mean the things I said."

I sprang from my chair into her arms as if propelled. She clutched me tightly, murmuring, "I've got you, it's all right, I've got you." She held me till I calmed, sobs fading into rasps.

"Vanessa, I don't know what's happening to me. Everything you said was true. I'm so scared."

"We're going to get you some help, Kate. There are things that people just can't handle by themselves. You taught me that." She brushed the hair from my forehead and smiled sweetly. I never knew Vanessa capable of such gentleness. "C'mon," she said, "Annie wants to tell us what happened. From what she's said already, I think you're in for a shock."

I shrank back. "No, Vanessa, I can't face her. I can't."

"How many times have I told you that in the last few weeks? And how many times have I gotten the same damn answer, 'Yes you can.' Yes you can, Kate."

"Screw you," I said, words muffled in her shoulder.

She laughed out loud, a real and infectious sound. "Now that's the Kate I know." She poked my ribs a few times, tickling me into concession.

"Cut it out," I said. "You're ruining a perfectly good depression."

"Don't worry, there'll be plenty more to come. C'mon, Annie needs you."

"Give me a minute, okay? I need to pull myself together. I feel so guilty, Van." I faced her, eye to eye. She nodded soberly. "I'll be out in a minute. Really." She gave me a quick hug and left.

I threw water on my face and used the dishtowel to dry my eyes. Leaning on the counter, I covered my mouth with one hand and thought. There were very few options. My eyes wandered wistfully to the back door, but where would I go? It had come to that. These women were my last connection to the human race and if I broke it, I might never get back. Shoulders rounded in surrender, I left the solace of the empty kitchen. Entering the living room, the first thing I saw was Annie's face.

It was worse than I remembered. I closed my eyes, swaying against the arm of the couch. Oola compressed her lips sympathetically, but let me make my own way. I folded at the foot of Annie's chair. I was Judas in front of Christ, there was no penance possible. The enormity of what David and I had done swelled Annie's face to twice its size.

"It started last night and then David left work early. You really scared him, Kate," Annie said haltingly, pressing a gauze pad to her lip. "He gets very worried about what people think."

"I'm sorry, Annie. I am so sorry."

She continued dreamily, as if she hadn't heard. "I was mad at you, Kate. I still was when I got here. But this isn't your fault. I'm the one who allowed it . . ."

All our no's came down at once, outraged by Annie's words and for her wounds, as if she had tried to inflict them on us. Yet something firm but quiet in her expression silenced us. When she continued speaking, it was an inner voice we were hearing, as if we were only present in her mind.

"I should have stopped it a long time ago," she began. "Not just David, the three of you, too. What you were doing. It was just too hard to defend David to you."

"There is no defending him, Annie," interrupted Vanessa.

"See, that's what I mean. But you don't really know, Vanessa. You either, Kate," she added as I opened my mouth. "In spite of what I've let you think, this is the first time he's ever hit me. Our marriage has been far from perfect, but he's never hit me."

"But your arm . . ." Oola began. She quickly fell silent before Annie's one good eye.

"I broke my arm. I fell down the stairs just like I told you. I knew what you thought. And I let you think it. It was more than just not wanting to explain, I wanted to have you on my side. And I knew that if I told you everything, you wouldn't understand." I started to protest, but Annie waved me silent. "See how that lie came back to haunt me. Kate's phone call set in motion the very thing I let you believe. It almost serves me right."

"Jesus, Annie," Vanessa muttered. This served nobody right.

"I know how you see me, like I'm some wide-eyed innocent, that victim we've talked so much about lately. Well, I'm no victim." Her smile was so pitiful I wasn't surprised to see tears in Oola's eyes. Annie seemed to retreat from the contact and her voice was dreamy again when she resumed.

"I don't know what happened to David and me. It didn't start out like this, you know that, Kate. After Carla was born, we seemed to stop talking. I was so tired, David was working so much, trying to carry the expense of a child, then two. It seemed like the only time we communicated was when we fought. When he was mad he could get everything off his chest. I'd yell right back. The relief was enormous, and pretty soon it was a regular thing. I felt so guilty because I knew it scared the girls. I think that's when I had to start justifying it, you know. You guys helped with that."

She stopped to listen for the children's voices in the next room where they were unpacking their toys. So her kids were still there for her, even if she was talking to us like figures in a dream.

"David doesn't have a lot of friends. The closeness between us is hard for him. He's jealous, you know, because I have something with you that I don't have with him. Still, he was shocked by Kate's call."

"Annie," I started. She kept on talking.

"He realized I'd lied to you."

"You didn't lie."

"Yes, I did. And though he would never admit it, that hurt him. The call hurt, too. He thought you liked him, Kate. And he liked you."

I looked at her face and hated his guts. I didn't care what she said, David was a monster.

"But what happened, Annie?" Vanessa asked. She answered in a monotone.

"I was trying to clean up the lunch dishes. He was so mad, kept ranting about Kate's call. Why did she think that, what had I said. I felt cornered, he kept crowding me. I yelled at him to leave me alone, get away from me. He kept stepping in front of me when I turned to the cupboard or the sink. I felt like if he didn't get away from me, I was going to break apart. Then I . . ." She stopped, a tiny shudder running across her shoulders.

"Go on, Annie," Oola prompted gently.

"I jabbed him. In the ribs with my elbow. It just happened. He was standing right behind me, I felt like I couldn't breathe so I jabbed him." Her good eye closed, tears on the lashes. "He hit me back and once he started he couldn't stop. I tried to get away, hit at him, scratched him, too. We were . . . it was . . . both so out of control." She broke down entirely and Oola moved to her side.

"It's okay, it's okay."

It wasn't the least bit okay! Was I hearing this wrong or were we letting David off the hook?

"What about Lindsay," I sputtered. "He hit your daughter!"

The look Annie gave me wasn't pitiful but pitying.

"That's the saddest part of all. I don't really know how Lindsay got hurt, I just know when. Everything is a blur. It could have been him. It might have been me." She looked me squarely in the eye. "Either way, we both left our children in the middle of a war zone until they had no choice but to try and make the peace. I'm not about to absolve myself. I love my girls and David does too. Look what it took for us to see what we'd been doing to them."

All of us were subdued when Annie finished. Even Oola skipped the opportunity to lecture. When Annie asked, she offered the name of a marriage counselor. Annie was sure that David would be willing to go. David was a little late, in my opinion. Vanessa was quiet.

"Are you going to let him see the girls?" she asked. Of course not, I thought.

"Of course," Annie replied. "The kids have been through enough and they don't deserve to lose their father." Vanessa nodded, a little bit wistful. "What they do deserve is for us to grow up and get some help. We're the adults, we're responsible for fixing this."

"There's got to be something worth fixing first, Annie," I insisted.

"I think there is, Kate. I know it doesn't look like it right now." She touched her face ruefully. "What David did was wrong, I know that. Please believe me I do. And I'm angry and I'm hurt and I'm tired. Scared too. But this is a marriage, not Psych 101. I'm not a case history," she added with a glance at Oola. "We're real people, both of us."

I turned away, frustrated by this woman I didn't know. Vanessa leaned over and handed Annie a clean gauze pad. Annie looked up at her.

"I'm sorry about this, Vanessa. You have so much going on, I just didn't know where else to go . . ."

"Annie, please! Of course you should have come here. I wouldn't have it any other way. Kate came, didn't she? You don't see her worrying about it!"

I beg your pardon?

"But Kate can't help what she does."

"Excuse me, I don't think Kate is the problem here," I said loudly. Vanessa looked from me to Annie's face and back. I shut up.

"Life is full of problems," Oola said. "It's how we handle them. "

"Though it does get a little nuts when they all come to a head at once," Vanessa added.

"Maybe so, but look at us. Fighting Jake has brought us together, stronger than we've ever been, even in college. Maybe now is the right time to bring things out in the open while we're sure of each other's support."

"Being alone is a lot harder," I agreed, feeling safer than I had all day. "It's like I'm always getting sucker-punched and . . . oh. Sorry, Annie."

"I know what you meant." She smiled with cracked lips. I was suddenly so tired, relief as much a factor as anything. I yawned widely, covering my mouth with my hand.

"I'm tired too," Annie said. "I need to get the girls settled, then I'd like to take a bath before I go to bed."

"You'll love the jacuzzi," Vanessa assured her. "We'll put you and the girls in Kate's room. I'll make up the sofa in my office for you, Kate. C'mon, let's get you to bed."

Stumbling and bumbling I let her lead me from the room. As if by magic Vanessa swathed the couch in crisp, Downey-fresh sheets that crinkled softly as I sat. I kicked off my loafers and lay down, head sinking gratefully into a full feather pillow. I was asleep before Vanessa could snug the comforter around my neck.

I woke the next morning, at first uncertain where I was.

The night came flooding back. I sat up, head pounding, mouth dry, hungover from emotions, not elixirs. It felt exactly the same. No one else was up, so I made coffee with shaking hands and searched the cupboards for relief. I had just swallowed some Tylenol when Vanessa came down the stairs.

"Hey," she said.

I nodded. "Is Oola still here?"

"No, she went home last night, after we got Annie settled. She's gonna call this morning." Vanessa pulled a box of Special K from the cupboard and looked at it quizzically. "Do kids eat Special K?"

"How the hell would I know?"

"I'm just asking. I don't know what kids eat." She set a package of strawberry breakfast bars on the counter and opened the refrigerator. "I suppose I could make pancakes or french toast. I think there's some syrup in here somewhere."

"Toaster waffles," I suggested impatiently, waiting at the coffee maker, empty mug in hand.

"I don't have any toaster waffles," she responded crossly.

Annie appeared in the doorway. In the morning light, her bruises were vibrant splashes of color on a pale and stretched canvas. She smiled tentatively and Vanessa grinned in response.

"Annie, just who I need. Kate and I are stymied by what to give the girls." She held up a banana hopefully. "What do you feed them?"

Annie's smile broadened. "Vanessa, they're kids, not exotic birds. They eat what we eat, cereal will be fine," she said, giving her seal of approval to the Special K. Vanessa dramatically wiped her brow. "Sit down before you hurt yourself," Annie went on, "I'll get their breakfast ready."

Vanessa sat gratefully and we sipped our coffee, listening to the first stirrings of activity from upstairs. Annie hummed a little, comforted by the simple acts of slicing bananas and pouring juice.

While Annie got breakfast, Vanessa brought her up to date on Jake. She told her about the credit cards and the garage and the supermarket, playing it for laughs. Annie followed intently, with the occasional ooohs and gasps of an attentive listener. Vanessa made a few bosom jokes at my expense and I entered the fray with zest.

"At least I'm not wearing a WonderBra," I retorted, eyes meeting Vanessa's bust, two on two.

"I do not own a WonderBra, thank you very much!"

"I don't know, those boobs look awfully perky for a woman your age," I replied skeptically. She swatted me with a copy of the *Village Voice*. I ducked and grabbed the paper, then hit her back.

"I love you guys," Annie said.

"What bothers me the most is the mail," Vanessa told her when things settled down. "I hate to think of him reading my mail."

"It's frightening how easy it was," I said.

"I'm amazed someone would even think of it."

"Jake Romano has ceased to amaze me," Vanessa said grimly. She got up and refilled our coffee as I flipped mindlessly through the *Voice*. Suddenly a headline caught my eye. The wheels in my tiny brain began to turn, then spit out an idea. A wonderfully spiteful and malicious idea.

"You know, maybe we're approaching this the wrong way," I announced. "If Jake wants mail, maybe we should let him have it." I grinned mysteriously.

Annie squinted at me, then said, "What are you up to Kate? I know that look."

"What if we gave Jake some mail, not necessarily Vanessa's mail, but mail of his very own," I drawled.

"What on earth are you getting at," Vanessa wanted to know.

"Look, Jake is obviously lonely. Anybody who knows him has to hate his guts. So where do you go in the nineties when you're hard up for friends? Or better yet, a date?" I extended my arms, palms up. They looked at me blankly. I grinned again, pointing my index finger at the large type on the top of the page. "The personal ads."

From Vanessa's expression I could tell she was starting to see the beauty of it.

"I don't get it," Annie said. "Why would Jake take out a personal ad?"

"He's not, but we are," Vanessa answered, wiggling her eyebrows.

"Come on, let's do it!" Finally I was in charge of something. "Get some paper and a pen," I ordered Vanessa. "Annie,

sit. Let's figure out what category we're going under." Armed
with pen and paper, the three of us perused the personal ads
of New York City's alternative weekly. Judging from the content of some of the ads, alternative is a major understatement.

"Listen to this one," I said, reading aloud. " 'BiWF, blonde,
blue-eyed Valkyrie seeks soldiers to mount her. Two hundred
and forty pounds of female flesh await the brave, showers of
gold for the truly adventurous.' Wow!" I squeaked.

"Holy shit, these people are too weird," said Vanessa.

"I don't think we should do this, Kate, what Jake is doing
isn't a joke."

"Annie, I'm not trying to be funny. Think, Vanessa. G-W-
M . . ."

"I don't want anyone to get hurt, Kate. Think about the
feelings of someone who answers that ad."

"I'd rather think about Jake reading the responses. Come
on, Vanessa!"

"Maybe she's got a point, Kate. I'm not saying these people
aren't a little off base, but look." She pointed to the paper. "A
lot of these are people with AIDS."

"I don't want to hurt anybody who has AIDS," Annie interrupted. "Strange or not, people with AIDS, well, it must be
hard for them to meet people. I don't want them to send a
letter, thinking they might meet somebody and never get a
response."

"Worse yet, Jake will answer. You're absolutely right, Annie," Vanessa said. "It was a good idea while it lasted, Kate."

"Wait a minute," I said. "I don't want to hurt anybody
either, but there's got to be a way to creep him out. Who's
politically incorrect these days?"

"This is a bad idea, Kate," Annie scolded. "Let it go."

"I suppose somebody who messes with kids," Vanessa
mused, almost to herself.

"Oh Vanessa, how could you even think that," Annie turned
away.

"That's exactly the kind of person he is," I exclaimed.
"That's it Vanessa. They deserve each other."

Carla straggled uncertainly into the kitchen. Lindsay trailed
behind, thumb in mouth, doll cradled in one arm, and Disney
animals frolicking on her nightgown. Annie silenced us with
a shush. She hugged her daughters and they snuggled into her.

She led them to the table, placing bowls of fruit and cereal within their reach. Vanessa and I made kid chatter the best we could and failed to get a response. They slopped their milk and dropped Special K on the floor. Lindsay spilled her juice, then cowered when I sprang to save it. That said it all.

Gently Annie hugged her shoulders, murmuring softly. She wiped the juice from table and hands while both kids watched her with big puppy eyes. Carla couldn't look at her mother's face. She kept her gaze directed downward, stirring her cereal with increasingly agitated strokes. Lindsay ate quietly, propping her doll in front of her bowl, occasionally reaching out to touch its cheek. Annie looked on with an expression of pain that became a twisted smile when one of the kids glanced up.

When they had played with their food long enough, Annie squatted between their chairs. "Did you know that Kate has her kitties here? I bet the kitties would love to have someone to play with." I bet not. But if I could cope with children, so could they. It was about time they did their part, I thought vengefully, recalling every scratch, bite and flea.

"Take some aluminum foil," I suggested helpfully. "They like to chase balls of it." Vanessa pulled the foil from a drawer, tearing off a sheet for each child. The girls pondered this, then Carla slowly crumbled the sheet into a lumpy, mutant sphere. Lindsay's little hands struggled and Annie cupped her fingers, helping her to achieve a round shape.

"Girls, I want you to go upstairs and get dressed first. And don't forget to brush your teeth. Your toothbrushes are in the bathroom. Carla, help your sister, okay?"

"Oh mom," Carla replied, in the age-old voice of older sisters everywhere.

"Carla . . ."

"All right," she conceded gracelessly. "C'mon Lindsay, hurry up."

"Coming," said Lindsay. "Gotta bring baby." She toppled from her chair with the doll, somehow landing upright, and took her sister's hand. They went up the stairs together, Annie following to the foot, watching their ascent. Within minutes, we heard the sounds of a toothpaste war, Lindsay crying and Carla yelling. Annie raced up the stairs to quell the riot.

I grabbed the pen and paper. "Come on, Vanessa, you're the writer."

"Kate, people can get arrested for this."

"Do you really care if any of these creeps get arrested. Including Jake?"

It was sickening, what we wrote. Even I knew that. We kept the wording somewhat subtle, at Vanessa's insistence. It was going on her credit card, after all. When we finished, I read it out loud.

"I don't know about this. It makes me ill. What if this provokes . . ."

"Jake deserves it," I insisted stubbornly.

"The children don't."

"These kind of people, they're like this already, we're not starting anything. Besides, we're not doing this for them, it's for Jake."

"We get more like Jake every day."

"Look, he has no problem playing hardball. Jake wasn't worried about his knife act in the cellar." It wasn't fair. He got to do anything he wanted but I was restricted by an ethics committee. "I'm willing to do whatever I have to stop him. I'm beginning to think I'm the only one who is. Where do you stand, Vanessa? Are you going to wait until someone gets hurt?"

She lit a cigarette, eyes brooding, then picked up the phone and placed the ad. I didn't feel triumphant, this wasn't as much fun as I had hoped. But Jake would know who did this, and that was worth it all. As I heard children patter down the stairs, I pushed away thoughts of the people the ad was calling.

"What are you two doing in there?" Annie called.

"Nothing!" we yelled in unison. The unmistakable yowl of an endangered feline split the air, interrupting the mood. We heard Carla calling, "Here, kitty, kitty, kitty, nice kitty." The nice kitty screeched a blood-curdling warning, prepping for a plea of self-defense. Annie hurried to rescue Carla and I to rescue the cat when the phone rang.

"I'll get it," I called.

"Katie, how are you?"

His concern was touching. "Just dandy, how 'bout you?"

"I miss Vanessa. I must find time to drop by and see her."

"Don't bother. We're doing just fine without you."

"Your friend didn't look so fine."

"Which friend you talking about?" It made me squirm when he let me know he was watching the house.

"The one with the little girls. I love little girls, remember?" He was referring to the scene at the airport. I thought about the ad.

"Jake, I don't have time for your bullshit today, so buzz off!" I hung up nervously. It was already placed. The personals ran on Wednesday.

"Who was it?" Vanessa called from the office.

"Who do you think?" I yelled back.

"Oh."

I wandered into the kitchen where Annie had somehow engaged the cats with a piece of string knotted around a paper towel. The kids giggled happily, sneaking quick pats on the cats' fur as they writhed and twisted after the string. I munched a breakfast bar, watching the kids as much as the cats, all four having all kinds of fun. I scribbled Jake's call on the calendar and picked up the portable phone.

"I'm gonna call Oola." I strolled to the living room. Oola's secretary answered. Oola was finishing an important call, would I wait? I would. There was a click and Gregorian chants were vibrating in my ear. Only Oola would turn loose a crowd of monks while you were on hold. It was kind of peaceful actually, and I was startled when Oola's voice broke in.

"Kate! Is everything okay?"

"Yeah, we're fine. Or as least as fine as can be expected."

"How are the girls?"

"Right now, watching the cats gut a paper towel."

"Good, I'm glad. Poor little things, they must be very confused. So," she added briskly, "what's the game plan for today?"

"I figured if you were free, maybe we could do the Jake thing."

"We could, if you're up to it."

"I'm fine. He just called. He's at the office."

"All right. I have a number for you, Kate. Do you have a pen?" She waited until I found one and then repeated a Long Island exchange.

"Whose number is this?"

"My friend, the psychologist, remember? I told you about

her—Ellen. She's the one in AA." Oola didn't fill my silence, just waited for a reply.

"Oh."

"She lives out on the Island, not too far from Vanessa's. She really wants you to call her."

"Great, can't wait."

"Kate, she wants to help."

"Christ, Oola, don't you think I should have a little say in this. I'm not too thrilled at having to spill my guts to a total stranger."

"That's exactly what you did the other night, Kate."

"It's a little harder when you're sober."

"But it has to be done, Kate. You're an alcoholic and so is she," Oola replied evenly.

"Fine, you gave me the number. You wanna dial it for me?"

"Sarcasm is not going to help anything."

"I'm sorry. Can we talk about Jake?" Anything to stop the twitching.

"Why don't you come into the city? We'll go over to his office and take it from there."

"Okay, but meet me in Queens."

We agreed upon a place near Jake's office and hung up. I showered, got dressed and said my goodbyes, after borrowing thirty dollars from Vanessa's purse. I drove to the expressway, passing the sign for Warm Beer and Bad Food. To compensate for my surge of anxiety, I drove like a maniac, cutting people off at every turn. If you didn't count the Listerine, it was my second day without a drink.

20

I thought about not drinking on the ride to Jake's. I was sure there were people who didn't drink. Of course I didn't know any, except Oola and she didn't count. There was Jerry too, but that meant the AA thing. I still wasn't sure about that. Now I had to deal with this Ellen character, too, I thought, pounding the horn at a pickup truck. I flew by a twenty-foot Coors on the side of the road. There were a hell of a lot of billboards for beer, I mused. What about the Super Bowl, whispered the little voice. How can you watch the Super Bowl without a beer? I didn't know. Suppose someone gets married, added the second, what about the reception? I guess I can't go, I thought, with just a hint of self-pity. Open bar, mourned voice number two. Firmly I dragged the memory of Annie's battered face to the forefront of my brain. I would never drink again as long as I lived. That was it, end of discussion.

Jake was the real problem. Now that I had the proper motivation, I could stop drinking—granted I'd be miserable for the rest of my life, but that was nothing new. Jake on the other hand was harder to handle. The only comfort was in knowing that if I couldn't control him, he sure as hell couldn't control me either. It had to piss him off.

Oola was parked down the block and across the street from his office. She sipped from an Evian water and read the *Times*, folded neatly in thirds to fit a single gloved hand. I parked in an alley near a dumpster, walked over and got in the Blazer.

"Hi. Have you seen him?"

"No, but his car is in the lot over there." Oola pointed toward where she had been waiting. "How are you feeling?"

Was she overly solicitous or was I overly defensive? "I'm fine."

."Good. Do you want part of the paper while we wait?"

Reading the *New York Times* was normally not an option, unless my only other choice was the *Wall Street Journal*. But the paper was preferable to conversation, so I took on the Leisure section. I didn't have time to get into it.

Jake came out of his office with two men at a little after twelve. They all shook hands and walked to the parking lot. The two men got into a blue sedan and Jake started the BMW When he came out of the lot, sunglasses hiding his eyes, we slid down in our seats. He turned the corner and Oola followed as best she could. Following people was not as easy as they made it look on TV, I thought resentfully. First of all, you had to run a lot more lights. If I had been driving that wouldn't have been a problem, but Oola always had been a stickler for the rules.

He wound his way through all kinds of side streets and we nearly lost him twice. I shouted directions and Oola kept pace, all thoughts of discretion forgotten. If he saw us, he saw us. That was the point, after all. He finally turned into another lot, using a key card to open the gate. We watched as the BMW glided around the corner of the building and disappeared from view.

There was nothing to do but wait. Oola parked the Blazer down the street, then we decided to turn it around so we'd be ready to follow when he left. After that there was nothing to do, so we sat. It made me uncomfortable.

"So," I said brightly, "how's Andrew?"

"Fine. On a trip right now, to Turkey."

"Turkey! God, he's always somewhere. Doesn't it get lonely, Oola?" I was truly curious. Could someone like Oola ever be lonely? I didn't think so.

"Sure, I miss him a lot. But he loves his work and I respect that." Oola leaned forward to scrutinize her side mirror. I craned my neck to look, but she shook her head and settled back. "Andrew's worked hard to get where he is."

"King of the computer nerds," I muttered. The last time I'd seen Andrew was last Fourth of July. I was minding my own business, talking to the bartender, when he came up with a bunch of other computer types. I had tried to be sociable. I'd even pulled out my best joke, the one about the parrot and the nun. How was I supposed to know Andrew's boss was a die-hard Catholic? The man had no sense of humor.

"I wish you two could get along better," Oola replied.

"Yeah, well . . ." I wish I knew what the hell you see in him, I thought. From the minute I had met Andrew, I knew Oola could do better. I'd tried to explain that to her at the rehearsal dinner for her wedding, but she wouldn't listen. Now she was stuck with him, the pompous ass. "You made your bed . . ." I murmured.

"What are you talking about, Kate?"

"Nothing."

"Are you going to call Ellen?"

"Lighten up on Ellen, will you? I said I'd call."

"When?"

"Look, Oola, after what happened to Annie, there's nothing that could make me take a drink. Look what I did to her. You don't have to worry, Ellen or no Ellen, I'm never gonna drink again."

"I do worry, Kate."

No one trusts you, said the voice. It isn't fair, said the other. "I'm not drinking, Oola," I said, just a hint of underlying anger. "Now can we please let it go!"

She did, but it hung in the Blazer like smoke from Vanessa's cigarettes. Oola went back to the paper and I tried to do the crossword, but quickly gave up. There was nothing like the *Times* crossword to make you feel like a moron. I tossed the paper onto the back seat.

"How long has he been in there?"

She checked her watch. "A little over an hour."

"It looks like it's going to storm." Angry clouds had piled up on the horizon, gray and laden with snow. Oola nodded.

"Why don't we give him another twenty minutes? If he hasn't come out, I'll take you back to your car. We don't want to get stuck."

We gave him thirty. By then the sky was dark and tiny snowflakes had started to fall. There was still no sign of Jake or the BMW. With an anticlimactic sigh, I gave the okay and Oola started the Blazer. We got lost finding our way back but finally I saw the tail of the Phoenix and Oola slid to a stop.

"Okay, I'll call you later," she said as I got out of the car. "Be careful driving home, Kate."

"I will. You too." I tapped the hood of the Blazer and stepped back to let her go. She beeped a salute and I walked back to my car. The back window was already dusted with white. I had a snow brush somewhere, but if I wanted any heat on the way home, I'd have to let the car warm up. I slipped into the driver's seat and turned the key.

"I've been waiting for you, Katie."

His breath froze the back of my neck. I fought back a scream, a hand on my heart as if to hold it down. Carefully, I looked over my right shoulder. He leaned between the seats and showed me a crooked smile and shining eyes.

"Get out of my car!"

"But I've been waiting so long . . ."

"Now! Get out or I'll scream."

"That's getting tired, Katie. Works much better in airports than in alleys. Look around." There was no one on the streets. The snow was falling harder. "Scream. Go ahead, get it out of your system."

Wind whipped around the car, drifting snow across the hood. I bit my lip, hands on the steering wheel. I had to stay calm, had to think clearly. The car was a two-door. I could get out and run, get a head start. Even as I turned, his gloved hand flattened the lock.

"We need to have a talk, Katie. This has gotten out of hand." With his right hand he turned my head back to him. He was smiling his prettiest smile, making his eyes look sincere.

Snow clung to the side windows, front and back were already covered. Frost nibbled at the edges of the glass. The car was a lonely cave. I had to get out of here, find some people.

"Shitty way of getting things in hand, you ask me, locking me in a car." I met his eyes. They glowed with warmth—had no trouble meeting mine.

Jake suddenly lurched forward. I flattened myself against the door. "You touch me and I'll . . ." I didn't know what, but it would be bad. I doubled my mittens into fists. He clambered between the seats and heaved himself into the passenger side, dismissing my fuzzy blue boxing gloves with a glance of amused contempt.

"Katie, you embarrass yourself." Tears prickled the backs of my eyes and I blinked hard.

"I want you to get out."

"And I want us to talk."

"Fine. You wanna talk, I'll talk, but not here." I folded my arms, set my lips and we glared at each other, then his face changed again. Jake the reasonable, Jake the willing.

"Okay, there's a place up the street." He opened the door and slid into the snow. "Follow me," he said.

"That's the point, all right," I muttered as the door closed. In that second, I could have started the engine. I had the keys, he was out of the car. But if Jake wanted to talk to me, I wanted to talk to him. Whatever his plan was, one of my own was already forming. He thought he could feed me a bunch of bullshit and get me out of the way. Fine. Let him play his little game and I'd gather information. I'd find something to use against him, some way to hurt him, scare him, nail him, jail him. I got out of the car.

He waited, wind ruffling his hair, snow stuck to his lashes. If someone had passed then . . . If a woman came by she'd have thought how lucky I was to have a man like that waiting. Without a word, I followed him up the street and around the corner toward a dull red glow at the end of the block. Morey's, said the chipped paint on the dirty picture window.

It reminded me of Petrillo's. A couple of old men huddled at the far end of a long bar. A few booths were scattered around the fringes and an empty steam table sat next to the back wall. Fine dining at Morey's saloon. Jake took a table across from the center of the bar where the bartender was drawing a draft. The beer foamed over the glass, even more golden to eyes like mine, still full of white. I will never drink again. Not even during the Super Bowl, reminded the voice.

The bartender served the beer and came back, making token chitchat about the weather. Jake ordered two Molsons. "No glass, right, Katie?"

"No nothing. I'm choosy who I drink with." The bartender set the bottles down on fresh white napkins.

"Have any coffee?" I asked the apron-clad old man.

He nodded. "Right away," he said over his shoulder. "Fresh pot.

"Not drinking?"

"Just freezing. You wanted to talk, so talk."

Jake poured some beer, tipping his glass to keep the head down. I watched it fill, mouth suddenly wet. I looked away.

Out of the corner of my eye I could see him still making a production out of filling his glass.

"I want us to be friends," he began finally. "Vanessa is an important part of my life and we've put her in a terrible situation."

"*We've* put her?"

"We're making her choose between us. It's got her so upset she isn't thinking clearly. How else could you explain a scene like the one in my office? That's just not the Vanessa I know." He took a swallow and the smell of the Molson cut through the coffee. I shivered. "Still cold?" He tossed his overcoat back from his shoulders. I took a sip and scalded my tongue.

"Ow! Shit!" The Molson held its chill, beads of sweat just starting to trickle down the sides. My tongue burned. I thought of Annie, the bruised angel who was going to help to keep me sober, and let my breath out in a whoosh.

"Are you okay?"

"I'm fine," I snapped. "You were saying?"

"I know you think I've been trying to make Vanessa miserable, but you're wrong, Katie." So sincere. "At first I thought . . . maybe if I was persistent I could help her make up her mind." He was staring at a place over my head, wincing. His hands were flat on the table, only the bubbles in his beer were moving. "Look, I know I went too far . . . But I thought . . . If she could know how much she meant to me. How much time I devote to her. How much time I spend thinking about her . . . us . . ."

"Come on, there never was any *us*." I was watching his eyes to see if I could bring him back to me. He didn't budge.

"Oh yes there was. There was us. I could have been good for her. It would have been perfect for me."

"I'm not buying this, Jake. I know too much about you. I know what you've done. It was you in the basement that time. If you really do want a relationship of some kind with Vanessa it's just to have more control over her. Keep her in your own basement, maybe, so torturing her is more convenient."

He looked hard at me. Now I had him. But maybe not, he was just confused.

"What basement? How could you think that? I would never do anything to hurt her. I love her. I want her to be with me." He lifted his glass. I wrapped my fingers around my mug.

"Really. Okay, so you love her and you want us to be friends." He nodded earnestly, took another swallow. The bastard. "Then maybe you can help me clear a few things up."

"Anything you want to know, ask. I've always liked you, Katie. But you never liked me." The eyes were so blue, so beautiful. "What have you got against me? Most women like me. You know it's true. I'm just curious, what makes you different?"

"I hate self-centered guys who need attention all the time. Could that be it, Jake? All the sick, twisted shit you do is just to get a rise out of people. Right? Just to let them know how well you get around, how easy it is for you to pop up out of nowhere."

I heard the sound of my voice teasing him and didn't like it. I could say just what I thought of him at Vanessa's, where I felt threatened by him, but I felt safe in public. The incident at the airport had proved how easy it was to get the better of him. Then Vanessa had made a complete fool out of him right in his office. Jake may have been clever, but he seemed vulnerable at the moment, and though I knew I hated him, and with good reason, I didn't feel much hatred at the moment.

"You think I like the way it's been going?" he was saying. "I know I've got some kind of hang-up about Vanessa, fixation, call it what you will. But there's a reason. I hardly knew my parents. My mother was always cold to me. It's usually the fathers who wonder if a particular kid really belongs to them, but this was a mother, someone who was supposed to have carried me in her belly. How come she never gave a damn about me?"

You've been having the same effect on women ever since, I thought. "Your birth mother?"

"Sometimes I wished she wasn't. Yeah, I hated her. And sometimes the anger flares and I hate Vanessa the same way. For trying to pretend she doesn't feel anything, she doesn't care how much I have to say to her, how much I feel."

Whoa, I found myself thinking. This guy believes his own bullshit.

"Bullshit!" He had been tipping his bottle at me while making his last point. "Stop it!" I grabbed the bottle angrily and our hands met. It was like an electric shock. He pulled away first and left the bottle in my hand.

"Do you really hate me as much as you want me to think?" His whisper was almost sultry. His scent filled my nose, deep and musky, and rage began to stifle me. My elbow bent with it, the beer rising automatically to my lips. The bottle clinked against my teeth. Shit. No drinking. Ever. Reluctantly, I set the bottle on the bar.

"Sadistic morons don't appeal to me."

"That's not what I've heard."

"Now that's the Jake we all know and love." But I didn't want to find out who he meant by that crack. Could he have been watching me, too, while we all thought he was only after Vanessa? "Anyway, you're the one with the tale of woe. So sorry about your troubled childhood. What if you were adopted?"

He shook his head slowly but his eyes were somewhere else. I wasn't getting to him. When Jake wasn't fencing with me he was a big bore.

"What about your dad? He ignore you, too? Or just knock you around all the time?"

He actually grinned now. "No, we were great buds. He took me places. He was proud of his son."

"Maybe that's why scaring women is such a turn-on. Where love and affection are concerned you only respond to men."

"Careful, Katie."

That was the voice I knew from the phone, but dammit, I could tell from his eyes I still hadn't touched a nerve. I was figuring him out, though. Getting close to the truth of something that had been giving me nightmares. If Jake was really as pathetic as he wanted me to believe, it didn't make him less dangerous, but it made him a whole lot less scary.

"The places my father took me," he went on, "were mostly bars. Same thing with your dad, I understand."

"What do you know about my father?" I came flying out of my seat and the edge of the table sat me down again.

"Hey, relax." But he was gloating, the bastard. "She told me about her friends while we were still talking, while things were going right for us."

"She told you about my *father*?"

"In the context of your drinking problem, yes."

"She said I had a *drinking problem*?"

All right, laugh, you bastard, I thought, but you're gonna tell me everything she said.

"It's what people do, Katie. You were her best friend. She just wanted me to have something to go on when I met you. I told her about my father, then, too. She was the first one to point out how much we have in common."

"You and me? So our fathers were drunks, what else did she think we had in common . . . *back then*?"

"Our personalities. You know, being aggressive. Saying what we think even when it rubs people the wrong way. Going overboard for the things we like . . ."

"So now you're going to tell me you've got a problem about booze, too. That it?"

"She said it would be easier to know me, she knew you so well . . . No, I never had a problem of not knowing when to quit. I saw my dad drunk too many times. Sometimes I feel like wanting to go deeper. You would know. It calls to me."

Yes, I would know all right. How could I sit here and listen to Jake Romano's version of things, knowing better the whole time. If I was looking for a weakness in his defenses, lies I could catch him on, facts I could use against him, he was feeling me out, too. What was odd, though—I couldn't help feeling he was sincere in wanting me for a friend, or if not that, at least in wanting me not to be an enemy. He must have known he could never have my approval of anything he'd done, but if he could make me understand why he got so twisted that would be the beginning of forgiveness. Sure, it was a setup.

"You think I'm going to go to Vanessa and tell her, 'Look, Van, now that I've heard Jake's side of things, he's not such a bad guy and he really does love you a lot.' "

"No, she wouldn't listen," he said, draining his beer. "It's all my fault, you don't have to tell me. The lines have been drawn. Hey, bartender."

"Looks like we're going to be snowed in, folks. More coffee, Miss?"

"I . . . all right."

"I'll have another beer." Then he shouted after him, "And a double shot of Jameson's."

"You're trying to get me started," I said, hating him more than ever.

"Why look at it that way?" he said matter-of-factly. "If I feel like a few drinks more than usual tonight it's because it's hard for me to talk about myself . . . and what I've been doing with my life lately. And it's a way to handle being attracted to you, because it's clear as anything you hate my guts. I'll never forget what happened at the airport. That was worse than you two doing guerrilla theater at my office. Fortunately, those three guys were there to ask a favor."

"About the airport . . . One fucking minute, *attracted?* Am I supposed to be flattered because you've taken the time to spy on me lately as much as you did on Vanessa and come popping up out the dark the way you did tonight? I should be doubled up on the floor, laughing, right? Except that I wouldn't give you the satisfaction of seeing me doubled up on the floor for any reason. Yeah, the airport . . . That was when we all knew how far you were willing to go."

"That was when you made me out to be a child molester in front of a room full of people just because I wanted to make sure that the woman I loved was really leaving town the way she said."

"Gotcha, Jake! She said she was leaving town the day before."

He looked offended and waved me off with the back of his hand. "But she didn't leave then, so I had to try to find out when. I knew she was terrified after what happened. She still suspected me and was trying to keep me from knowing where she was. I had to be content to watch from a distance. For now, that's all I can have. I've come to accept that."

After what happened? Vanessa had never told him about the cellar. We had all been there when she called. I knew it! I knew if I talked to him long enough, the prick would hang himself!

"What do you mean, *after what happened?* How do you know what happened?"

"I was there, Katie, remember?" He smiled.

Time stopped. Everything was frozen, every nerve alert.

The coffee arrived, his beer, and the whiskey in a rock glass. I started adding sugar. He held the whiskey toward me and the smell of it wrapped around me like a quilt. Ummm, murmured the voice. I took a deep breath. No. A sip, crooned the second. No!

"Have a drink, Katie."

He tipped his glass forward.

"Did I just hear you say you were there, in the basement?" My voice was higher than intended, anxiety setting the pitch. I took a sip of my coffee but it tasted like mud. The whiskey winked on the bar. There was room in the mug. No. Never again. I added more sugar.

"The basement?" He was puzzled, shaking his head, his confusion adorable. "What are you talking about? We found the rose on the mantle, in the living room. I was there, with Vanessa, remember?" He lifted the Jameson's and held it up to the light. "There's nobody like the Irish for good whiskey. Why aren't you drinking, Katie?"

"I don't want to." Yes you do.

"Yes you do."

"No, I don't." Weaker than I wanted.

"Don't tell me you're on the wagon?" Jake leaned back in his stool, face a picture of astonishment. "Katie, I'm surprised. You can handle your liquor sometimes, can't you?"

My fingers clamped on his wrist like vise. "I can handle anything I want, including you."

One of the old-timers dropped a dollar in the jukebox. Frank Sinatra's voice crackled through ancient speakers. The skin of his hairy wrist was hot and dry. I kept my hand there a long time. It was a kind of weird embrace, staring into each other's eyes. But there was nothing in his, not even wariness, and I knew there was nothing in mine.

A bead of sweat ran down my ribcage. To warm me up . . . I let go of him.

"I thought you *loved* Vanessa." The wind howled outside. Jake smiled, tipped his glass. The coffee tasted burnt. I pushed the mug away.

"I do."

"What do you see in her, Jake? Let's hear it. What has she got that could make you want to risk your whole career . . ."

"I see her the same way you do. Beautiful, talented, successful . . . But that's a small part of it. I've got the looks, the clothes, the car and some success doing what I do. But it's not what she's got, it's who she is. She's strong, Katie. She doesn't need anyone, I don't think she ever has. In the business—books, movies, it's all the same—you need people. Patronage. I don't care what you call it—someone to believe in you, someone to put a value on the work you do."

"You work, Jake? Really? With all the running around you do keeping tabs on us . . ."

That stopped him, and I saw the hurt expression I'd been waiting for, but I didn't feel good about it. Maybe the bastard really could feel pain. Sure, that was what he wanted me to think, but maybe all tonight represented was some elaborate backhanded way of getting me to see the truth about his feelings. And he was telling the right person about Vanessa because I'd always wondered the same thing about her. How could she be so independent? How come she didn't need love as much as I did?

Frank Sinatra had faded into Tony Bennett.

"You're right." He sighed. He still hadn't taken a drink since the new round arrived. "I'm out of the office way too much. No one can find me. I'm going to lose my backers if I don't get some of my projects in the can."

"What if those men in your office had been your backers, Jake? Think of it. If you don't stay the hell away from Vanessa, she'll ruin you. That was just the beginning."

"You think she has me on the run by making it appear that I was persecuting her? Think again. I saw right through her and so did my friends. Hate and love are opposite sides of the same coin. To try to disgrace me in front of my associates was such a low blow—the kind of hate that could only come from great pain. And so much pain could only come from disappointed love."

A jeering sound, a bray, escaped me involuntarily. "You expect me to believe . . ." I couldn't bring myself to say it: You're a wimp, Jake! You're so afraid of being dropped by a woman that you gotta figure love's behind it somehow when she's kicking you in the balls! Tell me more! Never had he looked so pathetic as he did now. What if it was all an act, though? Was that possible? "C'mon Jake, Vanessa may have been hurt for a couple of seconds when she realized that any sort of relationship would be impossible, but she got over it right away. All you've been since then is a pain in the ass. Go into therapy. Seriously. Get help before you hurt someone or someone hurts you. Think of all you've got to lose."

"I still love her, but I know I can't have her yet. She's got to respect me first. I've got to have the upper hand. What happened before, as soon as she saw how much I needed her she pushed me away. Maybe I've just been telling myself I've got to have her to salvage some self-respect. Does that make sense?"

"No," I said frankly.

"Sure it does. If I keep thinking I can have anything I want and deserve anything I want to have, it's only her being a hardheaded bitch that's stopping me, I don't have to admit being hurt. And if I can hurt her . . ." He started paying attention to his drink again. "If I can hurt her, she can still need me for something."

"Right. To stop. So why don't you?"

"I don't want to think about it. C'mon and drink with me. You know we do have things in common. We could be friends. Don't believe all that crap about one drink leading to another. You were having a tough time after your husband left, that's the only reason you couldn't handle it."

"She told you that, too!"

"Look, don't we all drink too much after a busted relationship? I could have done the same, much as I hate to drink alone. Sometimes after a few drinks your enemy can turn out to be someone a lot like you." He pulled on his beer but left the glass of Jameson's full between us. "Afraid we'd agree about too many things if you started talking . . . ?"

You're snowed in anyway, said the first voice. You and Jake aren't going anywhere, said voice number two.

"Well, we're snowed in anyway. I wouldn't put anything past you, but there's only so much you can try on me in here."

"I'll tell you things about Vanessa you might be surprised to know. For one, she's a prude. She's afraid to let go with a man. She never really gives herself. But I won't say she puts too high a price on herself, either. If she didn't have so much to give I'd never have thought she was worth the game."

"Game? You call it a game the way you've pursued her?"

"No. She's the game, though. I'm the hunter."

"The stalker, you mean."

"Call it that if you want. It's something hunters do."

"You think it's some kind of man thing, don't you?"

"It was for thousands of years. Do you think men have changed that much? Look, I can take the rejection and the things she does to make me look bad. But if you think I'll give up trying to have her, think again. You don't know what persistence is. Don't worry, I'll never have to give up—she'll give in."

Jake's lips were dark red from the alcohol and his dark blue eyes were dewy and wistful. He was coming across as vulnerable and attractive and I realized with a jolt that the only way I could make this work and keep drawing him out was if I wasn't myself. Things were getting too chummy with him telling me all his sob stories. I needed to slip back inside the familiar armor of my contempt for him. And if he saw me weaken and start drinking he'd feel contempt for *me* again. He would can all the "I want to be your friend" crap he'd been feeding me and go back on the prowl looking for some way to hurt me, or hurt his "game animal of choice," Vanessa.

". . . To a true hunter the chase is everything, you know . . . " he was saying.

"So if you're a true hunter why do you want to wound Vanessa with your cheap shots. Even if you think of her as nothing but a trophy, which makes you a wacko, at least you'd want her in good condition. When you're ready to make the kill . . ." I couldn't believe I'd said that, ". . . you wouldn't want her all worn out from defending against your dirty tricks, all the crummy little ways you've gained the advantage."

"You have a point . . . Maybe I credit her with being a better opponent than she really is. I must admit it's refreshing to know that I've been getting through to her."

"Bastard."

"You don't think so, though. To us, Katie," he said, raising his beer. Calling my bluff.

All right, you bastard, I thought. I know you're making this up as you go along. Attracted to me? Still believing Vanessa loves you after the way she dissed you right in front of your important friends? But you'll be telling the truth soon enough, pal. Because nobody gauges sobriety more keenly than a heavy drinker who's not drinking. And, Jake, you've got a nice buzz on. But after what I've been putting away lately, I've got the tolerance of a Russian diplomat. I'm going to drink you under the table, *Jakie,* and you're going to tell me *everything* . . . And someone else will have to scrape you off the men's room floor.

Slowly I brought the glass of whiskey toward my lips, hand suddenly trembling. Never drink again. Don't do it.

"To friendship and understanding," said Jake again, relentless. "If we can understand ourselves so well, surely we can understand each other."

"To Vanessa," I said as the first of the whiskeys slid down my throat. You don't want to feel like a traitor for finding out a few things about her life, said voice number one. You've got to see where this is going, insisted voice number two.

"I don't want to feel like a traitor to my friend." My voice was suddenly husky as if the center had been scorched out of it. "But I do want to hear more."

21

"So I says to him, I says, Frankie, what the fuck, ya ain't gotta treat me that way. Right? Am I right?" The woman leaned into the mirror, filling the purple lines around her lips with maroon. "So I hit him with the fuckin' bottle, ya know, and the lousy bastard bled all over my car. Can ya believe it? Can ya?"

She was talking to me. Suddenly, out of nowhere, I was in a bathroom with a stranger, a stranger with teased hair and a low-cut dress with a short skirt. Large breasts bubbled up over the edge of her bodice and a butterfly tattoo sat on top, wings spread for flight.

"Are you listening to me, honey? Katie, ya okay?"

Katie. Where was I? I was leaning against the door of a compact but clean bathroom while the stranger did her face. There were stripes of blush on her cheeks and black eyeliner had been applied with a liberal hand. Two stalls were stuck in a corner. Her purse sat on a shelf over the sink. I looked down and saw mine on the floor at my feet. Loud music strained against the shell-pink walls. No Sinatra here. Where was I? Who was she? How did I get here?

A fist from the outside pounded the door, bam, bam, bam. I jumped away, frightened, slopping my drink on my shoes. The smell of beer. The stranger's perfume. Reeling. "Aaaa, hold your fucking horses," she yelled nasally, "we'll be out in a fuckin' minute."

I took a deep breath. The last I knew I was at Morey's. Jameson's. Jake talking, explaining, telling. Friends. We were going to be good friends. Clinking glasses, tossing back shots. Singing to the jukebox. "You know, Romano, for an asshole, you're not a bad guy." I almost lost my balance, grabbing at a stall door that swung open, tipping me toward the toilet.

"Hey, ya sure you're okay?" She turned from the mirror to look at me, one hand on her hip. "You ain't gonna puke or nothing, are ya?" she asked suspiciously. I shook my head. Partly to clear my brain. Struggling to remember. Somehow I had gotten from there to here. "Good." She turned back, added some more hairspray to the stiff pile on her head. The person outside pounded again. She pulled a tiny vial from her pocket, twisted off the cap and tapped some powder into two piles on the back of her hand. Expertly, she placed a nostril over each one in turn and sniffed. The coke was gone. "Ya wanna another hit, Katie? Ya look like ya could use it." She held out the vial. Another? I didn't do drugs. Mutely, I shook my head. "Okay." She tucked the vial back in her pocket and tugged at her skirt, then cupped a breast in each hand to arrange her neckline. "C'mon honey, the boys are waiting."

With a last satisfied look in the mirror, she unlocked the door. The music was so loud it was solid, a wall of sound, blasting like a windstorm that pulled at my face and hair. The pounder was wearing leather, a tiny girl, young, all but wrapped around an older man who grinned foolishly. Drunk, very drunk. "About time," the leather girl mumbled. "Fuck you," Madame Butterfly replied cheerfully. The leather girl flipped us off and dragged the old man into the john.

"Do you see Frankie?" the stranger shouted. The music was so loud. She peered out into the darkness, head swiveling. My eyes struggled with the blackness, people moving in it. Red and blue lights scattered around the edges. Winking. Far away, a door with light. Everything moving, blurry, black, people, music, smoke, very smoky. Cigarette lighters flaring, dying. "I told him to wait!"

Determinedly she started forward. I had no choice but to follow. She plunged into the crowd, working her way toward the door with the light. I clutched my purse and my drink and prayed I wouldn't lose her. It was another world, unworldly, lumps and globs zooming into faces, breasts, body parts glowing in the dark. There were couches filled with people, intertwined and silent, separate and laughing. Some just sitting dazed, off in a darkness of their own. I felt them pull at me. I know you, they called. I knew them too.

The stranger stopped and screamed at a woman sitting on the end of a couch. Something about Frankie. "Ya lose your

ole man again, Charlene?" the woman yelled. Charlene. The
name meant nothing. I didn't know her. "Well, it ain't my turn
to watch him, but I did see him head thataway." She waved
vaguely toward the door. Charlene lunged forward again.

"Who's the looker with him, Char," she called. "Don't forget your friends."

She cackled obscenely, blowing smoke as I started past. I
stumbled and fell forward, dumping drink and dropping purse.
Her drink spilled too and she jumped up angrily, pushing me
off her, cursing. I fell backwards into a wall of moving bodies,
people pushing, kicking my bag. Faces loomed in and out,
hostile voices, shrill screams of laughter, no point of origin. I
dropped to my knees, feeling for the shoulder strap, frantically
slapping about on the floor. Feet and faces, light and dark, so
much smoke, too much sound. Another world, unworldly.
Feeling desperate, everything loud and moving, nothing still.
Blind, in the darkness, gagging, anxiety attacking. No purse.
Where was I?

"Help me!" No one heard or no one cared. Music screeching. Panic rising. What was I doing here? I had to get out!
Desperately, I crawled forward, pushing, not caring where I
went, fingers trampled, elbows kicked. My hand came down
on a piece of leather. Not a shoe, a shoulder strap. I grabbed
it, clutching the purse to my chest like a baby, and struggled
to my feet. A stranger snarling as I bumped into his leg, a
woman looking disdainfully down, curling her lip. Upright
now in the mass of writhing bodies, too many people, not
enough light. Charlene was gone. All alone. Dazed and drunk,
I let the crowd tumble me, still clutching my purse. A piece
of trash in a stormy ocean, unwanted, unwelcome, just riding
the tide. Fingers wrapped around my upper arm.

"Where the hell are you going?" Charlene screeched. "They
gotta be at the bar!" She gestured toward the lighted door and
dragged me forward, fingers digging into my arm. I bumped
along in her wake, like a toy on a string, catching on everything and everyone in our path. She hauled me past a dance
floor where light flickered furiously on gyrating bodies.

When we stepped through the doorway, the music dropped
to a dull roar. Charlene pulled me into a circular booth on the
far wall, her purse resting next to a candle burning in a red

globe. It was too dark to see, but I had to find out where I was. "Charlene, where are we?"

"Where are we, that's a good one, Katie. Who the hell knows." She laughed and pulled the candle over to light a long skinny cigarette. Her face was grotesque, lit red from beneath, a gargoyle covered with graffiti. I whimpered, breath coming in short spurts, faster, tears trembling at the edge of my eyes. I could feel the scream building and worked to fight it back. "Hey, don't get yourself all upset." Charlene patted my hand. "Have another drink, you'll be okay."

Have another drink. "I want to go home."

"Yeah, sure." She was getting bored with me. No one likes a whiner, whispered the voice. "The guys must be getting us a drink. Talk to your old man. Maybe he'll take ya home."

My old man? I almost gagged, remembering Mike the maintenance man, thinking for one crazy moment that he was here. "What do you mean, my old man?" Have another drink.

"Whadda ya mean, whadda I mean? Your ole man, honey, the babe who brought ya." I looked blank. She shook her head in exasperation. "Lookit, honey, let me give ya some advice. You gotta nice figure, face, but when you go out with a hunk like the one you got, you gotta stay on your toes. There's plenty out there who got no problem taking over where you left off, ya know what I mean, Katie? Women are bitches, right?"

"My old man . . . You mean Jake?"

"Ya gotta know him better'n that, Katie. The way he was braggin' about ya lately."

"You knew him before tonight?"

"Sure, honey. He works around here. We never saw him much until a few days ago, though. Like he only came in here to brag on you. We told him there'd be room at our place, he wanted to party."

"We're supposed to party at your house?"

"I love it. Now you've forgotten that, too. What ya been drinking? Kid, you're gonna blow it with this guy, I swear to God. We gave you the bedroom. Don't tell me you didn't know that was the plan. You can go back now, you wanna clear your head. Take a shower. How about it? That must be where they are, him and Frankie. Can you believe this shit, though, all the business I give this place, the bar girls can't keep our glasses full or come and give me a message. Don't worry, one of these bitches knows where they went. They're prob'ly already tired of waiting. Hey, where ya goin'?"

I forced my way past the lights, past the dance floor, pushing, stumbling, angry voices from behind. People grabbing, cursing, pushing, me not looking to see who followed. Had to leave, had to go. Not my friend! Please! Finally, finally, finding the way, pushing past the bouncer, big and courteous, opening up the door. Fresh air. Freedom. Freezing. I had no coat. I didn't care.

It must have been very late. In the distance the city glowed weakly against the dark sky, the eastern horizon was starting to get light. The snow was pristine. I raced down the street to look at the sign. I'd never been after-hours except in Manhattan, a sad little joint on Sullivan Street. I was in Queens and I didn't know Queens at all. I couldn't think. I had to go home. Vanessa would be worried. Not after she knows what you've done, sneered the voice. Had he really had his hands on me? His lips? I was too numb to know. "I'm her friend," I cried. Some friend, the voice replied.

A man was opening a public garage down the street. I ran to him, crying now, nose running in the cold. He turned and looked me over—coatless, close to hysterical—"Take it easy, girlie,"—retreating warily, hand holding a conspicuous nightstick, telling me how I must look. As calmly as I could, I asked him where I was. He stared. I mentioned Morey's and his face cleared. Not glad to help me, but wanting to send me on my way. Four or five blocks, only two turns. I walked away, faster, found myself jogging, running. I turned the second corner. Morey's.

The same picture window. If I closed my eyes, I was back inside, everything familiar. I had spent most of my life at Morey's. These places were my life. I ducked my head and started by when my feet stopped. My brain screamed hurry but my feet refused. I gazed into the window. Let myself remember what I could, not all, bits and pieces, ugly pieces. My life a series of ugly pieces too hideous to recall, too shameful to forget. I took one last look at Morey's and walked away.

By the time I got to the Phoenix, I was frozen, fingers stiff, body shaking. I brushed off the windows with bare hands and sat in the alley, motor running, willing heat from the too cold engine. My shoulders sagged, then the words *no more* formed in my mind; not one of my little voices, something more like a thought that stood out from the jumble. A kind of calm settled over me, warmer than my quilt had ever been. No more. It was that simple. And it scared me. Because like that man without a country, I would be a woman without a life. I was suddenly sober. "No more," I repeated, comforted by the sound. I sat for a moment longer, then pulled out into the street. I headed for my apartment, too tired to drive out to Long Island, and probably still too drunk not to be a danger. And I didn't want my friends to see me this way. Would they have waited up? Not after the way I'd been drinking lately. Called the police in Jake's precinct? Probably not. And if they were worried about me they would keep calling my place. I could change the message, tell them I needed some space.

It was afternoon when I awoke and I'd turned off the phone without changing the message. Still, if I cleaned up enough, I reasoned, I could just drive out there . . . They'd probably be relieved to see me.

When I reached Vanessa's there was a police car parked in her driveway. Just for a second I wanted to run, and keep running the way I had from that after-hours place. But only for a second. I walked the steps to the kitchen door. Turned my key in the lock. Took a deep breath.

"Hello?"

They raced to the kitchen, Annie, Vanessa and Oola too. I swayed in front of them, deluged by hugs and hands and kisses, all of them trying to touch me at once. From the shelter of their arms I smelled the whiskey oozing from my pores. Knew that they could too. No one said a word about drinking.

"Oh, Kate! You're all right!"

"We've been worried sick!"

"We thought you were with Oola . . ." Vanessa.

"I couldn't get home. I stayed in the city because of the storm . . ." Oola.

"So she didn't get our message until she got up. I'm so glad to see you." Annie with tears in her eyes.

"We didn't know if you had an accident or . . ."

"If Jake had gotten you, so we called the police and . . ."

"Please," I interrupted. "I really need to sit down."

"Ms. Clayton," said a man's voice. "There's something you need to hear." It wasn't Lieutenant Meese. Thankfully not Moroski. The smoker, Officer Clyde.

"Kate's home." Vanessa waved dismissively. I sank into a chair at the kitchen table. Annie's hands rested on my shoulders and Oola stood protectively between me and the police. "Do you want something, Kate? Coffee, something to eat?"

"I've got Mr. Romano on the phone, Ms. Clayton. You wanted us to call him. I think you should listen to what he has to say."

An ocean roared in my ears. A breath was an effort. Everyone looked from the officer to me. My eyes were dull and downward. There was no point in pretending. I knew what he would say.

"Ms. Clayton?"

Vanessa's eyes were locked to my face. "Kate?" Worried. Wary?

I didn't look up. "Go ahead, Vanessa. We'll talk when you're done." Nervously, she followed him from the room. Oola too. A tangible darkness seemed to follow them. Annie sat at the kitchen table and held my hand.

"It's all right now, Kate. You're home."

"It's not all right, Annie. You don't know what I've done."

"I don't care what you've done." I closed my eyes against the tears. The minutes ticked by, muted sounds from the other room.

"Ms. Greerson?" His voice boomed. "Can you come here, please." Not a request. I didn't move. "Ms. Greerson."

I forced myself up from the chair, Annie moving with me like a shadow. Vanessa sat in the armchair, dazed. Oola leaned against the mantle, face ashen. An officer I didn't know stood next to Bobby's tape machine (which had replaced Vanessa's message machine, and differed from it in that it would take two hours worth of messages). No one met my eyes.

"Ms. Greerson, I want you to identify the voices on this tape. Can you do that." A huge lump in my throat. Almost impossible to nod. The tape rolled.

"What is it, you don't want me, Katie . . ."

"I do . . . Just let me . . . I'm not ready . . ."

"You know I'm real choosy about the women I fuck."

"I want you . . . Don't stop . . . It feels so good . . . Right there . . . Thassa way . . ."

Then I was moaning. Loud. I. Me.

I was too humiliated to say anything.

"Stop it!" It was Annie, screaming. "Turn it off!"

She pushed past the officer who was running the tape. "I said turn it off." She angrily flipped the switch, right in the middle of series of shrieks, rising in pitch, that became sobs when they broke. It was anybody's guess what he was doing, but it was clearly something I wanted. At the time. God knows why. My brain was in darkness. Why wasn't my body just as numb. He put something in my drink? Could be. With all the drinking I'd been doing lately it would have taken a lot to black me out.

"What exactly is the point here, officers?" Annie's eyes blazed and Officer Clyde had the grace to be embarrassed. He mumbled something about identification. "Identify what? Kate's voice? Yes, it's her voice. I've known her since kindergarten, is that good enough for you?"

"Ma'am, you're the ones who made accusations about Mr. Romano. You asked me to speak to him. I got him on the phone. He told me he was going to play a tape for our machine—I guess he knows you've got this thing—"

"Can't you tell she's drunk out of her mind? She didn't mean any of those things." Annie's scorn was all the more powerful for those of us who knew her. Still, her last statement had them smirking, the pigs.

"Ms. Greerson, Mr. Romano says that you willingly accompanied him to a drinking establishment in Queens called . . ." He paused to flip through his notes.

"Morey's."

"That's right," he said, surprised. "From this, uh, Morey's, you left together for another establishment called Frank's Motel. One of the owners," again he consulted his notes, "a Ms. Charlene Morrow, took you to a social club," he cleared his throat, addressing the room now, "known as the Starbrite. The four of you had cocktails until Ms. Greerson became ill and had to leave." He stopped and looked at me. "Mr. Romano has stated that you were a willing participant. Is that correct?" I didn't answer. Annie stepped behind the couch, put a hand on my shoulder. Both of us were trembling. "I can call and confirm his story, Ms. Greerson," he prodded.

"Yes."

Vanessa smothered a cry, leaning forward, a hand over her mouth, rocking in her chair. Oola pushed off the mantle and came to sit at my side. I kept my head down. Officer Clyde closed his notebook with a snap.

"Ms. Clayton, we're too busy to waste time on any more of these calls claiming harassment. You ladies can work out the details of who gets Mr. Romano, but in the . . ."

"Get out!" Vanessa was on her feet, moving toward the door.

"I beg your pardon?" Officer Clyde was more accustomed to the Vanessa who sauntered and smiled.

"I said, get out of my house!"

"Look, we're just trying to do our job."

"Well, do it someplace else." She threw open the door.

"Next time you should give some thought before calling in a false report. Ma'am." Stiffly, angrily, following his partner out onto the porch.

"Next time I won't bother calling!" Slamming the door in his face.

I buried my face in my hands. Felt Vanessa's weight on the couch.

"I'm sorry," I whispered.

"I know," she said.

In a halting voice, I told them everything I could remember. It wasn't much and not all of it made sense. But they all believed me about wanting to trap Jake into saying something damaging while I was sober. No one could understand how I could drink with him, though.

"I just couldn't stand being myself while he was coming on to me," I said. "I was finding out a lot of stuff and wanted to find out more, but when I started drinking, I thought we were snowed in, that's what the bartender said. I had the feeling I was going to be listening to Jake for a while, and I really did want to hear more. But he'd been planning the whole thing, the son of a bitch. Even the snow! Telling me all that shit about his poor childhood, the mother who never spoke to him, the father who was a drunk like mine and dragged him to all the bars . . ."

"His father was no drunk," Vanessa said scornfully. "He was an attorney for the entertainment business—that's what he said. Probably for the mob. But not a drunk. And I think his mother died just before his teen years. That's what he said. He was raised by a series of bimbos that his father had taken as mistresses. I'll bet they fussed over him every minute, trying to get him to like them so that their sugar-daddy would see them as a wife and mother instead of an occasional parking place for his prick."

"How could I be so naive?" I asked Vanessa. "I was the first one to catch onto Jake. I knew he was trying to shine me on last night, but everything he said made sense in explaining his behavior. He was even a little sheepish, believe it or not. Hearing a confession from a guy like that . . . He was telling me, like, 'I know I'm twisted. I can't help it. I'm out of hand. I know I am, but that doesn't mean I can *stop* having feelings for Vanessa.' "

"Wow, he's good," said Vanessa coldly. "He did a better number on you than he did on me. Even if there's nothing true about what he told me, either. He spent some time setting this up. How did he know we'd be in the area, though? He scouted the motel, described you to that Charlene lady. How'd he figure he'd get you there last night?"

"Look, plots are your specialty," I told Vanessa.

"Well, he must have known the places we would be watching," she said.

"Anyway, I'm sorry I was such a sucker," I said. "Sorry to all of you for letting you down, but most of all to you, Vanessa. Everything that happened after we talked at that first bar . . . I never saw any of it coming. Whatever he did, he didn't do it to *me*. Will you still hate me?"

"I don't hate you, Kate." I began to sob and buried my face in her shoulder. "Listen to me. Through this whole thing, you've watched over me. I don't care what the cops say, Jake says, anyone says, I believe you, Kate." The others murmured assent. I raised my face. There were tears in her eyes.

"I shouldn't have had a drink." My voice was cracking. "I promised I wouldn't drink."

"Kate, you paid a big price to try and help me. It's not your . . ."

Before she could say it, I flung myself up, brushing aside

hers and Oola's arms. I whirled to face them, Annie a statue behind the couch.

"It is my fault! Don't you understand, I let him touch me. I drank with him, I let him touch me. All it takes is a few drinks and I'm fucking a man who makes my stomach turn." I wiped my nose with the back of my hand, angry tears, wanting them to hate me, too. "Whatever that bastard did to me was rape, and there I was telling him I liked it." I slammed my fist against the fireplace and a picture wobbled on the mantel and fell.

Vanessa and I were staring at each other. "All I know is, I'm sorry, Kate," she said. "I'm so sorry for what happened to you."

It was more than I could bear. I ran from the room. They didn't follow. I lay down on the couch in the office and cried myself to sleep.

It was dark when I woke up, still hungover and depressed. The children were scampering around the kitchen as I poured a cup of coffee. Carla jarred the table, reaching for—and missing—her sister. Lindsay crawled between the legs of my chair and I spilled hot coffee on my hand. Stifling a curse, I carefully suggested they play elsewhere. Carla's "Okay, Aunt Kate," was obnoxiously loud. I gritted my teeth till they were gone.

Annie came into the kitchen a few minutes later.

"Hi," she said. I nodded without speaking. "I hope the girls aren't bothering you."

"No, of course not."

She rinsed the few dishes in the sink and placed them in the rack. The swelling around her eye had receded some. I could see fleeting glimpses of iris and pupil, the white pink with broken veins.

"I promised you, Annie."

"I know."

"Aren't you mad at me?"

"No, not even a little bit." She smiled, wiping her hands on cloth.

"I got drunk, Annie. After what happened to you, I got drunk."

"Kate, it's not what happened to me, it's what's happening to you. It's like watching someone you love turn into a ghost, slipping away until there's only the faintest image of the person that you knew."

"I feel like a ghost, almost invisible. The only time I know people see me is when I do something bad." No need for an example.

"Kate, I'm not making excuses for you, but don't forget about Jake. He knew that if he could get you drinking, he could take advantage of you. And he did."

I nodded my thanks, but I knew I was no victim, I had been a volunteer. I should have known better. I did know better.

The clock ticked on the kitchen wall.

"I can't stop, Annie, especially once I start. I don't know how to explain it so you can understand." I ran my fingers through my hair. "I know I shouldn't drink. Lots of times I don't even want to, but I can't stop myself." She stared at me. "I know it's crazy, never mind."

"No, no, Kate, I do understand. It's like David and me. I don't know when it changed, but somewhere along the line, we got to a place where we couldn't stop. Even when we wanted to."

"Oh, Annie. This is the last thing you need right now."

"I'll be all right, Kate. I'm going to get through this. And whatever happens, it'll be better than it was. It has to be."

"I don't know."

"You know, the other night . . ." She swallowed hard. "When Lindsay got hurt, it shocked me. David too. We had been on this collision course for so long, but neither us saw what was coming. Maybe it had to happen, for us to see."

"I don't like what I see."

"But you have to look. Otherwise you'll just keep doing the same things over and over. Like David and me."

We sat at the table in silence.

"He never hit you before, Annie, for real? Not even a slap?"

"Not even a slap."

I wanted to believe her, but I wasn't sure. If Annie's marriage was like my drinking, then minimizing disaster was necessary to survive.

22

We were a strange group. No more blustering or pretending. Acceptance. Of the fear and the danger and the willingness to proceed despite it. For however long it took, for whatever we had to do. The calm I had felt the other night sitting in the Phoenix had returned, as if I were bathed in light. No more, I thought. From drinking, from Jake Romano, no more.

Carla pounced on Annie, Lindsay right behind. They told the same story at the same time, something about the play house next door. They had to have one. Annie leaned down and took them by the hand, nodding and listening but not committing. They played every card they could think of, from tears to logic to lies. Children were weasels, worse than cats. Vanessa took their side and Oola chatted with the young mother named Heather who was Vanessa's neighbor.

I went through the back door to the kitchen and looked at the phone. I dug the number from my purse and dialed. A machine picked up, Van Morrison singing "Moondance" in the background. No one was home, wait for the beep. "Ellen, I . . . I need someone to help me. I've tried, but I keep . . . I can't stop. I want to but I can't. I don't know why, it seems so stupid, please. I . . ."

"Kate, I'm leaving," Oola called from the kitchen door. Quickly I hung up the phone. I hadn't even left my name, I realized. But I had told the truth. There was comfort in that. I walked Oola to the Blazer, said goodbye, and Vanessa and I went back to the house. Annie stayed talking to Heather, giving the children a few more minutes outside.

"Did you check the messages, Kate?" Vanessa asked, shutting the door.

"No," I replied.

She went in the living room and played back the machine. Annie and the kids came through the door.

"The lieutenant called," Vanessa yelled from the living room. "I'm gonna call him back."

"Can we have a soda, Mommy?" Carla asked. Annie said yes. I was closest, so I opened the refrigerator and handed them out. Two Coors sat on the bottom shelf. Silver bullets. Death by my own hand. I took a Diet Pepsi for me and Annie and closed the door.

Vanessa came back in the kitchen. "Where's my cigarettes? I need a cigarette." Everything came to halt while we looked. She lit up and leaned against the counter. "I just talked to Lieutenant Meese."

"Yeah?"

"If I don't leave Jake alone, he's going to file for an order of protection against me."

"What!" The uproar took a second to die down, Annie and I for once equally shocked and appalled.

"He has rights, too, you know."

"And Meese bought this!" I demanded. "Just when I thought I knew a cop whose IQ was bigger than his shoe size."

"It's not his fault," Annie murmured. "What did he say, Vanessa? "

"He talked to Officer Clyde." Nobody looked at me. "I'm not sure what he thought. But Jake was complaining that we've been threatening him."

"It's all my fault. He was the only cop who believed us."

"Kate, we don't have time for that crap. What's done is done." Vanessa stubbed her cigarette in the ashtray. "We've lost some ground. We can't pretend we haven't, but so what? They never believed us in the first place."

"What about the order of protection, Vanessa?"

"Excuse me," I interrupted, "I know what I did was wrong, but tell me, how the hell could he get an order of protection? How does that happen?"

"An order of protection is just a piece of paper signed by a judge. They're not that hard to get, a lawyer can ask for one, like in a divorce. If there's any question of abuse, the judge usually signs it," Annie added. We looked at her and she flushed. "I looked into it for Oola," she mumbled.

"Throw me a soda, Kate," Vanessa said. "Gary said . . ."

"Gary?"

"The lieutenant." Vanessa's turn to blush. I rolled my eyes. She never ceased to amaze me. I was hard-pressed for men, period, and the ones who asked me out had more tattoos than teeth. I remembered Jake's gorgeous face bending toward me and shuddered. "He said we're on very shaky ground, especially after what happened at Jake's office."

"Did Gary," I said, dragging out his name, "tell you if he got the order?"

"Mom, can we go outside?"

"No, Carla. It's dark out."

"In the back yard, Mom. The lights are on. Come on."

"Carla."

"Mommmmm!"

"No." Carla wailed loudly. Conversation ceased while Annie took her up the stairs to their room. Lindsay trailed behind, crying sympathetic tears. Ozzie stood by the back door and yowled for freedom. Resigned, I opened up the door and let him out.

"Sorry," said Annie, sliding back into her seat. "What did the lieutenant say?"

Meese had played Jake well, slightly submissive and certainly in agreement. Jake was confident, explaining the latest twist to his story, my sexual betrayal, Vanessa's outrage. The lieutenant listened sympathetically before informing Jake that he had spoken to Vanessa after the incident with the painted obscenity on her garage. Vanessa, said the lieutenant, was adamant that she was the one being harassed.

"That set him off. I was unstable, irrational, emotionally volatile. Gary calmed him down, then told him that I said I had proof. A caller ID box. Jake got kinda quiet. The way it was left—Jake wanted to get the order, Gary would serve it, but Jake had better be prepared for me to make trouble. If Jake preferred, Gary would speak to me officially and see if that would put a stop to it. Jake agreed." She smiled grimly. "I'm supposed to stay away from Jake, period. That's what he said."

"Did anyone explain that to Jake?" I interjected.

"Well that's what we need to do then," Annie said, sounding almost relieved.

"That's what Vanessa needs to do," I corrected. "There's no order of protection against me."

"I don't know, Kate. This is getting scary. The lieutenant thinks we need to back off before we get hurt."

The phone rang and we all knew who it would be. Annie was closest, so she picked it up.

"Hello. No, this is Annie. May I tell her who's calling?" She covered the mouthpiece with her hand. "It's him!"

"Hang up, Annie," Vanessa said.

"What?" She responded to Jake. "How do you know about that?" Annie had never really dealt with Jake in person, just in theory. "I don't think that's any of your business. And you're no one to talk about David, after what you've done!" Annie said heatedly. Without even thinking, I snatched the phone from her hand.

"For someone who needs an order of protection, you seem to have trouble leaving us alone."

"Katie," he said, genuinely pleased to have an experienced player on the line.

"Jake," I replied conversationally, "did you know that every time you've called we have had a little box record your number. We've had it from the start, we're a high-tech household." No point in telling him we could record what he said now too or he wouldn't give us anything to use against him.

"Miss me?"

"No."

"I think you do."

"You're wrong, as always. As I was saying, that box shows a record of . . ."

"Let's get together. Have another drink. You left too soon, Katie."

"Not soon enough from where I'm sitting." The calm draped itself across my shoulders. I floated there, half-listening to his answer, forgetting that Annie and Vanessa were hanging on each reply.

"You know, sober I would have died before I let you touch me."

"But I did touch you."

"And it killed me," I continued.

"You liked it," he interrupted.

"Killed a part of me that needed to die," I insisted, talking over him. "I owe you for that."

"Is that a threat?"

"It's a thank-you."

He was silent, trying to guess where I was headed.

"It's over, Jake. All of it."

"Have a drink, Katie. You'll change your mind."

"No."

Gently I hung up the phone.

"I don't understand, Kate," Annie asked. "What did he say?"

"Kate, stay off the phone. Don't talk to him again," Vanessa warned.

"He can't hurt me anymore."

"I don't believe you!" She rose angrily and paced the kitchen. "After everything that's happened, how can you be so naive. He will hurt you! Even the lieutenant thinks he's dangerous." She was shouting now. "Every time you talk to him you're daring him to hurt you! I want you to stop!"

"Hey, we're all on the same side," said Annie. "Everybody slow down, okay?" Deep breaths all around. "I think Vanessa is right, Kate. He'd have no qualms about hurting you if he got the opportunity."

"And he'll make one if he has to," Vanessa insisted. "He's already proven that."

"Okay, okay."

"So what can we do," Annie asked, "to protect ourselves?" While Vanessa and I wallowed in the problem, Annie sought solutions. All those years of watching Mr. Rogers were finally paying off.

"Well," I said, "we probably shouldn't count much on the cops."

"No, I don't think so," Annie agreed.

"Maybe we should get a dog, one of those pit bulls," Vanessa suggested.

"Oh, wouldn't the cats love that! Isn't one homicidal maniac enough?"

Annie spoke quickly. "I wouldn't be comfortable with a dog like that around the girls. What else could we do?"

We all thought while Vanessa smoked up a storm.

"Didn't Kate's friend give you that pepper spray?"

Shit, I had forgotten all about those canisters. Where the hell were they?

"Where did you put them, Vanessa?" I poked around in the kitchen drawer.

"Me!"

"Here they are," I exclaimed, gathering them up. I held out one to each of them. Annie took hers gingerly, as if it were a loaded gun. Vanessa checked the label.

"This makes me nervous," Annie said. "I don't like the implication."

"You were one who wanted to know what we could do," I reminded her.

"Just keep them away from the girls," she said.

Vanessa and I put a canister in each of our purses and she went into the office to work. Annie went up stairs and herded the girls to the bathroom over loud protests. Bath time at the barn.

Alone at the kitchen table, I thought about me and Jake. What he had planned for me. How I had followed the plan. I sighed and felt something physical shift inside me. I had stopped drinking, I realized. I had had my last drink. I knew it. Not like the other times, no voices, no excuses, no exceptions. But I would need some help. If I had had my last drink, I would need help. I didn't know how to stop yet, but at least I knew I had to.

But there was still Jake. Two stalkers in my life, both destined to destroy me. Stopping one was not enough. I picked some nail polish off my fingers, noticing the pale strip of skin where I had worn my wedding band. Wedding, wife! That was it!

I dialed Charlie Harrington and caught him as he was leaving. I needed Natalie Romano for a campaign. I had to have her and nobody else. Charlie demurred. He didn't represent her and didn't have a clue where she was.

"But Charlie, I need her and we're just too jammed up to track her down," I improvised. "Come on, I'll give you a finder's fee." I named a number. "You get me Natalie Romano and Steve will cut you a check that day! Promise." If lying was an art form, I was Michelangelo. We haggled over the terms, but in the end, he agreed to try.

We ate dinner sitting around the living room. At Lindsay's request, we ended dinner with a Make-Your-Own-Sundae contest. The girls went for form—towering structures with advanced ideas about function and design. The women went for calories. Peanuts and semi-sweet chocolate were not kid stuff.

It was probably about nine-thirty when the phone rang. The girls had been wiped clean of chocolate sauce and tucked into bed. Vanessa was reading by the fire while Annie and I watched a video.

Vanessa closed her book with a snap. "I haven't had a turn in a while." She picked up the portable in the kitchen. The slap of slippers continued till she was back in the living room entry. "May I tell her who's calling," she asked. She held the phone against her thigh. "Kate? Somebody named Ellen?"

I leapt from my chair. How did she find me? Annie put the video on pause, but I signaled her to go on. I wanted as much background noise as possible. I took the phone back to the kitchen, pausing nonchalantly by the tape recorder and secretly flicking the switch. No way anyone was getting their ears on this conversation. As I left the living room, I heard Van asking Annie, "Who's Ellen?"

"This is Kate."

"Hi, Kate, this is Ellen, Oola's friend. I hope you don't mind, she gave me your number." I don't know why, I wanted her help, but I was suddenly panicked. Immediately I took the offensive, explaining away Oola as co-dependent and deluded. Lying, just like always.

"Oola's worried about you Kate, that's all," she responded pleasantly. "People who don't drink like us don't really understand. It's hard for them. Just ask my husband," she laughed. "I put the poor man through hell!"

" 'Fraid I can't relate. My husband dumped me." I was on edge, poised for battle, determined to fight off the one person who could help me."

"I'm sorry, Kate. If it's any consolation, Ned and I were filing for divorce before I stopped drinking. It took a lot of work, but after I got sober, we managed to put our marriage back together."

"I don't think Steve has the least interest in putting our marriage back together."

"I understand you've been having some trouble. I was always in trouble," she added ruefully. Somehow I couldn't get the image of the beer in the refrigerator out of my mind. "I'd always plan on having just one beer. One beer couldn't hurt."

I froze. The woman was psychic. "You know, Kate, I hardly ever had one beer. Once I had the first one, the second one made more sense. Pretty soon I'd had twenty and was puking my guts out in somebody's car." Her laugh was self-effacing and sincere. I moved further from the refrigerator, amazèd that I had even considered the beer in there . . . I needed help.

"I'm sorry I'm being such a bitch," I murmured.

"It's okay. It's scary to think about quitting."

"I want to, so bad, I do, but I don't know how I can," I blurted desperately. "Drinking is my whole life."

"I know, I felt the same way. That's why I went to AA. There were people there who knew how to live without it. It's that simple."

"I'm afraid," I whispered.

"I'll help you, Kate."

"Why?" What was with this woman! Normal people didn't act this way. They didn't go out of their way for a stranger unless they had a reason. "You don't even know me! Why would you want to help me?"

"But I do know you, Kate. You and I have lived the same life, just in different places." I remembered the night with Jerry. "Ten years ago, I thought it was hopeless, and then a woman brought me to AA. It's gotten better ever since. You need it to get better, don't you?"

"It can't get any worse."

"Oh trust me, Kate, it can. Keep drinking and it'll get worse, I guarantee it. C'mon, let me take you to a meeting. If you don't like it, you don't have to come back."

I wavered, torn between fear and hope. What if I tried this and it didn't work? I'd really be shit out of luck then. Alcoholics Anonymous was a last resort, an ace in the hole that I didn't want to play too soon.

"You can do it, Kate," Ellen said, reading my mind again. "If I can do it, so can you."

We agreed that she'd pick me up at five the next day. As soon as we had set the time I felt relieved and gratified and a little ashamed of myself for resisting. How could I be crying out for help and then reluctant to take it when it came, or picky about the form it would take? Ellen didn't need to hear all that. She stopped me when I started to apologize. She knew.

I skulked back to the living room, feigning total absorption in the video to avoid Vanessa's questions. I don't remember watching it. I just gazed toward the TV, letting my life play out in my head. There were lots of good times, insisted the voice, Jake's the problem. Sitting in Petrillo's, watching old men's hands shake as they reached for a glass. Going to AA, murmured the second, that's for losers. Annie laughed out loud at a scene in the movie, turning her head to share a smile with me. I bared my teeth, pretending to know the joke, while the bluish reflection of the TV played across her battered face. I was the problem. I thought about my Pop, Steve, the guy I pushed in the street. Every bedroom I'd woken up in. Every bathroom floor I'd been lying on. The bounced checks, the unpaid bills. I was the loser. I wanted to stop. I just didn't know if I could.

23

I slept restlessly, tossing and turning into the early morning hours. My body ached and though my period wasn't due, I felt bloated and bitchy nonetheless. Mysterious twinges and prickles wreaked havoc with my nerves. I'd have sworn there were thousands of ants crawling around in the sheets. I only knew there weren't because I checked. Repeatedly.

Groaning, I finally pulled myself off the couch at ten of six. I was hesitant to equate my first day of abstinence to the reaction in my body. Jerry had told me about his withdrawal symptoms: drinking dreams and sleeplessness, nausea, irritability, headaches. Withdrawal was something junkies went through, not me—heroin addicts or crackheads kicking the habit with sweats and restraints. I felt lightheaded and nauseous. If this was life without drinking, I was all for a short life.

I made coffee and watched the sun come up in the kitchen. Annie got up a little after seven. Since I wasn't normally an early riser, my presence impressed her. My appearance, on the other hand, probably scared her. I looked and felt ill, dark circles under my eyes, skin that was clammy and ashen. She fussed over me, placing her palm on my forehead.

"Cut it out, Annie," I barked. "No one can read a temperature that way. I feel bad enough without you crawling all over me."

"You look so sick!"

"I *am* sick! I'm sick of ever one watching me like I'm some kind of laboratory rat!" Where the anger came from I didn't know. "Why don't I just take a Breath-a-lizer every morning? Would that satisfy you?"

"What are you talking about, Kate?"

"Can the innocent act!" I pointed at her accusingly. "I know what you're doing. You and Vanessa and Oola, sniffing around me all the time, waiting for a whiff of Budweiser. Well, screw you!"

"And a very good morning to you too, Kate," Vanessa said from the door. "Remember, Oola said she'd be irritable," she reassured Annie. "It's like somebody who's trying to quit smoking."

I hated being spoken about as if I were not in the room. "Speaking of which, let's take a look at your habit, Vanessa."

"I don't go sneaking off for hours on end to smoke cigarettes with nasty old men till I end up rolling around on rest room floors or in bed with the first psychopath I meet. If it comes to that, I'll quit."

I was able to let that one slide without fighting back or crying. If I'd cried she would have started to feel sorry for me again. The way I felt at the moment more pity would have been as bad as the rest room floor.

I sulked in my chair while they made breakfast. I ignored Annie's questions about eggs or toast and soon they ignored me back. It sucked, giving the silent treatment to people who liked it. I didn't know why I was acting this way. It wasn't that I didn't want to stop, but wanting and doing were two different things.

The girls tumbled down the stairs a half an hour later, chattering incessantly about Kevin and Calvin next door. Through mouthfuls of toast they informed their mother of their plans for the day. Nintendo for Carla, Fisher Price farm set for Lindsay. No such toys at Vanessa's, Annie reminded them. Kevin and Calvin had them, they cried. Though it didn't faze Annie, Vanessa was a sucker of the first order.

She put in a call to Heather and wheedled permission for a return visit. Vanessa passed this on to Annie, who gave in willingly. The children ceased whining instantly, smug in their victory. The old ask-for-one-thing, settle-for-what-you-really-wanted ploy, I thought admiringly. It took another hour for the kids to get ready and go. Annie had just walked in the door after dropping them off when the phone rang. I looked up from the paper as she picked it up. Vanessa was in the office, committing mass murder on her computer.

"Hello?" Her face paled and she leaned against the counter.

"Who is it, Annie?" I asked, sure it was Jake.

"Hold on, please," she said into the phone. She pushed the mute button before replying. "It's David."

I wanted to insist on handling it but my resume wasn't exactly up to speed. Annie put her hand over the mouthpiece and looked at me, nodding toward the door with her head. It wasn't easy but I forced myself to go. She seemed sadder after the call, coming to join me in the living room.

"Are you okay?" I asked.

"I think so. There's still so much anger."

"You have a right to be angry, Annie!"

"Kate," she sighed, "this isn't as one-sided as you want it to be!"

From the looks of Annie's profile, it was as one-sided as it could get. What was it with women who got beat up and kept going back for more of the same? It set the rest of us up to be idiots. After all, we only had Annie's story about the broken arm, the elbow jab. If she wanted me to believe she was lying before, then how could I be sure she wasn't lying now.

"Annie, you have to face this! The guy pounded the crap out of you! Let me give you the number of the lawyer who handled my divorce."

"Divorce?" Annie squeaked. "I'm not ready for a divorce."

"Who's shouting in here," Vanessa said, coming out of her office.

"Annie's planning on going back to play a little more pattycake with David." Vanessa would set her straight.

"I don't know much about working things out," she answered. "I never stayed around long enough to try. Just stay safe," she said to Annie, adding to me, "It's her life, Kate."

It might have been Annie's life, but I knew one thing for sure. If I was going to an AA meeting, she was divorcing David. It was only fair.

Oola called mid-morning with a cold and a scratchy throat. It was snowing in Connecticut and she was staying home. It was trying to snow here with little success, more like rain with an attitude. She asked if Ellen had called and I cast around for a way to change the subject. Stupidly I picked the personal ad.

"So come Wednesday, we won't have to worry. Jake will be busy making plans with Chester the Molester."

"Don't you dare joke, Kate. How could you do this!"

"Oh, come on Oola. Don't tell me you're concerned about Jake's feelings."

"I don't give a damn about Jake's feelings," she responded. "How could you write an ad to someone who rapes children." She didn't have to be so harsh. That wasn't what I'd done.

"Oola, this isn't about children . . ."

"No you are absolutely right, Kate," she interrupted. "This is about you! I can't believe you even considered this idea, much less actually carried it out. Of course it's about the children! And you used their predators, you called up their predators just to get a reaction from Jake!"

"Don't you protect him, Oola, not to me!"

"Protect him! I'm trying to protect you, from becoming just like him!"

"Look, it's not the same thing." Trust Oola to psychoanalyze an innocent prank, sneered the voice. "Jake and the creeps who answer this ad . . . they deserve each other!"

"Who are you to . . ." She broke off with an frustrated sigh. "I am not going to argue about this. Next time, Kate, before any actions are taken, all of us should be involved in the decision," she said, not giving an inch. "I'm very upset with you."

"No kidding," I muttered.

Oola hung up abruptly. I stuck my hands in my pockets and sulked. I was not a mean person. Oola was trying to make this something it wasn't.

"I had to do it," I said out loud, convincing myself.

"Had to do what?" asked Annie, returning from the bathroom.

"Oh, Oola's upset about the personal ad."

"What ad?" Annie said anxiously. "Oh no, Kate. We agreed it was a bad idea. Why?"

"He does it! He called Vanessa's mom, dated that girl from the publishing house, even messed with Oola's own patient," I blurted defensively. "I wanted him to see how awful he really is."

Annie looked solemn. "And what Oola saw is how awful we could be."

That shut me up. But it wasn't fair.

"Annie, we have to fight back!"

"I know and I'm sure Oola does, too. It's how we fight,

Kate. Maybe you went a little too far." We walked back to the kitchen, Annie subdued, me annoyed. I had been looking forward to Jake getting his mail but now that expectation was tainted. I needed to do something to perk myself up. I didn't give the little voice a chance.

"Why don't we go find him, Annie? The kids are at Heather's anyway and Vanessa will be home."

"You mean to follow Jake? The lieutenant said . . ."

"The lieutenant meant Vanessa," I replied. "If we don't do it, he's going to think we're scared."

"I *am* scared."

"I am too. But we can't let him know. Come on, we'll stay in the car."

"I suppose we could. I've never done it." There was a little spark of excitement in her voice.

"I'm going to take a shower," I told her. "If you want, call around to see if you can find him. That way we'll know where to start."

I went upstairs and hopped in the shower. The Listerine bottle no longer scared me, but the mirror was definitely not my friend. Stepping from the stall, I wrapped a towel around my body to avoid the sight and brushed my teeth as fast as possible. I dug through a pile of doll clothes and coloring books in my old room, looking for anything clean to wear. Laundry was a definite need. I finally located a pair of black leggings and a huge gray sweater that covered most of my thighs. Annie was waiting downstairs.

"I called Oola back," she said. "It's okay."

I really didn't care. I was tired of everyone second-guessing my decisions. Let Oola come out and deal—see how she did!

"Let's go," I replied. We got in the car and headed for the city, stopping to gas up before we got on the highway. My VISA card was maxed, so Annie laid out the cash while I tried to recall my last payment. Definitely nothing since Thanksgiving, I decided guiltily.

Annie buckled her seat belt and gave me the eye as we pulled onto the expressway. My driving reputation preceded me. I made a point of using my turn signals and kept my speed below sixty-five. She fiddled with the radio and found a classic rock station in the midst of a Beatles marathon.

"Did you find out where he is?" I asked her. We were about twenty minutes from the Queens exit.

"No," she replied. "There was no answer at his house and his secretary said she wasn't sure when he'd be in."

"Did you try the car?"

"No, I forgot."

We decided to swing by the office first, in case he had shown up. The rain had trailed off into grungy sunshine. Suddenly Annie sat up straight.

"Kate, look!"

"Look where?" I answered.

"Behind us! I think he's behind us!" She scrunched in her seat, peering at the side mirror.

"What!" I twisted to look over my shoulder. The steering wheel followed my lead and the car in the next lane beeped indignantly. "Shit!" I straightened the wheels and sneered at the other driver, who was telling me off with both hands. "Where? I don't see him. Are you sure, Annie?" I kept one eye on the road and one eye on the rearview mirror.

"I'm pretty sure," she answered, peeking over her shoulder. "There! Right behind the brown van. See him, Kate?"

A gray BMW slid past the van and fell in behind a blue Nissan three cars back and one lane over. The driver was the BMW's sole occupant. A silver sheen floated above the steering wheel and I realized it was a reflection from mirrored sunglasses. I clenched my jaw angrily.

"It's him. The son of a bitch must have been out at the barn." I was pissed. How dare he follow us when we were going to follow him!

"What should we do?" Annie asked nervously.

I didn't answer. Instead I whipped into the right lane, keeping my eyes on the mirror. My foot left the accelerator and the car slowed, much to the frustration of the driver behind. He swerved angrily around us, flipping me the bird.

We had dropped back a car length and Jake was only two cars behind in the middle lane. I didn't know if he saw us, but assumed he did. He followed the blue Nissan closely, hugging its bumper. I dropped back even with it, then cut my wheels sharply to the left.

The driver of the Nissan jolted sideways, lunging into the far lane to avoid the Phoenix's fender. Horns blasted and Annie shrieked, but I forced the car into the lane, planting us directly in front of the BMW. Jake hit the brakes and his car skidded to the left before straightening behind us. I looked grimly in the mirror, sweaty palms stuck to the wheel. His face was twisted in a snarl. That was worth every obscenity the other drivers threw at me.

"Kate, please be careful," Annie pleaded.

"I am," I replied through clenched teeth. He pulled up behind us, cars so tight they were almost touching. I accelerated to gain a little ground, then took my foot off the gas and quickly flicked my lights on and off. The red glow from behind flashed back to me in the mirror. He reacted reflexively, pumping the brake pedal to avoid an imagined collision. I accelerated again, pulling away. I saw him push his hair from his forehead and lean into the wheel. He came up on us again.

We were getting close to the city now. Traffic was tying up; there would be less opportunity to control the situation. The Beatles were surreal now, like listening to Muzak while you're trapped in an elevator.

"Annie, I've got to get us off the highway. There's an exit coming up and we're taking it. So hold on, okay?" I looked over at her. She was clutching the door handle, eyes wide with fright.

"Kate, I'm scared. I'm really scared!"

"That's what he wants, Annie. Just hold on and it'll be okay."

"Kate, look out!"

I looked up. The rearview mirror reflected a green Toyota. The BMW was gone. "He's coming up on the right, Kate. On the right!"

He was in my blind spot. I had to turn my head to see him. He was almost abreast of Annie's door, a fixed smile on his mirrored face. The exit was approaching fast. I was getting off, I thought stubbornly, and he wasn't going to stop me. No more. I swerved a trifle to scare him, but he didn't give ground. I was still doing sixty, my driving skills stretched to the limit.

"Hold on, Annie, I'm getting off!"

"Kate, you can't! There's no room!" She was near panic.

"I'm gonna make room. Just hold the fuck on!" He wouldn't let me in the lane. Less than fifty yards away, the exit ramp split from the highway. A large concrete buttress sat between the two, directly in our path, yellow and black stripes screaming for attention. I forced air out of my lungs. I had been holding my breath. Less than twenty-five yards now and he still didn't give.

"Kate," Annie screamed.

I slashed the wheel to the right. The Phoenix surged forward, spread-eagled across the exit lane. He had no choice but to slam on the brakes or hit us dead on. Though I'm sure he was tempted, his tires screamed, black rubber skid marks commemorating the spot. Annie yelped as her seat belt battled the momentum. I cut the wheel back and the car lurched into position with a shudder, half on the ramp, half on the shoulder. He was still struggling to control his car. All I had to do was hit the gas and we were out of there. I pressed the accelerator, escape at hand. The Phoenix, pushed beyond its endurance, stalled.

"Come on, baby, come on." I cranked the ignition desperately, but it didn't respond. I put the car in neutral, and it rolled a few yards down the ramp. "Not now, dammit, come on!" I cranked again, the engine close to flooding. I hit the steering wheel in frustration, and he pulled up in front of us, blocking our way.

"Kate! Oh god, Kate!" Annie said, looking frantically from me to Jake's car. His door sprang open and he burst out of the BMW, as angry as I'd ever seen him. "Kate, he's coming! Go, go!" She grabbed my upper arm.

"I can't!" I shook her off. The panic was suffocating. He was coming up on the car, hand reaching for my door, keys dangling from his gloved fingers. A second too late, I reached for the lock button. Before I tumbled from the car as he jerked the door open, the shoulder strap yanked me back into place. Buckle up for safety, I thought crazily.

"What the fuck is wrong with you? Stupid bitch!" His fury was impressive, good looks blazing with heat. I shrank back into my seat.

"Get away from my car," I squeaked, betrayed by my own voice. Splashes of bright light danced in front of my eyes and I felt faint. I heard a door open and slam and suddenly Annie was standing in front of the car. Oh no.

She rounded the hood and faced him off by the Phoenix's

left front tire. He gave her the consideration an elephant gives a flea, intent on his real prey.

"You leave her alone!" Annie shouted, the open door between them. "Get away from her, right now!" There was a ludicrous side to this that I knew I'd appreciate later. Annie was speaking to Jake as if he were Carla, certain he would obey her in fear of being sent to his room.

He looked her over cruelly. "Nice face! Shut up and stay out of this! Get out of the car, Katie!" He reached into the Phoenix to pull me from the seat. I scrambled backwards, still tangled in my seat belt. I was trapped.

Annie reached over the door and jerked his coat sleeve, hard. His arm flew up and the back of his hand smacked the roof of the Phoenix where it curved to meet the door. There was a satisfying crack as bone met steel—the rubber sealant around my doors had long since rotted away. The keys to the BMW dropped, skittering off the steering wheel and landing on the floor hump between the seats.

"Ow! You bitch!" He growled, attention now focused on Annie. A car whizzed by us, then another, the second driver staring curiously. Have a car phone, I prayed, call the police. Jake reached over the door and grabbed the front of Annie's coat. Her weight swung the door against him and he stepped to the side, pulling Annie with him. Her face was set, but calm. Another car passed by and suddenly my rage took hold.

The seat belt finally released, I leapt from the car, throwing the door wide. It brushed the back of his right leg, and his knee gave way. I charged at him, pounding his shoulder with the side of my fist. Annie squirmed free and he wheeled to face me.

"Get away from us!" I yelled, winding up to hit him again.

I never had a chance. He jabbed two gloved fingers into the hollow of my throat. My ranting ceased instantly, as did my breathing, and I staggered back against the car. I bounced off the Phoenix, struggling to regain my balance. I watched him move toward me as if in slow motion. I saw his face loom, his tightly clenched teeth framed between thinly stretched lips. I attempted to dodge away but he clobbered me with the flat of his palm, the blow landing squarely on the tip of my nose.

The pain was excruciating. For a second, I thought the bone

had been driven into my brain. Blood gushed from each nostril, and I slid down the car to the ground, legs wide and ungainly. Annie rushed to me, pushing past him to squat at my side. Dizzy, I choked and blew blood bubbles out my nose.

There was red blood on Jake's coat, or perhaps it was just my eyes. I watched his feet walk away, and Annie jumped up. Now the red was on her. It seemed to be flashing. Comprehension dawned when I heard her say, "Officer, he hit my friend. Don't let him leave."

Who says cops are never around when you need them? The officers had wandered upon us after exiting the expressway and thought they were at the scene of an accident. Jake and Annie battled for their attention while I bled all over myself. The pain in my nose had diminished to a dull ache, but the gushing continued unabated. I made no attempt to stem its flow. A bloody victim is a believable one.

I stayed on the ground, letting Annie explain. One of the officers knelt beside me, asking if I was all right. I nodded and gurgled. She instructed me to tilt my head back and went to the patrol car for Kleenex. I packed my nose with the tissue as ordered and played victim to the hilt.

Jake attempted to explain, an outrageous tale of being forced from the road by a crazy person, presumably me. Annie defended me like F. Lee Bailey, eloquently pointing from Jake to my nose. The officer squatted beside me again. Did I want to press charges?

You bet your ass I did. I struggled to my feet, staggering a bit for effect and watched them handcuff Jake Romano. He'd turned to stone, recently molten stone still radiating heat.

The officers gave us directions to a nearby emergency room and handed Annie a business card. We would need to come to the station and sign a statement. I was becoming an old hand at police procedure. I smiled bravely, an honest citizen willing to do my part in the war on crime. I risked a quick triumphant glance at Jake, my eyes gleaming. He stared straight ahead from the back seat of the patrol car, nostrils flared, body rigid. Forget the excitement of the chase, there was nothing quite so thrilling as the capture.

24

Annie got behind the wheel and started the Phoenix. It coughed a bit before complying. She backed away from the BMW while the officer radioed for a tow, and I turned for one more look at Jake. Annie's hands were shaking on the wheel. She drove only a few blocks before pulling over on a side street, turning off the car and resting her head on the wheel.

"I never want to go through something like that again," she said, turning a drawn face to me. "I though he was going to kill you, Kate. Just like Vanessa said."

"It'll take more than Jake to kill me." Though my nose still hurt, I was exhilarated. I relished the thought of Jake in jail, fingerprinted and strip-searched. "I bet Jake's gonna make a lot of friends in the slammer," I joked, "pretty as he is."

"I don't know how you can laugh about it, Kate," Annie scolded. "We could have been killed. Why did you have to try and get off when he wouldn't let you in the lane?" Her voice rose accusingly. I squirmed in response. "He would have crashed right into me!"

"I don't know. Ever since he had his hands on me I've been mad and so calm at the same time. I know it seems reckless to you, but I feel like nothing can happen to me. I may be the lowest person on earth, but Jake Romano won't get the best of me. And look how it turned out—Jake's a jailbird."

"And you think I'm naive! He'll be back at his office in a couple of hours, Kate. What do you think he'll do then?"

I hadn't considered that. A queasy feeling settled in my stomach. Vanessa was alone at the house. We needed to step up our protective measures. I thought for a moment, then it hit me. Bobby! Bobby could help us. Given today's situation, it was time to bring in a professional.

"C'mon Annie, let's go. We're going into the city," I said, meaning Manhattan.

"Kate, you need to see a doctor," she protested. "And we have to go to the police station."

"We can do that on the way back. They think I'm going to the emergency room anyway," I argued.

I lowered the window visor and looked at my nose in the vanity mirror. Nothing to be vain about here. Red and swollen but not broken, I thought, gingerly touching the tip.

"I'm okay, Annie, really. It's mostly blood. I wanna go see Bobby, the guy who gave us the spray." Annie just looked at me, making no move to start the car. "You're right. We need more help. Come on, start the car." Shaking her head, Annie turned the ignition. The Phoenix jolted forward and the keys slid down the hump onto my foot. It took a split second to remember where they came from and less than that to scoop them up.

"This is definitely against my better judgment, Kate. You should go to the hospital and home. Stop bending over, you're supposed to keep your head back."

"Look," I said, obediently leaning back against the seat, "I don't wanna present this mess to Vanessa without something to lessen the shock. After we talk to Bobby, I promise I'll go home and be good. Girl Scout's honor." I held up four fingers, switched to three, then back to four.

"Obviously your honor is rusty," Annie commented wryly. "If I recall correctly, Kate, you never made it out of the Brownies. Didn't you push Susie Ingston's face into her hand-print clay?"

"I did not. I can't believe you said that," I answered indignantly.

"You did, too! I sat right next to you and watched you do it! The poor girl had clay in her eyelashes."

Annie reentered the expressway as we bickered. I fingered the keys in my pocket as we talked, letting an idea form. We crossed into Manhattan and I directed a nervous Annie uptown, wincing as she repeatedly gave ground to more aggressive drivers. It made me crazy. People from the suburbs should learn how to drive. Between them and the jerks from Jersey, they gave New Yorkers a bad name.

We circled the block of Bobby's office numerous times

before I coaxed Annie into a parking garage. If we waited for a space that suited her, we'd be members of the AARP. We got our ticket and went to Bobby's building, stopping in the lobby restroom for a cleanup.

My already sparse wardrobe was taking a serious beating these days. The gray sweater was streaked with rusty maroon from collar to bust. My face was smeared with blood, enough to earn me a guest spot in one of Vanessa's books. I scrubbed my face, unearthing a ghostly but blackening shadow beneath one eye. Good, I thought, the worse I look, the worse it's going to be for Jake.

We rode up the elevator to the sixteenth floor. From behind a large but tasteful floral arrangement, an exquisitely groomed receptionist gave me a careful once-over. Her suspicions were confirmed by my lack of appointment. Some microscopic adjustment was turning her smile into a sneer. Mr. Rourke was on the phone, she said, meaning Bobby. A number of lines and lights blinked on her master phone, so I couldn't debate the statement though I didn't necessarily buy it. Annie had seated herself on the beige leather couch. I plopped into an armchair where I could stare a hole through the receptionist's forehead. She answered calls and took messages unperturbed. Bitch.

She spoke discreetly into the phone, face pointedly turned away from me. She called to me from across the room, requesting my name once again. A cheap shot. I spelled it for her, and she curled her lip in response. Annie thumbed through a magazine, oblivious to my latest battle. I pulled my trump card and asserted my personal friendship with Bobby's uncle, just so she knew who she was dealing with. She'd obviously dealt with Uncle Chubb because her disdainful expression never wavered. I was imagining her hair pulling her face into a paper shredder when Bobby strode into the room.

"Kate," he said, hand outstretched. He stopped as he got his first clear look at my face. "What happened? Tina," he ordered Miss Priss. "Bring some ice and clean towels to my office. And some sandwiches from next door. You ladies are hungry, right? The pastrami's good. They have turkey."

We ordered turkey and pastrami, to please Bobby, mainly. I was still too excited to think about food and I'm sure Annie was, too.

After I'd introduced Annie he ushered us toward his office. Tina came in with the ice just after we were seated. I applied it to my nose while Annie told the tale. Bobby sighed and twisted his mouth, warning signs of an impending I-told-you-so. I beat him to the punch.

"I know you told me not to handle this on my own, Bobby. That's why we're here."

"Thank you for seeing us without an appointment," Annie said. "I'm sure you're very busy."

"Kate, only you," he replied, nodding at Annie. "I warned you not to get in the middle of this. You're crazy!"

"Okay, all right." I gave ground grudgingly, just to keep things moving. "I've gotten in a little over my head, I'll grant you that. But we've got him on the run, Bobby!"

"Oh yeah, I can see that by your face!" Bobby came around the desk and carefully removed my ice pack. He examined my nose gently.

"Well, your nose isn't broken."

"I'm almost sorry. That would be more to nail Jake with. Look, Bobby, we need some help. Are you gonna help us or not?"

I gathered up my coat, as if to leave. Before he could reply the lovely Tina opened the door. She carried a cardboard box of sandwiches with a noticeable lack of enthusiasm which I countered with a yawn.

"Kate's been under a lot of strain lately," Annie explained. "She needs a rest."

"What Kate really needs is a stiff drink," he answered, his back to us while he fiddled with a cabinet behind the desk. He turned around saying, "What's your pleasure, ladies? There's some wine, a little rum and some Tanqueray. How about a gin and tonic, Kate?"

Yes, my body screamed.

"No," my mouth replied. The traitor. "I'll just have a soda."

"Me too," said Annie.

"On the wagon, Kate?" Bobby asked, setting out plastic glasses with ice.

"No, I just don't feel like having a drink," I lied. "Look, I didn't come here for cocktails. Are you going to help us or not?"

"Of course I'm going to help you, Kate." He was distributing the sandwiches.

I pushed aside my sandwich and leaned forward in my chair. "Bobby, can I get a restraining order or whatever it is? I mean, since he hit me?"

He chewed thoughtfully. "You could try, Kate, but I doubt it. You said he's filed a complaint against you?

"Against Vanessa, but only kind of. There's no paper work."

"But there is a record," Bobby said. "Face it, Kate. He beat you to the punch. Once his attorney gets hold of this, you'll be the bad guy."

"This is not about me," I replied hotly. "This is about Jake."

"I know who it's about, Kate. I'm just trying to answer your question."

"Mr. Rourke," Annie said, "what do we need to do?"

"We need to be able to prove that he's repeatedly demonstrated malicious intent. And please, call me Bob." He smiled at Annie. "I think you need to understand how the law works. It's a common misperception that in New York state there's a quote, stalking law, unquote. That's not quite true."

Annie looked puzzled. "But I thought they passed that law a couple of years ago?" I nodded vigorously, my mouth full of pastrami.

"What actually occurred was an elevation of degree for two existing laws. I looked it up after Kate and I first talked." Bobby shoved a quarter of a sandwich in his mouth and chewed. My head bobbed in rhythm with his jaws. He swallowed a huge lump of food that rolled past his Adam's apple, then wiped the Russian dressing from his chin. "The best our legal system could do in regards to stalking was some statutes pertaining to harassment and menacing. Here, let me pull it up." He settled himself behind the computer and punched in a file name.

"Okay, let's look at harassment first. Prior to the change in law, first-degree harassment was considered a violation, kind of like a traffic ticket. You pay your fine and that's that. The new law demoted the violation offense to second-degree and wrote a new statute for first-degree harassment. That was designated a Class B misdemeanor, which has criminal penalties attached. Are you with me so far?"

"Yes," Annie and I said together.

"Good," Bobby continued. "The new harassment statute focused on repeated acts. Let me read it. Umm, 'guilty . . . when repeatedly harasses another person by following such person . . . or by repeatedly committing acts which place such person in reasonable fear of physical injury.' The big issue then becomes what constitutes reasonable fear."

"Didn't this come up during the Bernard Goetz trial?" Annie asked. "Something about his previous muggings as a basis for his defense?"

"You're right. It was a different application, but the idea was the same. So to prosecute for first-degree harassment, we have to show a malicious pattern of repeated acts that place the victim in reasonable fear." Bobby paused to read further down the screen. "Now, the menacing statute was broken up into three degrees. Like harassment, the original offense became the lowest of them."

"It's unbelievable that someone can do the things Jake does and have it called menacing! He's a terrorist, plain and simple," I griped.

"Menacing under the current penal law is considered a form of attempted assault, Kate." Bobby stopped for a sip of his Coke. "Though the victim is not actually assaulted, because he or she believes an attack is pending, he or she experiences reasonable fear of serious physical injury."

"I've experienced reasonable reality of serious physical injury! Doesn't that count for anything?"

"You were hit, Kate," Bobby chided. "That's a different statute. The law is very specific and complex."

"Kill all the lawyers," I muttered.

"Come on, Kate, listen," Annie told me. "Go on, Bob."

"The new second-degree menacing statute does confer a higher penalty as a Class A misdemeanor. But the really important change was that repeat offenders of either second-degree menacing or first-degree harassment are subject to prosecution for a higher classification of crime. Repeated offenses fall under the new first-degree menacing statute, which is a Class E felony."

"How many offenses?"

"That's discretionary, Kate."

"So," Annie processed slowly, "Jake has to be arrested and

convicted more than once before the law recognizes him as a stalker. And we don't even know how many times it takes. That makes it hard."

"Hard, it's ridiculous!" I snapped.

"It's the law. Call your legislator and bitch at him," Bobby replied. "So, the question is, can the DA prove repeated acts that place Vanessa in reasonable fear?"

"Of course not," I answered. "Even the lieutenant's backing off and he was the only one on our side. Jake knows exactly how to work the system."

"He didn't do so hot today," Bobby pointed out.

"But what happened today was scary," Annie protested. "And dangerous. Look what he did to Kate. There's got to be another solution."

"I don't mean to pry," Bobby asked her gently. "But did Romano have anything to do with your face?"

Once again, I'd completely forgotten about Annie's bruises. Their color had faded to yellowish green with scattered patches of purple showing under the skin. Her eye was fairly normal, the cuts closed and scabbed. Despite the vast improvement, it was no wonder Tina had been suspicious. Between my nose and Annie's face, we looked like escapees from a plastic surgery clinic in some third-world hell. I watched as a blush mottled her already colorful skin.

"No. This has nothing to do with Jake," she answered, head down. Nobody replied and she cleared her throat. "My husband and I had a fight. We're staying with Kate and Vanessa until I figure out what to do."

Bobby looked at her carefully and shifted his weight in the chair, debating comment. "There's a lot more help out there these days for you and your husband," he said quietly. "Good luck with it."

"So what are we going to do? About Jake, I mean?" I was still uncomfortable discussing Annie's marriage. "What if we hire you to follow him, Bobby? Then we could prove repetition and intent."

"We do offer bodyguard services, Kate."

"I don't want a guard. I need a tracker," I insisted. "Can't you keep him under surveillance, you know, with a bunch of guys hiding in a van?" I was liking the sound of that. I could see myself on a stakeout, surrounded by high-tech equipment, using night-scopes and listening devices.

"Kate, Romano's not the only one who's subject to criminal penalties," Bobby answered. "Whether you like it or not, he's got rights, too."

"You could follow him, couldn't you? Like a private detective does for a divorce, when one person wants dirt on the other. They do it all the time," I asserted scornfully.

"In the movies they do it all the time."

Annie spoke up. "What if you could follow him—not bug his phone or anything—but just follow his car? If we paid you to keep track of his movements, then we'd have evidence to prove what he's doing. Could you do that?"

Bobby nodded. "Yeah, but it would take a lot of people and a lot of cash. And it might go on for a long time. Given the arrest, he'll probably rethink his strategy."

"Do you think it will make him stop?" asked Annie.

"It could, but I doubt it," he replied. "If he's pissed off enough, it might even motivate him."

"Trust me, he's plenty pissed off. Hey, wait." I had thought of something. "Bobby, couldn't you put one of those things on his car?" I touched my pocket to reassure myself the keys were still there. "You know, a homing device? Like the FBI uses to trace the delivery of a ransom without alerting the kidnappers? Then it wouldn't take a lot of people," I added excitedly, "and Jake wouldn't even know you were around."

"Jesus, Kate! You can't just tap into someone's life without their knowledge."

I stood, waving my arms at him. "Get real, Bobby! You could do it and you know it. You have the equipment, don't you?" He avoided my eyes. "I thought so! Give us a week. Come on, do it for one week. If we don't get anything we can use, we'll take it off and nobody will ever know," I coaxed.

Bobby squirmed uncomfortably. "I don't know, Kate."

"It would really help," Annie added softly. "With everything he's doing, don't you think we deserve an edge? I'm afraid of what might happen if he isn't stopped." Her simple statement, delivered from her damaged face, had more impact than all my arguments put together. Bobby crumbled like stale toast.

"One week," he conceded. "And nobody knows, except us!"

"Thank you," Annie said.

"We have to tell Vanessa," I pointed out.

"Okay, but no one else."

"Oola," I added hurriedly.

"Jesus, why don't we just send out a press release!"

"That's it, honest! You're great, Bobby, the best!"

"Crazy is more like it. What I want from you is information on his whereabouts. I need access to his car when I'm sure he's otherwise occupied." We nodded and he looked at his watch. "Shit! I'm late for a meeting. Annie, it was good meeting you. Kate, say hi to Chubb when you see him." He rose and extended an arm toward the door. Annie stood obediently.

"Bobby," I said, not moving from my chair. "Do you mind if we stay for a minute and use the phone?" I never could quit when I was ahead. He rolled his eyes in response.

"Take the whole office!" He waved his arms expansively. "How about some money? Wanna borrow my car?"

"Thank you," I said sweetly. He glared and slammed some papers in a briefcase. He nodded again at Annie and left, hopefully validating our presence with Tina.

"Kate, you have no shame," Annie said as soon as he'd gone.

"Bobby doesn't mind." I brushed away petty concerns of courtesy as I dialed. "I want to call Vanessa and fill her in. We still have to stop at the police station, and I don't want her to worry."

Vanessa's reaction was as expected—big. I repeatedly assured her we were fine, playing up the outcome, not the incident. She insisted on speaking to Annie, clearly unwilling to rely on my version of the truth. I swirled the ice in my soda, and looked at the clock on Bobby's desk. In less than four hours, Ellen was coming. My stomach churned. I needed more time.

"Can you pick the girls up from Heather's?" Annie was saying. "We have to stop at the police station. It will be after four at least before we get home, even later if we get stuck in rush hour." I sat up straight. Annie was winding down the conversation, and I gestured for the phone.

"Hold on, Kate wants to talk to you," she said, handing over the receiver.

"Vanessa, can you do me a favor? Call Oola and tell her what happened. Then tell her this for me. I was supposed to go somewhere tonight with a friend of hers. I'm not going to be able to make it back on time, and I need Oola to call her for me." How perfect. I didn't have to go to the meeting, but best of all, I didn't have to cancel. "I'd do it myself, but I don't have the number with me," I lied.

"What friend of Oola's? Where were you going?" Vanessa wanted to know.

"Could you just do it, please, without the third degree!" People could make such a big deal out of the simplest things. "Look, we have to go. Bobby needs his office back," I was avoiding Annie's eyes. "See you in a little while."

I hung up and headed for the door. Now that our schedule was cleared, I had a plan. All I had to do was talk Annie into it. She trailed behind me, pursing her lips. As we neared Tina, busy at her desk, I slowed to a halt, the flowers a barricade between us. Annie continued past me and rang for the elevator.

Tina looked up with narrowed eyes and deliberately I reached into the bowl and yanked a red carnation from the mix. "Hey," she said, glaring furiously. I nodded and tucked the flower under my coat as the elevator arrived. Annie saw it anyway and scolded me on the trip down, but I didn't care. I could afford to be magnanimous. Life had taken an unexpected turn for the good and it was about to get better.

25

I insisted on driving back to Queens. Though Annie protested, I knew she was relieved. The whole way there I thought about how to broach my idea. Annie was pretty straightlaced; it wouldn't be easy. We made it to the police station in record time, though the cops took my statement with little interest. We tried to find out Jake's current status but no one seemed to know where he was nor were they inclined to find out. He might have been in holding, or he might have been arraigned and released. The thought made me nervous. His confinement was very pertinent to my plan. But, as Annie pointed out patiently and repeatedly, there was no point in arguing. I got the feeling that everyone knew something about dealing with the police that I didn't.

"Annie, before we go home, there's something I have to do."

"What now, Kate? I'm tired and the girls will need to eat."

"Vanessa will feed them. Or Heather." I waited, then it came. "Annie, are you sure you can handle this thing with Jake?"

"Of course I can. What do you mean?"

"Well, you did get pretty upset in the car," I replied, avoiding the expressway and turning the car downtown. "I mean, when you grabbed my arm . . . well . . . I was trying to steer and maybe you just panicked, but . . . we could have really gotten hurt." She bit like a trout on a fly.

"That wasn't my fault. I was scared, yeah, but you were the one who drove like a maniac."

I let her go on, sticking in just enough concerned doubts to work her up. There was nothing wrong with not being able to handle something, I told her, but for everyone's safety we needed to know.

"Kate, I am more than capable of doing my part in this. Whatever it takes. I'm just as willing as you are!" Perfect!

"I'm glad to hear that, Annie."

She glared out the window, still mulling over her indignation and muttering while I drove. It wasn't until we swung the corner near Prospect Park that she realized what I was up to.

"Kate," she hissed. "This is Brooklyn. What are you doing in Brooklyn?"

"Bobby wanted us to find out about Jake's schedule. You said you were willing to help."

The innocent approach never worked for me. Annie was hollering before I even found the right street. I bickered back to keep her diverted and found a spot in front of a hydrant three buildings down from Jake's. I turned off the car and waited for her to wind down.

"I will not be a peeping . . ." She was saying as I opened the car door. "Kate," she screeched, grabbing at the tail of my coat. "Where are you going?"

"Annie, there's got to be something in that apartment that will prove who Jake is, and I'm going to get it," I answered. "If you want to come with me, fine, but I'm going." I shook her hand off my coat and grabbed the carnation off the dashboard. I stood in front of his building, looking up at the blank windows when Annie hustled up.

"Kate . . ." I held up my hand to silence her. The afternoon light was dwindling. Shadows of the trees stroked the brownstone with skinny, arthritic fingers. The chill in the air gathered around the nape of my neck and I shivered in my coat. The enemy lived here. I felt the fear start, my fingertips and feet tingling as if they had been asleep. The keys were heavy in my pocket, their weight almost ominous. Maybe Annie was right, I thought.

"Kate," she whispered, though no one else was near us on the street. "You can't do this. It's wrong." I thought of Jake Romano sitting in his car, watching Vanessa, hour after hour. Wrong was just not the right word.

I started forward, shushing Annie's whispered "How . . . ?" by pulling the keys from my pocket. The BMW emblem glinted in the fading daylight. I swallowed nervously and checked the intercom speakers to the left of the door. J. Romano was in apartment 3C. It took two tries to find the right key, but the heavy wooden door swung open into a long narrow corridor.

"Kate, please." Annie pleaded, but followed me in. My eyes adjusted to the overhead light and I located a stairway at the end of the hall. I forced my feet to move and headed toward it. "What if he's here?" she hissed.

What if he was? It was too late. My foot was on the first step when I looked back at her, still hovering by the door. "We have the keys. He can't be here." I turned my back and started climbing. She caught up with me on the landing and we continued together. In silence. Every footstep boomed. Sounds drifted from passing apartments, a radio, children squabbling. Normal sounds exaggerated and harsh.

There was the door. A square buzzer with a round button sat underneath a tiny peephole. Two locks above the knob. I swallowed hard and lifted the keys with a shaking hand. I had just touched a key to the surface of the first lock when Annie cried out.

"Wait! We can't do this!"

"Dammit, Annie, you scared me half to death," I growled, glancing around the empty hallway. "Look, I scratched the fucking lock plate. Jesus!" I spit on my finger and rubbed at the shiny scratch in the dull metal, as if it were important. I cut her a nasty look and she subsided. I turned the first key and fumbled for another. This one was harder to find, but after a couple of tries, a key fit. I stood for second, a spasm teasing my shoulders, and took a deep breath.

"Wait," Annie said again, over my shoulder. I glared, annoyed but curiously relieved. She reached past me and pushed the button on the door. We could hear the muffled bing-bong of the doorbell. I held my breath and waited. She pushed it again. Nothing, but the fading memory of the sound. Both of us committed now, I put my hand on the knob. It turned.

We stepped hesitantly into the apartment. Annie clutched the back of my coat and I could hear her breathing. The quiet was smothering. I closed the door and the click of the locks joining made both of us twitch. With my first deep breath I smelled him. Every hair on my arms stood up and I rubbed my coat sleeve to make them go away.

Neither one of us had moved. Annie was huddled behind

me like a shy child behind her mother's skirt. I pushed myself forward and walked into the living room, the mangled red carnation drooping in my hand.

The room was good-sized, especially for New York. A wall of exposed brick no doubt upped the rent and a tiny galley kitchen was tucked behind a cutaway arch. Three blond stools sat at the counter it formed, one placed in front of a sleek black matte phone. I pictured him there, murmuring into the phone, his lips caressing the mouthpiece, fingers stroking the countertop. Thinking. Planning. A shudder shook me and the carnation fell, the walls of Jake Romano's home closing in around me.

"Annie!" She wasn't there. Panic-stricken, I turned, heading blindly for the door when I heard her answer. My heart raced and I leaned against the wall to breathe, knocking a picture cockeyed on its nail. It was a Picasso reprint of flowers in a bowl. I had the same one in my kitchen, red frame instead of gray.

I followed the sound of Annie's voice and found her standing by a window that looked out on the street. She had the Levolors tilted and was peeking out, shifting her weight nervously. The living room was gorgeous, white and vacant. Each piece of furniture so perfect it jarred the eye. No cat hair, no Ben & Jerry stains. Not a cigarette butt or a beer bottle or a threadbare quilt. High-tech stereo and television. Two VCRs. A black leather couch as cold and beautiful as its owner.

"Kate, this is too creepy. Let's go."

"Let's get what we came for," I replied, ignoring the alarm bells in my head. I cast around the room for something. There was nothing. I started down another hallway. A bathroom off to the right. The navy shower curtain and the gray striped towels. Not a hair on the sink, an electric razor sitting neatly in its case. His smell was so strong here it drove me from the room. I pushed open another door and exposed the bedroom behind it.

The walls were a deep maroon, very dark, almost bloody. The bed dominated the space, huge, overwhelming. I stared at it, the pinstripe comforter fat and ripe. I ripped my eyes away. On the nightstand sat an old-fashioned picture in silver frame. Vanessa's mom. A girlish Virginia Mae. I could barely breathe, hearing the effort of the air working its way to my lungs. I trembled in the doorway. I had to go in . . .

"Kate!" Annie's desperate whisper carried from the living room. "There's a truck outside. A locksmith!"

I bolted forward as the words sunk in. No more time to be squeamish. The color of the room saturated my consciousness, cloying and disorienting. I snatched the picture and started to run, bumping a black lacquered desk stacked high with paperwork and mail. She kept calling to me, racing frantically from the window to the door. His mail. I forced myself to stop, to read. Fumbling, skimming, struggling to comprehend. Bill, bill, bank statement, bill.

"He's coming. Up the street. Oh my god, it's him."

The texture of an envelope tugged at my fingers. An invitation, rich cream with ragged golden edges. I dropped it on the floor, clipping my head on the corner of the desk as I bent to pick it up.

"Kate!"

I finally forced the card from its envelope, nearly ripping the heavy bond. I made my eyes focus, shutting out Annie's frenzied warnings. Read, Kate, read. A banquet. A film society. The Plaza. Friday. This Friday, cocktails at 7:00 p.m. I shoved the invitation back into its envelope and buried it in the pile. I raced toward the doorway, drawn to look back as if passing an accident on the highway. I slammed full force into Annie, freeing up her scream. I clapped my hand over her mouth and she grabbed my upper arms, fingers digging in.

"Be quiet," I hissed, everything shaking, letting her loose.

"I can't see them anymore," she chattered through moving teeth. "They're working the door. We have to get out. Now, Kate, now!"

We fled down the bathroom hallway, through the living room, past the Picasso. My hand was reaching for the door. Suddenly the air was split with sound. We froze. On the second ring, the machine kicked on and his voice snaked through the empty apartment. Outside a door opened and closed. Annie moaned as footsteps came down the hall. Closer. In front of the door. Slowing? Passing by.

"Annie. Open the door a crack. Make sure no one's out there."

She responded obediently, a robot, face gray. I looked over my shoulder at Jake's apartment one last time, keys slapping

against my leg. With escape so near, the fear finally trans-
formed into fury. The fucking son of a bitch. I had been so
afraid I'd almost forgotten. I spun around and raced back to
the bedroom, grabbing the flower from the counter as I went.
With careful precision, I placed the carnation where the frame
had been, wishing I had a white rose. Only Annie calling
pulled me from the task.

"I can hear him. Kate, they're in. Downstairs. Come on!"
The last ripped from her throat and I responded. Back through
the living room, flying back toward Annie. She slipped
through the door and I followed, slamming it shut, so loud,
too loud. She started for the stairway, heading down and I
grabbed her coat, yanking her nearly off her feet. She yelped
and, putting a finger to my lips, I dragged her to the upper
staircase. We climbed quickly, hearing our footsteps mimicked
on the stairs below. We crouched on the landing, listening to
Jake talk with the locksmith as he worked to open his lair. By
the time the second lock gave, my thigh muscles were screaming. Annie was shaking so badly I thought for sure she'd tumble down the stairs. They stepped inside for Jake to write the
check and the door swung closed.

I popped to my feet, ignoring my legs, and jerked Annie's
arm. We raced down the stairs, floors flying by, radios still
playing, children still tussling. I struggled with the lobby door,
feeling the screams build up inside me, the demons behind.
Finally it opened and we rushed out, knocking into a woman
on the stoop, briefcase flying from her hands. Even Annie
didn't stop to apologize, we just ran.

We leaned against the car, panting, neither of us speaking.
Annie was crying. It took both hands to guide the key into the
lock as I opened her door. She just stood there so I gave her
a nudge and she slid into her seat. I went around to the driver's
side, waiting. She sat motionless, staring straight ahead. I
knocked on the window, and finally she reached across the
seats and pulled the lock up. I climbed into the car and put
the key in the ignition. The locksmith's truck was double-
parked in the rearview mirror.

A chuckle escaped me, then a snort. Annie glared, wiping
tears with the back of her hand. I started the car, trying not to
laugh but losing control. Rested my head on the steering
wheel, laughing till I choked. Against her will, Annie joined

me, nerves at last released, safety and triumph bubbling forth in hysterics.

I told her about the invitation, the details engraved on my mind like the words on the paper. Bobby could do the car this Friday! She smiled a real smile . . . and then lost it when she said she would never have the stomach for being a cat burglar again. I boasted about not being afraid. She didn't believe me, but then neither did I. As we entered the expressway, I turned the heat on until it blasted, but I couldn't get warm. The cold was on the inside, and nothing from the outside would change it.

We caught the tail end of rush hour. Our chatter slowly faded into silence, exhilaration turning to fatigue. I fought it, cursing other drivers and laying on the horn with abandon.

I was exhausted by the time we pulled into the driveway. So much had happened, it was taking its toll. My nose throbbed, and I wanted to lie down. Carla and Lindsay were jumping up and down behind the front window when we arrived. Annie hurried from the car, but I took my time, not yet ready for explanations or rebuttal.

Through the window, I saw her sweep the children up in her arms. A familiar ache settled in my body. Loneliness. Always on the outside looking in, that was me. All around me, lights were coming on in homes where families lived, eating dinner, watching TV. It occurred to me that at times like this, all alone, thoughts of suicide came to people who were too decent to want revenge.

26

The day ended in depression. It permeated the household, even Carla and Lindsay were subdued. The only ones seemingly unaffected were the cats. They were far too intent on seeking revenge for the invasion of the children from the suburbs. Both were quite content to narrow their eyes and knead their claws into an unsuspecting lap, purring innocently at each yelp of pain.

Annie made a dinner that no one ate. She and girls went to bed together, all exhausted by a hard day at play. Vanessa had listened with morbid fascination to the scene at Jake's apartment. When I handed her the picture, she looked from it to me, forehead bunching. She traced the faces on the glass.

"Don't ever do anything like this again. Do you understand me?" Her eyes filled with tears and she clutched it to her chest. I nodded. She set the picture on the table and hugged me fiercely. "I'm so grateful to have this back, but if anything had happened . . . Kate, please, you went too far." I had expected more enthusiasm, at bare minimum a hero's welcome. Her reaction left me guilty and uncertain, and I kept remembering Jake's Picasso. The day's excursion had forged yet another bond between us, and our sameness rubbed me raw.

Vanessa went into the living room and built a fire, smoking and staring as the logs burnt down into embers. I joined her in body, though not in spirit, and we sat in the dark until she rose for bed and silently left the room. I stayed up late, too tired to sleep, lost in my own mind, dreaming of wine and gin and sanctuary. I finally fell asleep on the living room couch, waking cramped and uncomfortable a little after six.

Annie was making coffee in the kitchen. I didn't think twice about it until I noticed her half-full mug and realized this was a second pot. We both moved slowly, as if weighted down, and I didn't bother asking how she'd slept.

When the coffee finished brewing, Annie poured me a cup. I loaded it with sugar and a dash of milk, noticing my hands were steady for the first time in days. Though I wondered where Jake was and when he'd call, I couldn't muster the energy to work myself up. I was overwhelmed by my life and the lives of the women around me. Everything was so big and I was so small.

My nose, on the other hand, was not small. What little evidence there was of bruising could be hidden with a cover stick. That would leave me with a perfectly flesh-toned mountain in the middle of my face, reminiscent of Karl Malden. The good thing about having no self-esteem was that ugliness came as less of a blow. I'd always hated the way I looked, and now I had solid evidence to back it up.

People didn't understand about not being pretty. They were always trying to tell you that you were when you weren't. Checking their hair in the mirror, they told you beauty was only skin-deep. Then let me have the skin, I wanted to say. When I was thirteen, my Pop had set me straight. He took a fistful of my shirt, lifted me off the floor and told me in no uncertain terms what a dog I really was. He inventoried my knobby knees and frizzy hair, my height, my loud laugh. He told me why no man would ever want me and how women would giggle behind my back. He was wrong. I turned out a lot better than either of us had thought I would when I was thirteen. But I remember the bourbon on his breath and how he dropped me on the floor when he was finished, and stepped over me, laughing as he went out the door. I'd lived ever since with emotional toilet paper stuck to my shoe.

Annie and I didn't talk this morning. No review of the previous day, no memories of childhood pranks or talk of future plans. We were both stuck in the moment, desperate to move forward and terrified to try. Sighing, I went upstairs to shower.

Vanessa's door was closed. The girls slept soundly, tangled in the sheets and each other. I turned the shower on full blast and scrubbed my skin pink. Afterwards, I wrapped myself in my battered bathrobe and fuzzy slippers and headed downstairs for more coffee. Today would be spent in solitude. Noth-

ing could induce me to go out into the world to be chased by
men or drinks or demons.

Annie looked weary and drawn where she sat at the table
next to the phone. Without looking up she said, "I talked to
Oola. She said to tell you Ellen would pick you up at eleven-
thirty." Panic!

"I didn't hear the phone ring. Shit, why didn't you let me
talk to her?" Damn! Eleven-thirty! Oola had a lot of nerve
making plans for me. So much for all of us being involved in
making decisions!

"I called her. I needed to talk to her about something."

Maybe it was Annie's lack of apology, or just the monotone
in which she spoke. Something penetrated my paranoia, and I
looked at her curiously. She still stared into nowhere, fingers
now tight around the cup.

"Annie, are you okay?"

She folded her lips and shook her head no. I wanted to feel
compassion, but I was dried up inside, barren. Another crisis
was more than I could bear. I had to force myself to reach
across the table and touch her fingers.

"I'm meeting Oola this morning. We're going to the
house." No question about whose house, I thought, but why?
Annie continued with my answer. "I need to pick up a few
more things for the girls, and I want to get Andrew's computer . . ."

Annie blew her nose in a paper napkin. "David's going to
meet us. He insisted. But maybe with Oola there, we'll be able
to talk. I'm willing to try, but I'm scared." She looked up at
me. "I love him, you know, but sometimes I wonder if I
should." She stood up, took her cup to the sink and rinsed it
out. "I'm going upstairs to get ready. I need to make sure
Vanessa can watch the girls while you're gone. I don't know
how long I'll be." She left me alone, the reminder of my appointment ringing in my ears.

I had to do something. There was no point in calling Oola;
she was the instigator of this whole mess. I paced the kitchen.
I would call Ellen and put a stop to this. This was my decision
and I wasn't going to be forced into it. I dug up her number
and dialed. The music had changed and so had the message.

"Hi, this is Ellen," she said, over the sounds of Eric Clap-
ton. "I'll be unavailable all morning and have plans for lunch.

But please leave a message and I'll call you later this afternoon. Wait for the beep!" I slammed the phone down without responding. How goddamn convenient for Ellen and Oola—unavailable all morning with plans for lunch! We'd see about that!

I scowled over my coffee and sat at the table looking for a way out. I had examined and discarded hiding or defiance and even considered getting drunk—surely drunks were not allowed in Alcoholics Anonymous—when I finally settled on injury. No one could be expected to go to their first AA meeting with a hurt nose. Vanessa came into the kitchen as I peered in the mirror. A few well-placed smudges of mascara and my bruises would have newfound vitality. I jumped when she said good morning and quickly resumed my seat.

"Annie says you're going out. Who is this Ellen person anyway?" Vanessa asked, making conversation over coffee.

"None of your business."

"Pardon me!"

"I have a life of my own, you know." Vanessa cocked an eyebrow. "I do! I can have lunch with someone if I want to."

"Fine, have lunch. Geez, what a grouch!" Vanessa turned to the cupboards in search of food. Wait a minute, I thought. What just happened here? I didn't want to go to lunch . . .

"I'm not going anyway," I muttered sullenly. "Oola has no right to make plans for me. If I want a secretary, I'll hire one!"

"What does Oola have to do with it?" Vanessa split a bagel and plopped it into the toaster. "Oh, that's right. Ellen must be the friend you blew off yesterday."

"I didn't blow her off," I responded. "I was hurt, it wasn't my fault. I couldn't go to the stupid meeting!" Me and my big mouth. Vanessa turned around, cream cheese in hand. She was like a submarine with its periscope up.

"Meeting? What kind of meeting?"

"An AA meeting! Are you happy now?"

"Yes, actually, I am." She chewed and swallowed. "So why aren't you going?"

"Because I don't want to. And because Oola had no right to make my schedule!"

"That's pretty lame."

"It's none of your business, so just shut up."

"No, I think you should go. You promised Annie and

everyone you were going to get some help." She smeared the cream cheese on her bagel and bit down.

"I'm going to. I just want a little time to think about it."

"A little time and a twelve-pack," Vanessa drawled between bites.

"Drop it, all right? I've barely had my coffee."

I crossed to the pot and refilled my mug. She shrugged and ate the rest of her bagel while I thumbed through the paper. I read an article full of sour grapes about the no-smoking laws for restaurants in the city. She waved disdainfully. Vanessa had always acted as if she were above discussions of public policy or ideology. Until Jake Romano I'd never seen her forced to do something against her will. If I wasn't such a good person, I'd almost think it served her right.

I got dressed and took Annie to the station a bit before nine. She and Oola would meet in the city and drive the Blazer up to White Plains. I dropped her off with a hug and squeeze and she stood on the platform, small and forlorn. I waited in the car till she boarded her train, thinking about courage. For all my talk of winning, it was Annie who was fighting back.

I drove home and sat in the kitchen, Vanessa in the shower. The children watched videos in the living room, after informing me that Aunt Vanessa was taking them shopping. Goodie for Aunt Vanessa, I thought, the brown nose. I watched the clock, minutes ticking off, time broken into increments that got smaller as eleven-thirty got closer.

Vanessa packed up the kids at quarter to eleven, leading them out the back door to the Volvo. Jake hadn't called. The phone hadn't rung. We hoped his arrest had slowed his pace. Vanessa was confident he would keep his distance, at least for a few days.

"Good luck," Vanessa said, stopping at the door. Ozzie yowled at her feet, looking for a way out.

"Screw you," I replied, toning down my language in deference to the kids. Vanessa tossed the cat back into the room and closed the door. I was alone.

The next forty minutes passed in a blur. Thoughts raced through my head and numerous times I got up and paced the house. Twice I grabbed my coat and keys to run and twice I stopped. I lived on a treadmill, going round and round, always ending up in the same place. I didn't really believe there was a way to get off. The doorbell rang.

I stood behind the front door until the bell rang again. I checked the alarm to make sure it was off. As if in my sleep, I swung the door open and saw a women in her early fifties standing on the porch. She was slim with short silver hair and blue-gray eyes. She smiled warmly and put out her hand.

"Hi! I'm Ellen Simon. You must be Kate." I nodded. "Can I come in?"

"Oh, I'm sorry," I mumbled, stepping clear of the doorway. I led her into the kitchen. "Do you want some coffee?"

"Sure, half a cup. We've got a minute." She hung her jacket over the back of the chair. "How are you feeling?"

"Fine."

"Good. I was worried when Oola called yesterday. I'm glad you're all right." She was relaxed and comfortable. I was not. "I was really scared when I went to my first meeting. I was hung over and felt like shit."

"I'm not hung over."

"That's good. How long since you've had a drink?"

"Two days," I muttered.

"Fantastic!" She exclaimed. What's the big deal, I thought. Don't patronize me. "You've already got some experience being sober."

Hurray for me.

She checked her watch and I checked the clock. "Well, I think we better go. Are you ready?"

No, I thought.

"Yes," I said.

I pulled on my coat and followed her numbly through the house. I reset the alarm and climbed into the passenger seat of her pickup truck. As she drove, she chattered about her passion for gardening, antiques and architecture. "Your friend's house is fascinating. I'd love to talk to her sometime about the renovation." I gazed out the window blindly, on the way to my doom.

We turned into a small church parking lot at ten of twelve. The lot was half full, with others pulling in behind us. Ellen parked the truck, turned off the ignition, and looked over at me. "This is the hard part, Kate. I promise you'll never have to go to your first meeting again." She smiled. I wanted to hit her.

She got out of the truck and waved at a woman and man who were walking toward the door. They smiled cheerfully and waved in return, waiting for her to catch up. She stopped and turned back. I was still in the truck. I opened the door and stepped out. She came over and took my arm, half-dragging me toward the others.

"Dick, Laurie, this is Kate," she said, receiving a hug from each of them. They better not touch me, I thought.

"Hey, Kate. Nice to meet you," said Laurie.

"Hi," said Dick. He was finishing a cigarette and told a story about three alcoholics in a bar that made everyone laugh. I didn't get what was so funny. This was deadly serious as far as I was concerned. Miserable, I stood to the side, wondering if all these AA people were on some kind of drug. They were too goddamn happy to be real.

"We better get in there," Laurie said.

We went through the door and down the steps into a large, open room in the basement. Three long tables were set up in a horseshoe shape, folding chairs around them. Another table sat to the side, with two large coffee pots and a plate of cookies. We moved toward it as a group. It was getting hard to breathe. My legs trembled. I was afraid my knees would buckle.

"Kate, why don't you sit down over there," Ellen suggested, pointing toward two empty chairs. "I'll get the coffee. Cream and sugar?"

"Lots of sugar and a little cream," I croaked and made it to a chair.

I kept my head down, cheating glances at the other attendees without meeting their eyes. There was no one wearing a dirty trenchcoat and everyone appeared to be recently groomed. They talked happily among themselves, calling out greetings to new arrivals, laughter bursting forth more than once. Again, I wondered what was so funny and gave myself a mental once-over to make sure it wasn't me. Everything was zipped and buttoned, so unless I had something hanging from my nose, I was safe.

The people appeared to be normal, a mix of white and black, suits and jeans, all different ages. At the table in the front sat an older man who looked vaguely familiar, a woman around my age and a teenage girl. I couldn't believe they let people bring their children; it didn't seem right. Ellen slid into the seat beside me, handing me a cup of coffee that I had no desire to drink. She smiled at me and gave my hand a little squeeze.

"Hi everyone," said the woman in front. "I'm Marla and I'm an alcoholic."

"Hi Marla," they said to her. Holy shit, I said to myself.

"Can you help me open this meeting with a moment of silence, followed by the Serenity Prayer." She bowed her head, and the room hushed. Great, religion! I should have figured it when I saw the church. I'm out of here, I thought, wishing I had driven my own car.

The group recited a short prayer. Marla read a few announcements about anniversaries and something about studying a big book. As opposed to a little book, I thought.

Marla read a paragraph about Alcoholics Anonymous, then other people around the room read some lists. Each time, the person reading gave their name and identified themselves as an alcoholic. Each time, the group roared their name in response. I thought I might throw up. I was dizzy, and there was a loud buzzing in my ears.

"Is there anyone here for their first contact with Alcoholics Anonymous? Their very first meeting?" I looked at Ellen accusingly. Hey! Nobody told me about this part. She nudged me, and grudgingly I raised my hand a few inches from the table.

"Over here, Marla," said a man two seats away from me. I glared at him. He smiled back.

"Hi," said Marla warmly. "Welcome! What's your name?"

The whole room was looking at me expectantly. "Kate," I managed.

"Hi, Kate," they boomed. "Welcome." People smiled and nodded at me, and I wanted to crawl under my chair. This was worse than I could have ever dreamed.

"Kate, we're so glad you're here," Marla said. I bet, I thought, nothing like fresh meat. "People are going to tell you how it was for them before and how it's changed. Just sit back and try to listen. With that, I'd like to introduce today's speaker. Please welcome Robin." She turned to the young girl beside her.

You could have knocked me over with a feather when the girl opened her mouth and said, "Hi everybody. I'm Robin and I'm an alcoholic and a drug addict."

What a waste of time this was going to be! What the hell could this kid tell me about drinking? She didn't even look old enough to drink, much less to stop. I folded my arms in disgust and slid down in my seat. At least I wouldn't have to come back, and nobody could say I hadn't given it a fair shot.

"Kate, welcome." Robin smiled at me.

Okay, I get it already—I'm welcome?

"This makes me think about my first meeting," Robin continued. "I sat there, looking around at all those old people, wondering what the hell they could possibly tell me!"

The group laughed appreciatively. I sat up a little straighter, trying to remember if any of the lists had mentioned mind-reading.

Robin was older than she looked—twenty-four—and had been sober three years. Her story began with sneaking beers from neighborhood block parties when she was only nine. The drinking made her feel different. Included. Not on the outside looking in. It was good to fit in, so soon she carried pint bottles in her knapsack everywhere she went. Morning or night, at school, in the park, to celebrate, to forget, to feel anything at all, the bottle was always there.

I don't know exactly when I started crying. She joked about fist fights and blackouts and mouthing off to cops. But her voice grew quiet as she acknowledged the girl behind the façade, a frightened, miserable, lonely girl who didn't know what to do. I was only as sick as my secrets, she said. That scared me. I must be pretty sick. She told me about how different it was for her now. She had completed school, just started a new job, a new life. After twenty minutes or so, she stopped and called on others around room.

They told me things that they had done and the things they did today. I heard stuff I'd joked about—one day at a time, sponsors, twelve steps. A petite black woman told of losing her children, and how today she was earning back their trust. A jovial, red-faced man with three DWIs laughed as he explained how lucky he was to be there. A large husky man spoke softly of wanting to die, then he beamed as he shared the birth of a son less than a month ago. Their honesty was too raw to be less than sincere.

It went on and on, the hour speeding by, me sobbing through it all. At some point, Ellen handed me a tissue, and the man who pointed me out to Marla dropped two cookies by my cup. I didn't understand a lot of what was said, but one thing was undeniable. I belonged here.

It hit me like a punch in the stomach. I hadn't belonged anywhere in so long. But here, with these people, I fit. They drank like me, they did the things I thought only I had done. Yet they were, for the most part, happy and at peace with themselves, things I had forgotten how to feel if I had ever known.

"Kate," Marla was saying. "We passed around a schedule of meetings and the women have put their phone numbers on it. Pick up the phone before you pick up a drink, okay?" She waved a booklet and smiled. "Would you like to say anything?"

I cleared my throat and tried to make the words come out. Ellen patted my shoulder reassuringly. Everyone looked at me, nodding their encouragement. I wiped my eyes, sniffing to clear my nose.

"I'm Kate," I stammered, "and I'm an alcoholic." Out loud, for the first time. Tears choked me, and blindly I reached for Ellen's hand. She gripped my fingers firmly. "I didn't know." My words were a hoarse whisper. "I mean, I always knew there was something wrong with me. But I never knew what it was. Thank you."

"Keep coming back," people called.

"Thank you for letting me chair," said Marla. "We have a nice way of closing."

We joined hands and stood in a circle, saying The Lord's Prayer. I hadn't said a prayer in years, except to bargain with God when I was in trouble. It felt different, nicer now. After the prayer, the meeting broke up. Ellen hugged me, and I felt as if a thousand pounds had rolled off my back.

Two women came up and introduced themselves. Marla handed me the meeting schedule and asked for my number. They invited Ellen and me to lunch, but I couldn't do it. Ellen suggested another time, so Robin invited me for coffee before tomorrow's meeting. Tentatively I accepted, and she beamed as if I'd just handed her a winning lottery ticket. Slowly, we made our way out of the building and got into the truck.

Wisely, Ellen said little on the way home. I said nothing at all. We pulled into the driveway and she looked me. "This is the beginning, Kate. You have a chance to make it all different. Don't drink, just for today."

"Thank you, Ellen," I said. From my heart. "There's just one thing. Maybe it's not the time to go into it."

"I've got the time."

"When Oola spoke to you . . . Did she tell you about Jake? What happened?"

I saw her guard go up. "She said your drinking had compromised you with a man you hated. Those were her exact words."

"That sounds like Oola, all right." We shared a brief smile.

"She said she couldn't go into more detail, but that you needed help right away. You know, she's always very concerned about her clients, but seemed especially concerned about you."

"Yeah. Well. I'm grateful, now that I know a little about AA. And how it works for you. But it's probably worse than you think. Damn it, I was sure I wouldn't start crying again."

"Go ahead, Kate. By now you know that there's no such thing as 'other people's dirty laundry' where we're concerned. You're not going to shock me."

As briefly as I could I told her everything that had happened. As soon as I began telling her, the tears did stop. The way I lined up the facts and described the psychological ramifications of Jake's behavior for the rest of us, I had a feeling of self-control that I hadn't known since I was good at things in school.

It really did take less time to tell it all than I would have thought.

"There you have it. Did I reach my 'bottom,' as you say?"

"Probably. It's a relative thing. But what really sounds good to me is the way you thanked Jake. Even before you had any help in understanding the problem you hit on the very core of how our program works. You saw how alcohol betrays the best that is in you. At some point you thought you had to be someone else to carry out your plan. I'd have thought the same—most of us would. How well I remember feeling that life had loaded me down with more than one person could carry. And in your case, the excuse for drinking was even more compelling . . ."

"Excuse for drinking? You think I went with Jake to have an excuse to drink?"

"Not at the time. I'm sure when you followed him you had a noble motive. And it always helps at times like that to put your head right in the lion's jaws and go someplace where not drinking will be very hard."

"I swear, Jake had it all planned out. He tricked me."

"I'm sure he did. But you tricked yourself, too. Ask yourself how would you feel if he were giving you that Irish whiskey right now, putting it under your nose . . ."

"Like putting a knife into his throat!"

"That's why I think you're so lucky. You know it, too. That's why you thanked Jake. Thanks to him you won't be creating any new bulletproof Kates to do your dirty work for you. Trust me, before too long you're going to like being you, and that's the best revenge."

I'd been hit by a ton of bricks and she knew it. That small smile of hers and the pat on the hand she gave me before I got out of the truck were so kind: a blessing. It was only one-thirty-five. In less than two hours my whole life had changed.

Vanessa and the kids weren't home; neither was Annie. I sat in the kitchen and thought about the meeting and the people I'd met. The packet Marla had given me was in my jacket pocket. I took it out and thumbed through it. There was a pamphlet on alcoholism, a schedule of meetings with phone numbers written on it, and a small folding card that would fit in my wallet. It listed the Twelve Steps and Twelve Traditions and the paragraph Marla had read at the beginning of the meeting was on the front. On the back was a short prayer.

"God, grant me the serenity to accept the things I cannot change, the courage to change the things I can, and the wisdom to know the difference," I read out loud.

I got up and walked into the living room. The tape machine sat there. I stopped in front of it for several minutes before I pushed the button to rewind. And then I played the tape. All of it. Listened to the woman on the tape giving up everything, morals, convictions, beliefs and friendships, all for the price of a drink. Accept the things I cannot change.

I was throwing the tape in the garbage can when I heard someone pull into the driveway. I got up and checked out the window, finding a florist's van. I opened the back door as a man removed a huge wreath from the back of the van. Red carnations stared accusingly from the midst of purple mums.

"Hi," I called. He looked up and came toward me.

"Vanessa Clayton?"

"No, but this is her house."

"Delivery," he replied succinctly, leaning the wreath against the steps. "Sign here, please," he added, indicating a clipboard.

"Are you sure this is for us?" I scribbled my name on the sheet.

"That's what it says," he said, already heading back to the van.

I hefted the heavy wreath and lugged it into the kitchen, a familiar queasiness starting in my stomach. I laid it on the table and saw the black ribbon that stretched across its opening. WITH GREAT SYMPATHY, it read, in silver script. This was a funeral arrangement.

Chilled, I pushed it away from me, knocking the sugar bowl onto the floor. I left it, staring at the graveyard flowers and the mocking message. There was no card. Where was Vanessa? Should she have been back by now?

I pushed away guilty thoughts of red carnations and cursed Jake Romano. I ran to the machine, hoping for a reassuring message, and saw the blinking light. I played it back: a call from Mindy, a man selling insurance and finally Virginia Mae. Her voice crackled across the tape, elderly but never feeble. She too had received a floral display, a large papier mache vase of gladioli with an unsigned note offering sympathy on the loss of her child. Angrily, with just the slightest edge of worry, she demanded that Vanessa call. Her parting words were, "This is about that white boy, I know it."

I went into Vanessa's office and went through the Rolodex for Virginia Mae's number. I called her down in Georgia and assured her that Vanessa was OK. Though she said she hadn't been worried, I could tell that she had. I promised to have her daughter call as soon as she got home.

I went back to the kitchen and dragged the wreath out to the garbage cans by the garage. I found Ozzie hiding in a nearby bush, and carried him back to the house, scolding all the way. The sugar on the floor stuck to the bottom of my shoes, so I came back and cleaned it up. I was thirsty and the beers were still there when I opened the refrigerator looking for something to drink.

I remembered what somebody at the meeting had said about dumping her booze down the sink. She said it symbolized the lack of value alcohol had in her new life. Abruptly, I reached into the refrigerator with both hands and came out with both beers.

I had popped the top of the first can when the back door opened. Annie stopped in surprise, dropping her bags, registering the beer in my hands. Her eyes flew to my face.

"What are you doing, Kate?"

"This," I replied, turning the can upside down over the sink. The amber beer foamed as it hit the stainless steel. I watched it settle into the drain, the foam surviving longer than the liquid. Courage to change the things I can. I opened the second and did the same, feeling relieved they were gone.

"I'm so proud of you," Annie said, hugging me.

"Thanks. What about you? What happened?"

"I can't really get into it now. It was better, a little. At least we're headed in the right direction."

I told her about the flowers and the message from Vanessa's mom. There was no longer any outrage in our reactions, just simple resignation. While we waited for Vanessa and the girls to return, two more floral deliveries arrived. Twenty-four white roses in a black ceramic bowl and another arrangement of mums, this time standing on wire legs. Both offered condolences in our time of sorrow. Neither were signed. They joined the wreath in the pile by the garage. Jake hadn't called all day.

We ate a late lunch of peanut butter and jelly sandwiches which Annie automatically cut in quarters. The small squares reminded me of paper bag lunches and hopscotch lines chalked on the sidewalk. All the time I was little, I had wanted to be big. Now I'd trade my entire adult life for one day of crayons and kickball.

The Volvo roared into the driveway around three, disgorg-

ing girls and bags and Burger King crowns. The children
swarmed into the kitchen, eager to share news of their pur-
chases. Annie bustled them upstairs to stow their loot, so I
could give Vanessa the latest. She listened grimly, staring out
the window at the discarded flowers.

"Well, the implication's clear. I don't suppose there was a
card."

"No. Different florists too."

"Damn him! Where's my lighter?" She fumbled around in
her purse and emptied the pockets of her jeans. Finally, she
stooped and lit a cigarette off the stove. "I'm going to go call
Mom. I could wring his neck for scaring her."

I followed her as far as the living room when she stopped
at her office door. "Hey, Kate. Did you go?"

"Yeah." I hesitated. "It was okay."

"I'm glad. How'd it go for Annie?"

"Okay, I guess. She wasn't very talkative, but at least nothing awful happened."

"Two down, one to go. Funny, isn't it?" She leaned against
the doorway.

"What's funny?"

"How this thing with Jake has changed everything. For you
and Annie." She exhaled. "But for me, it's all still the same."

She gave a sad smile and walked into her office, shutting
the door. I wanted to follow and tell her it would be all right,
that we would stop him. But in truth, I didn't know if we
could. I wasn't sure when it would end. So I stayed where I
was, offering nothing, wondering if this was the wisdom to
know the difference.

27

Everything had been so calm, the deliveries stopped, Jake didn't call, just a quiet evening at home. The highlight of my night was a call from Charlie Harrington. He had found Natalie Ellinwood Romano. Or Rachel Linwood as she was now apparently known. Stage name or alias, I wasn't totally sure. She lived somewhere down in Alphabet City, the Lower East Side. A land of freaks and weirdos, junkies, artists and outcasts, all finding a place to light. He didn't have the address yet because she didn't work anymore. Hadn't in years. He thought he could work on the guy who used to represent her, though. "Is this chick wanted by the cops or something?"

I refrained from commenting on "chick" and thanked him for all he'd done so far. He'd get his check, I said, as soon as we had an address. He agreed that "alive in the East Village" wasn't what we were paying him for. I sensed that the reason for his call was to find out why Natalie Romano was worth so much time and trouble. He had to be happy with "she means an awful lot to us, that's all I can tell you."

We all went to bed early. For the first time in over a week, I slept solidly. I didn't wake up till nearly ten a.m. I showered and dressed quickly to meet Robin at the diner at eleven. Annie was fiddling with the little laptop, Vanessa cursing as she struggled to connect the new Nintendo the girls had wheedled from her during yesterday's jaunt to the mall. Carla and Lindsay huddled around her, pointing, asking and helping Aunt Vanessa out of her mind. I chuckled evilly at Vanessa's restrained response as I waved goodbye.

Robin and I had coffee, our alcoholism a strong and common bond between two strangers more different than alike. When we got to the meeting, I was surprised at the people who remembered my name. They acted glad to see me again, but I felt the same glimmer of paranoia as before.

The elderly man I thought I had recognized yesterday came up and introduced himself as George. He asked if I remembered him from the Grand Union. He was the tomato lady's husband, I realized in shock. Embarrassed at being in an AA meeting with someone who had seen me buying beer, I nodded quickly and escaped, taking a seat on the other side of the room. Robin joined me and the meeting began.

There was nobody new today. The speaker was a middle-aged man named Tom. When he finished talking, the group discussed anger and denial, both focal points of his story. Near the middle of the meeting, the chairperson called on me. My face got red, but I tried to talk like the others. I told how I couldn't control myself when I got mad, how I held grudges and nursed thoughts of revenge. I had never been a person to stuff my anger, I said. I was much more apt to stuff the person I was angry at. Everybody laughed. It felt good to be part of something, anchored instead of a fly-away kite with a snapped string.

When the meeting was over I drove home whistling. There was something about the meetings that made me feel good. I debated whether they put something in the coffee, just to help them get through. Probably not, I finally decided, though not completely convinced. They were an awfully perky group.

Everyone was gathered at the kitchen table when I came in. There were mugs of tomato soup made with milk and half-eaten grilled cheese sandwiches. Annie got up and made me one while Lindsay tried to teach me a rhyming game that was incomprehensible to anyone over eight.

"Wait a minute," I said as Lindsay and Carla dissolved into giggles. "Why can't I say that? Puppy rhymes with guppy!" The children were nearly choking at my stupidity. Evidently I still failed to grasp some essential element of this game. "I don't get it," I said, giving up. I waved a paper towel as a white flag and the girls went off into hysterics again.

"Try this, Kate. Dumb and plumb. Or maybe just plumb dumb," Vanessa sniped.

"How 'bout witch and bit . . ."

"Kate," Annie interrupted, setting my sandwich in front of me. The girls giggled anyway. They knew very well what

Aunt Kate intended to say. "Girls, let Kate eat. Finish your soup, Lindsay. Carla, you have to eat at least half your sandwich before you can watch TV. Get to it."

"Has he called?" I asked Vanessa.

"Not a word."

"I'm not sure if that's good or bad."

"Let's enjoy it while we can," Annie said. "Jake will be back soon enough." The girls giggled again, little heads close together.

"The ad's out. I wonder how Jake's liking his mail," I said slyly. Again the girls giggled, seemingly provoked by Jake's name. Annie looked at them sternly.

"Auntie Vanessa sitting in a tree," chanted Carla.

"K-i-s-s-i-n-g," lisped Lindsay.

"What are you girls talking about?" Annie asked, hands on hips.

"First comes love, then comes marriage," they sang. "Then comes Vanessa with the baby carriage!" The last line was garbled by laughter, the children titillated and embarrassed by the murky connection between kissing and babies.

"I don't know what has gotten into you two," Annie said.

"Maybe they've taken silly pills," Vanessa suggested, smiling at the girls.

"What do you two know about kissing," I teased. "Do you have a boyfriend? Do you?" I swooped down on Lindsay, tickling her off her chair and into a wriggling lump on the floor. "Do you?" I asked again.

"No, stop," she gasped. "Not my boyfriend! Aunt Vanessa's!"

"Lindsay!" Carla yelped. "You weren't supposed to tell!"

All heads turned. The adults froze as Lindsay's giggles died out into gasps. Under our stares, Carla slid lower in her seat, looking to join her sister under the table. Her mother put an end to that.

"Carla, sit still. Lindsay, I want you to come up here in your seat. Right now." Annie's anxiety gave an extra edge to the command. The children looked wary now. Lindsay clambered back into her chair, and Vanessa put a hand on her head.

"Lindsay, what did you mean, about my having a boyfriend?" Lindsay gazed back at Vanessa mutely. "You can tell me, it's all right. No one will be mad."

Lindsay looked at her sister uncertainly. Carla pursed her lips. Solemnly, Lindsay imitated her, closing her tiny lips and turning an imaginary key to lock them tight.

"Lindsay, answer Vanessa," Annie ordered. The child squirmed but didn't respond.

"Lindsay," I caroled, dragging out her name, "I'm gonna get you." I leaned playfully toward her. Her eyes were huge, watchful. I slid an arm around her waist and began to tickle. She writhed in silent laughter, and I plucked her from the chair, pulling her across my lap. "If I can unlock your lips you have to tell me." She struggled to keep silent. I tickled her mercilessly, waiting for her mouth to open.

"Aunt Kate, stop! I'm gonna pee my pants," she shrieked indignantly. Quickly, I turned the imaginary key and pocketed it.

"There! I win! Now you have to tell me the secret," I said to her, pulling her upright. Her head quivered under my chin as she played with the hem of her cotton shirt. I leaned closer and whispered in her ear. "It's okay to tell. Cross my heart and hope to die, stick a needle in my eye." She twisted around to look at me, debating.

"Aunt Vanessa has a boyfriend," she confided. Vanessa took a sharp breath, and Annie smothered a gasp. Lindsay looked up nervously.

"It's all right," I soothed. "How do you know Aunt Vanessa has a boyfriend?"

"He told me."

"It was our secret," Carla cried plaintively. "You spoiled it, Lindsay!"

Lindsay's lip quivered. Annie shushed Carla. I tipped Lindsay's chin up and smiled trustingly. "Did he tell you his name?"

"Yes."

This was like pulling teeth. "What was it?"

"Jack."

"It was Jake, you stupid," said Carla scornfully.

"Carla, don't call your sister stupid," Annie responded automatically, eyes fixed on Lindsay's face.

"Jack and Jake sound a lot alike," I said, plaiting a section of Lindsay's hair.

"He said I could call him Jack if I wanted," Lindsay answered, making a face at her sister.

"That's 'cause you're a little baby who can't talk right," Carla muttered.

"Am not!"

"Are too!"

"Am not a baby!" Lindsay grappled for a better view of her sister, using my thigh and left breast as stepping-stones.

"Baby! Baby, teeny-weeny baby!" Carla taunted.

"Ouch! Lindsay, sweetie, you're hurting Aunt Kate," I exclaimed, in fear of losing a nipple.

"Lindsay, sit still. Carla, be quiet."

Annie sounded just like every other I-mean-business mom I've ever heard. That voice had to result from hormonal changes during pregnancy. I'd never heard it in a woman without children. She looked at them sternly.

"I've talked to you about speaking to strangers, haven't I?" They nodded slowly, all the fun gone out of this situation. "I want you to tell me exactly what happened—what this man said to you, when and where. Do you hear me? Right now!"

"Mom, he wasn't a stranger," Carla explained. "He's Aunt Vanessa's boyfriend." She tried to smother what she knew to be an inappropriate giggle. "He likes to kiss her."

"Carla, honey, that man was only pretending to be my boyfriend. He's a bad man, do you understand?" Vanessa stroked Carla's hair. "He wasn't telling you the truth."

"But he was nice. He said I was pretty." Carla was clearly confused. "You aren't supposed to lie."

"What did he tell you, honey?" Vanessa asked.

Lindsay tugged on the lapel of my blazer. "Just a minute, sweetie," I said, eyes on her sister.

She tugged again impatiently. "What do you want, Lindsay?" I finally snapped.

Her face got red. "What's gressif mean, Aunt Kate?"

"What? Gressif? That's not a real word, Lindsay."

"Yes it is," she said indignantly. "Jack told it to me." If Lindsay was looking for my attention, she got it.

"Be quiet," I told Vanessa and Annie, who were still prying details from Carla. "Lindsay, what exactly did Jack say?"

"He said to ask you, Aunt Kate. He said I was a gressif,

and when I asked what that meant, he said to ask you," she replied.

"Aggressive? He said you were aggressive?"

"Yes," Lindsay beamed, having finally managed to communicate with that lower life-form known as the grown-up. I felt the dread deep in my belly.

"Is that all, Lindsay?"

The room was as tight as a dry cleaning bag stretched over our faces, cutting off our air.

"He said I looked like I was bigger," she told me proudly, twirling her braid. "He's funny. He thought I was eleven." She made a little face to let me know she knew a line when she heard one. "That's when he asked me if I was a gressif. Then he had me blow." The last was very matter-of-fact.

Annie half-rose from her chair, but Vanessa grabbed her arm, holding her back. I kept the same stupid smile on my face, all the while my mind and stomach churning. I could hear myself at the airport, pretending to be drunk, spouting mindlessly about his alleged molestation of an eleven-year-old girl. Lindsay looked up trustingly into my face.

"He made you blow?" I asked softly. "You mean, like blow your nose?"

"No," she responded slowly, pondering how to explain. "We did this," she said, puffing her cheeks with air and sucking in and out rhythmically. "He showed us. I did it better than Carla."

"You did not!"

"I did too! Jack said so! He said I could get a job blowing," she finished importantly. The children bickered as the adults reeled.

Suddenly, Annie brushed off Vanessa's arm and grabbed Carla with both hands. She shook her, frightening both children into tearful silence. "Did he touch you? Carla, did he touch you or your sister in any way?"

"No! No! Mom, you're hurting me," Carla cried.

Lindsay burst into tears, wailing, "Jack's nice, Mommy. He's not like Daddy!" Raw with pain, Annie's gaze found her youngest daughter.

"Annie, let go," I said, taking her by both wrists. Slowly, she loosened her grip from Carla's upper arms. I pushed her gently into a chair. Her face was white as paper, blotched only by her bruises. "Calm down. They're all right."

"Girls," said Vanessa calmly. "I think you should go and play Donkey Kong. Go on, I've got it all hooked up. I'll give you a half an hour to practice, then I'll come in and beat you. Bad," she promised, grinning. They timidly grinned back, grateful for a return to something they could understand. Carla glanced nervously at her mother, still uncertain as to whether permission was granted. "Go on, hurry up," urged Vanessa. "I'm gonna beat you."

"Oh Aunt Vanessa, you can't play good," scoffed Carla, sliding off her chair.

"We'll see," Vanessa answered. "Hurry up, Lindsay."

"Okay," Lindsay replied, heading for the living room. She stopped in the doorway, and turned back, saying seriously, "But I get a head start, Aunt Vanessa, 'cause I'm little and you're big."

Annie sat unmoving. I didn't know what to say. As soon as the girls were gone, Vanessa spoke with quiet authority.

"We have to get the children out of here. It's not safe. Annie, where can they go?" Annie looked up at the sound of her name, dazed. She didn't answer.

"Annie," I said sharply, giving her shoulder a shake. "They're all right. He didn't hurt them. They didn't even understand what he meant." She still didn't reply, just sat slumped as if she had no bones. "Vanessa?"

She knelt beside Annie's chair. "Hey, snap out of it, Annie!" She shook her chin gently. "Kate, call Oola. See if she can come out here."

She picked up one of Annie's hands and rubbed it briskly as I reached for the phone. I dialed the beeper number and waited anxiously for the return call. When it came, I tersely told Oola what had happened. She and Andrew were shopping in Manhattan. She would head out immediately. She said to help Annie lie down and elevate her feet, to put a cool cloth on her head and keep her warm. I repeated the instructions before she hung up and begged her to hurry.

Vanessa and I walked Annie to the couch in the office and covered her with a blanket, placing my pillow beneath her feet. I ran to the bathroom and wet a washcloth for her forehead. Vanessa went to the living room and occupied the children while I stayed with Annie. Mostly she was quiet, but occasionally she moaned and tossed. Perhaps twenty minutes later the phone rang.

"Hello," I said, picking it up off Vanessa's desk on the first ring.

"Kate," he said softly.

"Who is this?"

"It's David. Don't hang up," he added quickly.

I glanced nervously at the couch but she hadn't moved.

"Kate, I know you're mad at me but I need to speak to my wife."

"She can't talk to you right now." I replied sternly, then softened. "Honest."

"Look, Kate you have the wrong idea about what's been going on . . ."

"And you have no idea what's going on." I glared guiltily at Annie on the couch. This wasn't what she wanted.

"We're going to a counselor. Didn't she tell you?"

"Yeah, she told me."

"It's gonna work out, I know it will. I just wanted her to know that. That I'm really going to try."

"I'll tell her, David." I waited for him to hang up.

"How are the kids?"

"The girls are fine," I fudged. "Look, I'll tell Annie you called and what you said. That's all I can do. We've got our own problems here."

"What problems?"

"Nothing you'd be concerned about. Just another jerk who likes to threaten women and frighten little girls. Annie tried to tell you about it, but you wouldn't listen."

"You mean the guy Vanessa was dating?"

"He's stalking her! He thinks he can do anything he wants to her and no one will stop him."

"Are Annie and the girls safe, Kate? I want the truth!"

"Yes. Look, I've gotta go. I'll tell Annie you called . . ." He was the first to hang up. Annie lay still as ever, eyes closed. I tiptoed toward the door for a soda, and maybe a call to Ellen. Annie spoke softly as I passed behind the couch.

"That was David."

"God, you scared me," I stalled. "Yeah, it was him. I would have given you the phone but I thought you were asleep," I lied.

"No you didn't."

"No, I didn't."

Annie sat up, pulling the warm soggy cloth from her head. "Where are the girls?"

"Kicking Vanessa's ass at Donkey Kong. They really are fine, Annie. We scared them more than Jake."

"This time, Kate. They're okay this time. But what he did was unspeakable and it terrifies me to think what he'll do next."

"I don't think he'd actually do anything to them. It's us he wants to get to," I said. Judging from the look on Annie's face, she didn't really care what I thought. There was too much at stake to value the opinion of a woman best known for hangovers and hindsight. "Not that we should take any chances," I added hurriedly. "Is there someplace you can send them, Annie?"

As I spoke, the doorbell rang.

"Who on earth is that?" Annie asked nervously.

"Oola," I answered, heading for the front door. Annie followed slowly, trying to shake off her fugue. Vanessa was already punching in the code when I met her at the door.

Oola stood under the porch light, silver streaks of light playing off her golden hair. Even in a crisis, Oola looked great.

"How is she?" she asked without formality.

"Better," I said, hearing a car door slam. "Who's out there?" I could see the outline of large Mercedes sedan.

Oola faced us, rather defiantly I thought. "Andrew is with me . . ."

"To what do we owe this great honor? . . ." But I only thought that. And thought better of "Whoopee!" But I managed "How nice" before I was looking at her back.

"I've been talking to the girls," Vanessa said, drawing Oola inside as she looked back uncertainly. "I don't think they have any idea of what he was talking about."

"Annie," said Oola, opening her arms, with one last glance over her shoulder.

I heard footsteps on the sidewalk and looked up. Andrew came up the walk, tall, slim and bespectacled. He looked none too thrilled to be here, but tried to make an effort.

"Kate."

"Andrew." We nodded and stiffly shook hands.

"It's nice to see you again," he added.

No it's not. "Yeah, right," I said gracelessly. His face flushed and he brushed past me up the stairs. Maybe I should have been nicer, but I didn't see much point in pretending. Andrew made me nervous and edgy and insecure and as I followed him into the house, I felt confrontation looming. To avoid it, I headed to the kitchen and did the lunch dishes while Oola and the rest of them talked to the children.

". . . as soon as we get their things packed," Annie said, entering the room, trailed by Andrew.

"What's going on?" I asked.

"Andrew and Oola are taking the kids home," she replied, pulling a six-pack of Juicy Juice from the fridge.

"Home? Home where?"

"Kate, they can't stay here and they've had enough up-heaval. David wants them to come home."

"Who cares what David wants?" I replied. "How can you even think of sending them there?"

"Kate, this is my decision," she said, face tight and angry.

I started to object again, but thought better of it. What did I know? It was plain as hell that the low opinion I'd had of David had owed a lot to my opinion of myself. Still, there were times when I was sure I knew what was best for Annie, and for her marriage and her kids, too. And Annie used to think so, too.

Within seconds, the phone rang. It was Ellen. "I was thinking about hitting the five-thirty meeting and wondered if you wanted to go." Grateful for the pretext to leave, I agreed eagerly. Ellen was on her way home from work and wouldn't have time to get me, so she gave me directions to a nearby church.

I went to the office for a clean shirt. I skirted the conversation in the living room, Oola and the kids still talking, Annie, Andrew and Vanessa looking on. There wasn't time for a shower, so I pinned my hair on top of my head and pulled on a sweater. Without explanation, I fled the house, gunning the Phoenix and peeling out of the driveway.

I found the meeting without much trouble. Though I had never been there before, I saw the usual slogan signs and AA literature. I'd found out at the last meeting what they meant by a big book. Actually, it was the Big Book, a volume of solutions to alcoholism by alcoholics, specifically those who helped found the organization some sixty years ago. Ellen had suggested I get one, but I wasn't much of a reader.

She slid into the chair next to me as the steps were being read. This meeting was run differently than the others I'd attended. There was no speaker. Instead, after the chairperson asked about new people, he surveyed the room for topics. Did anyone want to talk about a step, a tradition, or have a living problem they needed help with?

I had a problem. I was very misunderstood, something I knew these people would understand. I raised my hand, and when acknowledged, poured forth my tale of woe. After five minutes of righteously reiterating my story, I sat back to receive their affirmation and reassurance.

I didn't know what the hell had happened to AA, but ten minutes into the meeting I knew these people were messed up. Just like Jerry, they told stories from their own lives, but I knew what the deal was. The gist of it all was self-pity. Apparently mine.

In mid-meeting, a guy on my right rose to get coffee and gestured toward my empty cup. I jerked it from his reach and pushed back from the table indignantly, stomping to the ever-present coffee urn. He shrugged and followed, an amused grin playing around his lips. Laugh once, sport, I thought, and you're a dead man.

Ellen was speaking when I returned to my seat. I was fuming. No one understood at all. A bartender might, suggested voice one. Poor Kate, sympathized the second, this AA thing was a big mistake.

"When I was drinking, I had these nasty little voices in my head, telling me all kinds of crazy stuff. I was an insecure egomaniac, if that's possible." A few people at the table chuckled. I still felt betrayed but she had my attention. "You know, I had my life in such a mess by the time I got here, but that didn't stop me from telling everyone else how they should live."

My cheeks had gotten red as she spoke. People continued talking but I rolled her words around in my mind. She might have a point. I had decided how Annie should handle her marriage and I was shoving it down her throat. If I was really honest about it, my marriage didn't make me much of a role model.

This was just great. I came to AA to stop drinking so I would stop doing awful things. What did I get—an opportunity to have the awful things I did pointed out to me! At my first meeting, I wasn't a bad person trying to be good, but a sick person trying to get well. By day three, they were kicking my butt around the church basement. I'd hated mirrors all my life and now I sat in a room with about thirty-five of them. Belonging was not everything it had been cracked up to be.

The house was quiet when I came in. I heard Vanessa in the office and went there. She turned from the computer and looked me over.

"Have you been drinking?"

"How subtle, Vanessa," I replied. "Let me see. If I'd been drinking, would I tell the truth and get my ass kicked, or would I lie? Hmm, what's a girl to do?" I put my fist to my mouth and pretended to be in deep thought.

"Can the crap! Where have you been?"

"Where's your faith, Vanessa?"

"In the gutter with your track record, Kate."

"Your support is overwhelming. I've been to a meeting with Ellen."

"Oh. Sorry."

I plopped on the couch and waved her away. "Don't worry about it. Where's Annie?"

"Upstairs. The kids leaving shook her up a little."

"How come she didn't take them?" If this was such a good idea, sniped the voice.

"She figured the last thing they needed was another fight and things between her and David are still too raw."

"Oh," I said. "Poor kids, three hours in a car with Oola and Andrew."

"They're fine. They're going home. Now, Andrew, there was somebody who didn't look so fine."

"What's the matter with him?" I replied sullenly.

"Maybe he got some crazy impression that he wasn't welcome here."

"Maybe he shouldn't have thought he was doing us such a big favor by being here."

"He is kind of a priss," she conceded with a giggle, "but their marriage seems to work. Unless Oola stays with him as an inspiration to her clients."

For the life of me I couldn't see how being married to Andrew could be an inspiration for anything but suicide or divorce. "Only if they never meet him."

We laughed.

"Well, he's gone. And he did help Annie with the computer."

"Yeah, all right. Is Oola coming back?"

"No, they're going home after."

That was too bad. I liked it when we were all together. Oola was a pain at times, but having her here made me less afraid. As if she knew what I was thinking, Vanessa said, "Yeah, me too."

28

I went upstairs to Annie, truly apologetic. I tried to listen to her perspective and managed to back off about David. It wasn't my business and Annie deserved my support, no matter what she decided. Without having to actually promise, I agreed to apologize to Andrew, though I wasn't making it a priority. We came downstairs, got something to eat and took up our least favorite topic.

"What do you think Jake is doing?" Annie wondered.

"I don't know," Vanessa replied. "He's stopped calling. Even though it's been a nice break, it makes me nervous. Speaking of which, Kate, what happened to the tape in our new machine?"

I flushed. "After the thing with cops, I didn't want to record Jake saying anything about me and Annie being in his house. The taping was supposed to help us, not get used against us."

Vanessa nodded slowly. "I suppose you're right. But I know he isn't finished. And now we're operating in the dark."

"Well, we do have the flowers," I added flippantly. "There's a coupla hundred bucks sitting in the garbage can."

"But no one will help us. I still don't believe nothing happened with the mailbox. That's a federal offense, isn't it?" Annie pushed her plate away.

"Yeah, but only if you can make the cops believe you," I replied. "I have a feeling the feds have their doubts."

"Doubts about what?"

"Cops are the same, Annie. God forbid they get themselves caught in the midst of a lovers' quarrel," Vanessa said.

"So nobody even watched the box? To see who picked up Vanessa's mail?" Annie asked incredulously.

"Not that we know of," I replied. "And it pisses me off,

too. Not just for catching him, but we don't even know if he got the answers from our personal ad."

All that night, or so it seemed in the morning, my marriage played through my head like a bad movie. A parade of Steves and Kates locked in battle, the Steves pleading, arguing and yelling, the Kates screeching, blaming and denying. Then and there I decided I had a duty to tell Steve I was seeing some things he had seen all along.

The Phoenix got me to Steve's new offices about eleven. I couldn't believe how well it was driving. Or maybe I wasn't asking so much of it. As I entered the building the knots in my stomach would have done a sailor proud. There were some hard steps to the signboard to find the room and floor. WMFH, it said, seventh floor, Suite 721.

A little smile touched my face as I remembered the night we named the business. We had just gotten the loft and were drinking champagne in the middle of the floor on a blanket. Our furniture hadn't arrived and the popping cork and clinking crystal echoed in the empty loft. I was telling Steve some crazy story and he was laughing hysterically. When he finally got his bearings back, he told me I had a warped mind. Warped mind for hire, I had said. That's it, he'd said, that's what we'll call the agency. Warped Minds For Hire. We had made love then, rolling around on dusty tarps and unfinished floors, pausing only long enough for me to move the champagne within reach. Funny how I hadn't cared about the dirt or the hard floor, just the champagne. At that time, Steve hadn't even noticed. Later, he would notice every drink I took, so I started hiding bottles and sneaking drinks. It was for his own good, said the little voice. That's not true, I replied soundlessly. Normal people don't hide vodka bottles in the laundry hamper.

The elevator ride took forever and not quite long enough. The doors finally opened and I walked down the hall. I could see Amad sitting behind a high-topped, black lacquer desk in the reception area. I opened the doors and Amad looked up, professional smile in place. His eyes widened in recognition and the smile dwindled. He got a grip and smiled again, warily. Amad had known me back when and his reaction was a slap in the face.

"Kathy," he said. "How nice to see you. How are you?"

The words were right, but his tone was way off.

"It's Kate now, Amad. I'm great, thanks. How are you?

"Getting by," he replied. "So . . . Kate . . . what can I do for you?"

"Obviously I want to see Steve."

Quickly, he scanned the large appointment book in front of him. "Does he know you're coming?" he asked hopefully.

"Look, I don't want to put you on the spot, Amad, but I'm gonna see Steve and I'm gonna see him today. Now I can either sit out here and greet clients—" Amad's eyes widened in dismay. "Or you can tell him I'm here."

I smiled benignly. Amad punched some buttons on the phone and spoke quietly. To cut him some slack, I moved away from the desk. He whispered into the phone behind his hand. I caught him sneaking a look at me, and I knew what Steve had asked.

"I'm sober, Amad. Tell him I'm sober." Amad's face flushed and he hung up the phone. I waited five more humiliating minutes until I saw my ex-husband walk into the lobby. He grimaced at me and curtly gestured with his head to point me in the direction of his office. Nothing was said until the door was closed.

"What do you want, Kathleen?"

"I need to talk to you, Steve."

"I don't think we have anything to talk about."

"Yes, we do. I want . . ." I started

"You want what?" He interrupted. "Money? Need me to pay off your bar tab or did you just stop by for a free drink?" He strode angrily to the wall unit and threw open the cupboard where he kept liquor for clients. As he moved a strand of hair flopped across his forehead and I had a vivid memory of gently pushing it back one night as he lay next to me in our bed. I would not cry, I thought, chewing skin off my lip.

After a while it dawned on him I wasn't fighting back. He glared at me, then looked puzzled, and finally sat, his anger spent, at least for the moment.

"I want to apologize," I said.

"Apologize! For what? What kind of a game is this, Kathleen?"

"It isn't a game, Steve."

"So this is how you apologize to people," he sneered, voice

rising again. "Barge into their office unannounced, threaten their staff, demand to be seen! Typical!"

"I didn't threaten anyone. You're the one who's losing his temper."

"It's always me, isn't it, Kath. No matter what you do, it always ends up being my fault!"

"No!" I stood up, walked a few feet away, then turned to face him. "That's why I'm here. If you would just give me a chance . . ."

"A chance," he roared. "Jesus fucking Christ, how many chances do you need!"

He picked up a large file folder and slammed it down on the desk. I cringed at the noise, but it seemed to shake him from his fury. He closed his eyes for a second, gave a deep sigh and sank into his chair.

"Damn it, Kath, what is it about you that turns me into a stark raving lunatic?"

"I'm sorry," I said miserably. "I came to make things better, not get you upset." He didn't reply, just sat, shaking his head in futility. "But I was always good at getting you going," I added with a weak chuckle.

He gave a snort. "That's for sure." There was silence for a second. "What do you want, Kath?" I sat back down, took a deep breath and met his eyes across the desk.

"I started going to AA, Steve. I'm trying to stop drinking."

"Yeah, right, Kathleen," he replied, playing with a pencil.

"I am," I asserted again. "Look at me. I haven't had a drink in over a week."

I faced his inspection bravely. His eyes narrowed and he came around the desk, swooping close behind me. I was confused, uncertain of his motive, half-expecting him to nuzzle the nape of my neck the way he used to. Instead he sniffed loudly, the prick.

"Do you want me to pee in a cup!" Irritably, I flapped hands to shoo him away. "Jesus, Steve, I only came here to . . . I mean, since I stopped drinking, I realized some stuff."

"Really. And what was that?" He was back at his desk, arms folded, superiority oozing from every pore.

"I guess I deserve this," I said, letting out a big breath. "But you're not making it easy. I want to apologize for what I did. To our marriage and our business. I'm an alcoholic." I put my hand up to still his interruption. "I know, you told me that a long time ago. But I had to find out for myself." He was still looking at me suspiciously. "I'm pigheaded, remember? Nobody knows that better than you." I smiled tentatively with raised eyebrows. It took a minute, but slowly he smiled back.

"Is this for real, Kath? You've really stopped drinking, for good?"

"I'm not drinking today, that's how it works."

"Yeah, but what about tomorrow?"

"When tomorrow comes, it'll be today." He wanted to believe me, I could tell. That desire warred with our history and my promises from the past. "It's hard to explain but I was going crazy and didn't dare let anyone know. I was afraid if you knew you'd leave me. How could you stay? And you couldn't, could you?" I tried to smile and started crying instead.

He moved quickly, coming around the corner of the desk. I felt his arms around me and turned my face into his shoulder. We stayed like that for a while, me mumbling and weeping, Steve holding me and saying it was okay. When I had completely ruined one side of his suit jacket, I lifted my face and wiped my eyes.

"I've been such a jerk."

"Yeah, but you do it so well," he replied, grinning.

"Thanks, you're a pal."

"How 'bout this pal takes you to lunch?" I looked at him, surprised. "I don't hate you, Kathy. I hated the way things were. C'mon, I'll buy. You still eat, right?"

"Like a horse," I replied, feeling much better. "This will cost you."

"Please . . . Since your expense account was dropped, we've saved thousands. Of course, a couple of neighborhood saloons have gone belly up, but . . ."

"Cheap shot. For that, we're doing the Four Seasons. Break out the gold card, hotshot!"

"You're on," he said.

We gathered our stuff and breezed through the lobby past the astonished Amad. In the cab to the restaurant Steve gave me an update on WMFH. It was doing very well and to my surprise, I was honestly happy for him. We had just finished our salads when I started telling him about Jake and Vanessa. He listened straight through our entrees, shaking his head a lot.

"The bastard actually hit you? But you're okay?"

"Yeah. It'd take more than a little pop in the nose to slow me down."

"That makes me feel better. At least I was right."

"What?"

"There's been more than once I wanted to knock some sense into you, but I didn't think it would work. I was right. Decaf, please," he said to the waiter who cleared his plate.

"Very funny. You were just afraid I'd hit you back," I taunted. "Regular, extra sugar."

"Hit me back?" he joked. "You hit me first!"

My face flushed and I looked away.

"Hey, Kath, I'm sorry. I was kidding, really. Tell me more about this Jake guy. Is there anything I can do?"

"You've already done plenty, you just don't know it. Rented any P.O. boxes lately?" At his quizzical look, I explained about Vanessa's mail and the personal ad. His face darkened. "The son of a bitch used my name?"

"He wanted to see if he could push my buttons. I tried to push his back with the *Voice* ad, but I'm not sure if he got any of the letters. Now that he knows we're on to him he won't go back."

"Where's the box?" He asked.

"Midtown," I answered, giving the address.

In the cab on the way back to his office he told the driver to turn around. "I want to go downtown." He repeated the address of the mailbox location. "Let's deliver some mail, Kath."

"It's Kate now," I said absently. "Are you sure about this?"

"You bet. I don't like other people using my name or trying to scare my wife." I didn't bother to remind him I was his ex-wife.

When we reached our destination Steve paid the cab and strode confidently toward the counter.

"What about the police?" I hissed, suddenly nervous. "What if they arrest you?"

"You watch too much television." He flashed a brilliant smile at the woman behind the counter. "Hi. I'm Steve Meriden. I have box 1394, but I've forgotten my key." He pulled out his driver's license. Within minutes we were back on street, carrying two sacks of mail.

Steve flagged a cab and gave the driver the address in Queens. The cabbie started bitching about leaving Manhattan, but settled for mumbling curses under his breath when Steve asked for his license number.

"I can't believe you! You're the best!" I planted a kiss on his cheek.

"It ain't over yet. We gotta make the drop, doll," he joked, talking out of the side of his mouth.

We crossed the bridge and made it to Astoria in record time. While we rode, I dug through the mail sacks and finally found the reply from Gordon Sims. I placed it on top of the bag.

When we pulled up in front of Jake's office Steve handed some money over the seat. "This is for what's on the meter, but I want you to wait and take us back. Will an extra twenty on top of the bill cover your wait?" Our cabbie suddenly developed customer service skills, jumping out to open my door and promising to be here when we got out. As we climbed the stairs to Jake's office, my heart pounded. Steve walked confidently to the secretary's desk. Claire looked up and smiled.

"Is Mr. Romano in?"

"No, I'm sorry, he's not," she replied. "Did you have an appointment?" She looked at me puzzled and I could see her trying to remember how she knew me.

"No," Steve replied pleasantly. "I'm just here to clear up a little mixup. Mr. Romano's mail seems to have ended up in my box. I have a P.O. box and I have all this mail," he gestured toward the sacks on the floor, "that belongs to him."

"Oh," she said uncertainly.

"My wife and I were out in this area so I thought we'd drop it off," Steve added grandly. I did my part by gazing at him in an adoring fashion.

"Well, how nice," Claire replied. "That was Mr. and Mrs. . . . ?"

"Meriden," Steve said helpfully.

"Steve and Katie," I added.

"Have we met?"

"Why don't I just leave you my card," Steve interrupted. "That way if Mr. Romano has any further problems getting his mail, he knows where to reach me." He dropped the card on her desk and took my arm, leading me out into the hall. She was still looking from the card to the mail as we turned into the stairwell.

We laughed all the way to Manhattan, watched in the rearview mirror by our cabbie who probably wondered if the two crazies in the back would pay up as promised. We did, then stood on the sidewalk in front of the building, awkward again for the first time since lunch.

"Well, thanks for everything," I said. "This was great."

"It was," he agreed. "Like old times."

"Yeah."

We looked at each other and suddenly I felt like crying again. I think he did too, because he turned away, looking toward the lobby of the building as if he was expecting someone to come out. I played with the strap of my purse and shifted my weight from foot to foot.

"Well," he said crisply. "Take care of yourself, will you?"

"I will. Steve, I'm really sorry."

"I am too, Kath. You're not the only one who lost."

He hugged me hard and before I managed to respond, he let me go and hurried into the building. He didn't look back, though I watched to see if he would. Walking back to my car my emotions were in an uproar and I knew the little voices were about to start. I found a working pay phone, and using the little card Ellen had given me, located a meeting in fifteen minutes down on St. Mark's Place. I forced the Phoenix into traffic and made it to the meeting only five minutes late.

The traffic home was reasonably light. I felt light myself, unburdened and free. I yielded the right of way to a little old lady in a blue Camry and cheerfully ignored the opportunity to blast my horn at some idiot kid who blew by me in a Corvette. Not that he didn't deserve it, mind you, but there was nothing like forgiveness to make you feel forgiving.

The Blazer was in the driveway behind Annie's van, so I parked on the street. Oola had returned and everyone was sitting around the kitchen table, talking excitedly. Heads turned as I walked in.

"Where the hell have you been?" Vanessa.

"Where were you?" Oola.

"We were worried." Annie.

"I went to see Steve and hit a meeting on the way home," I answered casually and grabbed a soda from the fridge. "So what's goin' on?"

"Your friend Bob called," Oola informed me. "We told him about the banquet at the Plaza."

"And guess what," Annie added, all excited.

"What?" I mugged, jaw dropped and eyes wide.

"Guess who's going! Come on, guess!"

"Woody Allen?"

"Us! Vanessa fixed it!" Annie clapped her hands.

"I know everybody and everybody I know knows somebody else," Vanessa drawled. "There isn't a party in this town I can't get invited to if I put my mind to it."

"Not only did she get us in, they're gonna set up a table for us, right near Jake," Annie added.

There were lots of hugs and squeezes. For no reason we could articulate, we knew the banquet was our best chance yet. We had no idea what to expect, but he would be in public wearing his mask, and we would be there to expose the man behind it.

Eventually Oola got around to asking about Steve, just as I knew she would. I told her Steve was doing great and side-stepped the real issue.

Oola might have been too polite to push but Vanessa wasn't.

"What did you and Steve have to talk about?"

"Perhaps that's private," Oola suggested.

"Come on, Kate, spill it. If I have to live in a fish bowl . . ."

"I got to thinking about how things were for Steve when I was drinking. And they weren't too hot. I just wanted him to know I was sorry."

"That's wonderful, " Oola said, smiling. "Did it work out all right?"

"Better than all right. It was a little rocky at first, but after I apologized, Steve took me to lunch."

"Where?" Vanessa asked.

"Four Seasons."

"That must have been some apology."

"It was some divorce," I replied. "But listen to the best

part. I told Steve about Jake . . ." There was a sharp intake of breath all around. "About the mailbox, of course. Boy, was he pissed!" Vanessa at least was delighted.

"What do you say I take everybody out to dinner," said Vanessa. "Maybe it's premature, but I think we should celebrate!"

"Sounds great to me," Annie said.

"Me too," I said. "Let's do that Mexican place. I love their guacamole."

"If you want to fit into my clothes, you'd better forget the guacamole. Friday is only two days away, *comprende*?"

"*Chinga tu madre!*" I responded, proud of my accent. And my high school Spanish teacher had sworn I hadn't learned anything.

29

The next morning, I showered and dressed, then wandered restlessly about the house. Vanessa was shut up in her office. Annie was doing laundry like there was no tomorrow. I checked in with Bobby to see if everything was set for the Plaza. He wasn't there and Tina's voice was ice. Mine was a message he wouldn't get. Then I took a call that gave me plenty to do with the rest of my day. Charlie Harrington had come up with an address for Natalie Romano. No phone, but the address was fine. I told him I'd issue a check for him right away, sure at this point that Steve would be glad to help.

Vanessa came with me in my car. The Lower East Side was pretty quiet in the morning. The piercing shops and tattoo parlors were just pulling up their gates. Most of the residents of Alphabet City were vampires, clothed in black, covered with symbols, rising after darkness to party into the night.

Her building was scary. The front door didn't shut and the intercom had been ripped away. A painted swastika on the second floor was almost obliterated by fist holes in the sheet rock. Most of the apartments were unnumbered and so we knocked at random. At the third door, a woman answered.

"Hi, I'm looking for Rachel Linwood," I said. Vanessa stood behind me, keeping an eye on the hall. A man and a woman screamed in Spanish from the floor above. "Hello?"

"Who's asking?" she said, muffled by the door.

"I'm looking for Rachel Linwood," I repeated. "Do you know her?"

"Depends on who's looking." The door still hadn't opened. I resisted the urge to stick my eye against the peephole. I wouldn't be able to see anything, but I knew she was looking and I hated being watched.

"Oh, right. I'm Kate Meriden, I'm a partner in the WMFH

agency in Tribeca," I lied smoothly. "We're interested in hiring Ms. Linwood." I dug out my wallet and fumbled through the sections, looking for an old business card.

"For what?" Suspicion radiated through the battered wood and peeling paint.

"Do you know Rachel Linwood or not?" Vanessa was not the most patient person I'd ever met.

"Who's she?"

"My art director," I continued with a side glance at Van. This was her. I knew it. I had to get us in.

"Nah, I don't know her."

"Well, thanks anyway. I'm going slip my card under the door, if you should happen to meet her, this is a big job. Big money." Money bought safety. Silence from behind the door.

"Let's go, Kate." Vanessa was already four feet down the hall.

Still nothing. I waited another minute, then took my last shot.

"We'll be flying everyone out to L.A. Our expense, of course," I called as I hefted my bag and followed. The Spanish upstairs had picked up in volume and something crashed against a wall.

"Wait a minute." I hadn't heard the door open. We both turned back. A waif of a woman stood beside it, slim to the point of skinny. She wore a man's undershirt and her small breasts poked out just like her ribs. Her head was recently shaved, a haze of reddish regrowth just beginning to sprout. She wore huge gold earrings that framed her face and brushed her shoulders. Her large green eyes roamed over us, still checking, needing to be sure.

"I'm Rachel Linwood." She held out her hand. Vanessa reached her first, towering over her, strangely protective.

"Vanessa Clayton."

"Kate Meriden," I said. "Do you mind if we talk inside?"

She led us into the apartment. It was sparse and ugly, institutional yellow walls, bathtub in the kitchen. The room was hot, a radiator in the corner hissing steam, the valve broken away. A futon couch unfolded behind a cable spool table. There was an old rocker and a card table with four beat-up folding chairs. It was sad, a sad place, and the woman seemed the same. Suddenly, I felt less comfortable about what we were doing.

"So when would we be leaving? I mean, what's the campaign for?" Natalie asked. She didn't apologize for the apartment. Vanessa prowled the room, stopping to peer at a picture in a frame.

"Your mother?" Vanessa held it up. Natalie nodded. "Pretty. Does she live around here?"

"She used to. She's dead now."

"Oh. I'm sorry." Great, more guilt. I sat at the card table, touched by the single slender iris in a salad dressing bottle. She sat across from me and entwined her fingers, trying not to look eager. Afraid to hope.

"So, this campaign. What's the product?"

"Umm, mascara." I'd almost said shampoo. "I have to tell you, I almost didn't recognize you." She laughed and ran a hand over her bald head. Long polished nails. Vanessa leaned against the wall behind me. Watching her.

"I just did it last week. Wild, isn't it?" She grinned. She was a beautiful woman. Just like Vanessa. "If you're gonna live in this neighborhood, it makes sense to blend in." Especially if you're hiding. "Sorry about the thing at the door," she added. "There's a lot of crazies around here. You have to be careful."

Vanessa pushed herself off the wall and paced the room. I babbled on about some mythical mascara, unsure how to tell her why we'd come. I was hot in my coat, sticky and uncomfortable. I was trying to figure out how to convince Steve to hire her, when Vanessa spoke.

"Have you lived here long, Natalie?"

She turned in the chair with a smile. "No, only about . . ." The smile faded. The eyes were huge. "What did you call me?" She faltered, hesitant, scared but not wanting to believe that when the enemy knocked on the door she had let them in.

"Rachel, I meant Rachel. I'm terrible with names, I'm always . . ."

"Get out!"

"Wait, let me explain, I . . ." Vanessa stepped forward.

"Get out!" She screamed, her head twitching and cocking like a sparrow on a window sill. "Both of you!" I didn't move.

She threw back her chair and stood, arms gesturing wildly. "Did he send you? Is that it?" She raced to the window, pushing aside the dirty blinds to look out, then yanking the cord to shut them tight.

"Natalie . . ." Vanessa tried.

"Get out!!" She grabbed a soda bottle off the bookshelf between the windows and flung it. Vanessa ducked and it smashed against the wall. I jumped up, shocked, my chair clattering to the floor. She slid down the wall, still ordering us out, softer and softer, fist pounding the floor. We gaped at her, both of us unnerved and unprepared for the reaction we had wrought.

"Natalie," I said softly, crouching by her side. "He didn't send us. Honest he didn't." It was like touching a tuning fork. Her whole body hummed.

"Why would you help him? Don't you know what he is?"

Vanessa sank to her knees. "I would never help him. That's why I wanted to talk to you. I tried to call, but you had moved."

"I have to move . . ." We could barely hear her. "He finds me." Her whisper floated on the air. Tears rolled down Vanessa's cheeks. She tried to answer but couldn't find the words.

"Natalie, a few weeks ago a friend of ours called you. Do you remember?" She didn't answer but I pressed on. "She told you about a woman Jake was stalking." She raised her head from her knees, lashes wet and shining. "It's Vanessa. We came here to see if you could help." I put my hands on her shoulders and our eyes met. Then she threw my hands off and struggled to her feet. The blinds rocked against her back.

"I told her I couldn't get involved. I can't let him find me! How dare you track me down and lead him right to me!" She faced us both, eyes blazing.

"I need your help," Vanessa cried.

"I don't care!" Natalie spit the words at Vanessa's face. She flinched as if she'd been slapped.

"Well maybe you should care! You selfish bitch! I thought once you understood you'd want to help us stop him! But you don't care about that, you don't care about anyone but yourself. Well, fine, we're going. Lock your fucking door and hide in this goddamn rattrap until you die for all I care! But I'm not gonna let him keep doing this to Vanessa, because I'd hate like hell to see her end up like you!" She turned away halfway through, her whole body shaking, hands covering her face. Vanessa rose slowly from the floor and I put my arm around her shoulders. "Come on, Van. Let's go."

"You don't understand," she pleaded. "You don't understand what it's like."

"Yes, I do. Why won't you believe me—I do!"

They stood three feet apart, physically so different, but so much the same. Suddenly they were in each other's arms, in the middle of the room, Natalie's head buried just below Vanessa's shoulder.

"It's not that I don't want to help you. I can't," she said finally, pulling away. She checked the window nervously. Her skin seemed to itch, fingers endlessly scratching and rubbing and plucking. "I just can't. It cost me so much to get away. I can't let him find me."

"He's not going to find . . ." I began. Vanessa shushed me.

"I've been running for over seven years." She smiled at us, lips trembling. She gestured around the room. "You think I like living like this? I haven't had a home since I married him. Don't marry him," she said to Vanessa. I started to laugh, but she was serious.

"There's no chance of that now."

Natalie nodded, satisfied, and wiped at her nose with the back of her hand. She pulled a mangled pack of Marlboros from her jeans, lit one and took a deep drag. "You can't stop him. I hate to tell you that, but it's true." She walked to the window and peered out. "He's crazy. People don't believe that, and for a long time I thought it was me, but it's him." She sank into a chair at the card table. Vanessa got an old tuna fish can that served as an ashtray from the cable spool and sat down too. I took up the vigil at the window. It was getting dark now, more people prowled about, delivery trucks clotting the street.

"So crazy," she whispered again in a faraway voice. The cigarette hung from the corner of her mouth while she twisted a ring on her finger. "I never would have gotten away at all if it wasn't for my mom." She got up and brought the picture back to the table.

"My mom helps me too."

Her lips trembled and the cigarette fell. It lay there, burning a hole in the vinyl. "My mother's dead," she said dully, fingers tracing the picture's cheek. Vanessa picked up the cigarette and butted it in the can.

"You said so, I'm sorry."

I turned to the window and gazed blindly into the street.

"It was a hit and run." Voice like breaking glass. Eyes dark and angry. "No one would believe me, but I know Jake did it!"

Vanessa stared. I turned in shock, blinds slipping from my fingers, hiding the street from view. Vanessa started to speak.

Wait a minute. I lifted the blinds again, cautiously.

"What is it, Kate?"

He came out of the Korean fruit stand, tossing an apple in his hand. I stared out the window, breath stuck in my chest, fingers bending the blinds. He walked by the Phoenix, halfway up the block, and leaned against the BMW, double-parked behind a truck. He looked up. I released the blinds with a snap.

"What is it, Kate?" Vanessa asked again. I heard the panic in her voice and Natalie heard it too. She jumped up from the card table and pushed me aside.

"Nothing," I said quickly.

"Oh my god," Natalie cried, hand touching her lips.

"What! Tell me, what?" Now Vanessa was at the window too, the three of us huddling behind the slats, peering at the man who had hunted us down. "Oh my god," she echoed.

"Close the blinds," I hissed, yanking the cord.

"It's too late," Natalie whispered and spun away from the window, nearly knocking Vanessa down. She ran to a closet and pulled a large duffel bag from a hook on the door. Back to the kitchen, shoving things in spoons, plates, bowls.

"Natalie, calm down, we have to figure out what to do."

"I'm sorry," Vanessa pleaded, following her about the kitchen. "Nat, I'm sorry."

"No you're not, you got what you wanted, now go! He found me, that was it, wasn't it? Now maybe he'll leave you alone." She shoved past Vanessa and pulled open a bureau just right of the kitchen door.

"That wasn't it at all," I protested.

"Get out," she yelled, stuffing sweaters in the bag, silverware. "Haven't I done enough! Haven't I helped you?" Her words were painful, smarting like a carpet burn.

"Natalie, please. I'll go out there, I can draw him away . . ."

"Like you led him here? You still don't get it, do you! Jake doesn't lose! He'll find you wherever you go, whatever you do, even when he doesn't want you anymore, he will still find you! And you . . ." She pointed a shaking finger at Vanessa. "You're supposed to understand and you led him right to me." Her teeth were clenched, breath barely squeezing through. The hatred in her eyes scared us both. "Get out!"

"No," said Vanessa, suddenly calm. "We've got to stick together. We can get you out of this." She went into her purse and pulled out her checkbook.

"You think money will help?" Natalie was more hysterical if anything. "He'll spend any amount to finish me off, don't you know that?"

"Not if he doesn't know where you are. Hey, remember our story to get in here? A job in L.A. You were willing to consider it ten minutes ago. What if I make this for ten thousand dollars? Is it Rachel Linwood on your ID?"

"It's *useless!* Don't you get it? What good is money to a corpse?"

"You're giving up too soon." Vanessa wrote the check. "One of my books is being made into a movie, so I've got some contacts on the West Coast. There are some people I would trust—women! They'll see that you're safe till Jake is behind bars."

Natalie took the check, looked at it for a few seconds, then beyond it to the floor. I knew she was thinking of safety in terms of hours or days. It was too soon even for hope.

"We'll go to my bank and get you traveler's checks."

"He'll be right behind us!"

"We're used to that. But we can lose him. And you can lose him for good if you want to! Look, it's information he wants. He'll want to know where you're going so he can keep tabs on you. He's not going to try to kill all three of us in the street out there, or in midtown Manhattan! Not after it took him all these years to find you."

"Well . . ."

"That's right," I said, warming to Vanessa's idea, "he'll be behind us in that big car . . ."

"And we'll be in two cars as soon as we get the chance.

We can all go in Kate's old heap, but we'll stop along the way and put you in a cab."

"I can't! You don't understand!"

"Not alone. I'll go with you to my bank. Don't worry, I'm well known there. He's not going to leave that car and take on a bunch of security guards. Anyway, Kate will be keeping him busy . . . Running interference."

I was with her now. We were the same mind.

"We can make the calls to the airlines from inside the bank," said Vanessa, putting her arm around the much smaller woman, "just you and I."

"C'mon, Natalie, this is going to work!" I said. "Think how great it will be not to have worry about that scumsucking swine!"

"I agree, it's worth a try." Vanessa and I said "yes" so loud it sounded like a cheer. "But one thing, please, if you don't mind, call me Rachel."

Jake couldn't contain his excitement when he saw the three of us emerge. I was first onto the street, carrying Natalie's duffel bag. Vanessa and Natalie were right behind me, walking side by side, Vanessa's arm around her again so possessively that they looked like lovers. The hard look that Jake was giving Natalie told me that he'd never seen her without her hair.

There was a moment when I felt the danger of something he might do right there on the street. Then Jake made a quick move back to his car and all of us knew instantly that our plan was going to have a chance. We were exultant as we climbed in, closed and locked the doors.

We were in control. Jake had to keep us ahead of him, and even though our so-called plan was nothing but a bunch of ideas that might work if we spotted the right circumstances, we knew what those circumstances were and Jake didn't, yet.

Our first chance came when we turned uptown from Union Square. Vanessa shouted out of her open window for a cabbie to take "me and my friend all over town." We made the transfer with me alongside, and once the two of them were in the cab I stayed in place at the light and let them go ahead. Afraid of losing time, we decided to leave Natalie's big army bag with me.

Where Jake had been willing to let a car or two get between

us till now, he was right on my tail now that he had two cars to keep in view. I had no doubt that Jake would try to pass me and stay with Natalie and Vanessa if we divided up, so I had to stay with them, too.

What we had in mind was for me to stay in the middle lane going up Park Avenue South and try to block Jake if he tried to pass me on either side. He was making moves all the time now and I would squeeze him off. There were mostly cabs on the street so I heard plenty of honking and saw plenty of hands fly up in rage, but nothing could take the smile off my face.

The cab was unable to get more than one car, two cars, three cars ahead, but I could sense Jake's mounting rage. He had to know that I meant business after the other day. He wouldn't risk an accident because he would have to stop. Nothing could wipe the smile off my face, not even the thought of sacrificing the Phoenix.

Unfortunately the traffic was moving right along and I hadn't had a single opportunity to bottle him up. Vanessa's bank was up by Rockefeller Center, so we didn't have that much time. Up by Grand Central I was hoping for a snarl-up from which the cab ahead would emerge, while I just made things worse. Jake wouldn't be the only one trying to take my head off if I was at the heart of a traffic jam. I'd have dozens of men swearing at me in just as many languages. I could hardly wait! My mess was his mess!

I didn't have to wait for Grand Central. We were still in the thirty-something streets when I saw a delivery truck come to a stop in the right-hand lane almost a block ahead. That was Jake's lane at the moment, so I slowed enough, braking briefly again and again, as if in response to something I saw ahead in my own lane, luring him alongside. Of course he'd seen the truck by now, but he didn't hit the brake. He was going to put on a burst of speed and pass me on the right, but the second I saw him commit I swerved into him. My reaction was so fast our two cars were kissing, my right front bumper raking his front left.

The guy in the delivery truck had just stepped out when our tires began to squeal. He froze, waiting to see if his truck was going to get hit. When we came to a stop a few feet from it I was on the street telling him to stay put.

"What the hell?" he was saying. He was still having trouble

believing his eyes. So was I. "What the hell?" It was "Tony" speaking, according to the script in red thread above his shirt pocket.

"Don't leave! You'll be a witness!"

"That's right!" Jake was on us right away, in no apparent need of a cervical collar. "He saw you plow right into me, you crazy bitch!"

"I dunno, lady," said the deliveryman, who blinked his eyes back into his head and seemed to weigh about four hundred pounds now that he was just another New Yorker trying to make up his mind about something.

The cab with Natalie and Vanessa in it was out of sight by now, Jake must have been going out of his mind, but he wasn't going to try to leave the scene of an accident, not with Tony here as a witness, and he wasn't going to pop me in the face again, for the same reason.

"How come you ran into him, though?" (Which makes it hard to back you up the way I want to, I imagined him thinking.)

"He must have been in my blind spot. I was only trying to get over . . ."

"Bullshit! You stupid cunt! It was deliberate!"

"Jake gets like this when he doesn't get his way . . ."

"You two know each other?"

"Not very well. I mean, it's embarrassing, we only had one date. I wasn't much fun. I got drunk, he took me to some motel, raped me and made a tape to play on people's message machines."

"Raped you? You think anyone would take your word for that, you drunken slut?"

"Hey, pal, take it easy with the language. You'll get to tell your side of it."

Soon. There was a light flashing behind our two cars where they had come together as if vying for the chance to run into Tony.

Tony was around to hear about Jake's assault on me by the side of another New York highway just the other day. Actually, it was the first thing I told the officer, but he didn't run to his radio to check out my story, so what the hell. Why did I keep thinking the next cop I spoke to would be the one who gives a damn? However, thanks to the way Tony was playing favors the cop was telling us, by the way he looked and spoke and scratched his head, that he didn't think Jake was much of human being, even if he was a better driver than I was. For once Jake had the good sense to keep his mouth shut. The accident was eloquent—you didn't have to be a claims adjuster to see whose fault it was.

"But why would he risk an accident like this to get ahead of you?" the cop asked me.

"To catch up with the two women I'd just put in a cab. One was his ex-wife, who's been hiding from him for seven years after he nearly killed her with his bare hands. He did kill her mother, though—ran her down with one of his fancy cars. And oh, the other woman in the cab was my friend Vanessa, a successful novelist he's been stalking . . ."

"Sure you're not a novelist, too?" But he wasn't suspicious, he was buying it! And why shouldn't he? It was the plain truth, right? Even Tony believed me, I could tell.

The policeman had his shoulders in a fixed shrug and had turned his palms up, looking at each of us in turn with the goofy expression of someone trying hard not to smile.

"What the hell," I said. "Right, Tony?"

30

I wasn't able to get Vanessa till two that afternoon, at her editor's office, where she returned my call before starting her story conference.

"She went to Newark. She's on a hop to Dallas-Fort Worth, where she knows somebody. If that doesn't work out, she'll try L.A. Everything's ready out there."

"But what do we do with this bleeping bag of hers?"

"We'll send it to Dallas. She's in no hurry. With the money I gave her she can buy everything new. God knows she needs to buy some things, poor girl."

"That was great, what you did."

"You know, she never had any money all the time she was in hiding. He had tied up all the money precisely so she'd never be able to walk out on him."

"She couldn't work?"

"Not as an actress. Too much exposure. She had a job in an old bookstore on Third Avenue, helping some little old Jewish guy. He cried when she cut off her hair."

"He was in love with her?"

"He was reminded of the camps."

"Jesus . . . There but for the grace of God, eh, Van?"

"Right. She scared the shit out of me, but I loved her. She cheered up after we got away from Jake. I rode in the car with her to Newark and she was crying tears of joy. Look, I haven't got time to hear what you did to tie Jake up in traffic, but that'll keep us entertained tonight while we're on our way . . ."

But the details couldn't wait quite that long. My friends had to hear them half-dressed or with half their faces on while we were getting ready for our hot date with Jake. The details they savored most were: the look on Jake's purple face while I told the truth about him; the way words failed him; the way

Tony escorted him back to his car—Jake either had to go where he was being taken or lose an arm. My car was driveable, the policeman sent me on my way. But Jake? His tire had been slowly getting flat while we were talking with the cop. If Jake changed the tire he would have had to do so in his Italian suit. Probably he got a tow instead. The only downer was, the cop wouldn't have taken kindly to my staying around to watch. Still, driving away I felt like a big winner. But I knew that Natalie and Van would still be scared out of their wits, and that hurt. "If I could have told you how it came out, Van—told you to take it easy—it would have been perfect. Even so, he had to be hurting, didn't he? I can't wait to see what color he is tonight when we come in!"

Vanessa burst my adrenaline bubble when she reminded me that Natalie was sure Jake had killed her mother. "Just so you'll know what to expect if you get him mad enough."

We finally assembled in the living room. Oola was stunning in basic black and Annie looked exceptional, too, in an old-fashioned beaded gown with a lower neck than I'd ever seen her wear. I was pleased that my new shoes matched my gold lamé gown. I had good legs and my dress had slits to show them off. Our meeting of the mutual admiration society was cut short when Vanessa entered the room. Jaws dropped.

Her long nails were metallic gold, and her dress was a killer. It was emerald green and skintight with no back whatsoever. It seemed to grow out of her butt and curl around her belly and breasts like a nymphomaniacal vine. But that wasn't the shocker. Above the bare brown shoulders, Vanessa's hair had been cut so short it was a whisper. She held her head high and glorious, like an African idol with emeralds gleaming from her eyes, green contact lenses hiding the natural brown. Huge gold earrings completed the homage to Natalie Romano. Vanessa was more beautiful than I'd ever seen her.

We went to the Plaza in Annie's minivan. Vanessa was so stunning when she emerged from the back seat she could have been stepping from a pumpkin and no one would have noticed. All through the lobby people who watched her go by tried to stand straighter or otherwise look more dignified.

We checked our wraps and found the cocktail reception which was overflowing the room. Oola, Vanessa and Annie were laughing with a famous actor, his not-so-significant other and two New York party-types almost as stunning. I refused numerous glasses of champagne from polite waiters and finally worked my way to the bar for an orange juice. Twice I thought I saw him, my stomach knotting and muscles tensing, only to be wrong. While I was waiting to be served, eyes scanning the room, I felt a hand on the nape of my neck.

I whirled, clenched fist upraised, ready for combat. Bobby caught it in one large hand, like a child trapping a fly. I sagged for a second in relief, then angrily shook my wrist free.

"Jesus Christ, are you trying to give me a heart attack! Thank you," I snarled to the bartender as he handed me my juice. He rolled his eyes and Bobby laughed.

"I've been following him since he left his apartment. I figured I better make sure that he was gonna take the car. Maybe he'd hire a limo or something."

"Shit, I never even thought of that. Where is he?"

"Here, don't worry. And his car is in a garage on East 56th. Looks like he's been in a wreck."

"I'll tell you about it sometime. So did you plant the bug?"

"Oh sure. I went right up to him and said, 'Hey buddy, I need to tag your car.'"

"Keep your day job," I replied.

"This is my day job, and some people actually pay me to do it."

"All right," I acknowledged, "you are doing me a favor. Will you still take care of it tonight?"

"Yeah, I'll catch him on the trip home. How long do you think this thing will go?" he asked, looking at his watch.

"You mean you're leaving?" It was hard to keep the panic from my voice. "Bobby, I, I think he's, he's . . ."

"He's what, Kate? Has something happened?"

So I told him about Natalie and his face tightened. He took my elbow and led me away from the crowded bar.

"Katie," he said, not knowing that was what Jake called me. "I think he's losing it, which means he's twice as dangerous. I want you to be very careful." I nodded, not even trying for bravado. "I'll stick around, okay. Anything happens, anything," he emphasized, "you find me. And no more hanging around bars alone."

He gave my elbow a squeeze and told me to find my

friends. He didn't want Jake to see us talking too long and put us together. With a final squeeze he left me, alone with my orange juice in a roomful of strange people and familiar cocktails.

Suddenly I saw Oola and with a surge of relief headed toward her. The Goddess radar was on full alert, because she knew something was wrong before I got anywhere near her. She gracefully excused herself from her conversation and met me halfway.

"Kate?"

"I'm scared. He's here."

"I'm here, too." She tucked her arm through mine and we strolled toward the dining room, nonchalant. But we were on the alert, throats taut.

Annie and Vanessa were chatting near the double doors that led to the banquet hall. Oola went to get them. He was here. This was it. Annie clutched her bag nervously and I touched mine in response, reassured by the outline of a tiny canister through the satin pouch.

The cocktail lounge had nearly emptied out. Jake was nowhere to be seen. He had to be at his table. Like Dorothy, the Scarecrow, the Tin Man, and the Lion, we started forth to face the Wizard.

As we entered the huge ballroom, abuzz with people who probably weren't as happy to see each other as they wanted to seem, I flashed on those women in China. How it must have felt marching up that hill to face that man. Not tonight. We were sisters and we would always have each other.

We looked at the numbered cards on each of the tables, searching for #12, knowing who waited at the end of our search. People called out to Vanessa as she passed, and she waved and smiled, her eyes roaming, never stopping. There he was.

The blond woman beside him was laughing. All the seats at the table were filled. He was charming his dinner partners, toying with a fork as he talked. Everyone leaned toward him, their attention firmly anchored on his handsome face. The blue eyes flashed and crinkled. We stopped. Slightly to the front of his, a round table sat empty, except for four place settings and a large number twelve. He looked up.

There was no pretense. Right in mid-sentence his mouth

curled into a snarl and the blue eyes spit fire. When the girl-friend leaned forward in concern and touched his hand, he pushed hers away. She pouted angrily and still we stood motionless. His knuckles wrapped around the fork and he jabbed it viciously into the white linen cloth.

It shook the table. Water glasses jiggled and people started. He realized his error and began his explanations, smooth as ever. We moved forward and took our seats, passing his table without a glance. I seated myself directly in his line of vision, Vanessa beside me. Oola, the coolest of our lot, calmly placed her back to him. Annie filled in the space between. A party of four in a room full of eights. The only table of only women.

He watched us watch him, all the while making dinner chatter. We spoke only as necessary, passing the salt and the rolls. I snuck glances at him, avoiding his eyes, but even so the current of rage left me almost breathless. As the salads were served, I watched him glare at Vanessa's shorn head, fingers picking at the table top. Suddenly, as if my scent was in the air, his gaze turned and found mine. Our eyes locked.

Deliberately, he picked up his linen napkin, running its length between both hands. He stroked it, fondled it, caressing his lips with the tip. It was strangely obscene, yet mesmerizing. Slowly he twisted it, tighter and tighter and then suddenly, he jerked it taut between his fists, teeth clenched, violence in every motion. Our waiter bumped our table while filling our water glasses, breaking my trance.

"I'm frightened, Vanessa," Annie said, nearly spilling her drink. "He's really angry."

"I am too, Annie. I think of Natalie and . . ."

"And we're not gonna let him get away with it," I finished. I raised my water glass. "A toast. To taking back our lives."

We solemnly touched our glasses together and then turned slightly toward his table and tilted our glasses his way. All around us people chattered, paying no attention to our table, not knowing what had transpired. Where he sat, however, the gathering clouds grew darker. He was watching us with deadly concentration.

I babbled through the meal, rambling, philosophizing as if talk could protect me. The night had a surreal feel to it, Salvador Dali does dinner at the Plaza. Jake's gaze never wavered.

I've seen a million made-for-TV movies, probably seen a million murders. I've watched stalkers and stranglers, contract killers and serial psychopaths. There was absolutely no connection to what I was feeling now. The gut-wrenching certainty that he planned to kill me was unfathomable and yet completely real. It was as if I were split in two, one calm woman evaluating the situation for what it was, the other frantically trying to deny, diminish or disregard the truth.

It began to happen after dinner. The waiters had cleared the plates and coffee flowed from graceful silver urns. Brandies were poured and aperitifs ordered. Soon the speeches would begin. All around the room, nominees checked themselves, index cards were shuffled then tucked back into jacket pockets. Nervous smiles flashed and women touched their hair, their necklines and played with their rings. The blonde next to Jake pushed back her chair, gathered her tiny evening bag and started for the rest room, her fingers skimming the shoulder of his jacket as she passed. I watched and decided we'd been passive long enough.

"Vanessa," I said, "I have to go to the ladies room. Wanna come?" I jerked my head in the blonde's direction. She missed it entirely.

"No, I'm okay."

"Vanessa . . ." I wasn't sure if Oola would approve my latest strategy and didn't want to find out. If Vanessa would just pick up on this, I wouldn't have to.

"You can go alone, Kate, you've been doing it for at least a year now."

"But I wouldn't be alone, Vanessa," I replied just as irritably. "You never know who you'll meet in the ladies room." Jesus, did the woman need to be hit with a brick!

"Kate, is something wrong?" asked Annie.

"What if Jake can read my lips?"

"Jake's date just went to the ladies room, " Oola answered. "Kate wants to talk to her. Isn't that right?" I nodded, forlorn.

"Well, why didn't you say so! Let's go." Vanessa pushed back her chair, tossing her napkin to the table top. I waited, looking at Oola.

"I don't . . ." She stopped, our eyes meshed. "I don't think all of us should go, so we'll wait here, okay? Be careful, Kate." I shot from my chair like a bullet and planted a kiss on her cheek. Vanessa tapped her shoe impatiently.

"Come on, let's go before she comes back."

"Van, we have to go right by him. Are you sure you can do this?" I gathered my purse as I spoke.

"Yes," she said, almost defiant, her face denying her words. "I'll be right with you."

"Stay away from his table," Oola added, unable to resist.

Vanessa took the lead and ignored the advice, as if needing to prove she wasn't afraid. The five yards or so between him and us seemed twice as long. He watched our every step. She faltered as we came abreast of his table and I slipped past her. I walked within a foot of him without a flicker of recognition. He let me go but as Vanessa followed, he jumped into her path.

"Vanessa," he snarled sweetly, "you look so lovely." He leaned forward to peck her on the cheek and she shrank back.

"Let her by," I said firmly, turning back. He ignored me, his fingers glowing white against the dark flesh of her upper arm. The tips sank into her skin.

"I like your hair, Vanessa. It suits you," he continued, his eyes glittering next to her face.

"Let go," she whispered.

"It suits you," he repeated, "just like it suited her."

"Let her go," I said loudly. People at nearby tables were looking up. He turned his back, a barrier between me and Vanessa.

She tugged her arm, trying to pull free. The hysteria rolled off her. He leaned into her ear and whispered softly. Her eyes widened, she froze. He had her.

So I pushed him. Placed my hand between his shoulder blades and pushed him, hard. He stumbled forward into her and she stumbled back. I moved quickly, wedging myself between her and the table, in front of his girlfriend's chair.

"I'm so sorry," I cried. "Are you okay?"

Again I stepped forward, ostensibly to help. I twisted sideways and deliberately planted the stubby heel of my right shoe on top of his left. I ground it into his foot, with a flash of regret at having passed on some three-inch spike heels when I had been shopping that afternoon.

"Ow! Dammit!" He jerked his foot from under mine, automatically letting go of Vanessa. We all almost fell, Jake

stumbling against his chair, me against the table, Vanessa spinning backwards into air. I caught her arm and pushed off the
table, staggering forward. He lunged at me but missed.

"Bitch!"

"I said I was sorry," I replied indignantly, pushing Vanessa
out of reach. At a safe distance I turned back to the others at
his table, extended my arms palms up and shrugged my shoulders as if to say, "What's with him?"

We hit the ladies lounge like a bunch of ironworkers entering a union hall, the door pounding a small crater in the
wall. The entrance opened into a small sitting room, with up-
holstered furniture and a long, mirrored makeup table. The
actual toilet facilities were discreetly separated by a partially
open door, next to a delicate inlaid table with a large pewter
vase. The blonde was just shutting off the water at one of the
sinks. It had all taken less than two minutes, yet we were
breathing as if we had run for hours.

"Are you okay?"

"Yeah, just scared."

Two other women who had been doing their makeup before
our less-than-genteel arrival quickly gathered up their things
and left. The blonde strolled casually into their spot, turning
to look at the back of her hair and her gown before she settled
in a cushioned chair to address her face.

Vanessa took a deep breath and planted herself in the other
chair and smiled, pulling a lipstick from her bag.

"I love your dress," the blonde said admiringly.

"Thanks. Yours, too." Vanessa's lips were trembling. I
stepped up closer to the mirror, pretending to fuss with my
hair. The blonde casually noted my presence, then frowned as
a tear on Vanessa's cheek caught her unawares.

"Hey, are you all right?" she said, then twisted to look at
me.

"She just saw the ex-husband of a friend of ours," I answered, by way of explanation. "A real bastard."

"Aren't they all," the blonde sighed. "Nobody could ruin a
night faster than mine."

"That's what you think," I muttered. She gave me a puzzled
look and turned back to Vanessa.

"You're pretty upset. She must have been a really close
friend."

"Yeah, kind of. Actually I know him better than her. He's crazy. Beat the shit out of her." Vanessa carefully smudged eye shadow in the crease of her lid.

"My sister was married to an asshole like that! I could have killed him. What is wrong with men, anyway." She shook her head, checking her cheekbones in the mirror. "I hope she nailed his ass in the divorce."

"No, he screwed her over there too," Vanessa said.

"Sure. I'm Martha, by the way."

"Vanessa. That's Kate."

"Do I know you?" Martha asked, looking me over in the mirror. "You look familiar."

Before I could answer, Vanessa said, "Remember I told you I knew him better?"

"Yeah," she said, still focused on me.

"That's because I only met her after he started stalking me."

"Stalking? No! Really?"

"Yeah," I added, determined to get my two cents in. "He's been watching Vanessa for months, broke into her house, re-routed her mail, canceled her credit cards, he even sent a fake report of her death to her mother."

"Why don't the police arrest him?" Martha asked, lowering her mascara wand.

"Can't. Not enough evidence. So we decided that we would stalk him back. Let him know what it feels like, you know. That's when we found his ex-wife. She's been hiding from him for years."

"That is so cool," Martha said admiringly. "I mean, what you're doing about it. So, you came tonight because you're following him," Martha turned to Vanessa, "and he did something?" She sounded eager, as if she'd found herself in an Agatha Christie novel.

"Not yet. It's just a feeling. Like he's starting to crack and I don't know what's going to happen when he does."

"Wow, you hear about stuff like this on TV. How did you meet him? I mean, was he your boyfriend or something?"

"Something. He came to a lecture I gave and asked me out for lunch. He's very good-looking and can be really charming. At first. I dated him a few times and stuff started to happen. Welcome to my nightmare," Vanessa finished.

"God. I can't imagine," Martha shuddered, crimping a piece of hair over her ear.

"Oh yes you can," I murmured. "Try."

"What is that supposed to mean?"

"You haven't asked us who he is," Vanessa answered, meeting Martha's eyes in the mirror. Martha stared back, then her mouth dropped open. As realization dawned, she shook her head in disbelief.

"What are you trying to say?"

"How well do you know Jake Romano?"

"Are you saying this is Jake? My Jake? Oh please, what kind of scam is this!" Angrily, she started stuffing cosmetics back in her bag. "I don't know who you are, maybe some old girlfriend who just can't give it up, but I'm not falling for it, honey! Take your show on the road, and your dog and pony too," she added, jerking her head in my direction. She half-stood, shoving her chair from the table.

"How well do you know him!" Vanessa's hand shot out and circled her wrist.

"You're hurting me! Let go!"

Three sharp knocks made the door jump. Everybody froze. There was no time to answer before the pounding began in earnest, surely a fist against the heavy wooden door, slamming into it with increasing frenzy.

"Martha," he roared. "I want you out here and out here now!" Two more furious bangs. "I said now!"

Martha was a statue at the mirror, Vanessa still clutching her wrist. Her eyes swung to mine, to the door, to Vanessa's face.

"How well do you really know him, Martha?" Vanessa whispered. "What if I'm right? What will you do if I'm right?"

He hit the door again, this time with enough force to swing it open a few inches.

"He's coming in," I warned.

Martha's head swung back again, her face pale, her eyes enormous.

"I'll be right out," she called, voice brittle and forced.

"Now, Martha!" A hit or two for emphasis.

"I said, I'll be right out," she snapped, cheeks flushing red. "Stop acting like a deranged Neanderthal and wait for me at the table, Jake. I'll be back when I'm finished." She sagged back into the chair. She turned to Vanessa and started to say something, but Vanessa put a finger to her lips.

We waited. Thirty seconds. Silence. A minute. Nothing but our breathing.

Then, "Vanessa." Like a whisper on the wind.

"Vanessa, I'm watching your mother." Caressing, full of tender promise. "I watched Natalie's mother too."

Vanessa clapped a hand over her lips, releasing Martha's wrist, rising from her chair. She backed up until she hit the wall, eyes never leaving the door. I went over and took her hand.

"Oh my God," Martha murmured, dazed. "You're telling the truth."

It broke Vanessa's trance and she heaved a long, emptying sigh. It was as if we'd been battering a door that had finally given.

"It's okay, Van, he's gone," I said. "He's gone now."

"He'll never be gone," she replied tonelessly.

"Can I help?" Martha asked.

"Go back out there, before he decides to come in." I walked Vanessa to her chair. "But Martha, you should leave, now. He's losing it. You don't need to get hurt." Martha nodded grimly. She picked up her purse and paused by the door.

"If I had known, I never . . ." She faltered for the words, then pulled the door open an inch and peeked out. Evidently it was safe because she slipped through the crack, stopping just long enough to call, "Take care."

"Vanessa, it's all right."

"No it's not. Nothing's all right."

"Look at me." She wouldn't, so I put a hand on her cheek and turned her head. "We have to stop him. Remember why you did this," I added, now turning her face to the mirror, other hand gesturing toward her eyes and hair. "And for whom. " I took my hand from her cheek and whispered, "I won't let you give up." Shakily she rose from her chair, false green eyes glowing. "I can't lose you anymore than you can lose your mother. We can't let him win." In the mirror, her eyes met mine and slowly the graceful head on its slender neck nodded up and down.

We waited another half a minute before leaving. Annie met us ten feet from the door, obviously on her way to find us. I could see Oola anxiously watching and waved curtly.

"What happened?" Annie demanded anxiously. "Are you okay?"

"We're fine, Annie," Vanessa said, sounding anything but fine.

"What happened?" She repeated. "You've been in there forever! He's going crazy. It's like he doesn't care anymore, whether anyone knows or not. He's keeps getting up and pacing and mumbling, then sitting down again, slamming things. His girlfriend passed me. She looks awful."

"She's actually nice," Vanessa replied, biting her lip.

"Look, Annie, I need you to find Bobby. Right now, okay?"

"But I don't . . ."

"Go look for him, Annie, now! We need him. This is it. Jake's coming apart." I gave her a little push.

Annie hurried toward the back of the banquet room and we started for our table. I could see Martha at theirs, talking to him, rubbing her forehead as if she had a migraine. He was speaking fiercely and emphatically, jabbing his finger in her face, pointing beyond her to our table. His mood was easy to gauge, even from this distance. The other people at the table were distinctly uncomfortable, their bodies turned out, eyes away. Martha kept shaking her head and he gripped her wrist, then put his arm snugly around her shoulder.

We skirted their table and slid into our seats as the emcee took the stage, beginning the grueling monologue that was inevitable at these events. Polite laughter jittered around the room. I took Annie's seat to bring Oola up to date. Out of the corner of my eye, I could see Martha fidgeting. Jake still had an arm draped about her shoulders, keeping her in her seat. She'd given up reasoning for waiting. Something had to happen.

The second speaker was being announced. He was a famous, if ancient, Broadway director who had recently produced his first documentary. The audience clapped respectfully. Martha rolled her neck against Jake's arm and looked miserable. I watched as the speaker's well-known countenance approached the podium. The applause faded as he took his glasses from his pocket and took out his notes. He gave a sweet smile and began by unnecessarily introducing himself. Suddenly an idea hit me and I started to clap. Loudly and enthusiastically.

Clapping at a theatrical event was contagious. I jumped to my feet, applauding vigorously. I kicked Oola and she rose also. Vanessa followed suit, calling bravos and kudos that surprised but touched the elderly director. Celebrity wannabes who thought they were in the know stood as well. The momentum was too much for the crowd and by now the director had humbly stepped back from the podium to accept his tribute. The majority of guests had risen to their feet in standing ovation. Jake rose as well, his arm forced from Martha's shoulders as he joined in the salute. I tilted my head in Martha's direction, praying she'd recognize her chance to escape.

She did. She took two small steps backward and turned quickly, grabbing her purse as she went. As she backed away, he turned for her, but she was too fast. She flashed me a grateful smile as she darted into the crowd and disappeared. He stood, staring after her, palms curled into fists, then slowly traced her smile back to me. His face was contorted by rage. I thought he might throw his head back and howl in frustration.

The applause was dying now, people resuming their seats, programs returning to laps. The director stepped back to the microphone, murmuring his thanks as quiet returned. Heart pounding, I sat. Jake remained standing.

"Thank you. I'm overwhelmed," said the legend at the podium.

"You stupid cunt," said the one man in room still standing, his eyes burning into my face.

"I started in the theater as page," the director began.

"I've taken everything I'm going to take from you, you fucking cow," Jake continued loudly. People were staring at him. I didn't want to look but our connection pulled my eyes to his.

"Kate," snapped Vanessa urgently. "We have to go."

"C'mon, we're getting out of here now . . ." Oola took Vanessa's elbow protectively. I couldn't break from him.

". . . first time I saw Ethel Merman . . ." the director droned on.

"You're dead, cunt! You foul, fucking piece of shit!" He threw Martha's chair aside. A woman at the next table gave a short scream. Someone said he must be drunk. The director looked up from his index cards, confused.

"Kate! Get up! Move!" Vanessa yelled, pushing her chair back so hard it fell.

He was coming for me, intent and relentless. I finally understood why television portrayed extreme speed with slow motion. I watched him come, lost in his anger, knowing I had to get away yet not able to respond. Surely I had time. I turned to the table and grabbed for my purse.

His first blow caught me in the back of the head, just behind my ear, snapping my neck forward and flattening me against the table. No one moved until Vanessa flew forward, face twisted, nails curled into talons. She yelled something as he hit me again, a backhand that knocked me sideways, his heavy ring splitting my cheek. My face was exploding, the vision in my right eye lost to firebursts of color. My nose mashed into the carpet and I breathed against the fibers, struggling to gather my wits amidst the pain.

Vanessa was clawing at him, screeching incoherently. I heard a thud, then a whoosh and she doubled over, breathless. He carelessly withdrew his fist from her abdomen and turned back for me. People were standing for a better view. A waiter stepped between us and got chopped in the face. His mouth burst into blood. It was all happening so fast, yet with so much clarity.

Jake kicked my chair aside, his foot tangling in the legs. Oola was yelling for help and finally men were starting forward. Not soon enough for me. At last fear overcame confusion and I scrambled under the table, tasting the blood that trickled from my nose.

He kicked at my legs and connected hard with my shin. I curled into a ball and choked on the blood in my nostrils, pink bubbles floating on the air. For a second, surrounded by the hanging linen, I felt safe, as if a child hiding in her fort. Then he flung the table upward, glassware and silver flying, my fort destroyed, leaving me naked and exposed to attack. I heard people screaming and wondered if I was one of them.

I clambered backwards in a crab-walk until my shoulders hit the upturned table. Feebly I kicked out at him, knowing it wasn't enough. Someone called his name. Oola grabbed the back of his jacket and he pushed her away like a rag doll. She stumbled and fell.

I crossed my arms in front of my face knowing I was in for it and trying to save what I could. The kick landed just above my elbow, searching for my jaw. The force of it drove my arms backwards, and I punched myself in the face. I tumbled sideways, blinded by tears, my spine curling against the table. He gave a grunt of satisfaction.

The second kick was for the ribs and it drove the air from me, as well as the contents of my stomach. I vomited, a small puddle of the evening meal mingling with the blood from my mouth and nose. The pain was all-encompassing, leaving me helpless to defend. I surrendered myself to his next attack. And the next. There was warm blood all over me, quickly cold. I heard Annie screaming my name. Someone grabbed him. They were pulling him off.

They grabbed him by both arms, one of them calling him by name. His feet still reached for me, even as they dragged him away. I cowered on the floor, shivering, my face wet with blood and vomit and tears. Vanessa suddenly appeared in front of me, crying. She gathered my head into her lap and hugged it to her, murmuring my name over and over.

Waves of dizziness lapped at me and things popped in and out. I heard someone screaming "What's wrong with you?" Oola squealing something about the police. Annie appeared at her side, bathing my face with a cold cloth napkin. I wanted to thank her but couldn't make my lips work. They felt huge, as if someone had sewn two hot dogs to my mouth. Vanessa kept blubbering, cursing Jake and telling me I was going to be okay. She was hurting my head she was hugging so hard.

"Cut it out," I mumbled, spitting blood.

"What, honey? What?"

"Stop calling me honey," I sputtered, using my sleeve to wipe blood from my nose and mouth. "And let go of my head. I'm having enough trouble breathing as it is." I struggled to sit upright.

"Oh Kate," she cried, hugging my head again. "You're okay! Thank God!"

She propped me up against the table, Annie on the other side to catch me if I started to slide. My head spun as if I had been drinking martinis by the gallon. The functioning part of my brain registered that this was not a good feeling. Yet for years I'd been spending big money to achieve it.

"And all I ever had to do was get beat up," I informed Vanessa mournfully. "Why didn't anyone tell me?"

"What are you talking about? Kate, look at me. How many fingers am I holding up?" Vanessa's voice was anxious, but there was a lot of reverb. Where the hell did she get a microphone? Squinting my one working eye, I saw three raised fingers on three raised hands. Jesus Christ, I was halfway to being hamburger and she was playing party games!

"How many fucking fingers do you see, Vanessa?" I retorted groggily, unfurling my middle finger with difficulty. "I'm not in the mood for guessing games, I'm hurt, you know." Blood gurgled down my throat and I gagged, spraying a mouthful of red droplets everywhere. Each time I coughed my ribs took a bite out of my chest. I felt as if my chest was grasped by iron jaws and could only manage quick little sips of breath.

"I think I'd better lie down again," I suggested as I fell forward, faster than they could catch me, my face meeting the carpet once again.

31

I smelled the cognac before my eyes opened. This was not the first time I'd come awake with my nose stuck in a snifter. As in times past, too, everything on my body hurt, my head, my stomach, even my hair. Someone was talking to me, seemingly from far away. The voice was familiar, but I just couldn't place it, so I opened my eyes.

Bobby smiled down at me. His arm was around my shoulder and I was leaning against his chest. He held a small glass of brandy in his other hand and was telling me to take a sip. Finally someone with some common sense, said the little voice. It's not a drink, it's medicine, added the second. Just like the doctor. I licked my huge unwieldy lips.

"That's it, Kate. Wake up. Take a little sip, honey."

No more. Bobby rested the edge of the snifter against my mouth. The glass was cool and pleasant on my lips. I breathed deeply, relishing the dark, woodsy scent. I shuddered and pushed the glass away.

"What are you, a Saint Bernard? Get that outta my face, Bobby. The smell is making me sick," I lied. I pushed my hair back from my face. My cheekbone bulged like a bowler's belly. Wincing, I gingerly touched around my face, the swollen lips, the tender nose, the puffy eye. My fingers came back bloody. I need to wash my face, I thought.

"Where's Vanessa? Is she all right?"

"She's fine, Kate. More to the point, how are you?"

"Just goddamn dandy! How the hell do you think I am? I just got the shit kicked out of me!"

"Well," Bobby responded, "maybe not quite all of it."

I was in no mood for banter. "Help me . . ." He understood that I wanted to sit up and set the drink down within my reach. He put his hands under my armpits, pulled me up, and I gasped as the skin stretched across my ribs. My head pounded and there was a lump the size of a tennis ball behind my left ear. "Where is the bastard?" I asked.

"The paramedics should be here soon, and the police," he answered. "Let me get your friends. They were talking to security." He braced me against a chair and stood up.

"And where were you during all this?" I demanded. "Some bodyguard you are! I should sue!" My new lips came with a lisp, so it sounded more like, "I thould thue."

He laughed. "Same old Kate. You're okay. Look, before we move you, I need to know what's going on outside."

No sooner had he left than Oola was softly touching my face.

"Oh Kate." She stroked my good cheek while a tear or two rolled down her own.

"Don't cry," I said. I saw Annie behind her. She was crying too. My own eyes welled up and soon all of us were bawling like babies, on the floor of the Plaza.

"All right," Oola said finally, wiping her eyes. "Do you want to get up in a chair, Kate? Can you?"

"Yeah, I think so."

She and Annie each took an elbow and I got to my feet, head swimming. They held the chair and I sank into it gratefully, resting my elbows on my knees and my head in my hands. I had no shoes.

"What happened to my shoes?"

"Here's one," said Annie. "I'll look around. The other one's gotta be here somewhere." She gave my shoulder a careful squeeze and started poking among the ruins.

For the first time, I noticed the wreckage. Chairs were everywhere and every which way. Our table lay on its side, the jaunty number 12 ripped from its stand. There was broken glass all over the floor, glinting dangerously. Ugly brown blotches dotted the carpet and splattered the white linen. A lot of blood, most of it mine. A shiver ran through me.

"Where is the bastard?" I repeated.

"Here's your shoe, Kate," Annie said, slipping it on my foot. "And your purse," she added, dropping it in my lap.

"Oola, will you please tell me what's going on? Where's Jake? Did the police take him already or what?" She didn't answer. "Oola! I'm the victim here. I have a right to know what's going on."

Oola picked a chair up from the floor and set it on its legs. She pulled it next to mine and took my hand in both of hers. "We don't know where he is."

"What do you mean, we don't know?" My voice rose hysterically. "We don't know because we don't know where the police took him or we don't know because we don't know?"

"He got out before the police came, Kate," she answered calmly, trying to maintain eye contact.

"What are you saying?"

"How'd he get away? I don't believe this!"

Oola kept her voice low and steady. "One of the men who intervened was a colleague of Jake's. Had known him for years. I don't think he really understood the seriousness of the situation."

"Because Jake didn't have a chain saw? The stupid jerk!" I pounded my fist against my thigh.

"I don't understand either, Kate. But everything was so crazy, the place was in an uproar. The security people were getting the police, everyone was milling about. Jake's friend had taken him out by the bar. At some point—I don't know when—Jake must have turned it around, sounded like the man his friend thought he knew. You know how Jake can be. His friend never thought he would run."

"Why weren't you watching? Why didn't you check?"

"We were all concerned with you, Kate. I never thought about him at all." She put her arms around me and I leaned into her shoulder, crying. She rocked me and soothed me until I lifted my head.

"I wanna go home."

"You need to see a doctor, Kate."

"No," I said stubbornly. "I need to go home. Please, Oola, take me home."

"Miss Greerson?" A large balding man with a small pocket notebook stood hesitantly in front of me. "Are you able to answer a few questions, ma'am?"

"Officer, can't this wait? Kate's very upset and in a lot of pain."

"Yes, ma'am," he replied. "But if she could just tell us what brought this on. We need your help to find this guy," he fin-

ished, directing the statement to me. "He's out there somewhere. We want to catch him before he has a chance to get
out of town."

"It's all right, Oola," I said hoarsely. "Get my coat, okay?
See if you can find Bobby, too. He might be able to help."

Oola rose slowly, as if reluctant to leave me. The officer
waited patiently as I stumbled over words and thoughts, trying
to explain my relationship with Jake Romano. He asked about
where Jake might go. The only place I could think of was the
barn. He assured me they were watching. We were briefly
interrupted by Annie, bringing warm washcloths that came
away from my face rusty brown, then again by the paramedics.

The cop stepped back respectfully as the ambulance crew
took charge. They cleaned and dressed my cheek, laying a
butterfly bandage across the split skin. The woman gave me a
cold pack for the bump behind my ear and the guy felt up my
ribs.

"How do you feel?"

Brother! "My cheek is killing me, my head aches, my lips
feel like pumped-up Reeboks and you just ripped my rib cage
apart. Other than that . . ."

"There's another contusion on her shin," he said to his partner, as if he was used to such comments. "Okay. Let's take
her." The woman unbuckled a strap on the gurney while the
man turned to me.

"I'm not going anywhere but home."

"Ma'am, you're injured."

"If one more person calls me ma'am, *they're* going to be
injured."

He looked around helplessly, catching Annie's eye. She
hurried over.

"What's wrong?"

"She won't go to the hospital," the man said, folding his
arms with a smug look at me. What was Annie gonna do—
ground me? This guy was an idiot.

"Kate, you need to be looked at. You could have a con-
cussion. I'll ride right in the back with you," Annie coaxed.

"I am not going to the hospital, and I am certainly not going
to the hospital on *that* with *them.*" I too folded my arms.

The woman's radio crackled. She pulled it from her belt,

listened, then said, "Look, we've got another call. Either she's going or she's not."

"She's going," said Annie.

"She's not," said Kate.

"Fine," said the idiot, rolling his eyes. "*We're* going," he said, nodding to his partner. They placed their bags on the gurney, recited a canned speech about acting against medical advice and rolled themselves toward the door.

"Oh, Kate, you're impossible," Annie moaned.

"I'm the victim. I can do anything I want."

"Where are they going?" Vanessa hurried toward us, closely trailed by two policemen.

"Kate wouldn't go," she answered helplessly.

"What is wrong with you?" Vanessa demanded.

"I'm hurt," I replied indignantly. "Is that how you talk to someone who's hurt?"

"That's how I talk to someone who's crazy," she snapped. "Where's her stuff? Annie, get her stuff. We're taking her to the hospital."

"No you're not!"

They were going to ignore me. Annie found my purse. Vanessa gave one of the cops her card, scribbling her home number on the back. NYPD would stay with me until we got to the barn and then the Long Island police would take over. Until Jake was found, I would be living with cops outside my door. Suddenly I was less interested in leaving the hotel. He was out there. Somewhere. Watching. Waiting for his chance. He wasn't leaving town. Not without me.

"Someone will come out and take her complete statement tomorrow and she'll have to talk to the district attorney." They'd want all our documentation. If it took feeling this bad to get them to listen, it was almost worth it.

Oola returned carrying the coats and everyone took up discussion about which hospital to go to. Given how much everything hurt, I was somewhat less inclined to argue, but resented my lack of input. I flexed my swollen fingers and noticed brown smears on my knuckles that repeated up my arm.

"I have to go to the bathroom," I interjected.

They kept on talking with scarcely a glance at me.

"I have to go to the bathroom," I repeated loudly. "I wanna

wash my hands." They looked at me. Oola pursed her lips and Vanessa grimaced.

"I don't trust you out of my sight," she said. "Oola, why don't you and Annie take care of the van and I'll stay with Kate."

We separated, Vanessa and I making slow but steady progress toward the ladies room. We were almost there when an officer stopped us. Evidently, the news media were outside. They wouldn't have turned out for an ordinary beating, but it was certainly news when a celebrity dinner was disrupted by one.

I waited impatiently while the officer and Vanessa discussed various escape routes. They were debating a squad car in the back alley off the kitchen when I got tired of waiting.

I edged away from their conversation, alternately grateful and resentful at their lack of notice. I was a few yards from the ladies room when Vanessa called my name. I waved off her request to wait, and limped to the door. Though I was stiff as all hell and sore too, everything was in working order.

I pushed the door open carefully, relieved to see two women sitting at the makeup table. They were talking about Jake and me. Here in the ladies room, I had achieved celebrity status and without Vanessa, mind you. After bravely answering a few questions and allowing myself to be fussed over, I headed for the sink. I might have added a little oomph to my limp, but otherwise I played it straight. They murmured behind me, sympathetic and slightly titillated.

As I gazed into the mirror, I considered that maybe the others *had* been right. This was a face that belonged in the emergency room, its qualifications strongly supported by the fluorescent glare. With difficulty, I turned the facets and got the water running. As I leaned over the sink to splash some on my face, I heard a stall door open behind me.

I spun, water flying, terror rising so fast it belied my brave assertions to the women in the other room. Face dripping, its red and purple features contorted, I stood ready for Jake Romano. The woman who had come out of the toilet screamed. She'd stepped back and was clutching the pearls on her neck. We both froze there, staring, until I started laughing, a bit crazily. That was enough for her. She bolted from the ladies room without a thought for washing her hands.

"Are you okay?" one of the first women called. Yeah, I called back. I washed my hands up to my elbows, but everywhere I looked there seemed to be more blood, bruises or crud. There was a nasty carpet burn on my right knee, with little fibers stuck to it. I wet a bunch of paper towels and carried them back to the makeup table where I'd have room to work. The other women gave ground willingly and I settled myself, wishing but not quite believing that make-up could help.

We chatted as I cleaned up, but after a minute or two, even strangers got tired of Jake Romano. I built a pile of dirty paper towels on the counter and the women picked up their purses. I began to chuckle, imagining what that woman was telling her husband right now. Then the face in the mirror flagged me down and I dug in my purse for help.

His arm came around my throat, forcing my chin upwards. I never heard him coming, he was just there. Like a dream. Like a nightmare. My brain marched ahead doggedly, explaining the situation to the twisted face in the mirror. "He could have gotten away! He came back for you!" As I struggled to breathe, the panic and the pressure worked together, cutting off my air. In the mirror before me, Jake and I stared into each other's eyes. For the last time.

His blazed eerily, lit from within, crazy blue light sparkling and snapping; mine were dull with too much white around. I heard myself attempt a raspy plea for air. I clawed at the arm around my neck, sprained fingers and broken nails little help. He put his face down next to my ear, smiling. Watching in the mirror, I had a crazy flash of photo booths at Coney Island, me on Steve's lap, his face over my shoulder.

"No one ever needed you this much," my crazy brain was saying—about Jake, about now, but it should have been Steve. Again a flash of seeming fact: the woman Steve loved was about to die, but this crazy part of my brain that was commenting so calmly would survive and keep talking to Jake.

"How does it look to you, Katie?" He hissed. "You fucking cunt." He jerked his arm cruelly and I choked. "I'm going to kill you. And I'm giving you the chance to watch." He jerked again, three hard yanks and I felt my chest explode into flame. I slapped against his arm and pointed frantically at my reddening face. As if he would care. His hold tightened and he clapped his other hand over my nose and mouth.

All the while he talked to me, smiling, whispering of winning and stupidity and cunts. My arms flailed, no longer directed, hands searching for something, anything to let me breathe. The soggy paper towels were scattered and my purse spilled on the counter. As my eyes met the mirror, I watched my body convulsing, his fixed concentration. And I saw the pepper spray roll itself to a stop inches from my hand.

Fighting the blackness, I forced my fingers toward it. They seemed to crawl, I couldn't make them go faster. As they curled about the can, there were splashes of red and yellow light before my eyes. If I could just have one breath. I brought the spray upward, barely remembering to turn it from the face in the mirror. Everything was gray now, misty, and I never saw the spray leave the can.

The back spatter as it hit him splattered against my ear. The vise around my neck vanished instantly as he roared in pain. I gagged on air, gulping greedily, my body slumping forward. He swung out blindly with his fist, and knocked me from the chair. I scrambled on the floor, on hands and knees when the door suddenly opened.

"Help!" I screamed. The door swung closed. Whoever it was fled the room. "Help me!" I screamed again. Jake turned, drawn by the sound. He was still on his feet, blinded and burning but enraged beyond immobilization. I pulled myself up and staggered toward the bathroom door. He clawed the air, fingers brushing the tips of my hair. I shied away in terror and stumbled against the wall, cracking my hip against the decorative table and rocking the heavy vase.

I know now that he couldn't see me, there was no way he could have killed me, but all I knew then was that he was coming at me, just kept coming at me. Screaming. My name, foul names, screaming. I grabbed the lip of the vase. Flowers tumbled out as I raised it. I screeched at him to stay away. He kept coming. I swung, the heavy base connecting hard with the side of his head. A satisfying crack as cheekbone met pewter. He fell to his knees. I was still swinging when Vanessa burst through the door seconds later, cops in tow.

32

It was the first time I'd been out since it happened. We were
having lunch, me, Vanessa, Oola, Annie. We'd left familiar
haunts behind and sat in an almost empty, out-of-season hot
spot in the Hamptons. Vanessa knew the owner, so what else
is new.

I watched the ocean through the windows while the others
talked. I liked the water, the waves. From far away, I could
see a solitary man walking up the beach. His head was down,
dark hair ruffling in the breeze. He looked up and the sun
glinted off his dark glasses. My breath caught.

"It's okay, Kate," Annie said, gently touching my wrist. I
shook my mind free and could see the man's stocky build, his
chubby middle. I let my breath out as a dog raced forward,
dripping from the ocean, dragging a stick.

"So there she is," Vanessa was saying, "swinging this big
old metal vase in the air like a hatchet murderer, and there's
Jake on the floor, out cold."

"Excuse me for not having read Miss Manners, but this was
the first time anyone ever tried to kill me." I made a face to
hide a nervous twitch.

"She was fucking great!" Vanessa continued, lighting her
cigarette. "If I was still writing that kind of stuff, I'd steal it
in a heartbeat!"

"Not without a percentage you wouldn't."

"Have you heard from him, Vanessa?" Annie asked.

"No. Not a word." The table fell silent.

I still didn't really remember much of the afterwards. Vanessa said they had to convince me to put the vase down. I
had crouched against the wall, brandishing the urn, screaming
at them not to hurt me. I swung it a few times, wildly, incapable of determining friend or foe. He lay on the carpet in

front of me, a small pool of blood forming beneath his eye. When Vanessa finally coaxed the vase from my hand, its loss left me weightless. I slid down the wall to the floor, my feet almost touching his thigh. I remembered them rolling him over. One side of his perfect face was covered with angry red blotches, the other side completely caved in and partly sliced away. That's when the shaking started and I shivered against the wall, then against Vanessa, unable to answer the cops' questions, unable to talk at all. The ugly scarlet fingerprints around my neck apparently spoke for me, because they let Vanessa take me away.

The first two days home I slept, waking to Annie or Oola trying to tempt me to eat. I didn't. Mostly I went to the bath-room and went back to sleep. The barn was so familiar now and Harley and Ozzie never left me. By day three, the cops were there, with a man from the DA's office. They walked me through it again and again until I burst out crying and Oola made them leave. The next day they were back. Jesus, if they had paid a little more attention in the beginning, maybe none of this would ever have happened.

Nothing restored my faith in the justice system. Jake's attack on me was barely a felony. Evidently if you try and murder someone, it only counts if you get further than he did. If only he'd had a weapon, moaned the prosecutor. Oh sure, a butcher knife would have been good, I replied. He just shook his head as if I didn't know the score and I bit back colorful adjectives before sending him away.

I heard someone say my name and dragged myself back to the conversation. "What?"

"They're not pursuing the business about the pepper spray, are they?" Oola asked. Vanessa jumped in angrily.

"They better not even try, not unless they want me screaming my head off to every sleaze rag and cheap TV show out there. That really pissed me off!"

"I couldn't believe it, Kate," Oola continued. "How could they possibly consider filing charges against you for defending yourself?"

"How could Jake Romano walk away with a plea bargain that will get him less than three years?" I stopped for a bite of my shrimp scampi, then pushed the plate away. "Look, I don't want to talk about this part. We know it's fucked up, it's been fucked up from the beginning."

Jake and I had ended up at the same hospital that night. After getting shot up with pain medication, I remembered demanding separate checks. He was in a room down the hall in emergency when they let me go. Oola and Annie and Vanessa had surrounded me as we passed his door. I caught a glimpse of his feet on the gurney before they whisked me away. I wanted him to die, so badly that it scared me. I just didn't . . . I couldn't . . . I would never kill someone. And Jake Romano couldn't make me.

It was Bobby who came and told me about him. The doctors figured that the real damage had been done by my first blow to the side of his face, and one other across the top of his forehead as he fell. The second blow was glancing but the first had shattered the cheekbone. The damage to his profile was horrific and shards of bone had sliced his optic nerve and the muscles around his eye. It would be a while before they knew the extent of the permanent damage, but for now the eye was taped shut. After Bobby left, I brooded, thinking of that man in the street, David and Annie, Natalie Romano and the puddle of blood on the ladies room floor. I cried, not for Jake, but for myself.

". . . is how brave you are, Kate," said Annie. "Bob said you should work for him, that he'd hire you in . . ."

"Bobby's crazy, Annie, and so are you," I interrupted, squirming. "If you want a realistic evaluation of character, forget Bobby, call Andrew. Now there's one of my biggest fans."

"Andrew is very concerned about you, Kate," Oola replied, in her husband's defense. I crossed my eyes and Vanessa laughed. Oola shook her head, but couldn't help chuckling. Andrew and I were beyond even her control.

They're in the process of adopting now—somehow Andrew got guilted into it. They've found the child they want. She's six, a beautiful little girl who hasn't spoken a word since the police found her living in a box under a bridge. Andrew is teaching her to play games on his laptop and was the first one to make her laugh. Who would have believed it.

While Oola and Andrew undergo scrutiny to prove their fitness as parents, the rights of the biological mother seem to be the system's primary concern. She left the child in a box, I shriek to Annie in disbelief. It makes me angry, but Oola stoically endures it all, the probing, the prying, the waiting. She just wants to bring Hope home. That's what they call her. No one knows her name.

Annie is back at home with her girls. She and David go to the counselor once a week. I keep my mouth shut as much as possible. For the sake of the children, he's taken an apartment less than ten minutes from the house and they're trying to work things out. There are no definite plans for his return, but no divorce either, so I'm biding my time, watching David like a hawk. Annie's too busy to worry about either one of us. She's taken her teacher's advice and is going to school. She and Andrew are two geeks in a pod and he's going to help her get work once she's certified. If I didn't know better, I'd swear it was a conspiracy to make me look bad.

"I'm really excited about it," Vanessa was saying. "I've never written anything that I thought was important to say. All I ever cared about was the payoff."

"What's it about, Vanessa?" Annie asked.

"My mom. All this time, here was this amazing woman with a fantastic story and what have I been doing? Ripping apart adolescents with power tools."

I knew all about the new book since I was still staying out at the barn. She told me her idea one night, kind of shy about it at first. But then the passion of it caught her and by the end I could see it as she talked. She had signed off on the *Headstone* screenplay, and had no interest in the others. The queen of flash and trash had put away her party clothes and seemed more at peace than I could ever remember.

She leaves for Georgia next Tuesday. She's going down to spend a week with Virginia Mae and do research on the book. Virginia Mae is such a pisser. Vanessa wanted them to go on vacation, but her mother flatly refused. Why would Vanessa want to go to Hawaii—spend all that money—if she was writing a book about Georgia? The logic was hard to refute and it was great fun listening to Vanessa get lectured as if she were a little girl.

Natalie is still in Dallas. Vanessa has talked about going to see her sometime, but Natalie wrote a long letter to tell us how well she's doing, and expressing her thanks for the help, financial and otherwise, that changed her life. Vanessa thought the best way to discourage feelings of obligation would be to stay away.

All of us felt that rescuing Natalie had been the key factor in causing Jake to reveal himself for what he was, and more than once Vanessa had spoken of "money well spent." Still, Natalie would probably always be someone who would just get by, working in small stores. Jake's legacy to her psyche. Perhaps the days when Jake was such a big part of our lives were best forgotten.

Steve is going to look in on me while Vanessa's gone. I'm still afraid to be alone sometimes. He offered to come and stay, but I don't know. I understand a little better now how Annie feels. I might want him back, but I don't want to go back. Not to what we were. So for now, we talk and laugh. He brings me Mexican food and bags of baby peanut butter cups. I've only cried in front of him once, no reason why. It just came on when we were talking about old times.

"They have the most fabulous desserts here," Vanessa said, as the waiter wheeled a cart to our table. He pointed and named each concoction, ending with a chocolate cheesecake glazed with Grand Marnier. The velvety slice sat in a little golden puddle of fragrant orange liqueur. Not a single voice was heard.

"I'll have the deep dish apple pie," I said, "ice cream and whipped cream."

"Porker," said Vanessa, ordering the same.

These women had done so much for me. They thought I was courageous, but I knew I was only crazy.

Ellen and Robin had come to the barn twice a week while I recuperated, Jerry a couple of times too, and we held AA meetings in my room. They left me one of those Big Books and I started to read it. How did two dead men write a book about my life before I was even born?

I don't think about Jake as much anymore. Only sometimes, when a squirrel trips a floodlight or one of the cats tries to sneak out the back door. I think that maybe Jake Romano was just a manifestation of more personal demons. I hated him like I hated myself. He's in jail now. He stayed in the hospital while his lawyer cut the deal. His eye being what it was and the public nature of the attack, he skipped the trial and pled guilty to two lesser charges. He'll be eligible for parole in as little as eighteen months.

"At least it's over," Annie said, smiling around the table, cherry pie stuck to her lip.

"Here," said Vanessa, taking her chin and wiping her face. Annie squirmed and I saw the likeness to Lindsay.

"I hate to be a killjoy," Oola said, "but it's not really over."

"God, Oola, for someone who hates to be a killjoy, you're pretty goddamned good at it." Vanessa blew smoke at her and they bickered back and forth, just like they used to before Jake Romano.

I remembered something from the AA book about a daily reprieve. That's all you get with drinking, just one day. Pretty stingy—with Jake, I get a few hundred. I looked up as the waiter set the check down near my elbow. The women around the table argued and teased each other, laughing. It suddenly dawned on me that I was free. Free of it all, just right in this moment. Maybe not tomorrow, but right now, today, free.

"Hey," I interrupted, snagging the last bite of Annie's dessert and gesturing toward the check. "Don't even think I'm picking up the tab for this party. You guys owe me."

DENIAL

A novel of psychological suspense

KEITH ABLOW

He's in deep.

A series of grisly murders has forensic psychiatrist Frank Clevenger on the case of a lifetime and the fight of his life against a brutal killer with a horrific trademark and his own powerlessness over sexual compulsion, self-destruction and DENIAL.